Version 3.0
1st Edition

IMMINENT FAILURE

BOOK SIX IN THE RUINS OF THE GALAXY SERIES

J.N. CHANEY

CHRISTOPHER HOPPER

JOIN THE RUINS TRIBE

Visit **ruinsofthegalaxy.com** today and join the tribe.
Once there, you can sign up for our reader group, join our
Facebook community, and find us on Twitter and Instagram.

If you'd like to email us with comments or questions, we respond
to all emails sent to ruinsofthegalaxy@gmail.com, and love to
hear from our readers.

See you in the Ruins!

STAY UP TO DATE

J.N. Chaney posts updates, official art, previews, and other awesome stuff on his website. You can also follow him on **Instagram**, **Facebook**, and **Twitter**.

He also created a special **Facebook group** called "JN Chaney's Renegade Readers" specifically for readers to come together and share their lives and interests, discuss the series, and speak directly to me. Please check it out and join whenever you get the chance!

For updates about new releases, as well as exclusive promotions, visit his website, jnchaney.com and sign up for the VIP mailing list. Head there now to receive a free copy of *The Other Side of Nowhere*.

https://www.jnchaney.com/ruins-of-the-galaxy-subscribe

Stay Up To Date

Enjoying the series? Help others discover the Ruins of the Galaxy series by leaving a review on **Amazon.**

CONTENTS

PREVIOUSLY

Last time in *Ruins of the Galaxy Book 5: Black Labyrinth...*

MAGNUS LED a dangerous raid on the Paragon's flagship, the Black Labyrinth, to rescue Piper Stone from Moldark's clutches.

The Gladio Umbra slipped into the Super Dreadnaught undetected, thanks to some heroic pre-arrival sabotage by Ezo, Cyril, and T0-96. Once in the hangar bay, Taursar and Hedgebore Companies set up a perimeter around the escape shuttles while Magnus led Granther Company deep inside the enemy vessel.

However, the gladias' harrowing rescue attempt almost failed. Not only did Magnus's fire teams encounter significant gauntlet-style resistance, but Captains Forbes and Nelson faced off against dreaded TS40 Trench Sweepers. But teamwork, quick tactical thinking, and sheer determination of will kept both Gladio Umbra elements in the fight.

Finally, Magnus and his units came face to face with Moldark in the dark lord's observation deck. Blaster bolts, Unity forces, and Moldark's otherworldly powers collided as both sides fought over the galaxy's most gifted child. In the end, however, Magnus rescued Piper and raced for the hangar bay, risking his life in a treacherous spacewalk to ensure Piper's escape.

Meanwhile, the battle over Oorajee came to a catastrophic conclusion as Jujari ships rammed Third Fleet's warships in a final act of desperation. While the Jujari defense ultimately failed, Fang Company's starfighters, along with Sootriman's Magistrate squadrons, kept the Paragon ships occupied. The action not only allowed Magnus's units to return to Azelon's Spire but helped cover the Jujari's retreat, leaving Moldark fuming.

Now, questions linger about what the dark lord will do next, especially as Piper's unwitting collusion in brainwashing the Republic's First and Second Fleets comes to light. With Magnus and Piper's relationship restored, all eyes turn toward the fate of Capriana Prime and stopping what could be the bloodiest assault in the galaxy's history.

1

"I WANT those fighters back onboard faster than a hooker running into an admiral's lounge," Colonel Caldwell ordered.

TO-96 nodded and then opened a channel, and Ricio's face appeared in a side window overlaying the bridge's main display. "Commander Ricio, return to the *Spire*."

Caldwell gave the bot a stern look.

The bot nodded as if understanding the need to emphasize haste. "Like a morally ambiguous prostitute noticing gainful employment within an executive lounge full of overconfident ship commanders who believe they're above the law and any preexisting intimate relationships."

"What?" Rico asked.

"I believe the colonel wants you to hurry, sir."

Ricio grinned and gave a small chuckle. "Tell him we're on our way, 'Six."

TO-96 looked at Caldwell. "They are—"

"I heard the man, Brass Balls," Caldwell replied, and then looked at Azelon. "We have room for Sootriman's fighters, Smarty Pants?"

"Only half, sir," Azelon said. "And it will be very tight."

"Let her know we'll ferry as many as we can. The rest are on their own."

"Right away."

The colonel watched as more Jujari ships impaled Moldark's Third Fleet. In all his years in the Corps, in all his days aboard Navy ships, he'd never seen anything like what was unfolding before him. It began when a Pride-class Jujari Battleship named *A Glorious Day for Liberating the Exiles of Rugar Muda* rammed into the Paragon Battleship *Emergent Horizon*. The collision took out the enemy ship's propulsion and, more than likely, its life-support. The force was so strong that even the *Emergent's* conning tower tore from the main deck and fell backward.

Seconds later, a Jujari Dreadnaught and two Battlecruisers rammed into Paragon ships, rendering them inoperable. Caldwell watched as hundreds of escape pods jettisoned from the Jujari vessels, but he didn't need to count them to know that the majority of each ship's crew had perished in the suicidal attempt to make the Paragon bleed.

The first starship to make an attempt on the *Black Labyrinth* was a Jujari Battleship called *Terrified Enemies Hide in Dark Caves Awaiting Dawn that Will Never Come*. The most the battleship did was graze the *Labyrinth's* starboard hull. Anti-ship cannons pummeled the Jujari vessel, making it pay dearly for the brash attempt. The guns pulverized its bridge and drilled holes in its hull before the *Terrified* finally broke off and succumbed to Oora-jee's gravity well.

But the *Labyrinth* wasn't free yet. Bearing down on its stern was a Super Dreadnaught equivalent and the last flagship in the Jujari's fleet. *Wherever the Enemy Runs We Will Hunt Down and Slaughter Them in Droves by Order of Maw Snarlick* struck the *Labyrinth* on the port side aft. An entire engine cone was decimated in the collision, reducing the Paragon ship's thrust capabilities by at least a quarter, Caldwell guessed. The Jujari ship continued to burrow into the *Labyrinth*, tearing a furrow down the port side. Eventually, two Paragon Frigates that had been ordered to defend Moldark's Super Dreadnaught sacrificially, shoved the *Maw Snarlick* away.

Then, the full weight of Third Fleet's power leveled itself on the *Maw Snarlick*, blasting it apart in the largest display of ship fire Caldwell had ever seen. Whoever its captain, he or she was courageous, and one who had just purchased the *Spire* the window it needed to recover its fighters and exit the battle.

"Thank you," Caldwell whispered to the holo display. Never did he think he'd be thanking Jujari for saving his life. If anything, they had always been the enemy. And he'd killed his fair share of them in some brutal conflicts when he was fresh out of the academy. The truth was, he had hated them. Hated them bitterly. But if his short time in the Gladio Umbra had taught him anything, it was that everything was changing. He'd be damned if he was going to get left behind because he wasn't willing to change—*even if you are a stubborn ass son of a bitch.* "May you rest in peace, and may your survivors find safe passage to calm shores."

"I beg your pardon, sir?" TO-96 asked.

"Not for you, Ballsy," the colonel replied.

"Ah. Very good, sir."

Caldwell touched his in-ear comm and thought of Rohoar's name. His biotech interface identified the recipient and pinged the Jujari.

"Yes, Colonel Caldwell?" Rohoar said.

"I know what your people are doing right now, son. And I know you have some kind of pack connection to them or something. So I was wondering if you could get through, to tell them…" Caldwell struggled to find adequate words, so he settled on the simplest. "Thank you."

"It is an honor for the Jujari to defend our home," Rohoar replied. "But also to defend those who risk their lives for us. I will pass your words on."

"Thank you, son."

"Also, I am not your son. This is a strange miscalculation on your part."

Caldwell chuckled. "Duly noted. Caldwell out."

"Do you have a destination in mind, Colonel?" Azelon said, but Caldwell barely registered the question. He stood with his hands clasped behind his back and watched the battle's closing moments.

What a strange few months it had been. Witnessing all this, let alone experiencing it at the helm of an alien warship from another universe, felt surreal. Then again, his career had been fairly exceptional. Caldwell figured that people lived their most exciting years in their twenties and thirties. Hell, that's what he'd done—*sow your wild oats and burn the midnight mags away*—because no one figured they would live much past forty as a blaster-wielding ground-pounder. He'd been surprised to live past thirty. Yet here he was, at sixty years old, living out the most exhilarating days of his life.

The Jujari fleet had less than a dozen ships remaining, all of which were heading to the far side of Oorajee in retreat. The Sypeurlion and Dim-Telok, likewise, had abandoned their role in the fight, fleeing back to their respective star systems. If Moldark wanted to, he could finish off the Jujari ships and assault the planet. But judging from the massive losses the Paragon's Third Fleet had taken, and First and Second Fleets' disarray, Moldark would need to regroup and reassess his priorities—at least, that's what Caldwell would do.

Then again, whoever Moldark was, he was not the strategist that Kane was rumored to have been. Though impatient and ill-tempered, Kane was at least intelligent and dogmatic, if not ruthless. In contrast, Moldark had shown a brashness that was much less representative of the Republic's fine command tradition and more reminiscent of a fitful child. No starship commander would have ever let so many Jujari ships come in as close as Moldark did, which made Caldwell wonder about the man's motives.

The Paragon's enigmatic leader had been so distracted by Piper's rescue that he was willing to put his entire fleet in jeopardy against an already-won battle with the Jujari.

"A destination, Colonel?" Azelon asked again.

"He wants the child," Caldwell said to himself.

"I'm unfamiliar with that location, sir," Azelon said.

Caldwell ignored the misunderstanding and turned from the holo display. "We need to get Piper out of here. Let's head back to metaspace as soon as all of Fang Company and Sootriman's ships are secured."

"By your command, Colonel," Azelon said.

"Sir," TO-96 said. "Incoming call from Lieutenant Magnus for you."

"On screen," Caldwell replied.

A video image of Magnus appeared on the main holo. "Colonel, I've got something from Piper that's important."

"Go ahead."

"She's in sickbay here, in and out of consciousness still. But she's starting to talk about her grandfather."

"It's relevant?"

Magnus nodded. "She seems to think so, and so do I. She says she tried to help him open a void horizon quantum tunnel to metaspace."

"Mystics. Can she do that?"

"Well, I'm not sure. Awen's not sure either. But in any case, she failed."

Caldwell let out a sigh. "Well, that's a relief."

"It is, but she was successful at helping him with something else."

"Which was?"

"Convincing all three fleets to turn on Capriana."

Caldwell balked, then pulled his cigar from his mouth. "Come again?"

"I know—it's crazy if it's true. But it seems that Moldark is not only hellbent on crushing the Jujari but taking the fight to the capital too."

"You think she succeeded? You think he's headed there next?"

"I do, Colonel. And she seems to think so as well. With the Jujari force all but eliminated, I'll bet he's saving any cleanup work for later. The worst part is that Capriana's not gonna be ready for him, even with all the damage the Paragon has taken."

Magnus was right. Caldwell looked at Azelon's enemy force count in the main holo's sidebar. First Fleet was still the strongest with 74 warships and 11 Talon squadrons totaling 165 starfighters. Second Fleet came next with 50 remaining ships and 75 starfighters. And Third Fleet, which suffered the most losses, held onto 32 ships and only 15 Talons. If all three fleets turned on Capriana, it was game over. Hell, even if a quarter of them did and the planetary defense shield wasn't up, it was game over.

"We've got to warn them," Caldwell said. He stuffed his cigar back in his mouth. "They've got to raise the PDS if they have any hope of protecting the city."

Magnus took a deep breath and then started nodding. "For what it's worth, I agree. But it does beg the question—"

"How are we gonna pull that off?"

Magnus smiled. "You said it, not me, sir."

"Damn." Caldwell looked down. "My bridges are burned, Magnus. So are yours."

"Forbes and Nelson's too," Magnus replied. "Which means…"

"It means we're gonna have to do this the old-fashioned way, son. Face to face."

"We're going to Prime then?"

Caldwell chewed on his cigar and then spat out a chunk of tobacco. "Son of a bitch."

"Would you please define the destination Son of a Bitch, Colonel?" Azelon asked.

"It's Capriana Prime."

"Understood, sir. A course to Capriana Prime Son of a Bitch is laid in and awaiting your command."

Caldwell couldn't help at least a small smile. "How fast can you get us there, Smarty Pants? Faster than Moldark?"

"Given the damage sustained to his propulsion system and our faster speed, I would estimate we have a three-hour head start. Possibly more."

"It's not much," Magnus said. "But it's something."

"Agreed."

"Sir," TO-96 said to Caldwell. "Sootriman and Ezo are both hailing you. It seems they are taking issue with your order to recall their fighters."

"Splick. Now what's this about?" He looked at Magnus. "Stand by, son." Then Caldwell waved at TO-96. "Put them through, Brassy."

"Right away, sir," he replied.

Sootriman and Ezo's faces appeared in their own hexagonal

holo frames, both wearing flight helmets with their HUD visors lowered. "How can I help you?" Caldwell asked.

"Azelon says the *Spire* only has room for half my ships," Sootriman said.

"She's told me the same," the colonel replied.

"Then that's a no-go for us, Colonel. It's all or nothing. Plus, someone's gotta hang out here and make sure the Paragon doesn't get any bright ideas about going after those remaining Jujari ships. So far, we don't think the survivors have been spotted, but I don't want to take any chances."

"And you think you can fend the Paragon off?" Caldwell asked, his voice filled with suspicion. He wasn't trying to be disrespectful of her intentions, but it felt a little far-fetched, even with her Magistrates' numbers.

Sootriman shrugged. "Maybe not fend them off, but lead them away."

Caldwell bit the end of his cigar in thought. "I don't like it, queen. But I ain't your sugar daddy either. So you're gonna do what you're gonna do. You, on the other hand," Caldwell said to Ezo. "You have orders to—"

"Ezo isn't leaving his wife," the Nimprinth said.

Caldwell raised an eyebrow. He supposed he should have expected insubordination from this ragtag bunch of misfits at some point or another. This wasn't the Corps, after all. He just didn't expect it at such a pivotal moment. "Need I remind you that you're a squadron commander in the Gladio Umbra? So, you wanna run that by me again, commander?"

"I'm not leaving her," Ezo said. Caldwell knew the man meant business based on how he spoke of himself.

"Sir," TO-96 said, motioning Caldwell aside. "If I may. A word?"

"What is it, Ballsy?"

The bot lowered his volume. "If we are indeed preparing for a ground invasion of Capriana Prime, our airwing may be less necessary than it is right here."

"You're saying you agree with Ezo staying to help Sootriman lure the Paragon away?"

"I'm saying our immediate lack of need for the starfighters does provide a certain latitude that, should this course be one she does not show signs of being deterred from, it does not adversely affect us. Additionally, statistically speaking, she has a high probability of success. Therefore, I do not believe it is worth you winning the immediate skirmish only to lose the large scale conflict, as it were."

"It's win the fight, lose the war, bot."

"What is?"

"Never mind." Caldwell sighed, then turned back to Sootriman. "Fine. But I want you hot on our tails the moment you determine things here are on the up and up, you hear?"

"Yes, Colonel," Ezo said.

Sootriman, however, was less forthcoming. "Don't get your panties in a bundle, Colonel. We will get there."

Caldwell couldn't shake the sudden feeling that she was going to be more of a handful than anyone had bargained for. "Be careful. Caldwell, out." When the channel had closed and

Magnus's face reappeared, he said, "Rally Forbes, Nelson, and Willowood, and meet me in the war room." Caldwell turned to TO-96 and Azelon. "You bots need to be there too."

"Are we going to kick some ass, sir?" TO-96 asked. "Because I am quite learning to enjoy the kicking of some ass."

"Yes, bot," Caldwell replied. "We are most definitely going to be kicking some ass—probably a lot more than we bargained for. The trick is not to get ours kicked in return."

2

MOLDARK WAS ON HIS WAY. Magnus knew it—hell, they all did. It was only a matter of time before the maniac jumped out of subspace and showed up over Capriana, pounding the planet to dust with all three of his fleets.

But not without a fight, Magnus said to himself. The irony of his determination wasn't lost on him. Why defend the very capital that betrayed him? If anything, Magnus should wash his hands of the Republic and walk away. But he couldn't—if not for the Republic's sake, then for the billions of innocent lives that hung in the balance.

The *Spire* had beaten Moldark's fleets to Capriana Prime. Azelon commanded the faster ship, and Moldark's fleet, as well as the *Black Labyrinth,* had taken critical damage. With at least some margin secured, no matter how small, Magnus and the other commanders had thrown together the best plan they could, one that sought to ensure Capriana's protection and Awen's parents' rescue. Plus, with Sootriman and Ezo staying behind, they could keep the colonel informed on Moldark's movements. With a bit of hope and a whole lot of luck, Magnus figured the Gladio Umbra had a good chance of at least accomplishing one of their two goals.

"9.71%, sir," TO-96 said as Magnus doubled checked Cyril's maglock bond to Rix's back. All twenty-five members of Granther Company's Elites readied themselves in the *Spire's* main hangar bay.

"Come again, 'Six?" Magnus asked, looking up from his work.

"I have finished my calculations and estimate that you have a 9.71% chance of accomplishing one of the two ambitious goals you and Colonel Caldwell have set for this operation."

"Keep your voice down, would you?" Magnus could feel everyone's eyes bearing down on the back of his head. Magnus turned around with a big smile and then said in a loud voice, "97.1% chance of success? I'll take those odds, 'Six!"

"But, sir, I just said—"

Magnus got in TO-96's face and spoke through clenched teeth. "I know what you said, and you know what you said—"

"So do I," Cyril added.

"Me too," said Rix.

Magnus winced, then continued correcting the robot. "But that doesn't mean the whole world needs to know."

"I wasn't telling the whole world, sir. I was mere—"

"Six." Magnus held a finger up. "Don't make me isolate you from Azelon."

"You wouldn't."

"I would."

TO-96 tilted his head as if considering Magnus's threat, then turned up his external speaker volume. "Ha ha ha. You got me, Lieutenant. 97.1% it is."

Magnus rolled his eyes and went back to double checking Cyril's connection.

"Sir, are you absolutely ten ten certain that you absolutely need me down there, sir?" Cyril asked.

"If I didn't know better, kid, I'd say you're trying to get out of this jump," Magnus replied with a smile.

"Me? No, no, no. I love jumping out of a perfectly good starship into a planet's atmosphere. I do it all the time, actually."

Magnus raised an eyebrow. "Bullsplick."

"Holo games count."

"No, they don't." Magnus tugged the redundant safety harness, and Cyril winced. In case a suit took a lightning strike or was hit by an EMP, good old-fashioned carbon fiber webbing would keep Cyril from flying off into oblivion. Whatever Cyril had in the way of brains, he'd acquired it at the expense of athleticism. And what little athleticism he'd once had was beat out of him by his injuries back on Oorajee. Even with the Novian armor's flight assist, the kid wasn't making this jump without going tandem. "There's nothing to this jump, Cyril. Smooth and simple. Plus, you're our only code slicer, right?"

"Sure, sure, I am."

"And there's no way Zoll's squad is getting in that lab without a code slicer, correct?"

"Nope, no way, no how. None of his blasters will help with that. I mean, unless you're killing security guards, then his blasters will be green to go, sir."

"We need you then." Magnus patted Cyril on the shoulder and then handed him a helmet. "Remember what we told you, and don't squirm around on entry. You'll just piss Rix off and probably burn up."

Cyril let out a nervous laugh. "I definitely don't want to burn up."

"I'd be more worried about pissing off Rix," Magnus said. Rix gave a low growl over his shoulder.

"Right, right, right. No squirming. Promise."

"Good, kid. Now relax and enjoy the ride."

Magnus turned and saw Colonel Caldwell walking across the *Spire's* cargo bay. The old man's eyes were sharp, and his white mustache was forever stained by the cigar clenched between his teeth. He surveyed the Elites of Granther Company's First Platoon and then nodded to Magnus. "Everything in order?"

"Just about, Colonel. Azelon has our jump vectors?"

"I do, Lieutenant," Azelon said as her hard-light projection appeared a meter away. Her gleaming white body and blue eyes were a testament to the Novia Minoosh's tasteful engineering. She nodded once, and a translucent holo window appeared at head level. "Petty Officer Zoll will lead Charlie, Delta, and Echo Teams on the rescue attempt on the lab here." She pointed to a cluster of buildings toward the southern end of Capriana's atoll. A small yellow circle appeared around a nondescript facility near the western shore. "While you and Bravo Team will land atop Centennial Tower located adjacent to the Forum Republica's capital complex." A second circle appeared around a flat-topped building in a dense cluster of skyscrapers in Capriana's centrally located capital district. "Everything has been uploaded and sent to your team's biotech interfaces through the Novian Defense Architecture."

"You're so efficient it's sexy," Magnus replied.

"Strange."

"I'm just playing with you, bot."

"No," Azelon said, waving him off. "TO-96 says the same thing to me."

Magnus and Caldwell shared an awkward look as TO-96 fidgeted with his hands.

"Alrighty then," Caldwell said. "The rest of you good to go?"

"I think so," Awen said, struggling with a hip latch on her new Novian armor.

"Here, let me get that," Doc Campbell said.

"No, let me," Magnus replied, stepping forward to help Awen. "I've got it." Magnus secured the connection above her hip and then found his hand lingering as he examined her suit.

"Stay focused, Lieutenant," Awen said with a pat to his cheek. Then she turned to Caldwell. "I'd be lying if I said I wasn't nervous about this jump."

Caldwell chuckled. "You mean to tell me you can help three

companies of gladias escape a Super Dreadnaught, but you're nervous about an OTA jump in a state-of-the-art flight suit?"

"Maybe it's because I still don't know what all your acronyms mean."

"Orbital to atmosphere jump, miss," Azelon replied. "Standard Marine protocol for—"

"She knows what we're doing, Azie," Magnus replied.

"Of course, sir."

"Just follow the prompts in your HUD," Caldwell said. "The suit will practically fly itself, from what Azelon tells me."

"That is correct, Colonel," Azelon said. She faced Awen. "Not only will your Novian armor help maintain your flying posture and angle of incidence, but without it, improper entry could result in either skipping off the atmosphere and being incinerated or diving into the atmosphere and being incinerated, depending on your error deflection."

"Both of those are undesirable," Awen replied.

"Which is totally, absolutely why I'm not taking any chances me myself," Cyril said from Rix's back. "Trusting the big man here to get me where I need to go, on the double." Cyril tried to pat Rix's shoulder but had trouble reaching it, so the gesture looked more like a child just batting the air.

Awen smiled, then looked at the colonel. "Are you certain you don't wish me to help the other teams rescue my parents?"

Abimbola stepped forward, nodding his head. "I, too, wonder why I am not allowed to partake in that exploit."

"Because it's too personal," Caldwell replied. "For both of

you. And I can't have you making emotional decisions if things go sideways."

Awen raised her chin. "But, sir, I—"

"Awen, listen." Caldwell held up a hand. "I realize what this op means for you. Hell, if it were my parents, I'd be having the same conversation. So if it's any consolation, I have the utmost belief in Petty Officer Zoll and the rest of his squad. We are going to get your parents out. And I'll make sure you are kept in the loop the entire time. Your job, however, is to help get word to CENTCOM. I don't mean to downplay your parents' wellbeing, but you're tasked with the more important of the two missions. So keep your head down, eyes forward, and OTF until the job is done."

Magnus still winced at the use of the Marine mantra. "That's Own The Field," Magnus said to Awen, just in case she needed a refresher.

"I got it." Awen gave Magnus a small smile, and then looked back at the colonel. "I understand, sir."

"Good." Caldwell addressed everyone else. "And that goes for the rest of you too. We do this right and we save a few billion lives today. We get it wrong, and the Paragon will be liquifying your bodies along with every building in the capital. Stay focused, execute your objectives, and then get the hell out."

The members of Granther Company nodded at the colonel. No one needed a reminder of how much was riding on this mission, but it never hurt for the CO to bring everyone's attention back to the game plan—a game plan that was only a few hours old.

Had it not been for Piper and TO-96, none of this would be happening. First, it was TO-96 who had determined where Awen's parents were being held. After analyzing Bosworth's video, the bot had created a model of the laboratory and then compared it against Republic records. Contrary to what most everyone assumed, Bosworth was not confining his hostages to a ship's lab but a much larger ground-based facility on Capriana. Additionally, the coordinates that Bosworth had said to send Piper to happened to be near none other than Capriana Prime. *So if we're lucky*, Magnus thought, *we'll arrest the traitorous fat fool too.*

Second, before she'd passed out for the second time since being rescued, Piper had informed Magnus that Moldark was setting his sights on Capriana. She'd described her failure to help him achieve his first ambition—to create a new quantum tunnel —which led to her assisting him in his second one—turning the fleets' sailors against the Republic.

"He wants to destroy everything," she'd said from her bed in sickbay. "And you can't let him. You just can't." Magnus swore he'd stop the dark lord, and that he'd rather die than break a promise to Piper.

The child had also mentioned something about Moldark's hate for a group of leaders called the Circle of Nine. Unfortunately, Piper didn't know anything more about them, just that they were the ones ultimately responsible for so many of the bad things that had been happening. Magnus shared the intel with the commanders, but no one was familiar with the group, not even Colonel Caldwell.

Everyone's first idea of protecting Capriana from an imminent attack was the obvious one: have Caldwell contact a member of Galactic Republic Central Command—better known as CENTCOM—and let them know what was happening. Send some footage, corroborating data, and a few eyewitness testimonies, and the capital would begin powering up the planetary defense shield. Doing so would both spare the planet and buy the Republic valuable time to build a counterattack against Moldark.

However, like Magnus, Caldwell's, Forbes', and Nelson's bridges had all been burned, and there was no reliable way to get word to anyone's superiors, especially with such sensitive data. Were a general broadcast to go out, it would incite pandemonium across the planet. Instead, this had to be done through the proper channels. But security clearances had been revoked and new firewalls had been put in place—ones that not even Cyril or Azelon could slice. After all, this wasn't taking control of a torpedo or hacking a ship. This was attempting to infiltrate the Galactic Republic's upper echelons, which were locked down even tighter now that there'd been a raid on Worru.

The only way to warn Capriana was to do it the old-fashioned way. In person.

"I feel it is imperative to remind you that VNET may not be stable once you are outside CENTCOM's headquarters," Azelon said as the gladias finished preparing for their OTA jump.

"Yeah, yeah. She's really right," Cyril said from Rix's back.

Magnus caught himself chuckling. The code slicing genius looked like a baby chimp slung on his mother's back. Rix apparently saw Magnus laughing and mouthed the word, "What?"

But Cyril continued. "Once you're there, I'm guessing only

local IR comms will work in your helmets. They probably have jamming tech even better than the stuff the Zarkonian's use in *Galaxy Renegade*. It took me a few days to figure out how to maneuver my fireteams using traditional methods, and even then, the boss on level twenty was—"

"Cyril," Magnus barked.

"Ha ha. I'm rambling again, aren't I. Sorry."

"So, limited comms," Magnus said, looking back at the colonel. "And how long before the planetary defense shield is up?"

"It takes the PDS almost an hour to reach full power," Caldwell said. "Draws a huge amount of power across multiple relay points, and it has a lot of ground to cover. Literally. So that means you've got a lot of convincing to do before Moldark gets here."

Magnus nodded, then looked to Azelon. "And the last piece of the plan?"

"We have a transport shuttle ready to go," Azelon said. "I've placed emitters in a 3D printed child that will mimic a single life sign."

"Whoa—3D printed what?" Silk said.

"A child," Azelon said. "I took the liberty of fashioning a large doll, as you'd call it, to act as a stand-in for Piper. If we're going to draw the enemy out, we might as well make it as believable as possible."

"I wanna see this creep-bot," said Robillard. "Who wants to bet it's as ugly as Bliss's last attempt to shoot a grouping at a hundred meters?"

"I'll show you a tight grouping," Bliss replied, raising his NOV1.

"Easy, gladias," Magnus said. "We'll have plenty of time to see what the 3D printer can do later." He looked at Caldwell. "You think it'll work?"

"With any luck, Azelon's decoy will draw out some unfortunate lackey, and then blow them away," Caldwell said. "You and I both know it won't be Moldark or Bosworth. They'll be expecting a dummy. But they won't be able to resist the urge to at least investigate what we send."

"It would make everything a whole lot easier if Moldark went himself," Rohoar said through clenched teeth.

"You're telling me," Magnus replied.

"Correct, I *am* telling you."

"No, I mean—" Magnus waved off Rohoar. "Never mind. How do those sleeves feel?"

Rohoar looked down at the new additions to his kit: armored sleeves that covered his arms and lower legs. The Jujari's standard armor allowed the limbs to be exposed, granting the fighters greater dexterity to slice and maul. But the OTA required that the species' whole bodies be covered, including their muzzles, which also had new snout cones.

"I don't like them," Rohoar said in disgust. "But the robot says we Jujari will perish without them. So it is a necessary horror."

"You mean evil," Magnus said.

"What?"

Magnus held out his hand like he was offering a gift. "The expression is a *necessary evil*."

"No." Rohoar laid his ears back. "It is a horror, one I will refuse to tell my descendants about, lest they have nightmares."

An awkward pause filled the hangar until Caldwell clapped his hands. "Let's get this show on the road before someone's brother decides to propose to his sister. Remember, your time on target is one hour. The *Spire's* subspace speed bought us a head start, but we don't know how much. Get the PDS up, rescue Awen's parents, and we'll take care of the decoy. Azelon will have extraction transport waiting on the atoll of Simlia, as marked in your mission plan window. Easy in, easy out."

Magnus raised a hand. "Colonel, may I have a word?"

Caldwell stepped aside with Magnus. "What is it, son?"

"Ricio's wife and kid. He asked if there was a way to—"

"Already took care of it. Ricio was able to make contact with his wife on Capriana, and then he arranged for a little last-minute vacation care of some of his old Navy pals. I may have called in a favor or two as well."

"And no one is the wiser?"

Caldwell pulled his cigar out of his mouth. "Not a clue, son. Plus, who'd believe this splick anyway?"

"That's what I'm afraid of." Magnus chuckled. "Thank you, sir."

"Don't mention it. Just make sure you do your job."

"Colonel," Azelon said. "*Belvista Summit* will be coming into sensor range in sixty seconds." The ship was one of a handful of Ember-class Frigates that the Repub kept on orbital security around Capriana. But all of the ships combined would do little to thwart any serious enemy assault on the planet. The weak defense was just one more sign that the Republic had grown apathetic and was not prepared for what was about to jump out of subspace.

"Time to get a move on, Lieutenant," Caldwell said.

Magnus nodded, checked the mission clock, and then made the call. "Everyone to the line." All twenty-five Elites stepped up to the edge of the safety zone painted on the hangar bay floor about four meters from the environmental forcefield that separated life from hard vacuum. Magnus gave the command for helmets on and then ordered everyone to double-check the rig of the person on their right; Caldwell double-checked Magnus on the end. Once affirmation icons went down the chat window in his HUD, Magnus gave the order to advance to the red line against the shimmering translucent blue wall. The dark side of Capriana Prime loomed below them like an ominous black hole, punctuated by small dots of light wherever island cities poked above the watery surface.

"Ten seconds," Magnus said.

"Safe travels, Granther Company," Caldwell said over comms. "And mystics' speed."

———

MAGNUS LEAPED from the *Spire* and felt the weightlessness of low orbit tickle his gut. Unlike jumping from a vessel in-atmosphere, the gravity this high up wasn't enough to yank an object straight down. Instead, it was a gentle pull, noticeable only by referencing a larger stationary object—in this case, *Azelon's Spire*. Between his feet, he watched the hangar bay's doors close until the cloaked ship was invisible against Capriana Prime's night sky.

Apparent speed, acceleration, and altitude appeared in Magnus's HUD, along with a glide path and angle of incidence. The data was reasonably static at first. The only high number was the altitude, placing Granther Company 103 klicks above the planet in the lower thermosphere. The height also corresponded to a graph that represented the variation in acceleration due to gravity.

This moment of peace, Magnus knew, was the calm before the storm. Over the next few kilometers, things would go from tranquil to total chaos. The only gladias with battlefield experience for this type of jump were those who'd served in the Republic Marines—the rest had only done it in the enclosed combat simulation environment. Were it not for Azelon's suits and sophisticated automation, such a jump would be catastrophic for more than half of Magnus's company. There were still risks; no jump was ever "safe." But the Novian tech went a long way in ensuring everyone landed on target.

Not only was a night jump into the target area the surest way to avoid Capriana's defense network, but it was also the fastest. There was no need to fake ship logs, spoof scanners, or mess with hangar bay assignments. Instead, jumpers could head directly to their respective targets and start infiltration. As long as Magnus could convince CENTCOM of the situation, and Zoll could break out Awen's parents, there was no reason this entire op couldn't be finished before sunup.

Magnus glanced at his mission clock. It was 0300 local time—right on schedule.

"Remember," Magnus said over VNET. "Work with the suits, not against them. And Cyril?"

"Uh huh?"

"No squirming."

"Right, right, right. I'm roger that. Copy, sir."

Magnus watched on his HUD as the members of Granther Company began to fan out, making room for one another in case of a mishap. A blowout, satellite strike, or gear malfunction could spell disaster for more than one jumper if they flew too close together. Magnus had seen his share of emergencies, and he didn't need to witness any more today.

Fortunately, Azelon's handiwork didn't stop with the suits. She, TO-96, and Cyril had taken extra time to create a passthrough corridor that tracked with the jumpers during their entire descent. The *tech shadow*, as Cyril called it, temporarily rendered all planetary defense surveillance blind wherever the gladias passed by. It included blackouts of active thermal imaging, space displacement surveillance, and drone security. Only if the ground operators were really smart, Cyril had said, would anyone notice a pattern and discover the vectors. When Magnus asked about the likelihood of such a discovery, the code slicer just chuckled. "If everyone shared data like they were supposed to, they'd blast us in the first ten kilometers. But they don't, so we'll be alpha zulu good to go, sir."

The first test of the genius's plan came when Magnus noticed a satellite racing up to meet them. It boasted several solar panels, sensors, and a large central core. But unlike most orbital units he'd seen, this one looked like it had gone dark. No blinking lights, no glowing operations panels. The gladias were close enough that if it had been working, they'd be found out for sure. But instead, the teams ripped by without so much as a blip from the orbiting mass of metal.

"Dead as a dead corpse," Cyril said over comms. "You see that, Lieutenant, over?"

"I did, Cyril," Magnus replied. "Don't talk unless you have to, kid."

"Right, right. Sorry, sir, Lieutenant. Copy over." A beat later, Cyril's voice trembled. "Whoa, whoa! What's happening?"

"It's normal, kid. Just relax."

The first signs of entering the mesosphere were small vibrations that tingled Magnus's skin. He glanced at his altitude—85 klicks—and noticed his speed increasing. "Nice and easy, people," Magnus said. "Stay loose and ride it."

The vibrations increased, and small orange flames appeared on his visor. The HUD displayed a fast rise in external suit temperature as atmospheric friction increased. Magnus felt his limbs shudder and noticed the suit's smart pads expand to clamp down on his body. Just because an egg couldn't be fried inside a shell didn't mean it couldn't be scrambled instead.

Next came the roar.

The first time Magnus ever experienced the deafening sound of an exosuit entering an atmosphere, he'd thought he'd lost his hearing forever. And some guys did need surgery afterward. But rather than be afraid, Magnus felt exhilarated. Among the many experiences that constituted core Marine activities, orbital to atmo jumps were among Magnus's favorite. He was born to do this stuff and loved it as much now as he did the first time. Hearing the roar of fire against his body as it hurtled toward the planet was as hardcore as you could get.

"Woohoo," Magnus yelled, deciding to forgo comms discipline. Maybe if the newbs heard his enthusiasm, they wouldn't be as nervous—because mystics knew most of them were nervous. Hell, half had probably already spliced themselves. "Come on, Capriana! That all you got?"

Cyril's voice came over VNET in a soul-stuttering, teeth-chattering sound that made Magnus grin. "Yuh-yuh-y-y-you luh-luh-luh-lied-d-d t-t-t-to me!"

"I didn't want to spoil it," Magnus yelled back.

The violent forces reached their climax, shaking Magnus so hard it felt like the Novian armor would split open at any second. There was no way anything could survive this—an atmosphere was why asteroids blew apart. But he would survive it, just like he had dozens of times before, and as he double-checked the roster and team bioactivity, so would everyone else it looked like. Heart rates and blood pressures were up, but that was good—it meant they were alive and awake.

In another few moments, the flames died down, and the roar outside transitioned to the sound of whipping wind. The suit's temperature gauge also receded as the air cooled the red-hot panels. Azelon insisted that the telecolos finish wouldn't come off during their journey, which was good—they'd need all the cover the suit's chameleon mode could provide. But until Magnus saw it work again for himself, he wouldn't believe the cloaking tech could survive such a beating.

"Praise be to the gods of insanity," Abimbola said over comms. "I believe we flew through hell and survived."

"That's about the gist of it," Magnus replied. "Everyone good? Awen, you okay?"

When she spoke, it sounded like a child trying to talk through a mouthful of hot soup. "Not so much."

"Just spit it out," Magnus replied, guessing she'd vomited —*like always*. "Your suit will reclaim it." Then he heard her belch, followed by a juicy flow of something passing over the mic. "Feel better?"

"A little, yeah," she replied.

"I do not feel a little better," said Rohoar. "I believe Jujari were not meant to fly."

"Just hang in there, everyone," Magnus replied. "Stay on target. You're doing great."

A warning indicator went off in Magnus's HUD. The words Proximity Alert blinked in red letters, followed by a vector indicator pointing toward an object in the upper left frame. He willed his display to zoom in, and then identified the object as a drone hub—a two-meter-wide substation that deployed, resupplied, and serviced a dozen smaller drones at altitude. According to Cyril and the bots, the flight path was supposed to be clear of obstructions, but this unit was clearly off course, perhaps caused by some unforeseen side effect of the tech shadow. Worse, the drone hub was in the middle of Echo Team's flight path.

"Echo Lead," Magnus said, trying to keep his voice calm.

"Obstruction ahead," Zoll said, seeing what Magnus was. "Evade, evade, evade."

3

HANDLEY HIT the drone substation so hard that the sound traveled through Magnus's helmet. The unit flipped over and sent Handley's body flying off at an oblique angle. Then the substation surged to the left, trying to stabilize itself, and flew into Robillard's path. Robillard glanced off the side, giving little more than a grunt over comms. The substation spiraled away, unable to maintain altitude, leaving Handley and Robillard's bodies to tumble through the stratosphere.

Magnus looked at the roster and saw Handley's vitals flatline. Robillard, however, seemed relatively stable despite having a fractured humerus and ulna, along with two broken ribs and a hairline fracture in his right hip.

"Robillard," Zoll yelled. "Talk to me!"

"Damn drones," Robillard replied through gritted teeth. "Always knew they were trouble."

"You able to stabilize that spin you're in?"

"Roger." Within a few seconds, Robillard regained control and started slipping back toward Echo Team's formation. "Where's Handley?"

Magnus heard Zoll swear under his breath, then say, "He's gone."

"Splick."

"Stay focused, people," Magnus said, suppressing the anger he felt bubbling up from his gut. Not only was Echo Team's medic and demolition specialist dead, but the team's lead rifleman was badly injured. This was not the way to start a mission. Magnus had never been one for omens, but if the galaxy was going to send him a harbinger of doom, this was it. *The mission, Magnus,* he reminded himself. *Focus on the mission.*

Magnus opened a private channel to Robillard and Zoll. "You look hurt, Robillard."

"Nothing my suit can't handle, LT," he replied.

"I need to know you're good to go," Zoll said.

"Suit's pumping me with feel-goods, nanobots doing their thing, and I can feel the clamps on my arms already. I'm green."

"I'm good if Magnus is," Zoll replied.

"Roger that," Magnus said. To his credit, Robillard had been one of the toughest Marauders Magnus had seen come through training. Plus, Robillard was damn good in close quarters battle, and a crack shot too, so Magnus didn't want to lose the gladia to a stupid accident. Zoll's team would need him inside the lab if things got hot, especially now that they were down a man. "But Zoll and I need to know if you're unable to perform."

"You'll be the first to hear me whine," Robillard replied.

Satisfied, Magnus opened the company channel again. "Second squad, prepare to break off."

"Ready," Zoll replied.

"Waypoint hotel lima niner approaching in… five, four, three, two, one—break."

Zoll and his three fire teams banked south, diverging from Magnus's two teams. Second squad's course took them toward the research lab while Magnus continued toward the Forum Republica's capital complex. "Safe travels," Magnus said.

"See you at exfil," Zoll replied.

Forty klicks below, Capriana's atoll appeared like the jewels of a necklace, glowing golden yellow amidst a midnight black canvas. Smaller dots of light moved to and from the C-shaped island chain, designating water-bound cruisers and flying transport shuttles. From this height, it was hard to tell just how massive each island in the atoll truly was. But Magnus knew that each skyscraper-laden patch of land was equal in size to whole countries on other worlds. Only the ignorant thought of Capriana as a small cluster of islands.

Having grown up here as a kid, Magnus knew the city never slept. There was always someone needing to talk to somebody about something that couldn't wait. Then again, the fate of a hundred worlds rested on what happened on these massive islands, so there were legitimate excuses for the endless comings and goings of the galaxy's elite. But even with all the activity, a night incursion was far safer and more secretive than anything Granther Company might attempt in the day.

Magnus studied the flight path that appeared as augmented reality in his HUD. The line took them west of the atoll's wide center point, over the sea, and then curved inland. Glide assist would deploy at 1,000 meters above ground level, and then they'd traverse east, flaring atop Centennial Tower.

Magnus monitored each gladia's flight path, making sure everyone was staying on course. The only person straying a little too far outside the line was Czyz—the Jujari called up from Charlie Team to take Saladin's place. "You holding up, Czyz?" Magnus asked.

"I am not holding up," the Jujari replied. "I am falling."

Magnus smiled—*ever the literalists,* he mused to himself. "Right. Everything okay, though? You're straying from the flight path."

"This flying is not as easy as you humans make it seem."

"Well, that's only because I've had a little more practice than you. You do it long enough, it comes more naturally."

"I hope never to do it again," Czyz said. "Unless my mwadim forces me to under penalty of death."

"That's a little extreme," Magnus said.

"But it proves his displeasure," Rohoar added. "And Rohoar will endeavor never to ask him."

"Well, there you go," Magnus said to Czyz, noting Rohoar's curious self-identification.

"There," said Czyz. "I believe I am back on the trail."

"Yup, you are." Magnus noted the course correction. "Nice work."

"I only accept praise from my mwadim," Czyz said. "However, I recognize your approval of my achievement."

"Happy to hear that. First squad, deploy wing assist and proceed along vector path bearing 280°. Activate chameleon mode. Confirm."

Both fire teams acknowledged the heading and adjusted course. Magnus activated the wing assist feature, which deployed a carbon fiber fabric that spanned between arm and body, and between his knees. The new control surfaces gave him more stability as well as more maneuverability, allowing him to redirect along the west-bound flight path.

The squad soared out over the blackness of the Midnoric Ocean and then began a wide bank that brought them around to bear on the largest island. Buildings loomed ahead like a field of shiny opal columns reaching toward the stars. Magnus's glide path traversed the western beach and brought him into the city under the tallest buildings.

Magnus flared to bleed off a little speed and lowered the automation's assistance as he preferred to fly this route himself. Below him, hover cars and delivery transports went about their business, completely unaware of the eleven flying bodies overhead. To his left and right, he caught subtle flashes of camouflaged bodies as they whizzed across the skyscraper faces.

"900 meters to LZ," Magnus said. "Prepare for landing."

The overlaid flight path descended slowly as it headed toward a skyscraper that bordered a large clearing in the city's center. The medium height tower had a flat roof clear of obstructions, which made it a safe landing site for space divers. *If its designers only knew that it also made a perfect urban landing site*, Magnus thought to himself.

"Five hundred," he called out, and then began to flare. The wind buffeted his body, trying to throw him off course, but he managed to maintain proper trajectory with quick compensation movements. As he slowed, however, his flight stability lessened, and he risked losing lift altogether, which would cause him to tumble out of the sky.

Magnus and his teammates needed to stall directly over the LZ. Without AI assistance, such a feat would be almost impossible. Only the very best—or the luckiest—could pull it off without meeting a catastrophic end, either plastered against the side of the building or falling to the streets below. But with step-by-step guidance and full auto-assist for the least competent fliers, the difficulty was reduced significantly.

At 150 meters, Magnus sank below the building's top, flared, and then rose back up and over the summit just as his velocity dropped to under five meters per second. His boots touched down, and the suit's servos absorbed the majority of the kinetic energy. He still needed to take several steps across the gravel-covered rooftop before he came to a stop.

Magnus felt the carbon fiber control surfaces retract, and he turned around to watch the remainder of his teammates land. One by one, each gladia touched down on the rooftop—some skidding, others running. But only one made a perfect landing, sticking her feet to the roof on the first try.

"Seems you're a natural," Magnus said to Awen. "But I'm pretty sure you cheated."

"Me? Cheat?" Awen said, stepping forward with the poise of a princess. "I'm afraid you have mistaken me for someone else."

"Sure, I did." Magnus pointed to the rooftop's far side. "Bimby, Silk, set up the shot. Titus and Dutch, you're managing clip-ins and safety checks. Rohoar, you're first over, and I'm pulling up the rear. Cyril's tech shadow should keep us hidden from non-visual surveillance, but the closer we get to our target, the more suspicious we become, so keep your wits about you. Questions?" No one said a thing. "Let's do this, people."

Abimbola pulled an A-frame support rig off his back, spread the legs, and extended the feet. He placed it on the ground and then removed a bolt gun from the small of his back, firing anchors into both feet to secure the frame to the rooftop. He fired a third bolt into a winch plate, which he placed three meters behind the A-frame, and then tossed the small gun away.

Silk stood beside Abimbola, taking an SMMWS from Rohoar and hoisting it to her shoulder. Rohoar helped her charge the weapon as she aimed across the open expanse to the east. The shoulder-mounted multi-weapons system was Azelon's variation of the Repub SMDL—shoulder-mounted detonator launcher. But instead of only firing detonators, the SMMWS, or SMS for short, could fire an array of ordnance, including the explosive-tipped grappling anchor and zip cable that Rohoar had loaded from his hardshell backpack. Normally, Rohoar would operate his SMS as Alpha Teams heavy ordnance expert, but not at this range. This was a sniper's job, and he seemed only too happy to let the baldheaded, tattoo-covered former Marauder take the shot.

While Silk lined up, Abimbola motioned to Czyz and withdrew two planks from the Jujari's back. Abimbola unfolded each one to reveal a metal frame with a semi-translucent fabric in the middle. Quick button presses released spring-loaded support stands, and Abimbola set the screens on both sides of Silk.

"Might wanna stand clear, Nídira," Silk said, looking over her shoulder. The mystic stood directly behind Silk, apparently curious about the weapon and the screens. As a Luma, Nídira probably hadn't seen a whole lot of firearms, so this novelty must have seemed even more outlandish than standard blasters.

"Right," Nídira said. "Sorry." She stepped away as Silk resumed her firing posture. "But what are those?"

"Sonic disruptors," Magnus replied. "That SMS packs a mean bark, enough to draw more attention than we want. But the panels will help disorient sensors enough that they won't be able to pinpoint the source."

"Clever," Nídira said. "But why didn't you just ask one of us to help with that?"

Magnus looked from Nídira to Awen. "Well, because…"

"Would you like it to be fired in silence, Magnus?" Awen asked with a certain level of playfulness to her voice.

Abimbola and Silk both looked at Magnus before he replied, "Uh, that'd be great."

Awen nodded at Nídira, and then the two women produced a barely visible dome around Silk.

"Don't contain the blast," Silk said. "Just the sound, right?"

Magnus nodded at Awen. "If you contain it all, you'll rupture all Silk's soft tissue."

"Just the sound energy," Awen said. "We got it."

"Cool," Silk said, nodding slowly. "I'm down with this." Then she spread her legs, bent her knees, and lined up her shot. "Keep your panties on, everyone. Fire in the hole."

The SMS coughed flames out the front and back as the grappling anchor leaped from the tube and shot across the expanse. The only audio Magnus's helmet registered was a soft *whump* under his feet. Cable whipped out of the pile on the roof as the projectile streaked through the night and then slammed into the west side of Proconsul Tower. When the anchor struck, a small explosion emitted from the hole as the grapple's claws shot into the surrounding material.

Silk gave Abimbola a nod, and the Miblimbian yanked on the cable, pulling up the slack. Then he heaved the line over the A-frame, carried it to the rear anchor plate, and activated the small winch that pulled the cable through until it was taught.

"150th floor," Silk said to Magnus. "As ordered. You're all set, LT."

Magnus tipped his head toward her in thanks and then looked at Rohoar. "You're up."

"But Rohoar is going down," the Jujari replied, speaking of himself in the same weird way that Ezo did.

"Yes, but you' re—just get on the mysticsdamned cable and go cut the windowplex, would you?"

"You do not need to be snippy with Rohoar, scrumruk graulap." The Jujari approached the cable and raised a hand to it. Titus held Rohoar's wrist against the line while Dutch instructed Rohoar to activate his suit's traveler. A small gimbal mechanism protruded from Rohoar's wrist. Then a gate about the same size as the line snapped open. Titus pulled Rohoar's wrist in and the mechanism clamped down on the cable, giving a small chime and illuminating a green LED. Titus looked to Dutch, who then asked Rohoar to test his weight against the line. The Jujari pulled his knees up and began sliding.

"Whoa, whoa, big guy," Dutch said as she and Titus leaned in to stop the hyena-like beast from hurtling off the side. "Just a little test."

"Jujari do not test. We do, or we do not."

"Yeah?" Dutch said. "Well, not testing stuff gets you killed. And we like you too much for that."

Rohoar gave a low growl. "Is Rohoar ready to slide?"

Dutch nodded at Titus. "You're ready," Titus replied. "Happy trails."

"I see no trail, nor does it have feelings that would seem to indicate—" Rohoar was cut short as both Titus and Dutch sent him sailing over the edge. The Jujari howled so loudly that Magnus had to lower his interface volume. Rohoar's body sped along the cable, traversing the western quad of the Forum Republica campus far below.

Even from this height, Magnus could make out some of the ornate buildings, meandering garden pathways, and lit skywalks that composed the upper levels of the capital complex. It would still be two hours before the first staff populated the common spaces.

Magnus watched as Rohoar's now tiny body slid under the shadow of the docking platforms, some of which hosted government and civilian vessels. In another few seconds, Rohoar activated the brake in his wrist coupler and slowed until his body came to rest against the building.

With his HUD and bioteknia eyes working in tandem, Magnus zoomed in to see Rohoar remove his left gauntlet, maglock it to his thigh, and then stretch his left paw. He extended a single clawed digit and began scraping it across the windowplex in a full circle, large enough for his body to fit through. Rohoar traced the path twice more with his claw and then replaced his gauntlet. Then he pushed away from the building, out over the campus far below, and swung his whole weight at the freshly cut circle shape.

His boots struck the side, and, at first, nothing happened. Rohoar gave out an irritated snarl over comms and then pushed himself away again. His boots slammed into the windowplex a second time, but still, nothing happened. Another growl and Rohoar pushed off. This time, when he lunged forward, the Jujari disconnected his arm from the cable. Magnus was about to protest, but there wasn't time. Rohoar flew through the air and struck the circle hard enough that it gave way. Then the Jujari and the windowplex disk disappeared inside the tower.

"You crazy ass son of a bitch," Magnus said.

"No," the Jujari said. "Rohoar's ass is not crazy, nor is his mother a breeding hound used solely for producing progeny. Instead, she is a beautiful—"

"Don't finish that," Magnus said. "And let's just assume I believe you. Good job out there, Scruffy."

"Scruffy?"

Ignoring the question, Magnus turned to the rest of the gladias. "Who's next?"

One at a time, Titus and Dutch helped each person to the cable, attached their wrist-coupler, and then sent them across the expanse toward Rohoar's outstretched arms. After everyone had traversed the zip line, Magnus attached his coupler, stood with his toes over the edge, and then pushed off.

Magnus felt his body's weight yank on his arm as he flew out over the campus that lay nearly 400 meters below. He picked out a small stream that flowed around a seating area with soft, tree-mounted lighting. He also saw several small outbuildings that doubled as elevator terminals to speed people around the complex in the modular transport system.

Magnus picked up speed, listening to the sound of the cable whizzing through the coupler. He relaxed his body and let the active gimbal keep him aimed toward the hole in the building. Ahead, Magnus saw Rohoar's armored form waiting to receive him. Higher up, Magnus noted just how many transport shuttles slept against their docking platforms. Proconsul Tower not only served as the meeting place for the most important intergalactic dignitaries but offered easy access for their arrival by shuttle as well.

The wrist coupler started to brake, slowing Magnus as he neared the cable's end. Rohoar reached out and took hold of Magnus's free arm just as his feet touched the rounded window-plex edge.

"Rohoar has you," the Jujari said, pulling Magnus in as the wrist coupler released his other arm from the cable.

"Thanks," Magnus replied. "And what's with all this Rohoar business?"

The Jujari tilted his head. "Business?"

"Never mind." Magnus looked around and saw his two fire teams in an ample office, complete with an ornate wooden desk, brightly colored paintings, and opulent, low-slung guest seating. Abimbola had already made himself comfortable on one of the leather couches, putting his feet on the glass coffee table. "Bimby, I hate to cramp your style, but I need that line cut."

"On it," the Miblimbian said, sitting up and moving toward the hole.

Next, Magnus pulled up a building schematic in his HUD. The three-dimensional layout turned in his vision until an icon indicated the teams' position on the 150th floor. Magnus accessed the next waypoint, and it brought up a multi-point path that extended across their current floor, down an elevator shaft to sub-level twenty, and then into some sort of entrance hall. He populated the team's chat window with a link to the route and then moved toward the office door.

"We'll cross to the main elevator terminal on this floor," Magnus said, highlighting the route. "Then it's a straight shot 170 floors down. Keep chameleon mode active, and keep noise to a minimum. We should be able to spoof the low-grade office sensors, no problem. Weapons ready?"

Everyone nodded and brought their NOV1s to low ready position.

"Let's move."

4

ZOLL'S TARGET building was two blocks inland from the midpoint of Dalton Beach, which ran along the length of Terin Island's western shore. The long sandy strand made for a far easier landing than the one Magnus would have atop Centennial Tower. But that didn't mean a beach landing didn't come with its inherent risks—namely, people.

Despite the human's daily need for sleep, not everyone in the species chose to engage in it, especially star-crossed lovers on blankets or drug-saturated dimwits around campfires. Civilians were sometimes the most effective surveillance of all because unless you were going to detain them, or worse, kill them, they could raise the alarm just as effectively as automated sensors.

The upside of landing where civilians might be was that traditional surveillance was usually minimized. Wandering people not only set off automated systems, making their maintenance a nuisance, but acted as a form of passive security to deter would-be trespassers.

Of course, if you had invisible suits of armor, the very latest in stealth and mapping technology, and a little bit of luck, you could avoid the human and traditional surveillance altogether.

Zoll flared his suit just above a clear stretch of beach then let his boots dig furrows through the sand as he came to a halt. His fabric wings retracted, and he turned to see the others make landfall. To the naked eye, it would have looked as though small sand spouts had erupted across the beach. Zoll imagined some giant arachnids dancing around, making divots as they ambled above the surf.

"Dude, what the hell?" said a lazy voice. "You catch that?"

Zoll spun around to see two figures sitting in the sand about ten paces away. Somehow, he'd missed them when he scanned the strand. *Dammit.*

"Mystic spirits, bro," exclaimed the other, batting at his friend's shoulder and making a cigarette fall from his lips. "I told you the astrals were real. I told you!"

The first rip-smoker took a deep drag on his cigarette and then followed the movement in the sand as his eyes grew wide. "Splick, one's coming toward us, bro. It's coming toward us!"

The second junkie backed away at Zoll's advance. "They're gonna suck out our souls, bro! Run!"

The two hallucinating bums tried to scramble out of the sand but only made it a few paces before they ran into the invisible form of a Jujari warrior. The first man bounced off the armor and fell flat on his back. The second struck it and started screaming, arms flailing. Grahban ended the noise with a fist to the top of the man's head, sending him to the ground in a heap. The second tried backing away, crab style, but Grahban grabbed him by the ankle and hoisted him into the air. The victim writhed like he was about to be eaten by some invisible monster. Then the Jujari clocked the man on the side of the head and tossed his body away like a rag doll.

Zoll stared at Grahban for a second.

"What?" the Jujari asked. "They were annoying me."

"I can see that. You didn't need to kill them."

"Not dead, just sleeping for a long time. By the time they wake up, they will have good stories, and perhaps one more reason to become sober of mind."

Zoll chuckled. "That's one rehab program that may actually work."

"Thank you." Then Grahban hesitated. "What is this rehab program?"

"Don't worry about it," Zoll replied. Then, turning to the rest of his teams, he said, "Fall in."

The map for this portion of the city showed the research lab about 600 meters from their current location. They'd need to cross a boardwalk and then move east down a side street. Zoll talked his team through the approach.

"We'll use the loading dock in the back as infil. It will have the least sensors, and probably a security guard or two. Non-lethal force wherever possible."

"My rehab program?" Grahban asked.

"Yes, your rehab program. Rix, Dozer, we might need some

explosives on the main door. But if we can get in without drawing too much attention to ourselves, that's the priority. Wish, Telwin, Finderminth, see what your Unity powers can do for us."

The three mystics nodded. "We will," Wish replied.

Zoll brought up the building's schematic and made sure everyone had it in their HUDs. "Once we're in, we need to find out where they're keeping the assets. My guess is they've got them in a secured residence of some sort. But we won't know that without tapping a data node, located here. Cyril, that's you."

"Roger, copy that, bravo," the code slicer replied, still looking unstable after the jump.

"Once we've got a fix on the assets, we'll go from there. Any questions?"

Jaffrey's hand went up. He was Echo Team's sniper and the youngest member of Granther Company's second squad. He'd also trained with Handley the most. "What about Handley, sir?"

Zoll took a deep breath. "He was a good gladia. But he died doing what he believed in, so we honor that by making sure this mission isn't for nothing. Which means we all have to stay focused. Shoot now, grieve later—you got that, Jaffrey?"

"I do, sir." The kid nodded.

"And what about Robillard?" Bliss asked.

"What about me?" Robillard replied. "Do you think I'm not ready to kick some ass? Cause I can kick some ass right here, right now."

"Easy," Zoll said, raising a hand. "I think he's just checking to make sure you're okay after that drone strike."

"Me? You should see the drone," Robillard said, shrugging his shoulder away from Bliss. "I'm ready to go, Lead."

"All right," Zoll said. "But if you—"

"I'll let you know if anything goes south," Robillard said. "Don't you worry your pretty little hiney."

Zoll smiled. He liked the fight in this gladia. "All right, teams. Let's move."

"FEELS LIKE A LIFETIME since we were back on Oorjaee, doesn't it, Rix?" Zoll asked as the squad ran toward the lab.

Rix laughed. "Hell, where's Oorajee?"

"Copy that."

"Doesn't matter much anyway," Robillard said. "The way I see it, it's a different place but the same old story."

"Only this place has palm trees," Rix said.

"And bikini-clad babes when the sun is out," Bliss added.

"Good thing you're invisible, Bliss," Robillard said. "Or they'd be running."

"That's not what your girl said when she showed up at my quarters last night."

Robillard reached out and punched Bliss in the shoulder.

Bliss made a show of rubbing his arm. "That hurt *so* bad."

"All right, you two," Zoll said, but laughed as he spoke. "Knock it off."

"I know what you mean, Robillard," Rix said as they turned left at an intersection. "Not about Bliss and your woman.

Different place, same story. The powerful do horrible splick to the weak, and we're left to sort through the rubble."

"I'm not so sure about that, guys," Zoll said while he double checked his squad's six. "This feels different."

"How you figure that?" Bliss asked.

"'Cause now we've got cool armor and awesome weapons," Robillard said.

"Nah. But they're definitely legit." Zoll looked ahead toward the next intersection and signaled the team to turn right. "Somehow, with the Gladio Umbra, I feel like we're making a real difference. It's not just turf wars for the sake of pissing people off or fighting over scraps in the Dregs. We're actually doing something that people might remember."

"If anyone's left to remember it," Robillard said.

"Shut up," Bliss said as he returned the earlier punch. "He's being serious."

Even despite his guys' antics, Zoll knew what he'd said was true. The Gladio Umbra had given them all a chance to make something of their lives again, to lift themselves out of the desert sands and contribute to the cosmos. "We're making a difference. I know we are. I can feel it."

ON THE OUTSIDE, the lab looked like any other fancy office building in the high-end beach community—four stories of glass, metal, and wood arranged by some overpaid, overly artistic architect. The only notable thing to Zoll was the illuminated sign beneath a cluster of palm trees that read Burndale Home Furnishing Solutions.

"You sure this is the right place?" Bliss asked.

"You want to be the one to ask TO-96 to double-check his calculations?" Robillard replied before Zoll could say anything.

"Not if Azelon's around, I don't," Bliss said. "She's so defensive about him these days."

"Copy that," said Robillard.

"It's a front," Zoll said. "Stay low, and let's head around the back."

He led all three teams around the north side, over a grassy berm, and up to a security fence. Longchomps bit through the wire lattice and pulled open a hole for everyone to go through.

Zoll noticed several security cameras along the roofline and two in the loading bay. "Just be aware of the eyes on us," he said, marking the cameras on the HUD map.

The teams crossed the tarmac and moved up a set of stairs to a wide landing. Interestingly, there were still no guards to be seen, which was okay with Zoll. He'd take every advantage they could get. The extra-wide main door was really a reinforced blast door made to look like a loading bay port. Upon closer inspection, Zoll recognized the armor plating and telltale angular indents. He ran his fingers along the diagonal closure seam and turned back to the gladias.

"Now, why would a home design studio need thirty centimeters of reinforced armor plating on its back door?" Zoll looked around. "Anyone?"

"Bet they've got some expensive kitchen appliances," Reimer said.

"You cooking?" Bliss asked.

"Depends what you're willing to pay me."

Zoll raised a hand to quiet them. "Wish, a little help?"

"Certainly," said the woman. She stepped forward and lowered her head. Telwin and Finderminth came forward and joined her. Zoll wasn't sure they were doing anything until the sound of a latch mechanism released inside the door. A moment later the blast door's two primary leaves parted, exposing a narrow slit extending from the upper left to the lower right.

"Help me get this open," Zoll said. Longchomps, Grahban, and Redmarrow stepped forward and began separating the doors just enough that the other gladias could start sliding through. The metal groaned as the Jujari fought against the actuators buried in the frame.

"Come on, everyone through," Zoll ordered. "They'll be seeing this any second." All three teams slid through the gap, including the Jujari, before Zoll rolled over the lower of the two diagonal doors and landed safely on the other side. As soon as he was in, the sound of trotting footsteps came down a hall perpendicular to the main corridor. Zoll ordered everyone against the sidewalls and waited.

A security guard never appeared—but a Marine did, dressed in black armor with three white stripes on his left pauldron. The trooper turned toward the half-opened blast door and slowed, tilting his head to examine it. The moment his weapon lowered a centimeter, Zoll gave the order for Grahban to take him. "No rehab program." He could practically hear the Jujari smile.

Grahban swung a giant paw and struck the Paragon trooper in the back of the head so hard that the man's body flew forward and hit the ground, while his torso and legs carried over his back. The force was enough to split the man's spine, paralyzing him and—over the next few seconds—killing him.

"Leave him," Zoll ordered. "More will be coming to investigate, but we need to move." He led the way down the main corridor and followed his HUD's route to the first data node located one level up. "We'll take the stairs. Bliss, you take point."

"Copy," Bliss replied, then stepped through the sliding door and started up the switchback staircase.

Zoll waited for everyone else to follow, and then stepped halfway through himself when he heard more footsteps behind him. Three more Paragon troopers rounded the corner and knelt to examine their incapacitated counterpart. They shared looks between one another, but no alarm went off. Perhaps they thought it was an accident? After all, there were no blaster marks, and the security cameras wouldn't show anyone assaulting the trooper. Still, Zoll knew it wouldn't be long before they lost the element of surprise. He pulled back and let the door shut before bounding up the stairs.

On the second floor, Cyril was already at a data node, typing furiously on a holo console.

"Whaddya got?" Zoll asked.

"Working on it, big leader," Cyril replied.

Zoll looked up and down the new hallway when he heard Robillard chuckle. "What is it?" Zoll asked.

"I don't imagine a whole lot of customers find this ambiance accommodating." Robillard waved his NOV1 at all the Repub-styled bulkheads and trunk lines. It felt more like they were on a starship than in an office building.

"I don't know," Bliss said. "I kinda like the spartan look. Gives it a post-industrial feel."

"I'll give you a post in your industry feeler," Robillard said with a raised fist.

"Are they always like this?" Wish asked Zoll.

"Pretty much," he said. "Sometimes worse."

She gave a quick shake of her head. "Noted."

"Hey, hey, Mr. Zoll, leader man person?" Cyril asked.

Zoll detected a hint of concern in the code slicer's voice. "You find them?"

"Uh-huh. Yeah, I think so, yeah. But, we might have a problem. A big one."

Zoll crossed to Cyril's position. "Why? What is it?"

Cyril expanded a holo window and then pointed. The display showed the building schematic everyone was familiar with. Then it showed several additional floors—subterranean floors—as well as the words Bio Safety Level Four in red letters.

"Splick," Zoll said. "Is that what I think it is?"

Cyril nodded.

"Hold up," said Robillard. "What do you think it is?"

Zoll shook his head. "Seems TO-96 was only half right. This isn't just a lab; it's a bank for every deadly microbe in the galaxy."

"A what?" Bliss asked.

"A biohazard research facility," Cyril replied. "And Bosworth has Awen's parents locked up on level four."

"That's better than level five, right?" Robillard asked.

"There is no level five," Zoll replied.

Cyril nodded. "Four is as bad as you can get. And it's hard to break into for some very excellently important reasons."

A klaxon sounded and yellow lights began swirling down the hallway. Robillard nudged Zoll. "Looks like we've got some breaking in to do."

"And fast," Bliss said, raising his NOV1 to high ready position and pointing it down the hall. "'Cause here they come."

5

MAGNUS LED his two fire teams across a shared office workspace, down a hallway, and then toward a bank of elevator doors. He paid extra attention to the security cameras at each junction but rested in the fact that this floor didn't seem to be of much significance—as per TO-96's assumption—thus, the security measures were not very strict. Further down toward CENTCOM, however, Magnus knew the story would be different.

Alpha and Bravo Teams loaded into two transparent elevators with a view of the campus's north side. To the west, Magnus could see Centennial Tower and the remains of their A-frame rig peeking above the rooftop.

Abimbola and Titus held the doors, making sure to hit their destination buttons at the same time. Once pressed, the doors slid shut, and the pods sank. Magnus didn't like how vulnerable the teams were, but he reminded himself that to any onlookers, these empty elevators were simply being called to another floor. It was the people monitoring the security cameras and elevator sensors who concerned him. But he was playing the odds that at 0330, the security guards were more interested in their latest serial holo than whatever late-night illegal races the elevator pods were having with one another.

"All systems look nominal," TO-96 said in a private channel with Magnus. Video of his face filled a small window in the lower left of Magnus's HUD. "So far, I'm detecting no alarms or security calls."

"Let's hope it stays that way," Magnus replied.

"Indeed. Please remember that, as you descend, you may experience a comms blackout with us, as well as mild separation anxiety."

Magnus furrowed his brow. "Separation anxiety?"

"That is correct, sir. There is significant data on the human species, among others, which concludes you experience emotional distress when relieved of vital interpersonal relationships, either through physical or communicative separation."

"So, you're saying our relationship is vital?"

"Given all we've been through, I assume you feel a deep connection to me."

Magnus chuckled. "I mean, you are pretty attractive." When TO-96 didn't reply right away, Magnus said, "What is it, bot?"

"Sir, I regret to inform you that—well…"

"Spit it out, 'Six."

"I'm already spoken for, sir. In that way, I mean."

"Spoken for?" Magnus was doing his very best not to burst out laughing.

"Yes, sir. As in, someone has already expressed an interest in my particular affections."

Magnus could feel his armor bouncing as he silently laughed between clamped lips. But he also knew he couldn't afford to be too distracted, so he kept one eye on the descending floor numbers. "Let me guess. Is it Dutch?"

"No, sir. Though she would be a prime companion."

"Would she now?" Magnus brought Dutch into the channel as TO-96 replied.

"Yes, sir. Miss Aubrey Dutch exhibits several key characteristics essential for a healthy mating relationship."

Dutch turned to face him, and Magnus didn't need to have X-ray vision to know her eyebrows were raised in surprise. Magnus pointed to his ear as if to say, "Keep listening. It gets better."

"She is extremely faithful," TO-96 said. "As well as intelligent, strong, resilient, charming when she's not pointing a weapon at you, and she has ample hip displacement suitable for incubating and dispatching several progenies, perhaps in multiples."

Dutch seemed about to protest, but Magnus held a hand up. He was doing his best not to stop the bot with his hysterical laughter, and Magnus didn't want Dutch ruining it either, no matter how offensive she found it.

"Moreover, Miss Dutch's attributes would be wasted on me," TO-96 said. "For three primary reasons."

"Which are?" Magnus asked.

"First, I am not threatened by her threats of bodily injury, primarily those made with weapons—items that she loves so much. Therefore, as a mate, I would be improperly motivated to accommodate her needs if held at gunpoint."

Magnus stifled more laughter and glanced up at the floor count. They were almost there. "Fair enough. Next?"

"Second, I do not find myself attracted to Miss Dutch physically or hormonally. Granted, I lack the physiological systems necessary to facilitate copulation. However, I do feel that I understand the implications well enough to make certain hypothetical postulations about my preferences."

"Mystics knows I can't wait to hear what your preferences might be," Magnus replied. "And lastly?"

"Third, and closely related to the second point, I am unable to impregnate Miss Dutch, thus wasting both of our potential to preserve the species that are driven by the evolutionary desire for immortality. That said, however, I do believe I would be more than able to please Miss Dutch given my knowledge of—"

"And would you look at that," Dutch said, stepping toward the parting doors. "Here we are."

"Sorry, 'Six," Magnus said. "Looks like the rest of this convo's gonna have to wait."

"Ah, very good, sir. I will leave you to your work."

THE GOOD NEWS was that VNET still had integrity on sublevel twenty, at least in the vicinity of the elevator banks. The bad news was that the large corridor leading to CENTCOM's entrance was full of high-end security measures, at least as far as Magnus's bioteknia eyes could read. Point defense guns lay recessed in the ceiling while redundant multi-point sensor plates and multi-spectrum cameras ran along the walls and floor. Then there were the impregnable blast doors at the far end, operated by quantum encrypted ID panels—and all this was *before* anyone had even entered CENTCOM.

Two Marines in battle armor stood on either side of a luxurious check-in desk. An attractive woman seated behind the counter wore her hair pulled back into a ponytail and sported a combination headphone and mic. Apparently, people had stuff to do, even at this hour, because the secretary was busy taking calls, typing on three different holo screens, and attending to a short queue of people waiting to speak to her.

The guards held their weapons across their chests and kept their heads aimed at the line of people. Had it not been for the queue, Magnus felt certain the Marines would have noticed the elevator doors open. And when no one stepped out, they would have investigated. But as it was, Alpha and Bravo Teams' presence remained unnoticed.

While the space appeared pristine—no doubt designed to fit in with the capital complex's auspicious facade—Magnus guessed that what lay beyond the blast doors was hard-nosed military to the core. Here, glossy white surfaces with black trim and bright lighting reinforced the prestigious decor of the Galactic Republic.

But there, inside those doors, lay the heart of the industrial-military complex.

"So, what is the plan, buckethead?" Abimbola asked as the two teams pressed up against the sidewalls.

"We've got redundant multi-spectrum cameras along the entire hallway's ceiling," Magnus said. "Pressure sensors on the floor, thermal and motion on the walls. And point defense turrets hidden in the ceiling. Not to mention the quantum encrypted ID security and the big blast doors that none of us can shoot through."

"It's a damn kill box," Dutch said. "Splick."

"So, what you are saying is, it will be a walk in the park," Abimbola replied.

"Pretty much." Magnus looked back at the elevators. "Because I don't plan on going into CENTCOM."

"You don't?" Titus said, unable to hide the surprise in his voice.

Magnus shook his head. "Don't have to. While Cyril wasn't able to slice into CENTCOM's database, he was able to access a far less encrypted intel source."

"Which is?" Titus asked.

"General McCormick's personal calendar." Magnus could see all the gladias turn to look at him. "Turns out the General is an early riser and should be coming out one of these two elevators in approximately"—Magnus glanced at the mission clock in his HUD—"three minutes."

"You want us to pin him in the elevator and interrogate him there?" Titus asked.

"Could we not have done this while he was en route from his residence?" Abimbola asked.

"Negative." Magnus rolled his head to keep his neck and shoulders from getting too tense. "He's under personal escort throughout his day." Magnus waited a moment while everyone processed the information.

"Except when he takes the elevator down to CENTCOM," Titus finally said.

"Correct," Magnus replied. "It's the handoff between security details. Logic assumes no one is going to try and approach him between the ground floor of Proconsul Tower and the highly secured vestibule of CENTCOM."

"But we are," said Abimbola.

Magnus grinned. "Damn straight. I want all eyes on those doors. When you see the general, we push him back in, load up both pods, and peg it to the top floor, overriding any other floor requests. We'll have the whole ride for me to convince him of what I can."

"What if that's not enough time?" Awen said.

"It's gotta be."

"But what if it's not?"

Magnus worked his jaw. "Then we'll think of another way to raise the PDS ourselves."

"Which is what?"

Mystics, she just doesn't know when to quit. "Which is—"

"Heads up," Titus said, raising his weapon to one of the elevator's opening doors. "And a problem."

General McCormick was in the elevator—as was a second individual dressed in a senator's suit.

"Two for the price of one," Magnus said. "Here we go."

If either of the two Marines on security detail had looked at the elevators, they would have seen the general and the senator disappear as the gladias filled the pod. Only small hiccups in the telecolos rendering system would have betrayed the two men's presence. The same disappearing act went for anyone monitoring the cameras inside the elevator itself. But rather than take any chances, Magnus and the rest of Alpha Team repositioned the two men in the camera's blind spot as Awen pressed the button for the top floor. Then she keyed in the standard override code to ensure the trip was uninterrupted. Likewise, Dutch activated a local jammer on her forearm that took care of any attempts for the two men to call out—which they were doing.

"Security, this is Senator Blackman," the other man yelled into his lapel. "Elevator SB2, we have a—"

Rohoar batted the senator on the side of the head, stunning him. "Focus, human," Rohoar said over externals. "Your comms don't work. Pay attention."

The man sputtered, trying to focus on whoever it was that spoke to him. He was stocky with well-groomed grey hair and thick shoulders.

As for the general, the years behind the desk hadn't been kind to him—or maybe they had been, depending on your interpretation. The balloon in his gut and the extra chin on his neck told Magnus all he needed to know about the man's eating habits. But McCormick still wore his red hair tight on the sides and flat on top—a holdover from his years under a helmet. *If only he'd held on to PT the same way,* Magnus thought. *Let's hope he can think fast under pressure.*

"General Issac S. McCormick?" Magnus asked, still cloaked.

The general squinted at the mention of his name. "Who's there? What is the meaning of this?"

"My name is Adonis Olin Magnus, former lieutenant with—"

"Lieutenant Magnus?" the senator said, eyes still searching the empty pod. "But-but, you're charged with treason and—"

Rohoar slapped the man again. "Not focused."

"The 79th Reconnaissance Battalion," McCormick said, answering the rest of Magnus's opening statement. "Your company was assigned to Oorajee"

"Yes, General." Magnus felt uneasy that both men knew him by name. "At great risk to myself and my team, I've come to inform you that all three Republic Fleets have fallen into enemy hands and are currently headed toward Capriana with the intent of attacking the planet."

Whatever Magnus hoped would happen next, it didn't.

"You've got some nerve, Lieutenant," McCormick said.

"Former," Blackman added. Rohoar hit him again, and the man let out a yelp.

The general looked at his friend and then back in Magnus's direction. "Invading the capital, abducting a members of CENTCOM—"

"I know how it looks, General. I do. But the fate of the city rests in what you decide to do in these next few seconds."

"Correction," McCormick said. "Whatever you choose to do

in the next few seconds is going to be irrelevant when we reach the"—he looked at the touch screen—"top floor. Right now, my security detail is realizing that I failed to check in with my secretary. They've already deduced that I'm still in this pod, *and* they're tracking it to the top floor. When those doors open, you and whoever else is with you will be dead. So, on the contrary, Lieutenant Magnus, I think *your* fate rests in what happens over the next few seconds."

"Can we kill them both now?" Rohoar asked.

"No," Magnus replied.

"But they irritate me."

Magnus squared his shoulders. "General, you well know that Fleet Admiral Wendell Kane was tasked with commanding Third Fleet."

"Spare me the lesson, son."

"And you also know that you've lost all communication with him as well as First and Second Fleets."

McCormick's lips parted, but no words came out.

Finally, Magnus thought. *A foothold.* "Also, you probably know by now that Kane has taken control of all three fleets and has laid waste to the Jujari resistance. What you *don't* know is that he's headed here next for the sole purpose of wiping out the capital and a group he calls the Circle of Nine."

McCormick's back straightened. "How do I know what you're telling me is true, son?"

Magnus produced a small data card and slipped it into McCormick's breast pocket. The general jerked back when it touched him. "Easy, sir. I'm not going to hurt you. The data card in your pocket has tracking information indicating Kane's fleet movement, as well the subspace jump signature for their destination coordinates."

"Which is here above Capriana Prime, you say?"

"Yes, general."

McCormick pulled the data card from his pocket and examined it skeptically. "And you expect me to do what with this, Lieutenant?"

"I expect you to take it seriously and raise the planetary defense shield."

"The planetary defense shield?" McCormick raised an eyebrow. "Just like that?"

"Yes, general."

McCormick started to laugh. "I've got to hand it to you, son. Your grandfather had big stones. *Big* stones. But you, my boy? *Damn.* You're hung like a Pavroothian quarter stallion. And you're just as nearsighted too."

Now it was Magnus's turn to squint. "Sir?"

"Kane isn't coming back to attack Capriana, son," McCormick replied. "He's coming home." The general snapped the data drive in two and let the pieces fall to the floor.

Senator Blackman smiled.

Magnus felt like the rug had been pulled out from under him. Whatever secret organization had lost control of Kane, McCormick wasn't in on it. Or if he was, he was bluffing. Either way, this plan was falling apart fast. Still, Magnus had to keep trying. After all, this wasn't about rescuing a teammate or protecting the Gladio Umbra—this was about saving billions of people.

"General, we have a witness who spoke with Kane and knows about his plans."

"Do you? And where is this witness?" McCormick looked around. "Surely not cloaked here in the elevator pod with you, about to be arrested or shot."

"She's not here, no. However, her testimony was on the data drive you just compromised."

"And who is this woman?"

Silence filled the cramped pod.

When Magnus failed to answer, McCormick said, "I've heard enough."

"It's a child, sir. Daughter of Senator Stone. And Colonel William S. Caldwell will vouch for her statements."

Both officials' eyes widened. "Caldwell?" the senator said. "How would Caldwell know anything about this?"

"Because he's with us, attempting to stop Kane."

"Son," McCormick said. "I can assure you that Colonel Caldwell was killed during the raid on Worru. We lost a lot of good men in that conflict. So now I *know* you're here under pretenses. What those are, I do not know. But"—the general looked at the floor numbers again—"I don't have time to find out, and you've run out of time to manipulate me."

"General, sir. Please." Magnus put a hand on the man's chest. "You've got to raise the PDS."

McCormick grabbed Magnus's forearm with a surprising

amount of strength. "Son, I don't have to do a damn thing. And just so you know, you're about to be in a heap of trouble."

"Is that all you have to say, buckethead?" Abimbola asked over comms, nodding toward the floor count. "Because we are slowing down."

"This was not an excellent plan," Rohoar said. "Rohoar deems we kill them."

"Everyone relax," Magnus ordered, sorting through what to do next. "We're not killing them." Clearly, the general wasn't on board. Then again, Caldwell had told Magnus not to expect much. This part of the op was a long shot. But there were other ways to get the PDS up—this was just the least messy. And it had to be tried first, before the others, or Magnus knew he'd regret it.

"I recommend you surrender now," the senator said. "With or without Kane's assault, you've got nowhere to run."

"May Rohoar do a deed?" Rohoar asked Magnus.

"Just don't kill him," Magnus replied.

In the blink of an eye, Rohoar hit Blackman on the side of the head, and the man dropped to the carpeted floor. "This has pleased Rohoar very much."

"I'm happy to hear that," Magnus replied.

"Who are you people anyway?" McCormick asked, still unable to focus on anyone in the pod.

"No disrespect, General," Magnus said over externals. "But if you didn't believe me about the senator's daughter and the colonel, you'd never believe me when I tell you who was in this elevator with you. On that note, I'm sorry we have to do this, but you leave me no choice." Magnus gestured to Rohoar, and the Jujari dropped the general just like the senator. Then Magnus raised his NOV1 and pointed it toward the elevator's transparent exterior shell. "Titus, blow your elevator's glass. We're punching out. Everyone ready?"

"You've got to be kidding me right now," Awen said.

"Why? You and I have a thing about jumping off skyscrapers together."

"We did it *once*," Awen protested with her hands on her hips. "And I was unconscious."

"Still counts," Magnus said, feeling the elevator come to a stop. "So, it's a thing."

"It's not a *thing*."

"Then it will be after this," Magnus said, and then squeezed the trigger.

6

BOTH ELEVATOR's windowplex exteriors exploded like a shower of glittering jewels thrown into a moonlit sky.

"Everyone out," Magnus yelled. "Fly west. I'll drop an LZ marker when I have one." He looked across at the second elevator. "Titus, you coming?"

"We're on your heels, LT," Titus replied.

Abimbola, Rohoar, Awen, Silk, and Doc leaped from the opening and deployed their carbon fiber fabric wings. Magnus nodded at Titus. Bravo Team's leader pushed Czyz, Nídira, Dutch, and Haze out before following himself.

The elevator doors opened behind Magnus, and someone shouted at him to stand still. Magnus spun, lunged backward into the night air, and watched as his feet cleared the elevator. Gravity took hold of his body, and a second later he was clear of the enemy threat, diving toward the campus. He maglocked his

NOV1 to his back, deployed his wings, and rolled over. With a prompt in his HUD for adequate speed, Magnus flared into a nose-up position and banked left.

"You copy, 'Six?" Magnus asked.

"I see you and both fire teams heading westbound, sir," replied the bot.

"We need an LZ, ASAP."

"Understood. I'm sending one to you now. It will take you to the main island's western shore."

"Populate it."

A small icon appeared in Magnus's HUD. "Done," TO-96 said. "From there, you will be able to secure transport to Azelon's exfil coordinates."

"Negative, 'Six. We still have a mission to complete."

"But, sir—"

"I need a plan B."

TO-96 hesitated. "Plan B, sir? But I assumed you'd make entry into CENTCOM and activate the PDS yourselves if you weren't successful in convincing the officials."

"So did I, but it's locked down tight. Quantum encryption, impregnable blast doors, point defense guns, and redundant sensor security. We're talking splice that makes the *Black Labyrinth* look like child's play. So we're making this next bit up as we go."

"Improvising then, sir?"

"That's the word." Magnus adjusted course to follow the augmented reality flightpath in his HUD. He watched the other gladias lineup, preparing to fly through a long corridor of skyscrapers. "I need other ways to raise the shield besides doing it from inside CENTCOM. I need you to think like a badass."

"A badass, sir?"

"Hell, yeah. Break the rules. Think outside the box. Splick —hold on."

"Hold on?"

Magnus adjusted for a sudden crosswind. The gust tried to push him into the first oncoming building on his right. He banked left against the blast of wind, then corrected to fall back in line with the flight path.

"Okay, badass. Whaddya got?"

"Hypothetically speaking, it appears you could activate the PDS manually from inside the main generator station."

"See? Now you're talking like a badass."

"Thank you, sir. But I fail to ascertain how that makes me a badass."

"Just roll with it. Where's the station?" Magnus watched the line of gladias as they sailed between buildings along an ever-descending route above the capital's streets. Lights blurred in his vision while the sound of the rushing wind *whooshed* around his helmet.

"On the main island of the Elusian atoll," TO-96 replied.

Magnus grinned. "Now you're rolling. You feel that, buddy?"

"No, sir. I feel nothing."

"But you're thinking outside the box."

"No, I'm providing you a logical secondary option derived from an analysis of the PDS's infrastructure, utterly devoid of what you might call sexy peel."

"You mean sex appeal."

"Of course."

"Whatever works for you." Magnus grinned. "Just stay loose and keep the intel coming."

"According to the schematic I have, the core's main command console has a manual override function."

"Then that's where we're headed."

TO-96 nodded in his holo window. "You'll be able to initiate the start-up sequence with only minimal instruction from me."

"Nice. Thanks, bot."

"Because I'm a badass?"

Magnus chuckled. "Hell, yeah."

"I only wish I was with you to help take out the resistance you'll encounter."

"The what?" Without warning, another crosswind threw Magnus sideways. He was quick to compensate and avoided smacking into a mirror-finished building on his left.

"The resistance. The generator station is inside a military installation."

"And this is easier than breaking into CENTCOM?" Magnus said.

TO-96 tilted his head in Magnus's HUD. "Quantifiably, sir. You have a 0.0023% chance of getting through CENTCOM's front doors, not to mention certain entrapment and summary execution. So, yes, this plan B, as you say, has a much higher probability of success. Just guys with guns, as I overheard you saying once. But that is your specialty. You are going to break in there and kill everything that moves, sir."

"What?"

"No living soul shall survive. Your enemies will cower in abject fear. Future generations will marvel at the legend of your exploits."

Magnus chuckled as he increased his angle of attack, exchanging altitude for speed. "Relax, pal."

"Too much badass, sir?"

"A little."

"My apologies, sir. I will let you fly in peace."

Magnus thanked the bot, signed off, and then opened up the squad channel. "LZ's a wide stretch of beach. Avoid any civilians." Confirmation icons ran down his chat window, and Magnus flew the remaining distance with only the sound of the wind to keep him company.

The limited traffic below ran to where the streetlights met a hard intersection on the city's western edge. Beyond the city limits lay a dimly lit boardwalk and a dark strand that slid under the surf. And it couldn't be soon enough—Magnus was about to run out of altitude. The rest of the squad had room to spare, but Magnus was coming in under the projected flight path. A traffic control truss crossed the street about seven meters off the pavement ahead of him. Magnus decided not to attempt flying over it, so he dove, barely missing the structure, and emerged two meters above a hover skiff.

Magnus pulled up, trying to gain a little more altitude, and successfully flew over the cross traffic at the end of the street. He banked right to avoid a cluster of palms along the boardwalk, and then flared over the first open patch of sand. But Magnus came in too hot and was forced to roll out of his landing. Sand shot into the air as he spiraled forward, raining on his helmet once he'd taken a knee.

"All units check in," Magnus ordered. They did so, and he saw their icons spread out along the beach. Then he ordered his squad to fall in on his location, and the icons started to move closer until everyone was in a loose circle around him.

"I take it that did not go like you intended," Abimbola said.

Magnus shook his head. "Not quite. New plan. We're gonna activate the planetary defense shield ourselves. TO-96 said we could do so at the main generator core located here." Magnus populated a map in VNET and ordered everyone to open it. "The atoll is twenty-five klicks west of our current location, and home of Elusian Base and the PDS generator core. There are other relay cores located around the planet, but this is the big one and the only one with a manual override for the entire system."

"Manual override, as in we have to walk in there and physically throw the switch?" Titus asked.

"That's the idea." Magnus sent another packet of information to everyone. "TO-96 has already provided three routes into the base for us, all leading to the manual override terminal located here"—Magnus flashed a blue waypoint marker on an outbuilding connected to a sizable hangar-like facility—"next to the power core station."

"We flip that, and the PDS goes live, mission over?" Dutch asked.

Magnus nodded. "That's what I'm told."

"Did he say what kind of resistance we can expect?" Titus said.

"Based on the fact that we just broke into the Forum Republic, assaulted two high ranking Republic officials, and made quite the exit, I'd say the base will be on high alert. The good news is that the only two people who know we're interested in raising the PDS are currently unconscious. Until they wake up, no one knows where we're headed exactly."

"Rohoar should have slain them," Rohoar said.

"Speaking of slaying, we're going up against Marines," Magnus added. "So we're going to do our absolute best to minimize casualties. We're not here for them, and they're not the Paragon. We're here to get a shield up, copy?"

"This is all well and good," Awen said. "But how do you intended to get us twenty-five kilometers into the Midnoric Ocean?"

"With those." Magnus pointed toward a large beach hut with a sign that read Jules Sea Skimmer Rentals.

"You've got to be kidding me," Awen replied.

"If we ride in pairs, we can act like honeymooners."

Awen laughed once. "I'm riding my own. Thank you very much."

"What is honeymooners?" Rohoar asked. "And should Rohoar ride with Abimbola?"

"No," Abimbola said with a chop of his hand through the air.

"It means newlyweds," Titus said to Rohoar, then cocked his head sideways as if considering his explanation. "Uh, people who agree to be married. Family commitment?"

Rohoar jerked back. "You mean, mating rights?"

Titus raised both hands toward the Jujari. "There you go. Mating rights."

Then, with a sound of abject disgust, Rohoar stepped away from Abimbola. "Rohoar rides alone, like Awen."

THE SEA SKIMMERS were parked in a long line under a thatched awning that stretched out from either side of the main hut. Each unit was tethered to a charging station with a locking cable. Magnus asked Rohoar and Czyz to detach enough units for everyone and then raised Azelon over VNET.

"Any chance you can help us slice these, Azie?" Magnus asked.

"Please proceed to the procurement terminal," Azelon replied.

"The what?"

"I think she means the checkout counter," Awen said, pointing to the center desk under the main building.

"Right," said Magnus, then he vaulted over the counter and walked to a holo terminal. He waved his hand over the activation sensor, and a translucent keypad appeared at chest height.

"Standby," Azelon said. A few moments passed before she listed a series of numerals and letters, which Magnus entered. A green Accept indicator flashed, then opened to a user-friendly vehicle roster display with several easy-to-read tabs—no doubt designed for the cheap hourly labor that ran this touristy establishment. "Now, choose how many vehicles you would like, select Payment, and then enter your Republic account information."

Magnus hesitated. "Azie, my account is probably suspended, and I—"

"I'm producing offspring," Azelon replied.

"Huh?"

"It's *kidding*," TO-96 said, interjecting himself into her avatar frame. "We went over this already."

"Quite so. My apologies." Azelon looked back at Magnus. "I'm kidding."

"We don't have time for this," Magnus said but had to admit her attempt at humor was at least a little funny.

"But sir, you said, *keeping it light and punchy is a good way to dispel tension in combat.*"

"The slice, Azie."

"Stand by."

The holo screen flickered, and a few new screens appeared that looked more like Cyril's backend coding windows than anything an hourly employee would know how to navigate.

"I'm using your suit's sensors and your biotech interface to communicate with this business establishment's security proto-col," Azelon said.

"Looks like you're making quick work of it."

"It's a benign system." Several chimes began ringing down the rows of sea skimmers as the red lights on the locks changed from red to green. "There you are, sir."

"Thanks, Azie. Just two more things."

"Yes?"

"First, make sure you remove anything that might govern the speed and balance of our skimmers. Tourists might not want to kill themselves while surfing the waves, but we might."

"Curious, but easy enough. What's the second thing?"

Magnus looked at a stack of cheap poker chips that served as business cards for the proprietor's enterprise. "Make sure that Mr. Jules is well compensated for this little venture of ours when all this is over. Chances are, he won't be getting these skimmers back."

"Understood, sir. Also, Mr. Jules is Miss Jules."

Awen caught Magnus's eye and pointed toward several framed images on the back wall. An attractive woman in a wetsuit stood in front of a racing sea skimmer, or held various trophies and awards, or stood beside other racers or dignitaries.

Magnus whistled. "Nothing like stealing from a champ." Then he turned back to his squad and told everyone to find an open sea skimmer and prepare to move out.

SEA SKIMMERS WERE NOT COMPLICATED to operate when their automation was active, which was why almost any planet in the Republic with water had them. When tuned down, the skimmers made for great tourist excursions, as evidenced by Miss Jules's business, which—if Magnus had to guess—probably had franchises up and down the atoll. Plus, they looked amazing, so who wouldn't want to give one a try?

The skimmer's lack of complexity also made them extremely

fun to race, especially when souped-up with oversized drive cores, high-density repulsor panels, and customized steering modulators. The Intergalactic Sea Skimmer League was one of the most developed sporting organizations in the quadrant, right below spaceball, and Magnus had attended his share of races as a youth here in Capriana. He was surprised he'd never heard of Jules before but admitted it had been over ten years since he'd followed the sport.

Magnus hadn't ridden a skimmer since he was a teenager, but he knew it would come back to him in a flash. He made sure everyone found a unit suited to their size and weight before climbing on one himself. The entire fleet was painted in obnoxious neon colors and sported large racing numbers to make the tourists feel like they were pros.

The vehicles were mainly water-based hover sleds, but with several exceptions. The body was a narrow fuselage with a rounded nose in the front and vertical stabilizer for a tail. Small repulsor panels lined the bottom along the spine, making the vehicle hard to balance when standing still, but extremely maneuverable when at speed. While the addition of two small repulsor wings on each side of the body helped provide some stability, their primary purpose was to help roll the craft as they rotated along their axis. And, unlike repulsor technology used on land, the water-based equivalent afforded sea skimmer pilots a seemingly limitless, ever-increasing speed envelope, as well as the tightest turn radius of any vehicle in the Repub.

It was no surprise that the military routinely tried to purchase the vehicles. Still, the league consistently refused, not wishing their beloved racing sport to be sullied by the image of blasters strapped to the sides, riding into some interplanetary conflict that may or may not be supported by the league's diverse fan base. Most followers of the sport agreed with the league's decision, but not Magnus. *They would have changed the tide of the war for us on Caledonia,* he thought. Plus, he knew how badass Marines would look riding into battle on a fleet of them. Today, it seemed he'd get his wish, but with gladias instead of Marines.

Riders leaned forward against the skimmer's fuselage, nearly prone—hands on angled handlebars and feet on actuator pedals. The horizontal stabilizer in the rear, which sat atop the vertical fin, helped regulate the skimmer's pitch, and the pedals helped control the yaw. For most everyone, these input values were automated. All a pilot needed to do was turn the handlebars like a bike. But for the more experienced riders, which Magnus liked to think of himself as, automation could be reduced, with control given to the operator in varying degrees of intensity. The very best pilots could perform stunts and tricks that seemed to defy the laws of physics. Today, however, Magnus just needed the skimmer to serve as high-speed transfer sleds.

"Everyone ready?" Magnus looked up and down the line. "Throttle is in your left hand. Ease forward, find your balance, and then—"

All at once, Czyz shot forward and struck a media stand, knocking it over. Likewise, Doc Campbell surged forward, braked hard to compensate, and then dropped his sled. It fell sideways with a *thud* on the boardwalk. Similarly, Haze—the newest member of Granther Company, selected from Forbes's first platoon—bumped into Czyz's skimmer. The Jujari turned around and growled at Haze, but then dropped his sled in the sand.

Magnus shook his head. "Azelon, I'm having second thoughts. Can you return auto stabilization to everyone's skimmers?"

"Right away, sir. Please note, however, that it will adversely affect their top speed."

"I'm aware. And, right now"—Magnus winced as Rohoar smacked into Abimbola—"I'm fine with that."

7

SECOND SQUAD OPENED fire on the four men who came around the corner. Unarmored and brandishing only light sidearms, the security guards didn't have a chance against the NOV1s. Ultra high-output weapons fire ripped the guards' bodies to shreds in seconds. But the Paragon troopers who followed behind the security guards were *much* more prepared. The enemy took cover along the hallway's bulkhead-like separators and fired downrange toward the console station. Even though the troopers couldn't see anything, they must've known someone or something was there— the unauthorized node access and the dead bodies both here and in the loading bay gave it away.

"We need a plan," Zoll said, taking cover behind the mystics' shielding.

"And fast," Bliss added.

Zoll had hoped this would be a smooth snatch and grab. But

now that they were inside the high-security government bio-research facility, his hopes of getting back to the *Spire* before lunch were fading fast.

"You following all this?" Zoll asked to Caldwell over VNET.

"Affirmative, Zoll," the colonel replied. "Think you can still handle the objective?"

"I already canceled my breakfast reservations for this, so, since we're here, why not?"

Caldwell's mustache turned up at the ends. "Keep your heads down."

"Will do. Would you update Magnus for us?"

"Roger that."

"Thanks. Zoll out."

Without warning, a small detonator with a red blinking light rolled down the hallway toward Zoll.

"Fragger," Zoll yelled. He stepped forward to kick the enemy ordnance away, but it moved before he could get a boot on it. The detonator reversed course, flew through the air, and then exploded behind the bulkhead where the six troopers took cover. The sudden burst of light and sound shook the hallway and dimmed the lights. When Zoll looked around to see who or what had returned the enemy grenade, he saw Wish—Charlie Team's mystic—give him a little wave. "That was some fancy-ass splick."

"I try and make myself useful," Wish replied.

"Fine by me." Zoll turned from the six dead troopers and the four dead security guards to look at Cyril. "Give us a direction, kid."

"That way, on the double duty." Cyril pointed east, farther

down the present corridor. "Then north until we hit the lower elevator banks, ten four."

"Sounds good."

"But, but, sir. They're going to be locked down tight."

"Can't you do something about that?"

Cyril was back on the console, typing furiously. "Anything I do here could be nullified by the time we get down there. The building's AI is compartmentalizing systems as we speak. It's almost exactly like the level in *Blue Reaper* where you constantly have to stay ahead of the alien supermind that's trying to keep you from escaping from the—"

"Cyril," Zoll yelled. "We don't have time for this!"

"Oh, right. So sorry, sir. Yes."

"Can you slice the elevators?"

"Yeah, yeah. But, again, I'm not sure how long—"

"Do it. We'll improvise when the need arises. That's why we have you."

Cyril nodded and then entered several lines of code that made no sense to Zoll.

"Longchomps, Grahban, Redmarrow." Zoll pointed to the three Jujari. "I want you on point. Flip back your OTA extensions and get those snouts and claws ready. Azie's update on your telecolos covering should extend chameleon coverage to still keep your extremities cloaked. Wish, Telwin, Finderminth, cover our six, and keep Cyril cocooned while you're at it. Let's move."

As soon as Cyril was done slicing, the team left the data node and continued east down the hallway until they reached a T-intersection.

The three Jujari sniffed the air, and Longchomps raised a fist. "Hold," he said in a low tone. "I smell unbathed humans and energy mags."

"Which way?" Zoll said.

"Left. And right. Both stationary."

"They're set up on us," Bliss said. "Playing defense."

Zoll nodded, then looked back at Longchomps. "You go left toward the elevators. We'll cover right."

"With pleasure," Longchomps replied in a snarl. Before Zoll could move, the three Jujari dove at the far wall—*and ran along it*. Claws dug into the metal, and Redmarrow even raced along the ceiling. The Paragon troopers started firing, but their aim was imprecise. The Jujari remained clear as they advanced.

Zoll ordered his three snipers—Reimer, Bettger, and Jaffrey— to swing out and fire south, while Rix and Dozer provided covering fire. The gladias peeled out and took cover behind the bulkheads, NOV1s and CK360s pointed downrange, blaster bolts whizzing.

Northbound, the Jujari fell upon the defenders like a Bornark fessel pig that hadn't eaten in three days. Longchomps clothes-lined two troopers at once—one who was reloading, and a second who was firing right into the Jujari's chest. For Longchomps, that cost him 85% of his shield. But the two troopers hit the ground so hard their helmets flew off. Longchomps finished them by driving his palms into the heads, flattening them into a bloody pulp.

Grahban dropped to his side and slid along the glossy floor— his armor made a high-pitched squealing noise as he did. As he moved through the enemy's position, he reached out and slashed at the troopers' legs on either side of the hallway. Several men dropped to the ground, writhing. But for those who remained standing, Redmarrow dropped from the ceiling, rolled, and then pounced with all his weight. He pressed three troopers to the ground while closing his jaws on a fourth's torso.

The man in Redmarrow's mouth tried to raise his blaster high enough to fire down on the unseen force that crushed his ribs, but before he could get a shot off, the Jujari chewed his way through the stomach and spine, cleaving the trooper in two. The man's top half fell to the side, while Redmarrow held onto the bottom. When the Jujari turned around to look at Zoll, a pair of armored legs hung from his mouth. They only dropped to the ground when Redmarrow said, "Clear."

To the south, Reimer took out two troopers in quick succession, both with headshots. Bettger struck a third in the shoulder, flipping him to the ground, and finished him with a shot to the chest. Meanwhile, Jaffrey dropped a fourth trooper who maintained constant pressure on his trigger finger. The trooper's blaster continued firing as the man sprawled onto the floor, striking two other Paragon combatants in a deadly friendly fire accident.

"That counts as three kills," Jaffrey said.

"Does not," Bettger replied. "Unless you're that first guy—he gets two kills."

"South hall is clear," Robillard said, turning to face Zoll.

"Let's move," Zoll replied, then took off north toward the elevators.

The Jujari had already arrived at the four elevator doors when Zoll got there. So far, no other troopers had converged on their position, but he had a feeling the reprieve wouldn't last long.

Cyril walked up to a control panel and pressed the down button. "Okay, so, so, I guess it's time to see how far we get, right?"

"Right," Zoll replied. "Charlie and Delta, I want you defending this position. Echo, we're heading to the basement. Stay on comms, and stay alert." Everyone confirmed his orders in their HUDs, and then Zoll stepped into the open elevator. Echo Team loaded in, but Cyril remained on the outside. "Whaddya think you're doing?"

"Who, who, me?" Cyril pointed to his chest.

Zoll nodded.

"Well, ya see, I just thought that since—"

"Get in the damn elevator, Cyril."

"Sir, yes, sir. Copy over and out, sir."

Zoll reached out and yanked on the kid's arm, then punched the button for the fourth sub-level. The elevator doors closed, and the pod sank through its tube.

A small chime indicated that they'd passed by the first sub-level. Three seconds later, another chime sounded for the second sub-level. Then the pod slowed, but the third chime never came.

"What's happening?" Zoll asked.

"Well, sir, you see, that would be the AI," Cyril replied.

"Can't you get it going again?"

"Not likely," Cyril said.

"But you're a genius, I thought."

Cyril snickered. "I mean, it depends on who you ask but, like, the guys in my GAXCHAT forum? They say the real genius is—"

"For the love of mystics, kid! *Can you slice it?*"

"So sorry, sir. Let me see, sir." Cyril started tapping in the control panel and made discouraging sounds in the back of his throat.

"And?"

"I can't get root access from here, no. Sir, I'm sorry, sir."

The elevator started moving again, but this time it was going back up. "Oh no, you don't," Zoll said. "Wish, can you stop us?"

"On it," she replied. She raised her hands a little, and then a beat later, the pod's drive system gave a loud whine in protest, sending a tremor into the floor. The elevator shuddered and then began to slow as the sound grew louder. A loud bang sounded from underneath the floor, and the elevator jerked to a stop.

"Reimer, you've still got line, right?" Zoll asked, nodding at the sniper.

"Roger. How much?"

"Only one way to find out." Zoll turned to Longchomps and then pointed to the floor. "We need a hole."

The Jujari gave the menacing version of their species' smile and then began drawing a circle on the ground with his nail. The sound was horrifying but necessary. Like a can opener carving a furrow through soft metal, Longchomps completed his circuit and then punched down on the shoulder-width disc. The circle popped free and then fell into the darkness, clattering as it disappeared down the pit.

Reimer leaned over the hole and used his helmet's advanced range finder to determine the shaft's depth. "Forty-one point eight meters," the sniper replied. "But that's to the bottom. I have to imagine the fourth sub-level is somewhere above that."

"And you have enough line?"

"Fifty meters," Reimer said, patting the spool attached to his back.

"Run it. We'll follow." Zoll looked at Longchomps. "Can you make sure this pod doesn't go anywhere so Wish can stop working so hard?"

The Jujari nodded, turned, and then punched the sidewall. His fist left a dent ten centimeters deep. He repeated the blow in five more places around the pod, ensuring that the cart was bound to the narrow shaft it slid through.

"Try that," Zoll said to Wish.

She nodded and then seemed to release her hold on the elevator. When it didn't move for a moment, she said, "We're holding."

"Good." When Zoll looked back at Reimer, the sniper fired his cable anchor into the pod's underside, and then dropped through the floor's hole.

"It's holding," Reimer said, and then lowered himself down the shaft from his raised left hand. Zoll could hear the gentle whirr of the motor as it let out the nano cable. He watched Reimer's outline grow smaller as the gladia descended past the third subfloor and then head toward the fourth.

Unlike regular building stories that were four-meters high, these sub-level stories were far thicker—like Cyril had said, "for good reason." Breach control and containment were no small things when dealing with the galaxy's most deadly spores, viruses, and microscopic bad guys. Not for the first time, Zoll even wondered what jeopardy he was placing his team and himself in by gong this deep. Surely, there were safety measures and security protocols that sane people took when coming down here. But now they were punching holes in elevators and descending by cable.

"Almost there," Reimer said. "I see the door another fifteen—"

Reimer's voice cut off as the sound of metal sliding across metal filled the shaft.

"What the hell was that?" Zoll asked.

"Uh ohhh," Cyril said. "I was worried this would happen. I was worried, and now it's happening. It's happening!"

Zoll clapped his hands once in front of Cyril's face to get the code slicer to focus. "Talk to me, kid. What's going on?"

"Containment breach protocols. The AI thinks there's something nefarious going on."

"Because there *is* something nefarious going on!" Exasperated with Cyril, Zoll dropped to his knees and shined his headlamps toward Reimer. Where there should have been an open shaft, he saw a flat metal floor about five meters down. It looked like twelve metal leaves had spiraled inward, binding the cable at the center.

"It's, it's, it's a security wall," Cyril said. "Presumably shielded. That's why we've lost communication with Reimer."

"Let's just blow it," Longchomps said.

"And sever his cable?" Zoll asked.

"Not to mention blowing that panel straight down on top of his head," Rix added. "No way."

"So, what do we do now?" Cyril said.

"Bliss, Robillard," Zoll said. He waited a second before repeating the hail again. "Anyone? You there?"

"It's no good, roger copy, sir," Cyril said. "There's one of those walls above us too. The AI is trying to close in on us."

"So, what now?" Rix asked.

"Might I try to reopen the passage?" Wish said.

Zoll felt stupid for not thinking of such a thing sooner. This was, after all, the whole point of having fire teams comprised of individual specialists, wasn't it? He just wasn't used to having a mystic's uncanny powers at his disposal. "By all means," he said, stepping aside.

Wish smiled. "I don't need access to the hole."

"Right." Zoll shook his head. "Of course you don't."

Wish lowered her head, and everyone else waited. Several seconds passed before Wish said, "Okay, I see Reimer. He's managed to open the doors onto sub-level four."

"Excellent," Zoll said, relieved that the sniper hadn't sent himself plummeting to his death. "Are you able to speak to him?"

"Assuming he is settled enough in his mind, yes."

"Well—just—let him know we're coming, and to wait for us."

Wish nodded once. "It's done." She paused for another second. "All right, he says okay."

Zoll sighed. At least *that* was going right. "Can you open the security barrier?"

"I'm going to try, yes," Wish replied.

"If not, Rix can blow it," Longchomps said.

"No," Rix said. "The blowback alone in this confined space will kill us all."

"Not if I help contain the charge," Wish said. "But let me try opening it myself first. Please, everyone, I need to focus."

"Give her some space," Zoll said. "Come on." Longchomps, Rix, and Cyril stepped back, while Wish dipped her head again. At first, there was no sign that anything was happening. When the silence continued, Zoll thought of telling Wish to call it off, and then let Rix plant the explosives. But just as he was about to say something, a deep groan came from the barricade below them. Zoll dropped to his hands and knees again and looked into the shaft. "Well, I'll be," he said with a sense of wonder to his voice.

"Is the small mystic opening the hole?" Longchomps asked.

"Yes," Wish replied, her voice strained. "But do you mind giving me a hand?"

Longchomps touched his chest. "Me?"

"You have at least some power in the Unity, right?"

"Yes. We are raised as pups with a general awareness of—"

"Join me," Wish said. "I could use your help. This thing is strong."

"She's really not wrong," Cyril said. "The hydronic lock on that mechanism is said to make the unit unbreachable."

"I can still blow it," Rix said.

"Negative," Zoll replied. "Longchomps, join her."

The Jujari nodded and then closed his eyes. He gave a long

blast of air from his nostrils and then slowed his breathing. "Do you see my presence?"

"I do," Wish replied. "Do you see mine? Down here."

The Jujari nodded. "I'm coming to you."

"Good. Now, I need you to press along the leaves. Like this." Apparently, Wish was showing Longchomps something in the Unity down there. It was all very strange to Zoll, but he would be the last person to doubt it if, indeed, the pair could get the shaft opening again. "While you do that, I'm going to try and reverse or disable the locking mechanism. When I say go, I need you to push with all your might."

"But Madame Wish, I have not—"

"Go!"

Longchomps jerked back in surprise, but then started snarling as he did Wish's bidding. Watching the entire episode play out in the elevator was rather odd—a former Luma and a Jujari, grinding their teeth and moving their bodies around without anything else going on around them. It was a bit like watching two insane people have a conversation without using words.

"Almost—got—it," Wish said, hissing through the mic in her helmet. "Just—a little—bit—more."

"I do not think I can hold this much longer," Longchomps said.

"Just—a—little—"

A round *boom* rattled the shaft, echoing up and down it.

"Is everyone okay?" Zoll asked, unsure of what had happened.

Wish looked up Longchomps and placed a hand on his chest. "We did it."

"You—" The Jujari seemed at a loss for words. "You are very strong. And I am attracted to you. This unsettles me."

"—hear me, come in. I repeat, if can anyone can hear me, please come in."

"Reimer," Zoll exclaimed. "We hear you loud and clear."

"Thank the mystics," Reimer said.

"I will," Longchomps replied. He looked at Wish, and then said, "Thank you, tiny pretty human."

"I really wonder about you sometimes, Jujari," Rix said.

"Reimer, are you okay?" Zoll asked while staring at Longchomps and Wish, curious to see if the mystic would say anything back to the Jujari. The odd pair seemed to gaze at one another for a split second before Wish looked away. *Is she being coy with him?*

"I'm fine. I'm fine." Reimer sounded relieved. "Wasn't sure if I'd lost you guys there."

"Same," Zoll said. "But about you."

"Listen, that barricade split my cable."

Zoll balked. "With you on it?"

"No, no. I was able to descend to sub-level four and then open up the doors with my weapon. But as soon as that barricade opened, the cable came down. It obviously chomped it pretty good."

"Just glad you weren't on it," Zoll added.

"Me too. But now we've got ourselves another problem."

"How to get us down there," Zoll stated.

"Right."

Wish raised a hand. "I might have an idea. But I've never tried anything like it."

Zoll asked her to explain it. When she was done, Zoll looked at Longchomps, Rix, and Cyril. "Anyone have any better ideas?" They shook their heads, and Zoll put a hand on Wish's shoulder. "Looks like it's up to you again. Knock yourself out."

"What a horrible thing to tell her," Longchomps said. "And after what she just did for us. You humans disturb me."

8

It took three minutes for Magnus's squad to get off the beach. What had seemed like a bright idea at the beginning had turned into a comedic melee within seconds, as half the squad foundered with the sea skimmers. While the gladias made excellent gunfighters, they made horrible tourists—at least until Azelon turned the training hover plates back on. Everyone circled up and then shot off the beach, following Magnus into the low tide.

Their departure couldn't have come any sooner as several bystanders along the boardwalk started pointing fingers at what looked to be rogue sea skimmers driving around on their own. Magnus knew it would only be a matter of time before the police showed up. From there, officials would start connecting the break-in at the Forum Republica with the skimmer theft, and then the Repub would be on their heels.

Magnus looked over his shoulder at the tail of water shooting twenty meters into the air. His sled ripped across the wave crests, slicing through the white caps with ease, and maintaining speed over 160 kilometers per hour. To his left and right, his squad stretched out in a line 200 meters wide. He'd ordered everyone to keep the crafts' headlights off and operate using their helmet's night vision. Doing so would keep them from being tracked visually, both by those on Capriana and anyone watching from Elusian Base.

While the sea skimmers were capable of traversing the ocean faster with it off, keeping the automated stabilization controls on helped inexperienced riders from tipping over. But Magnus felt it was a fair trade-off—arriving at their waypoint a bit later would be better than only half of them arriving because of crashing. Even at half speed, the skimmer's drive core produced the characteristic scream known throughout the racing world. Magnus reflected on long walks down the shore as a kid. He could pick out sea skimmers a dozen klicks away just from their telltale wail. Unfortunately for him tonight, the same could be said of any enemies awaiting their arrival on the Elusian atoll.

"You're enjoying this, aren't you," Awen asked Magnus over a private channel on VNET.

"How can you tell?" he replied.

She chuckled. "I can hear you grinning."

"Guilty. I forgot how much fun these are."

"No, you didn't. And if I were a betting woman, I'd say we're not going fast enough for you."

"Damn, you're good."

"I know."

Magnus rolled his head in an attempt to loosen himself up—physically and emotionally. "Hey, Awen?"

She chuckled. "Yes?"

"Yeah. So, I know we haven't had a lot of time together lately—to talk and stuff."

"We've been a little busy."

"Right. But when we're not busy—later, I mean—would you like to walk?"

"Walk?" She laughed.

"Yeah. I mean, we can eat first, and then find a place to take a walk."

She giggled, and for the briefest moment, the sound transported Magnus to somewhere else, somewhere far away from Capriana and war and death.

"I'd like that," she replied. "You've got yourself a date."

"A date?"

"What did you think you were asking for?"

"Uh…"

Awen laughed again. "Don't answer that, Adonis."

"Okay." That hadn't gone like he imagined, but it hadn't gone worse either. He smiled, grateful for the diversion—for *hope*. Magnus took a moment to feel the fuselage's vibration rattle his body—to savor the wind and saltwater blasting his visor. "They're going to hear us coming, you know."

"Mm-hmm. I thought of that. How many guards you think they have stationed on the perimeter?"

"Midnight shift will be light, but I'm guessing more because of what we did in the capital."

"They're on alert then."

"And they're not the only ones," Colonel Caldwell said—his bushy white mustache appearing in a small window in Magnus's HUD.

"Colonel," Magnus said in acknowledgment.

The man must've noticed his proximity to the camera. He backed up and nodded at Magnus. "Seems Zoll's team has encountered more than they bargained for. Turns out TO-96's nondescript government lab is actually a secure biohazard research facility. Thing's got a security detail thicker than my sister's chastity belt and an AI that's smart enough to know how she gets out of it on the weekends."

"That bad?" Magnus asked, marveling at the colonel's endless treasure trove of one-liners. "Seems we've all got our hands full then." He looked at the mission clock. They had five minutes left before reaching the main island. "You listening, bots?"

"We are, sir," said TO-96, appearing with Azelon in their own window. "How can we help you?"

"Do you have access to any records on Elusian Base's force composition?"

TO-96 tilted his head and paused for a moment. "Affirmative, sir. It looks as though the installation can hold one company plus 100 civilian support staff."

"That seems excessive," Awen replied. "What is that, almost 300 people?"

Magnus grunted. "But that's maximum capacity, right 'Six? We're not talking that much strength now."

"Oh no, sir. There's much more on-site."

Magnus paused. "Come again?"

"There's another company there for training."

"Another company?" Awen cleared her throat. "Not to second guess you, Adonis, but are you sure this is the best idea?"

"It's still better than trying to break into CENTCOM," he replied. "We've got to try."

"To answer both your questions, the 9th Marines, 1st battalion, 2nd company is the second unit on location," TO-96 said.

Magnus rolled his eyes.

"I saw that," Awen said.

Damn. Some days, he wanted the old TACNET audio-only setup. "Azie," Magnus said. "Any chance of us sneaking onto post?"

"With the sound pressure level you're currently outputting, not likely," she said. "However, if you choose to slow your speed by 54% and approach from the south, you'll be able to make landfall on Cotter's Island here." A small island to the south of Elusian Base illuminated on Magnus's mission map. "Doing so should keep our presence largely undetected, at which point you can swim the channel between the two islands and approach the base in relative secrecy."

"How long's that gonna take?" Magnus asked.

"An additional forty-seven minutes, depending on your team's swimming efficiency."

"That's no good," Magnus said as a sense of frustration grew in his chest.

"Are you sure we can't afford the extra time?" Awen asked him. "It could mean fewer casualties on both sides."

"But it almost doubles our time on target," Magnus said.

"Whatever you decide, sir, it needs to be concluded in three minutes," TO-96 said.

"Understood." Magnus stretched his neck and felt the wind fight the motion. "Colonel, you got a preference?"

"I'm not sure that I do, son," the old man said. "I don't like that it extends your time down there. Plus, if Moldark shows up, that could spell disaster for Capriana faster than Aunt June's sweet yams give me the squirts. But assaulting the post head-on will most likely be a bloody affair. Even with your NOV1s and fancy armor, I'm worried you'll take heavy casualties."

"But can we hit the switch faster than forty-seven minutes?" Magnus asked. "Because, according to the mission parameters, that's the only question that needs answering."

Caldwell sighed and then looked offscreen. Based on how TO-96 and Azelon looked away too, Magnus guessed they were on the bridge and staring at one another. It was TO-96 who spoke next. "Again, you'll save the most time by assaulting the base head-on and making for the manual override switch in the substation control building."

"Then that's what we're doing," Magnus said.

"Sir, if I may," Azelon said.

"Go ahead."

"I have something you might find useful for this scenario. However, please be advised that it is not subtle."

Caldwell's bushy white eyebrows rose. "Darling, we're not looking for subtle. You save that for playing footsie with your boyfriend there. But you got something that will help them punch through? I say send it."

"Agreed," said Magnus. "Whaddya got?"

MAGNUS'S SQUAD made landfall on the island's north side sixty seconds later. By the number of the Marines taking their positions on the base's wall, either General McCormick and his senator had woken up to warn about a possible attack on the PDS, or the sea skimmers had woken everyone up. The floodlights were on, and the blaster rifles were warmed up.

With the sea skimmers at full power, Magnus ordered his squad to ride up the beachhead to a cluster of boulders. The giant rocks provided ample cover, allowing the gladias to dismount and regain the advantage of being invisible. The only aspect of the base that was visible from down here was the enormous tower that served to funnel the core's energy into the stratosphere.

Tactically, it would be ten minutes before Azelon's care package arrived, which meant Magnus needed to thin the enemy's ranks, open a breach in the base's wall, and make room for the drop. Although—to be fair to Azelon—armored crates propelled from orbit would clear their own way when they hit, he just didn't want any gladias in it.

"Bravo Team, you're going left," Magnus said. "Alpha Team, we're going right. And when Azelon tells us to get the hell away from the drop zone—"

"We get the hell away from the drop zone," Abimbola said.

"Right. Target the emplaced weapons first, and then pick off the sentries. Doc, Haze, I want two holes along the wall so they'll be forced to cover both of them, but hold the detonation until our delivery arrives. Then we'll take the gap closest to the substation, which will be to the west." He marked a spot along the base's right side. "That's infill. We press to the objective, and the first person to flip on the PDS wins a lifetime supply of Colonel Caldwell's cigars."

"Rohoar does not smoke," said the Jujari.

"Then you'd better learn, Scruffy, 'cause I want you tearing a path to that outbuilding."

"Rohoar will forfeit his reward to another person."

Magnus waved a hand. "Whatever you do, be sure not to hit the PDS generator tower. We damage that, and this whole mission's a wash. Let's thin their numbers and get those explosives deployed then clear out. Rohoar, Czyz, retract your armor extensions—we'll need your teeth and claws."

Magnus could sense everyone squaring up with the objectives. This was not going to be easy for more reasons than he cared to admit. For one, he was risking his life to protect—among other things—the Corps, the one that had double-crossed him. *But it wasn't really the military who betrayed you—right?* Magnus thought. *It was the Paragon.* Magnus bit his lower lip. *Just keep telling yourself that, Adonis.*

"LT?" Dutch said.

"Go ahead."

"Those are Marines in there." Before the words were even

out of her mouth, Magnus knew where this was going because he was thinking the same thing. Any member of the Corps would. "Not the Paragon. Marines."

"Hard copy."

But she wasn't done. "I just feel like—if we had more time, ya know? If we could talk to them, like you did with the Colonel and with Captain Forbes, then maybe…" She sighed. "I don't know what I'm saying."

To Magnus's surprise, it was Abimbola who replied first. "War is messy, Dutch. And you? You are a warrior. You will trade these lives for millions, because that is what warriors do." Abimbola lowered his head for a moment, but he wasn't done. "I have slain more of your brothers and sisters than I care to admit to you. Today, however, I take no pride in our killing—only in our saving. Without that, we are merciless. But if we keep the end in sight, perhaps redemption awaits us. Awaits us all. Let history decide later, but we decide now."

"Damn," Titus said, breaking the somber mood. "That was some good splick. La-raah."

"Thanks, Abimbola," Dutch said as she placed a hand on the Miblimbian's arm.

He nodded once in reply. "La-raah."

"Let's move," Magnus said. "Dominate."

"Liberate," they all replied.

Alpha Team left the boulders' cover and met a squad of Marines coming to investigate the sea skimmers. Magnus took aim at a trooper on the left who donned white Mark V armor. He fired a single round into the Marine's helmet. It was the most humane way to put a combatant down—instantaneous and, therefore, painless—assuming you didn't miss. And at such close proximity, Magnus knew he wouldn't miss. The trooper collapsed and rolled down the sandy embankment.

Upon seeing their fallen trooper and the flash of a random blaster bolt, the other Marines raised their weapons and fired into the darkness. At least one gladia took a hit to a personal shield, according to Magnus's HUD, but he was too preoccupied to see who it was.

Magnus's squad fired on the ill-fated search party, sending all twelve Marines to the sand, and rolling down to settle near the base of the boulders. Black-rimmed blaster holes pockmarked their white armor, while wisps of smoke rose through the flood-lamps' indirect light.

"Keep it smooth," Magnus said to Alpha Team. He moved around the bodies and ran up the hill, careful to keep his boots from stirring the sand too much—there would be plenty of snipers on the wall monitoring where their fellow Marines had disappeared. Magnus found cover behind some dune ferns and zoomed in on the fortified wall.

Elusian Base sat on a natural rise with about 300 meters of open sand between the boulders and the front gate. A ten-meter high blastcrete wall surrounded the complex, complete with watchtowers, electrified deterrents, and sniper nests. The main entrance itself was a five-meter blast door that was wide enough to accept amphibious transports directly from the sea. Floodlights adorned the towers, lighting a narrow trail of hardpack that went from the surf all the way to the gate.

"It looks like we have more company coming," Abimbola said. The gate opened, and a platoon of forty-eight Marines emerged, weapons in high ready position. They spread out in a V-formation, blaster's searing the horizon.

"Splick," Magnus said to himself.

"Looks like they didn't get the memo about your whole *low casualties* thing," Dutch said.

"No." Magnus chewed his lip. "They didn't." He doubled checked his NOV1 then hailed Titus and Abimbola. "You ready?"

"Let's do this," Titus said.

"We are ready," Abimbola replied.

"Open fire."

From two sides on the open ground, the Granthers fired on the advancing Marines. They dropped the center-most troopers first and then began working outward. The first ten combatants went down without a fight, but the remainder dropped to their bellies and virtually disappeared in the sand.

"They're going to ground," Magnus said. "Adjust fire and watch for those snipers."

Alpha Team moved further to the right, thinking to flank the prone Marines. Magnus dialed in the crest of a Repub helmet poking above a gentle rise in the sand and squeezed his trigger. His NOV1 whined as a single round raced toward the helmet and blew a hole in the top. The smoking bucket tipped sideways, and the trooper lay still.

Another trooper rose on one knee to fire at the invisible area where the Granther's blaster bolts were appearing from, and landed a direct hit on Rohoar's chest plate, dropping the Jujari's shield to 71%. Rohoar hissed something in his mother tongue—probably a curse against the Marine—and then returned fire, shredding the trooper's chest plate before the force knocked the man backward.

To Magnus's surprise, dozens of metal planks flipped up from the sand, standing like rectangular soldiers. They were positioned halfway between the Marines and the gladias, and cast long shadows across the open ground.

"Field walls," Magnus said above the scream of blaster fire. "Let's get to them first!"

At once, the Granthers were off and running, dashing toward the spring-loaded field walls in the field's center.

"I've got a runner," Silk said as she tracked a Marine running toward one of the barricades. She sighted in, squeezed off a round from her CK360 sniper rifle, and then ran toward a small boulder as the trooper flipped head over heels.

Magnus was the first to a field wall. It stood about a meter and a half high, and he crouched behind it, knowing there was a Marine on the other side. He reached around with his NOV1 and fired. But to his surprise, the Marine knocked the weapon out of his hand. Pissed and slightly embarrassed, Magnus withdrew his NCK and swung the blade around the wall. The weapon struck something hard that cracked under the blade's nearly indestructible point. Magnus grabbed the wall with his free hand to leverage himself, then he withdrew the knife and stabbed again and again until the person behind the wall fell away.

He peeked to see a Marine lying on the sand with bloody

holes in his back before turning to see the NOV1 laying a meter away. Magnus retrieved his weapon and then crouched with his back against the wall. After double-checking the weapons integrity and magazine level, Magnus leaned out the wall's other side and fired on a Marine who'd left his ass exposed. *Hell of a way to go*, Magnus noted, but all bets were off in a firefight. So he sighted in on the Marine's backside and fired. The first shot spun the victim out from behind the wall, and the second shot struck him in the chest. Magnus figured the trooper was dead before he hit the ground.

Magnus took off running for another field wall about twelve meters downrange. He slid to a stop and fired to his left, flanking an unsuspecting Marine with two shots in the ribs. The combatant slumped against the metal shield. To the right side, another Marine noticed the commotion and started shooting at Magnus's position. One blaster bolt managed to strike Magnus in the shoulder, reducing his shield by 18%. He returned fire, striking the Marine three times—once in the head and twice in the chest. The trooper fell backward, arms and legs sprawled.

Magnus went to move downrange again when the sniper fire started in earnest. The unmistakable shriek of MS900 rounds whizzed by Magnus's head and forced him to stay behind cover.

"Seems somebody finally decided to put their big boy pants on," Magnus said.

"They are already wearing pants," Czyz replied. "I do not understand your comment."

"He means thermal optics," Titus said from behind his own field wall. "They're able to see us now."

"I still do not understand what that has to do with young adult pants."

"Don't worry about it." Titus reached out to try a shot on the sniper nests, but the sniper rounds were too accurate. He pulled back and regrouped. "Too rich for my gut."

"Copy that," Magnus said. "Silk, Dutch, any help?" The two snipers had intentionally stayed back for this very reason. Now that he faced back toward the shore, Magnus noticed the women were set up behind small boulders, sighting in on the base.

"On it, LT," Dutch said. A beat later CK360 rounds tracked back to two sniper nests along the top of the wall. Magnus arched his head to see the first round drop a sniper into his metal bunker. The second Marine toppled forward and fell over the bunker's edge. His body flipped once in the air before landing in the sand with a *thud*. But before the impact, Dutch and Silk had fired on two more snipers, dropping them just as quickly as the first. It wasn't until their third shots that the remaining snipers along the wall zeroed in on the women and returned fire.

The momentary shift in focus gave Magnus and the others enough time to advance down two more rows of field walls before the enemy's fire returned in force. "Rohoar, Czyz. Think you can give us some SMS support on that left wall?"

"Yes," Rohoar replied. Magnus watched the Jujari pull the shoulder-fired launchers from their backs and take a knee. Rohoar readied the weapon and then used his HUD's aiming system to stick the tube outside of cover without placing his head in harm's way.

"Hole in the fire," Rohoar said. A beat later, a smoke trail blazed across the battlefield as a rocket-propelled detonator headed for the left wall. The round exploded, sending fire and sparks into the night air. But when the smoke cleared, the shot had done no damage, and the troopers reappeared, weapons firing.

The second round, however—this one from Czyz—caught five troopers by surprise, scattering them and their remains in all directions, and taking a chunk from the wall's railing. Another dozen Marines fell back from the position—either blown off the ramparts or driven to the sides.

"Good work, you two," Magnus said.

"Rohoar softened the target for me," Czyz said.

"Rohoar does not agree. Your shot was superior."

"Save it for your therapist." Magnus used the momentary lull to advance his squad one more row of wall planks. Knowing how to use the enemy's response to your advantage was critical in offensive maneuvers, and the Granthers needed every edge they could get.

The base hadn't shown its full strength still, and Magnus was worried about what would happen when they did. Granther Company needed to place charges on the walls—fast. Magnus took a distance reading on the wall—his HUD put it at eighty-six meters. They were closer than they'd been when this started, but still far enough that his two demolition operators would get taken out without adequate covering fire.

"Silk, Dutch, I'm gonna need a hard press on the sniper nests again."

"Almost in our new positions," Dutch replied.

"Good."

"You still sure this wasn't easier than knocking on CENT-COM's front door?" Dutch asked.

Magnus ignored the question. "Everyone else, we're laying down heavy covering fire so Doc and Haze can set charges on the wall. Azie?"

"Yes, sir," Azelon replied.

"What's the ETA on our care package?"

"Two minutes, sir."

Magnus sucked his teeth clean of saliva. "Then that gives us sixty seconds to plant the first charges, and sixty seconds to get clear of the inbound crates. Everyone ready?"

"Ready," Silk and Dutch said.

"Ready," said Doc and Haze. Everyone else pinged on the chat window.

"Bring the heat," Magnus replied, and then turned to fire on the wall with his NOV1 on full auto.

9

DESPITE BEING OUTNUMBERED thirty-six to one, Alpha and Bravo Teams laid down enough blaster fire to make any Marine think twice about firing on the two gladias advancing toward the wall. It seemed that only the enemy snipers had the necessary IR optics to track the demolition experts, so Dutch and Silk kept the sharpshooters from poking their heads up. Meanwhile, Awen and Nídira extended Unity shields around Doc and Haze, giving the two men added protection as they ran into the fortification's menacing shadow.

For his part, Magnus emptied two magazines as he raked the enemy line side to side. His NOV1 wailed, sending its withering stream of firepower into helmets and chest plates and vambraces. To his right and left, Magnus heard the distinct *kuh-thunk-woosh* of rocket-propelled detonators blast toward the enemy. Rohoar and Czyz leveled their SMSs against the densest pockets of resistance along the wall, blasting holes in the enemy ranks. Magnus's squad couldn't keep this up for long, but they didn't have to—they just needed to buy the demo boys enough time to plant their charges.

"How you looking?" Magnus asked as he swapped out for fresh mags.

"I'm set," Haze yelled. Magnus saw him duck as a sniper round drove down from above, blasting a hole in the sand less than a meter from his feet. Silk answered the attempt on her teammate by drilling the enemy sharpshooter through the top of the helmet. The Marine, who was already slumped over the railing, slid forward and fell down the wall. His body landed one stride behind Haze, who was now in full retreat.

"Doc?" Magnus watched the other demo expert struggle with something. "What's the holdup?"

"Charge isn't responding," Doc replied.

"Clarify."

"I've activated remote detonation, but it's not—just a second."

"You've got twenty-five seconds, Doc," Magnus ordered as he returned fire on a group of Marines who were regaining their courage.

"We're good," Doc said.

"Repeat?"

"I said, we're green to go." Doc rolled off the wall and double-timed it back toward the field walls.

"Good," Azelon said over the squad channel. "Because it's time to get the hell off the battlefield."

"Ceasefire, ceasefire!" Magnus waved his team off and then

gestured toward the north shore. He didn't want the enemy tracking blaster rounds back to their rifles. Plus, it was easier to run without shooting over your shoulder. "Fall back to the boulders."

Small plumes of sand and sparks leapt from the ground as Magnus raced north with the rest of his squad. He dodged the rows of field walls and ducked as several rounds pinged off the metal planks. Running in the sand was hard work, but his suit's servo-assist helped increase efficiency. Magnus poured on the speed and felt his lungs burn, watching his heart rate climb in his HUD. He also watched the Time to Impact counter tick backward. He had less than twenty seconds to get to cover.

The Jujari made it to the boulders first, bounding across the desert-like terrain on all fours. Awen and Nídira were next, followed by Dutch, Silk, Abimbola, and Titus. Doc and Haze picked up the rear with Magnus, already tired from their sprint to the wall and back. Magnus urged them forward, then he saw Haze trip. The gladia hit the sand hard, disrupting the ground enough that it drew the attention of several Marines. Blaster bolts pelted Haze's legs and backside, dropping his shield in under three seconds.

"Awen," Magnus roared. No sooner had he cried her name than a semi-translucent wall appeared behind Haze. Magnus dashed behind it and grabbed Haze under the shoulder. "Can you stand?"

"Yeah, I'm good," Haze said, climbing to his feet and retrieving his weapon.

Magnus thrust the man forward, trying to keep Awen's Unity

wall between them and the enemy. He waited for blaster rounds to strike him in the back, but none hit, which he was thankful for. He hated running from a fight, but according to Azelon, they needed to give the incoming crates as much leeway as possible. The mystics could have provided adequate protection against the expected blast force, but there was no way to know precisely where the crates would hit. Retreating to the boulders meant more running, but it was better than getting flattened. Magnus and Haze were just about to the embankment that ran down the side of the rocks when the orbital crates hit.

The concussive force struck Magnus in the back and flung him forward, clear over the boulders, and about twenty-five meters across the shore. He slammed into the sand and felt his suit plates bind at the joints, preventing his bones from bending in ways they weren't meant to. Still, the violent changes in inertia rattled his organs and sent waves of pain from head to toe.

When the blast wave had expired, and his body was done rolling toward the surf, Magnus pushed up and oriented himself. His ears were ringing, and he could taste copper on his tongue. He blinked several times and then willed his vision to focus. When he looked south, he saw darkness. The blast knocked out Elusian Base's floodlamps, which was good. With any luck, the lights wouldn't be the only things disabled.

Magnus heard a wet cough over comms. He looked right and saw Haze ten meters away.

"You good, Haze?" Magnus asked, watching the man find his feet.

"Roger, LT. Bit my lip, but I'm fine." The man shook his

helmet a little. "Think my HUD suffered some damage too. Sensors seem misaligned."

"Can you try a reboot?"

"Yeah."

Magnus pointed toward the boulders. "Do it as we run. Tap me if your comms go down."

"Copy that."

Magnus beat hard for the boulders. As he neared the squad, he gave a quick gesture toward the battlefield. "Up and over, Granthers. We gotta make this count."

The team broke off and went up both sides of the boulders, weapons ready. As soon as they crested the summit, Magnus saw three yellow containers standing five meters tall and three across. They sat at the bottom of wide craters in the field and bore scorch marks across their bases. Large stenciled numbers designated the containers as 1, 2, and 3 respectively, while smaller type read BATRIG Mk. I.

"I'm in number three," Magnus said. "Abimbola, Titus, you're in numbers one and two." Both men verbally assented and took off running. "Everyone else, keep us covered. And Doc and Haze? Get ready to blow those charges—assuming they're still active and on the wall."

"They are," Doc replied. "Ready when you are."

Magnus followed Abimbola and Titus toward the crates and then diverted to run down the bowl toward his container. So far, the enemy hadn't recovered from the blast, which was just fine with Magnus. He slid to a stop at the base of the crate and heard the metal creaking as it cooled. These units were meant for high-speed delivery of assets and were fairly common among most militaries. Like everything else she worked on with Magnus, Azelon's version had some modifications, which included directional thrusters and additional suspension to keep the contents from imploding on impact. But based on Magnus's limited understanding of what was inside, he doubted they'd need any white-glove treatment.

The security sensors detected his approach and unlocked with a soft chirp. Magnus stepped back and let the hatch swing open, then ducked inside and turned on his twin headlamps. The space was cramped, allowing him only enough room to squeeze around to the front and climb a set of recessed rungs. He was halfway to the pilot cockpit when blaster fire began resonating on the outside of the crate. The Marines were reengaging.

"You want us to light them up?" Doc asked.

"Not yet," Magnus replied. "Just a few more seconds."

"Copy that."

Magnus arrived at the cockpit and pulled himself inside, trying his best not to bump anything that he shouldn't touch. His ass landed in a small standing seat, and his feet found their way down leg tubes until they landed on base plates. Likewise, he reached forward and inserted his hands into control gloves that could double as manual actuators in the event his Novian biotech interface lost connectivity with the unit. As soon as his NBTI paired, a new tab appeared in his HUD. He allowed his eyes to hover on the tab marked Mech until a welcome screen appeared.

"Welcome to the Novian mechanized battle armament

system," Azelon's voice said, though Magnus realized it was a recording. "Your BATRIG mark one is equipped with—"

"Cancel," Magnus said. The voice went silent, while the sound of blaster fire against the outside of his crate grew more intense. It wouldn't be long before someone fired an SMDL on his position. "Initiate weapons systems."

"Initiating weapons systems," the voice replied. An outline of the BATRIG appeared in Magnus's HUD, and all the weapons systems glowed. "Weapons online."

"You boys ready?" Magnus asked Abimbola and Titus.

"Just say the word, buckethead," the Miblimbian replied.

"Ready," Titus said.

"Activate chameleon mode. Doc, Haze—blow the wall."

Magnus imagined flexing his arms, legs, back, and shoulders, and felt the suit respond. Limbs struck the container's walls, triggering the maglock system to decouple the crates panels. The container walls fell away, and a beat later, Magnus brought the mech to full height as the charges detonated. The explosions bathed the BATRIGs in bright orange light. Magnus got his first look at Abimbola and Titus's mechs as chunks of blastcrete and human flesh shot into the night sky.

The telecolos-covered white, blue, and black BATRIGs had wide multi-toed feet that could form over complex terrain. The robust legs employed the reversed bend of canine-like hind legs— which seemed fitting, given the Novian-minded designer. The torso, which housed the pilot's body, allowed only the operator's helmet to protrude and could deploy a canopy for additional protection if needed.

At the end of the right arm, Magnus saw a massive blaster barrel that he recognized from the assault on the *Black Labyrinth* in Nelson's company. In his HUD, the weapon was designated as a GU90M—no doubt the "Mech" version of the 90mm bore cannon that was responsible for giving Moldark's forces hell in the hangar bay. On the end of his left arm was a new weapon that consisted of a bisected barrel and a sleek charge generator. His HUD read RTD10. He opened the dropdown menu and glanced at the definition, which read Reticulating Torrent Disruptor, Version 1.0. While the description read a little like a similarly named Repub weapon, Magnus had no idea what to make of it. But if he knew Azelon at all, it was going to pack one hell of a punch.

The last weapon was a missile bay on the BATRIG's back, identified by the acronym VWMS. The designation stood for Variable Warhead Missile System, which had three primary options listed under the operations menu. But Magnus didn't have time to review the remaining information—his BATRIG was already taking fire from Marines along the wall.

"Let's see what these babies can do," Magnus said, and then brought his GU90M to bear on the wall's center section, above the main gate. Then he thought-ordered the mech to fire. Magnus felt the recoil before he saw the blaster round belch from the weapon and blow a hole in the wall's railing. Three Marines twirled through the air, their bodies maimed and trailing blood. Magnus spread his feet a little wider and fired a second round, blowing up a sniper nest. One moment, the Marine lined up a shot on Magnus—the next, he was vaporized as the large-caliber blaster round drove through the victim's head, down his spine, and out the souls of his boots.

Abimbola whooped as he tore through a cluster of defenders on the left side, while Titus made quick work of three Marines in a guard tower on the right.

Magnus brought his RTD10 forward and aimed it at two Marines setting up a MUT50—the Corps infamous 50mm ultra torrent tri-reticulating blaster. He didn't need to understand the BATRIG's armor capabilities to know that the MUT50 would inflict some severe damage against the mech. Magnus willed the targeting reticle to lock onto the men and then ordered the weapon to fire.

For a moment, nothing happened. Magnus only heard the whining sound of a capacitor charging up. He was a split second away from abandoning his weapon choice when the RTD10 let out a frenzied *blaaat*. The muzzle flash flowered outward as the high-frequency blaster rounds struck the two men and detonated their bodies. Their armor blew apart like shattering glass, and gore caked everyone next to the victims.

"Holy splick," Magnus said quietly, but loud enough that it went over comms.

"You can say that again," Titus said, using his RTD10 to liquefy three soldiers near the guard tower's base. Titus's rounds didn't just strike the men, however, but also hit the tower wall. The missing chunk destabilized the structure, causing the pillar to lean sideways and then pivot just enough that it tumbled over the barrier and crashed into the sand down front.

Refocused on the mission, Magnus ordered everyone to converge on the breach along the right side. "We'll cover you!"

The three mechs moved together, marching toward the hole while the gladias dashed toward the opening. They set up on either side of the gap, waiting for the mechs to ensure the way was clear. Magnus made it first then swung his GU90M into the breach and fired. The blast blew a giant pockmark in the ground and sent sand and blastcrete chunks shooting into the air, clearing the immediate area of enemies. Abimbola followed the explosion up with a spurt of RTD10 fire, ensuring that nothing remained to hinder the gladias on foot.

"Clear to advance," Magnus said. "Substation 120 meters, bearing 215°."

"Copy that," Rohoar replied. He and Czyz rounded the wall's charred edges first and then charged ahead. The rest of the squad went next, followed by Abimbola, Titus, and finally, Magnus. But as Magnus crossed through the wall, he felt his mech take fire on his left shoulder. He looked over to see two Marines running along the ramparts, firing MAR30s in his direction.

For whatever reason, Magnus's heart skipped a beat. The MAR30 was the signature weapon of his old unit. As if driving the point home, Magnus saw the 79th Recon insignia on one of the Marine's chest plates.

Magnus held short.

He shouldn't have hesitated. But he did.

Both Recon Marines leaped into the breach and landed on Magnus's mech. One brought his MAR30 up and placed the muzzle against Magnus's visor. But Magnus activated the mech's head cover, and a canopy deployed fast enough that it knocked the Marine's weapon wide. The second Marine fired into the mech's left shoulder joint, which sent warning notifications flaring in Magnus's HUD. The rounds continued to penetrate through the joint until the limb went limp, spurting fluid and sparks.

Magnus swung his right arm up and struck the first man in the back with the GU90M barrel, breaking bone. The man fell and landed in front of Magnus's feet. With a single step forward, Magnus pressed a foot down and ended the Marine's suffering.

The remaining Recon Marine fired into the canopy, but the shield deflected the blaster bolts. Magnus swung his GU90M at the combatant, but the Marine stayed clear, having learned his lesson from his fallen brother in arms. Magnus turned and backpedaled, slamming his back into the blastcrete wall, but the other man pulled himself away from the impact. Then Magnus heard the telltale sound of the wide displacement charge loading in the weapon. Just as the Marine fired toward the cockpit, Magnus lurched into the wall again. While the force wasn't enough to dislodge the man, it at least knocked the shot wide. Instead of cracking open the cockpit, the energy blast disabled the mech's right arm and right leg.

Partially immobile, the Recon Marine brought his MAR30 back up, and Magnus knew what would come next—because it's what he would do. He even saw the man select the distortion setting in the weapon's selector switch. He was going to incinerate Magnus inside the mech.

"Oh no, you don't," Magnus said. He activated the canopy's

emergency release, which shot the windowplex covering into the sky. It blew the Marine's MAR30 from his hands and left the man stunned, but still clinging to the mech's shoulder. Then Magnus withdrew his knife, freed his arm, and stabbed at the weak spot between the Marine's helmet and chest plate. A torrent of blood spurted down the knife and onto Magnus's gauntlet as the blade severed the jugular vein. The Marine grabbed onto Magnus's helmet and tried wrenching it sideways in an attempt to break Magnus's neck, but the strength was already leaving the fighter's body. Magnus thrust again, twisting the blade. It had the immediate response of draining the man of all will to fight. The Marine slumped onto Magnus's head and then flipped down the mech's front.

"Azelon," Magnus said. "My mech's done. Any chance I can use the missiles on the back to turn it into a parting gift when we leave?"

"By parting gift, do you mean self-destruct?" she asked.

"Sure do."

"Yes. You'll find it under the ordnance options in the VWN menu."

Magnus followed the path and found the Auto Destruct Sequence in the last row of options. More sparks blew out of the BATRIG as Magnus selected the option and set it for—*for how long?* he wondered.

"Abimbola, come in," Magnus said over VNET. He could see the other two mechs defending the substation. Both Marine companies had been fully activated, and the fighting was getting a lot worse. *So many lost lives*, Magnus noted, wishing McCormick had listened to him. But there'd be time enough to lament the mission's losses later—*if* he got out of this alive.

"What is it, buckethead?" Abimbola replied.

"How much time you need?"

"Awen is inside the substation now, along with Rohoar and Czyz. The rest of us are outside defending—"

"I see you. I just need a time."

"We're at the console," Awen replied, her voice strained. "I'm navigating the—" Awen's voice broke off, and Magnus heard growling in the background, followed by blaster fire, and then the sound of armor breaking apart.

"Awen?" Magnus said. "Talk to me!"

"I'm okay," she said, but her tone was far from convincing. "I'm activating the... *oh no.*"

"What's oh no?" Magnus winced as a small fire ignited in his mech's left shoulder. He needed to get out. More Marines were headed his way, apparently curious as to whether or not the machine was still a threat. "Awen? What's oh no?"

"Everyone out." Awen's eyes grew wide. "It's a trap!"

10

"IF YOU DROP US, mystic, I am going to devour you," Long-chomps said. He appeared to be the most nervous out of everyone that Wish was lowering in her "magic bubble," as he called it. Zoll felt his mistrust was ironic given the Jujari's quasi-abilities in the Unity. Perhaps it had something to do with seeing nothing but open air beneath his feet for over twenty meters.

"Pretty sure you'll be dead," Rix said.

"I will hunt her down in the afterlife."

Rix shrugged. "Fair enough."

Wish created the bubble's floor about two meters beneath the elevator. She told everyone to get through the hole and wait for her to climb down. It took Zoll a few seconds to trust the translucent surface beneath his feet before he let go of the elevator's floor. Wish pushed him aside with her feet and then dropped down.

As Wish lowered the team, Zoll said, "This is some crazy splick, you know that?"

Wish chuckled once. "You're welcome."

On the bright side, his unit was on the move again, and Reimer was safe. On the downside, they were disconnected from Delta and Echo Teams until Cyril or Wish found a way to reopen the elevator shaft. Then again, the pod was permanently stuck in the shaft, thanks to Longchomps's heavy-hitting, which—looking back on it—wasn't the brightest idea. *One problem at a time,* Zoll reminded himself.

"You are almost there," Longchomps said. "We are almost not dead."

"I'm not going to drop you, Longchomps," Wish said, her voice tight.

"I am not convinced."

"Would you shut up already?" Rix said, hitting Longchomps in the elbow. "She's got this."

The beast folded his arms. "Jujari were not meant to fly."

"We know, we know," Rix added. "Sheesh."

As Wish brought everyone even with sub-level four, Reimer appeared, extending his hand toward Zoll. Zoll clasped Reimer's forearm and stepped into the elevator landing room, followed by Cyril, Rix, Longchomps, and then Wish. The moment her first foot touched the ground, the magic bubble vanished.

"Nice work, Wish," Zoll said, patting her on the shoulder.

"Thank you."

Zoll looked around. The team stood in what appeared to be a security hold. The all-white brightly lit room was broken up by stenciled writing and panels of security glass on the walls, nozzles on the ceiling, and ducted fans under the floor grates. A single door led down a long hallway, while the largest window to the right looked in on a control room.

"Any bright ideas, Cyril?" Zoll asked.

The code slicer moved toward a control panel. "Give me a second." He tapped with one hand and then stood back as a small holo image appeared a few centimeters from the wall.

"You got something?" Rix asked, bending over to examine a series of geometric lattices that moved around one another.

"Actually, yes," Cyril replied. "Surprisingly. I seem to have access to the core matrix from down here. Which, I guess, is not really surprising, the more I think about it. But I'm surprised by how much I'm surprised because, if you think about it, we're actually closer to—"

"Cyril," Zoll said. "What do you have?"

"Until the AI kicks me out? Everything."

"What do you mean, everything?"

"I mean, access to the whole building."

Zoll winced, not sure he was following. "From right here?"

"Uh-huh."

"The whole building."

"Why do you keep repeating him?" Longchomps said. "It is irritating."

Zoll ignored the Jujari. "So you can get us through these doors?"

"Yeah, yeah, of course, roger. But I recommend we use

extreme caution and follow the suggested safety protocols. We wouldn't want to, you know, expose ourselves unnecessarily."

"I expose myself daily," Longchomps said.

Cyril let out a nervous laugh. "Ha ha. I mean, to contagions."

"My last mate says I carry contagions," Longchomps replied.

"Mystics, beast," Rix said in a disgusted tone. "Too far."

"What? I am truth-telling in an attempt to comply with the frail but brilliant human there." He pointed at Cyril.

Again, Cyril laughed, and then looked back at the holo. "So, so, first, let's keep the AI busy." His fingers worked at manipulating the geometric shapes before he continued typing on the small control pad again. "This should… give it something… to keep it occupied for a while."

"Like a roadblock?" Rix asked.

"Negative, Charlie."

"Charlie?"

"More like—like a word puzzle," Cyril said. "'Cause, there are some things computers can do better than sentients—most things, really. In fact, I once made a list of—"

"Hey, Cyril?" Zoll said, pointing to the terminal.

"Right, sorry. Anyway, but computers tend to—uh, to trip up on language, you know?"

"Clever," Zoll replied, though he rightly admitted he wasn't entirely sure what the code slicer was talking about. He just wanted to make sure the kid felt affirmed for his work. "Good job."

"Sir, thanks, sir."

"How much time you think that buys us?"

Cyril looked like he tried to scratch his head but forgot he was wearing a Novian battle helmet. Instead, he resorted to tapping his helmet and then brought his hand back down. "Maybe another fifteen minutes? It all depends on whether this AI is the Trimeric version 4.1 or 4.2. Because if it's 4.1, then we're safe for a while."

"But if it's the 4.2?" Zoll asked.

"We are safe for much less."

"Less than fifteen minutes?"

Cyril nodded. "Maybe three or four?"

"Minutes?" Zoll said. "Then let's get a move on."

"But, but, we need to decontaminate ourselves," Cyril said.

"We don't have time, kid."

"But, sir, remember that this facility must maintain its integrity well after we're gone."

Zoll froze. *Dammit.* He hadn't even thought about that.

"If Lieutenant Gladia Marine Magnus and his forces get the planetary defense shield up and save Capriana from Moldark's assault, it would be an epic fail if we did enough damage to this lab to wipe out the entire planet a few days from now, ha ha."

"That's the kind of stuff they have down here?" Rix asked, tugging on Cyril's sleeve. His voice held a certain child-like anxiety.

Cyril nodded.

"Do it all," Rix said, tapping the slicer on the shoulder. "Make us do all of the things."

"Roger copy, sir." Cyril began typing again, more quickly than before. A new security door closed over the elevator shaft, and then the nozzles overhead sprayed the gladias with a fine white powder. The ducted fans spun up, and Zoll watched the pressure gauge fluctuate in his HUD.

Once the powder was sucked away, a red LED on Cyril's console changed to green. "We're ready to proceed," he said. The door at the end of the chamber unlatched, unsealed, and then swung inward. Cyril led the way, stepping over the threshold, and then ducked into a side door. "Wait here."

"Wait?" Rix looked between Zoll and the retreating code slicer. "Where's he going now?"

"I'm just retrieving a data pad from the control room so I can monitor our AI friend."

"Why is it a friend when it wants to kill us?" Longchomps said.

"Ha ha. It doesn't want to kill us." Cyril reappeared, now holding a medium-sized data pad. "It just wants to keep anything from happening to the assets in this facility."

"I still feel like it wants to kill us," the Jujari said in a hushed tone.

Cyril brought up the floating geometric lattices again, studied them like a painter might study brush strokes and derive some cryptic meaning from them, and then pointed down the hall. "This way, double bravo."

The code slicer led them through several turns and down numerous hallways, each free of obstructions despite the many security doors and surveillance cameras they passed. Zoll looked in on half a dozen different labs behind windows on either side of the hallways. They were filled with fancy looking equipment and massive refrigeration vaults. Fortunately for the gladias, the one thing none of the labs contained were people.

"Yup, waypoint, copy," Cyril said at last. He stopped at a windowless door marked Habitat F.

"What's Habitat F mean?" Rix asked.

"We're about to find out," Zoll replied.

Cyril opened the door and stepped into yet another decontamination lock. Unlike the last one, this one was much narrower and didn't have any windows. When the door closed behind them, the code slicer fired up the sequence. The white powder came, went, and the red light changed to green.

Before the next door opened, Rix raised his weapon.

"Whoa, whoa, sir. What are you doing?" Cyril pushed the barrel down. "You can't shoot in here."

"Come on, kid. You've seen the holos. This is exactly the part in the movie where the guy like me gets eaten by some freak of nature, all because the director needed to kill off some gun-loving side character. Well, not today, bitches. Not today."

"It's okay," Zoll said, reaching toward Cyril. "He won't shoot anything unless he has to."

"But, sir, he really shouldn't be shooting at all. Sir."

Zoll leaned into Cyril's helmet and lowered his voice. "I know that. And you know that. But there's no way you're going to get Rix there to lower his weapon in a creepy-ass facility like this. And, like it or not, he has some good points. Plus, the last thing you want is for some tentacle-faced alien to impregnate you with its demon spore seed, only for the love child to burst out of your gut in the middle of your next shower, right? When that splick comes at you, Rix is the guy you want to keep it from shoving its wiggly ass arms in your belly button." He tapped Cyril's stomach with a finger. "Got it?"

Cyril swallowed hard over comms. "Ten four, got it."

"Good. Now tell Rix he can go in."

Cyril swiped something on his data pad, and the door's seal broke. "You may proceed, Mr. Rix."

"Thanks, kid." Rix shoved a fresh mag into his forward receiver. "And don't worry, I won't let them mess with you."

"Them?" Cyril looked back at Zoll. "You think there are more than one?"

"Just get moving, kid." Zoll pushed him forward and then motioned for Wish to follow. He was about to step through himself, but Longchomps grabbed Zoll's arm.

"Can they really do that to you?" the Jujari asked.

Zoll shrugged, let out a sound that neither confirmed nor denied the question, and then left the Jujari standing by himself in the lock.

"But can they?"

THE NEXT ROOM looked nothing like the rest of the facility. It looked nothing at all like the images TO-96 had stripped from Bosworth's transmission. Those had been scenes of Awen's parents inside what Zoll thought to be a typical lab setting. Sure, the bot had noticed various attributes that placed the lab on Capriana Prime in this specific building, all based on Repub records. And that was well and good, because, without that, Zoll wouldn't be standing here. But that lab—probably somewhere back on the main floors—was not this one.

The room itself was a large dome that rose ten or eleven meters high. Based on the spectrogram readings in Zoll's HUD, the projection of a star-filled night sky gave off the exact light specifications of an actual night scene on the planet's surface, including a small thumbnail of moonlight. Below the skyscape, Zoll was amazed to see several flowering trees, patches of ferns, and crawling vines draped from tree limbs and running along the lower walls. In the center of the garden stood some sort of elaborate laboratory divided into six sections, each with distinct workstations. They ranged from greenhouse-like tabletops and workbenches with microscopes, to refrigeration units and high-end holo consoles. If he'd been a science nerd, Zoll would have just found paradise—at least a strange outdoor form of it.

Along the room's perimeter were a dozen doorways and twice as many windows. A quick examination revealed rooms dedicated to human habitation: a large kitchen, a dining room, meeting rooms, a gym, bathrooms, and bedrooms. There was even a sign that read Pool.

"What the hell is this place?" Rix asked.

In a voice that sounded like he was helplessly in love, Cyril said, "It's wonderful."

"And we're still on the clock," Zoll said. "Check the bedrooms."

Everyone but Cyril nodded and headed toward the perimeter. The code slicer, meanwhile, seemed attracted to the lab spaces in the center of the garden like a Pladoni lilly fly heading toward a blue light.

"We're not gonna have time for any of that, kid," Zoll said.

"But, but—sir, there could be clues about whatever Bosworth was having them work on, sir."

"Balin and Giyel are the only assets we need."

"But, sir—"

"Found 'em," Wish called out. Zoll snapped his head toward her and then cut across the lab space to the room's far side. She stood outside a door labeled Quarters A-1.

"You sense them?" Zoll asked.

She nodded. "They're still asleep."

Zoll swiped a finger across the control pad, and the door slid open. The room was dark, aside from a small clock on a desk. "Mr. and Mrs. dau Lothlinium?" He heard someone stir, then he repeated himself.

Finally, a groggy male voice said, "Who's—who's there?"

"I am Petty Officer Kar Zoll with the Gladio Umbra. We're here to rescue you." Zoll touched a light pad on the wall and slid the lights up halfway. Then, realizing the assets would still not be able to see him, he deactivated chameleon mode. "We need you clothed and ready to move."

A slender man in black sleepwear rolled from the bed, his eyes wide. "Who are you?"

"Balin, what's happening?" the woman asked, sitting up. The moment she saw Zoll, she pulled the covers to her chin.

"I am Petty Officer Kar Zoll, and we're here to get you out of here. I must insist that you hurry."

Balin looked at his wife and then back at Zoll. "And you're with who again?"

"The Gladio Umbra, but there's no time to explain."

Balin paused. "Wait—how do we know this is not some sort of trick?"

"Because your daughter sent us."

Fortunately, Awen had prepared Zoll for this. He activated the projection system in his helmet and played the message Awen recorded for this moment.

"Hello, father, mother," Awen's holo said, floating half a meter in front of Zoll. She wore her power suit with her helmet slung under her arm.

"Oh, Awen," her mother exclaimed, putting a hand over her mouth. "She's alive?"

"Petty Officer Zoll and the rest of his team are here to liberate you," Awen continued. "I need you to listen to everything they tell you to do and don't delay for a second. Your lives are at risk, as are theirs. I—I miss you, and I'll be waiting for you on the transport shuttle."

The recording disappeared, and Awen's father blinked at Zoll while her mother wiped away tears.

"We need you to move, right now." Zoll turned toward the door. "We'll give you a few seconds to get your clothes."

LESS THAN A MINUTE LATER, Awen's parents emerged from their room, still rubbing their eyes. But they were dressed in white lab clothes and had shoes on. Balin had grey hair and blue eyes with the typical Elonian pointed ears, while Giyel had long black hair and purple eyes, just like Awen.

"I'm Balin dau Lothinlium," the man said, extending his hand in greeting.

"I know," Zoll replied, shaking his hand. "But we don't have time for introductions. We need to get you out of here."

But the man seemed hesitant.

"Trust me; we're going to take care of you."

"Who's we?"

Zoll forgot about his team's chameleon mode. He told them to de-cloak, much to the dau Lothlinium's surprise. But even after the couple acknowledged the other gladias, Balin looked at his wife with a concerned expression.

"What is it?" Zoll asked.

"We can't leave our work," Giyel replied.

Zoll glanced at Balin. "I don't think you understand. We don't have time for you to bring all that with you."

"That's not what she means," Balin said. "We don't *want* to bring it with us."

"We need to destroy it," Giyel replied.

"Destroy it?"

"That's right," Balin said. "All of it."

"And, and, and I would tend to agree with them," Cyril said from inside the garden. Zoll spun around to look at the code slicer. "Seems like they were making some very unpleasant microbes here. We're talking *Galaxy of the Undead* level splick, sir."

"I'm not sure what he means," Giyel said. "But the

unpleasant microbes comment is accurate. Only, it's much worse. We're talking planet-level extinction."

"Splick," Zoll said.

Her husband nodded. "If we leave this now, there's no telling what the Republic might do with it."

"It's not the Republic you need to be worried about," Zoll said. Balin raised one eyebrow at him, but Zoll didn't have time to explain. "What will it take to destroy everything?"

"Well," Giyel said, brushing some strands of hair behind her ear. "We'll need to initiate a decay cycle for the stage three embryos, and then program a degradation protocol for the—"

"I don't think you understand," Zoll said, waving her off. "Will the blast temperature of a thermal detonator wipe out your research?"

Balin thought about it. "How many do you have?"

Zoll turned to Rix. "I have four VODs, two XVODS, one LIMKIT4 mine, and whatever rounds Longchomps has left in his SMS."

"Two rounds remaining," Longcomps said.

"That might do the trick," Balin said. "Assuming those correlate to Repub ordnance of the same type. I'm unfamiliar with some of your acronyms."

It was Zoll's turn to raise an eyebrow, even though no one could see it. "Might? Do you understand how much firepower that is?"

"And do you understand what we were tasked to create?" Balin waited for Zoll to say something. When he didn't, Balin continued. "Then believe me when I say, even with all that, our work may still survive."

"Mystics. What the hell have you been doing down here?"

"As you said," Giyel replied. "We don't have time."

Zoll looked at Cyril. "I expect this place will go nova with all our explosives set to maximum yield."

"Ha ha, yeah. Sure, most likely," Cyril said. "I mean, I expect it to set off a chain reaction—if not chemically, at least structurally. Um, I think, based on what I've seen so far, we're looking at a catastrophic collapse, in the neighborhood of 83%, if I had to guess."

"That's a pretty specific guess," Rix said with a laugh.

"I'm paid to be accurate, not funny."

Rix's laugh faded away.

"Let's do it," Zoll said. "Balin, Giyel, I want you assisting Rix with the placement of the explosives. The rest of you, we need a way out of this pit. Once you have that, we'll know how long to set the delays for."

"No remote det?" Rix asked.

Zoll knew that Rix had some horrible memories of using delayed explosives when they worked for Abimbola. Hell, they both had bad memories of those crazy escapades in the Dregs. But this wasn't Ooragee, and these weren't expired Repub munitions. Plus, the Dregs wasn't full of bio-splick that could wipe out planets, or whatever it was the dau Lothliniums had been screwing with.

"No remote det," Zoll confirmed. "Not with the unreliability of this facility's defenses. If those barricades can cut comms, they'll cut det signals if we get on the wrong side of something."

"Copy that," Rix said with a sigh.

"So, so, yeah. I think we have exvac recon fill out for you, sir," Cyril said.

"What in *the* hell are you talking about, kid?" Zoll asked. He always remembered Cyril being a little too smart for his own good back in the Dregs, but ever since they'd joined the Gladio Umbra and spent more time with the former military guys, the code slicer was coming up with some funny-ass jargon.

"A way back to the surface," he said. "I think we figured it out."

Zoll left Rix and the dau Lothliniums and headed across the garden toward Cyril. The kid laid his data pad on a workstation and brought up a three-dimensional schematic of the sub levels.

"We're right here," Cyril said, indicating a blue dot on the lowest level. "Here's the elevator shaft."

"And you want to go back up it?" Zoll asked.

"Oh, no, no. Sorry to infer that, sir. We couldn't even if we wanted to."

"And why's that?"

"Well, well, because there are several more of these barricades, and I'm not sure Wish could manage those *and* lifting us in a magic bubble, sir. Even with Longchomps's help."

"It would be too much," Wish said. "My apologies."

Zoll studied the schematic again. "Then, what's your plan, kid? Because the only things I see connecting us to the upper levels are air vents and wire chases that are far too small for any of us to fit through."

"Totally, right, sir. Yeah, you're absolutely right. But, see, that's just the thing. We aren't going to go up."

"We're not," Zoll stated.

"Oh no. We're going down and out, as they say."

"Down and out?"

"Again with the repeating of words already spoken," Long-chomps said. "So irritating."

Cyril continued unabated. "Turns out that the architects were so busy keeping this complex's lower levels disconnected from the surface that they forgot to create adequate drainage for human waste into the city."

"The city sewers?" Zoll asked.

"Essentially, yes. Though it's rather more complicated than that. This facility's waste management is robust, as you might guess, especially given the sensitive nature of all the bio matter. But even a waste system needs a waste system."

"You're talking civil engineering and integration."

"Uh-huh. It's a lot like finding exploits in code slicing—the best gaps appear in between redundancies. People think that they're making a system stronger by adding in failsafes, but the more complex and tightly knit you make any system—"

"The more points of potential failure there are."

"Exactly, sir. That's—yes. Right. So here"—Cyril pointed to a subterranean building adjacent to sub-level four, separated by a large conduit—"this is the lab's own sewage management system. It's really well designed and can filter out anything they don't want. But they completely forgot that their system had to integrate with the city's system."

"So the city had to build a separate pump system"—Zoll reached forward and pointed at a secondary pipe that ran out of view—"right here."

"Precisely, sir."

"And where does it lead?"

Cyril raised his eyebrows. "Well, I don't exactly know that, but it leads away from here."

"And that's your plan?" Rix said, apparently done with the charges.

"Uh, yeah. That's *our* plan."

Rix rolled his shoulders like he was putting on a jacket. "We follow a sewage system, filled with stuff that can kill us, and then jump into a second public system that leads who knows where, and could potentially kill us."

Cyril laughed so fast Zoll thought the kid might hyperventilate. "More or less—ha-ha. But hopefully not as much *killing* as you just mentioned, Rix—ha-ha."

"It's the only way," Balin interjected.

Zoll turned to look at the man. "How so?"

"As far as we know, there is only one way back up." He pointed at the elevator shaft. "And that's it."

"He's right," Cyril said.

"In all the time we've been here, we haven't heard of any other way out of this sub-level. So if your code slicer here has found something, then I'd take him up on it."

"Then into the sewers we go," Zoll said. "Wish, can you get word to Charlie and Delta Teams? They need to know we're on the move."

"Yes," she said. "I'll let Telwin and Finderminth know."

"Good. Cyril, how long to get to that secondary system and into the sewer?"

"Uh—ha-ha. I'd say ten minutes?"

"Make it five." Then something on the map caught Zoll's eye. "What's that?"

"The ring, it's, uh, closing in on us," Cyril responded, nodding at the red circle. "That's the AI. I guess it finally solved my riddle, so it's locking down this floor."

"Then that's our cue to move."

11

Awen did her best to keep up with Rohoar and Czyz, but they were simply too fast. So she settled for keeping a shield around herself and one on each of them. Not that they needed protection yet—Magnus's new mechanized armor had done enough damage to keep the base reeling for several minutes. Like on Worru and the *Labyrinth*, the Gladio Umbra had killed dozens of Marines in a matter of minutes. Even though Awen knew her team had a mission to do—knew it was these lives or billions of civilians—she still found it difficult to stomach the sheer loss of life.

Magnus had tried to reassure her that the ends justified the means. Intellectually, she understood that. At least she thought she did. But coming face to face with means this gruesome, this horrifying, made it harder for her head to remain convinced—even harder for her heart. Somehow, troopers were able to compartmentalize the tragedies of war. Awen swore she'd never be able to understand that. But she guessed that, for many of them, compartmentalizing was not about virtue or moral rightness. It was about survival.

Body parts dotted the tarmac inside the base. Wherever she turned, she saw bodies, pools of blood, and victims crawling toward cover. One man had lost his helmet—and his legs. He pulled his way forward on his elbows, crying out for a medic, while two long red trails followed him.

Awen looked away and tried to keep from retching. To the other side, a large chunk of blastcrete sat smoking in a heap—until she realized it wasn't blastcrete at all. It was a limbless, headless torso. This time, Awen did retch, vomiting inside her helmet as she ran to catch up with the Jujari. But the emotion welling in her chest was stronger than she knew what to do with. Anxiety turned to panic. She spun around twice—she was having trouble remembering which way she was supposed to go.

"Are you still with us, *scrumnip braulick?*" Rohoar asked over VNET.

Awen hesitated, not sure who Rohoar was referencing. Then, as if on autopilot, her brain worked out the translation—*beautiful little peacemaker.*

All at once, Awen realized that Rohoar was talking about *her.* She had never heard a Jujari reference her with a nickname before. But it warmed Awen's heart, taking her back to when she first fell in love with the species.

At once, the feeling of panic ebbed, and then the anxiety. Rohaor's words seemed to call her back from the land of the dead. Awen's eyes focused again, and she noticed Rohoar standing two meters in front of her.

"Rohoar," Awen said, barely recognizing the sound of her voice. Where had he come from? "You're supposed to be in the substation."

"No, Rohoar is supposed to be protecting his teammates and accomplishing an objective."

"Yes, but—"

"Come. Rohoar will carry you."

Before Awen could protest, Rohoar scooped her body up with one arm and deposited her on his back, much like a father might do with his little child. She clung to his armor as his body resumed its lunging beat toward the substation. Within moments, blaster fire filled the quad as the rest of the gladias engaged the Marines attempting to defend their base against the invisible intruders.

Rohoar slowed and let Awen slide off his back as they arrived at the substation. It was a rather large structure, about the size of a three-story dormitory on Worru. But in comparison to the megastructures that her HUD said were the central core generator and its accompanying tower, one that seemed to stretch to the stars, the substation was little more than a shed.

"Stay behind us," Rohoar said. "And we will keep your path clear to the console."

"Thank you," Awen replied. "Let's go."

Rohoar nodded at Czyz, who slashed at the door with his claws. Sparks filled Awen's vision, and she looked away. Then the Jujari lodged his fingers inside the furrows he'd made and began separating the leaves. The sound of straining metal rattled Awen's head as Czyz forced the barricade open. Once it was large enough to pass through, Czyz stepped aside to allow Rohoar in.

Rohoar darted inside, followed by Czyz, with Awen in the rear. Clear of the carnage and the blaster fire, Awen felt her focus return, and she remembered that she had an important job to do: activate the manual override for the planetary shield generator. She reviewed the steps in her mind, recalling what Azelon had told her while on the beachhead. The bot had even sent a list of notes in a separate chat window. Focusing on the task made it easier for Awen to stay calm, especially when the killing began again.

The first person to pose a threat to the Jujari was a security guard who'd pointed his weapon at the odd shapes moving down the hall. He wore a black military uniform and matching beret.

"Stop where you are," the guard said. But Awen could tell by the quiver in his voice that the man was unsure of his command.

Rohoar bounded forward, grabbed the guard's blaster and forearm in one paw, and then yanked him forward. The guard's feet left the floor, and his head whiplashed, cracking against Rohoar's belly-plate. The guard bounced backward and then hit the ground without so much as a groan. Judging by the glazed look in his eyes and the blood streaming from his broken face, Awen guessed the guard was dead.

"Come," Rohoar said. "We must keep moving. This way." The Jujari followed the course outline in Awen's HUD, taking several turns and crossing more than one truss that was suspended over a deep cavern of energy wells, conduits, and monitoring stations. What the substation lacked in height, it made up for in depth.

Suddenly, two Marines in full armor stepped out of a side passage and raised their weapons. Unlike the first guard, the Marines didn't issue any orders—they just opened fire. Czyz took the first two hits while Rohoar took the third. But Awen's Unity shield absorbed them all, sparing either Jujari's personal shield or armor. In reply, Czyz stepped forward and slammed both Marine's helmets together. A deafening crack rang down the hallway as the bodies collapsed to the floor.

"Keep moving," Rohoar said. But another two guards appeared further down the hallway and started firing. Again, the Unity shield absorbed the blows. But it was Rohoar who took off running, running past the protective cover.

"Rohoar, wait," Awen yelled. But the warrior was not interested in heeding her words. So Awen was forced to move the shield forward as fast as she could. Only one enemy round struck Rohaor's shield before Awen's power caught up with him. But by then, the Jujari was upon the two Marines, slashing at their armor and divesting the men of their lives. He chomped down on one helmet, ripping it off the man's shoulders, along with his head. The second Marine lost his right arm as Rohoar's claws shredded it from its shoulder socket. The man still managed to fire several shots from the blaster in his remaining hand, but that arm was severed next and flopped on the hallway floor.

Rohoar spat the Marine's helmet out and then yelled to Awen to keep moving. "Just a little further."

Then the gladias came around a bend and entered a control room about 100 square meters. A wide console covered the far wall, and Awen instantly recognized it as the one in the image Azelon had provided. Two technicians looked up from their work and stared back at the entrance, but Awen could tell by the quizzical looks on their faces that they had no idea what they were seeing. That, and they were most likely terrified by the blaster fire both outside and inside the substation.

"Put your hands up, and no one gets hurt," Awen said. Both men raised their hands and looked at each other. But then one of them reached for his sidearm and fired. The bolt collided with Awen's Unity shield, and then Rohoar reached out and palmed the man's entire head. He twisted his wrist in a sharp motion, and the technician dropped to the ground.

The other man backed up, hands raised in surrender. The sight of his coworker's head randomly twisting surely put the fear of the mystics in him. "Please, don't hurt me."

"Let him live," Awen said to the Jujari.

"As you wish," Czyz said, knocking the man out with a strike to the side of his head.

"The console," Rohoar said as if presenting it to Awen for her inspection.

"I'm on it." Awen moved the main holo display and started swiping through it. As per Azelon's instructions, she found the manual override function in a subset of other miscellaneous menus. Apparently, this was not an option that Capriana wanted to be accessed easily, and for good reason.

Magnus's voice came to her over comms as she moved

through the required file path. She could tell he was under stress, and the sounds of weapons fire meant the rest of the gladias were in the thick of it.

"We're at the console," Awen said. "I'm navigating the—"

Rohoar growled and then snapped at something. Awen turned and saw three Marines who'd accidentally walked into the Jujari's backsides. The men fired several rounds into the room, a few of which struck equipment against the adjacent walls. Czyz lunged at one of the troopers and drove his claws into the man's chest. Chest armor split open like a cracked egg, and then the Jujari flung the man aside, letting his torso slip off his nails.

Rohoar chomped down three times, splitting armor and blowing up a blaster's energy mag. He yelped as an explosion filled the control room with a quick blast of white light. Then the two Marine bodies hit the deck, and Rohoar and Czyz turned back to face Awen.

"Awen?" Magnus asked. "Talk to me!"

Awen saw blood running out of Rohoar's mouth, but he raised his chops at her in the Jujari version of a smile.

"I'm okay," Awen said, and then returned to the holo screen to initiate the final step. "I'm activating the…" A new screen appeared. Her eyes took in the readout, and she caught her breath. "*Oh no.*"

"What's oh no?" Magnus asked.

Awen stared at the screen a moment longer to be sure it was saying what she thought it was saying. A large timer was counting down from thirty seconds with the title Substation Auto Destruct.

Magnus called her name again and asked her to clarify the situation, but her mind was in overdrive.

"Everyone out," Awen yelled, turning to Rohoar and Czyz. "It's a trap!"

AWEN WAS on Rohoar's back, riding down the hallway. Czyz was in the lead, slashing at troopers unfortunate enough to try and stop the trio. The least Awen could do was to put up a shield as a rearguard, absorbing enemy fire. But the Marine attempts to thwart the gladias seemed halfhearted, and presumably for good reason. The klaxon and swirling red emergency lights meant that anyone who valued their life should get out of the building.

"Self-destruct sequence initiated," the automated voice announced in a smooth female tone. "Fifteen seconds remaining."

"Faster, Rohoar," Awen said, urging the Jujari forward.

Rohoar claw's dug into the floor as he slowed at the first intersection, then he pushed off the wall as he made a 90° turn. He continued to bound down the hallway, tearing up the ground and leaping walls. At the end of the last hallway, Awen felt Rohoar accelerate as he and Czyz headed toward the exit. A dozen troopers turned toward the commotion, but they were still unable to see anything beyond blurry edges and semi-translucent shielding. A few fired on what they must've considered strange anomalies, but the rest of the Marines pushed through the blast doors and into the night.

Czyz barreled through the remaining troopers, opening a space for Rohoar and Awen. As they leaped out of the building, Awen yelled, "Everyone, get clear!"

She noticed as several gladias looked in her direction then back away. She was about to repeat herself when the structure detonated, giving off four separate explosions that rippled down the building. The sound cracked like lightning, rattling her body and making her ears ring. Awen was ripped off Rohoar's back and felt herself fly through the air, unable to tell which way was up. As a last-ditch effort to protect herself, she enclosed herself in a small forcefield. Then her body slammed against something hard. Even with the extra protection from the Unity, the shock made her vision grow dark and her head hurt.

"I have you, daughter of dau Lothlinium House," a deep voice said. She thought the sound belonged to Abimbola, but she couldn't be sure. A cold metal hand slid underneath her back and hoisted her off the ground. "It is time for us to leave."

12

Magnus had just finished setting his BATRIG's self-destruct sequence and was climbing down the side when Czyz and Rohoar burst out of the substation. Marines went flying from the doors as the two Jujari appeared, lunging on all fours.

"Everyone, get clear," Awen yelled, but Magnus still couldn't see her. Had they left her somewhere inside the building? "The facility is going to blow!"

Then Magnus saw her, straddling Rohoar's back like a child might try to ride their dog. Had he not been so preoccupied with keeping his team alive, he would have smiled. The Jujari made it three more strides before a series of explosions rippled down the substation. The exterior walls buckled as torrents of orange fire burst through the seams, blowing the plate metal apart like old rubbertrex tires under too much pressure.

"Awen," Magnus yelled, but the explosion's roar drowned out

his protest. Rohoar, Czyz, and Awen flew forward, backlit by the bombastic release of energy. Magnus's visor adjusted for the sudden brightness a split second before the shockwave slammed into his body. He fell backward but quickly righted himself—eyes searching for Awen's vector.

Her body lay amongst a pile of burning debris forty-five meters away. The two Jujari were close by as well, both gaining their feet. Magnus was about to order them to help her when he saw Abimbola's mech step beside Awen and reach down.

"I have you, daughter of dau Lothlinium House," Abimbola said. "It is time for us to leave."

"Thank you, Abimbola," Magnus said.

"Thank the gods," the Miblimbian replied.

"Technically, it was Azelon who provided the mechanized armament system," TO-96 said on a private channel to Magnus. "Giving praise to her seems far more fitting."

Magnus ignored the bot's point of clarity. "'Six, is there another switch in this base?"

"If you are referring to a way to activate the PDS manually, no, I'm afraid not," the bot replied.

"You're sure."

"I am 100% certain, sir. The only other way to activate the shield is from within CENTCOM, as previously discussed."

Magnus cursed, then opened up the squad channel. "Fire teams, fall back to the skimmers!" Acknowledgment icons ran down his comms window, and everyone began heading toward the gap in the wall. Doc checked in on Rohoar and Czyz, but both Jujari seemed fine. Miraculously, everyone's biometrics appeared nominal—aside from elevated heart rates and blood pressure.

Magnus stood beside his BATRIG as Abimbola lumbered past, followed by Titus. But Titus turned and started laying down a base of fire as the rest of the squad headed toward the breach.

"Go," Titus said to Magnus. "I'll buy us some time."

"No hero splick, Titus," Magnus said, pointing a finger up at the mech's operator.

"I have no intention of becoming a martyr, LT," Titus replied. "Just holding back the buckets until you say the word." There was a brief pause as Titus seemed to be working through the suit's systems. "Might wanna stand back."

"For what?" Magnus took a few steps away from Titus's BATRIG and then blocked his visor with an arm as half a dozen missiles launched from the backside. At first, they streaked upward like Vordic fangback snakes hissing at the night. Bright white engine cones traced lines through the darkened sky. Then the missiles pulled high-G turns and pointed back toward the ground, spreading out as they did. This was Azelon's variable warhead missile system, on display for the first time. Magnus guessed that Titus had selected the multiple target option, given that the six missiles were careening toward different points inside the base.

"Run," Titus yelled.

Magnus backpedaled, kicking his way through the rubble in the breached wall and turning toward the open sand. A moment later, six blasts billowed against the sky's black canvas, shooting out flames and fountains of sparks. Titus opened fire with his

GU90M and swept it back and forth, surely making every Marine think twice before closing on the monster in the breach. *Mystics know I would*, Magnus thought as he ran.

"Come on, Titus," Magnus said. "That's enough."

"Copy that." Titus's mech icon began moving away from the wall on Magnus's topo map. Meanwhile, the rest of the unit was advancing across the open field and making good time. He glanced at HUD to check the countdown timer, noting the self-destruct sequence still had thirty-three seconds to go.

More blaster fire erupted from the walls, hunting down the gladias with renewed enthusiasm.

The futility of the whole operation frustrated Magnus. Here he was, trying to kill Marines in order to save the planet from annihilation. They were just trying to defend themselves, and Magnus had no choice but to fire back. He hated the fact that the end really did justify the means—*but it's a backassward means*, he thought.

"A little help?" Magnus asked Titus.

"On it." Titus aimed his RTD10 and fired. The weapon's muzzle flash lit up the battlefield, bathing the sand in light. Bodies detonated along the wall as Titus swept the weapon from left to right. Magnus thought he heard Titus yelling from the cockpit but couldn't be sure over the noise.

Titus's assault had the desired effect—the enemy's blaster fire momentarily subsided. But Titus's barrage also gave the enemy a specific target, one that pointed their focus toward the northern shoreline. Blaster rounds were closing on the gladias retreat, and several members took direct hits to their shields.

"Don't slow down," Magnus ordered—as if anyone needed the reminder. But he knew encouragement was imperative. "Keep moving. Keep moving!"

He glanced at his BATRIG's timer. It had nine seconds remaining. Plumes erupted on either side of his feet, showering his armor with superheated sand. Magnus's leg muscles burned even with his servo assist, but he focused on the ledge ahead and willed himself forward. Gladias were starting to drop behind the boulders' cover, vanishing from view as they skirted down the embankment.

The timer reached zero. Magnus looked over his shoulder to see a series of missiles shoot skyward as the breach filled with smoke. More than a dozen white lines soared overhead, disappearing from the reach of the base's fires and floodlights. For a second, Magnus wondered if the software had been faulty—*hadn't Titus's missiles turned down sooner than this?* Then, as if appearing from the clouds like lightning strikes, the projectiles slammed into the mech with laser-guided precision.

The explosion made the horizon look like a small starship had lifted off. Fire billowed out from the wall, blowing everything and everyone off the ramparts. Bodies disappeared in the red plumes, as did the watchtowers, gun emplacements, and sniper nests. The air crackled as if torn apart, and debris blew out in an artificial sandstorm.

Magnus looked ahead and saw the ledge a few paces away. There was no time to run down the embankment, so he leaped. His body flew through the air, backlit by the exploding BATRIG, and then crashed into the sand some eight meters below. His servos whined, and he heard something crack. As his body rolled to a stop, he checked his HUD. The sound wasn't a bone—just his suit's right knee joint. *I can live with that,* Magnus said to himself, looking at the suit's diagnostic alerts.

With fire still swelling into the sky from the explosion, Magnus ordered everyone onto the sea skimmers. Abimbola set Awen down on her back, and Magnus grabbed her hands. "Can you stand?"

Awen nodded. "Yes, I believe so."

"Good." Magnus helped her up, hugged her, and then watched Titus's mech slide down the boulders. "Titus, Abimbola, get out and grab skimmers."

"But we just got these," Titus said, already opening the cockpit.

"And I hate giving toys back," Abimbola added.

"Well, if I know Azelon, I'm sure she's making more. Plus, it'll take a while for troopers to put these things down." That statement gave Magnus an idea. "Hey, Azie? Any chance those BATRIGs have some sort of sentinel mode?"

"Indeed they do, sir. Would you like me to activate it for you?"

Magnus smiled. "By all means. And I want to make sure the tech doesn't fall into Repub hands, at least not until this whole mess is sorted out."

"Understood, sir. I will initiate appropriate preventative measures."

Magnus thought of how his BATRIG auto-destructed and imagined the impact of two mechs going nova at the same time.

For the Marines' sake, he hoped none were close when it happened.

Magnus thanked Azelon and then made sure everyone had a sea skimmer before picking out the one he'd arrived on. He ordered them off the beach just as several defenders started firing on the north shore from observation posts along the antenna's base. Their aim was much better because, unlike the Novian armor and battle mechs, the sea skimmers lacked a telecolos finish. Magnus punched the throttle and surged past the surf, accelerating toward the rest of the squad.

"Sir," said TO-96. "I'm detecting movement from the island's east end."

"What kind of movement?" Magnus asked.

"Considering the fact that the objects appear to be moving across the water, I'd say either fighters or—"

"Kestrels," Magnus said. "Dammit."

"Should we be worried about something?" Awen asked.

"Kestrels?" Abimbola said. "I am guessing you do not mean the small bird of prey."

"I mean the Republic KT40 water speeders," Magnus replied.

"I'm guessing they have guns," Titus said.

"And light shielding," TO-96 added. "I have the unit's full specifications list and training manual pulled up. I might add that the manuscript's introduction is written with an extremely cheerful tone, congratulating users on their new—"

"'Six," Magnus yelled. "Shut up!"

"My apologies, sir."

"We need their icons on our HUDs," Magnus said. Azelon complied, populating the NBTI with new enemy targets. "Listen up, people. The Kestrels don't have a wide field of fire, but they can turn like a bull mutt on a rattler."

"Do bull mutts turn quickly?" Czyz asked.

"I believe that is the implication, yes," Rohoar answered. "Though I suspect it depends on the veracity of the rattlesnake in Magnus's analogy."

"As I was saying," Magnus said. "They are only shielded in front, so if you can get to the side or aft, you'll have a better chance of taking out the pilot or damaging the stabilizers."

"Then we'd better look sharp," Titus said. "Because here they come."

Magnus's HUD showed five Kestrels converging in a V-formation about 500 meters back. The enemy's first shots streaked past Magnus's skimmer and threw three water spouts into the air. The spray beat against his helmet, but he was moving far too fast for the water to impede his vision. Two more shots split through the white caps and ended against a massive wave.

"Awen and Nídira, give us some protection," Magnus said. "The rest of Bravo Team, peel off and double-back. Everyone else, stay with me. Assault formation with 100-meter spread. And for mystic's sake, watch the crossfire."

Everyone in Bravo Team but Nídira split off while the two mystics raised a Unity shield. Magnus accelerated to take the lead and watched as Alpha Team moved out to his right and left. In his HUD, the enemies split up. Two Kestrels shifted to intercept courses in a flanking movement, while the remaining three vehicles moved into attack formation, focusing on Magnus in the center of the line.

The next blaster rounds struck the Unity shields. The energy blew out in dazzling prismatic splotches that were simultaneously soaked by the skimmers' torrential wakes. The defense rendered the enemy fire ineffective but beautiful.

On his HUD, Magnus watched Dutch and Haze turn left with a Kestrel running an intercept course on their left flank. Just when Magnus thought the pair might get sideswiped by enemy fire, Dutch's sea skimmer slowed, creating a gap ahead of the enemy. It was a brilliant maneuver, one that forced the Repub pilot to choose which target to go after. Either way, Magnus knew the Kestrel was beaten.

The pilot chose Haze's skimmer, most likely because it was closer in range. He banked left after the gladia, and as soon as the Repub pilot committed, Dutch accelerated and opened fire with her NOV1. Even from two klicks out, the blaster rounds glimmered across the waves and slammed into the Kestrel's stern. Sparks danced on the vehicle's tail before it succumbed, folding into the waves.

"Nice shooting," Magnus said.

Following the same strategy, Silk and Doc spread apart on the right flank. This time, the Kestrel followed the slower inside skimmer. Silk opened fire as the pilot closed on her right side. Magnus noticed her shield's power drop to 10% before a spray of NOV1 erupted on the Kestrel's starboard side. Magnus zoomed in just as the Repub pilot was blown from his speeder and tumbled into the water at over 175 kilometers per hour. The pilotless Kestrel clipped Silk's skimmer and sent her flying.

"Silk," Magnus shouted, watching her icon divert from her vehicle and then stop in the sea. "Doc!"

"I'm on it," the medic replied.

The three remaining Kestrels continued firing on Alpha Team until they came up against the Unity shield. The lead pilot nudged his speeder's nose against it and then fired point-blank.

"You got something more, Awen?" Magnus asked in a way that he hoped invited her to do something creative. He could practically hear her smiling over comms.

"Maybe," she said.

Magnus looked over his shoulder just as the Unity shield stopped in place. Two of the three Kestrels slammed into it and detonated as if they'd struck a granite wall. The third, however, went wide, avoiding the wall and the exploding debris, and then came back in line. When the pilot fired again, Awen and Nídira's wall had dissipated, and the blaster rounds struck Rohoar's skimmer. The Jujari roared as he flew into the waves. Magnus only hoped the Novian armor made the high-speed impact survivable.

"I've got this," Magnus said. He looked over his shoulder again, gauging the Kestrel's trajectory, and then squeezed his skimmer's brakes. The vehicle lurched, and the rest of the sea skimmers flew ahead. The last Kestrel had no time to react, and screamed past Magnus less than two meters away. As soon as he could see through the spray left behind by the passing vehicle, Magnus pegged the throttle, and the sea skimmer dashed forward. Then he raised his NOV1, used his bioteknia eyes to help assist aiming for the one-handed shot, and squeezed.

The blaster rounds bit into the twin hydrofoil stabilizers, cutting them out from under the craft. Without them, the Kestrel skipped along the wave tops, bouncing like a skipped stone. Unlike a rock, the hops of which got shorter and shorter, the Kestrel's leaps became higher and more unstable, until its final jump sent it tumbling through the air only to crash into the bottom of a deep roller.

"You good back there?" Awen asked.

"Fine."

"Magnus," TO-96 said. "Watch out!"

A sixth Kestrel appeared out of the darkness and fired on Magnus. He didn't even have time to respond to the bot's warning before blaster fire blew his skimmer's tail off and sent his vehicle sideways into the water.

Magnus felt his insides pitch as his body spun through the air. Then Magnus struck the water with the force of a skiff hauler hitting him in the chest. He gasped as everything went dark, including his HUD. Had he not cried against the pain that jarred his body, he would have guessed he was unconscious. Instead, he was suspended in the sea, unable to tell which way was up.

As soon as the pain subsided enough to move, Magnus swished his arms and legs in an attempt to regain some semblance of control. Then his HUD rebooted, and the Welcome prompt initiated. Before icons populated his vision, he heard several voices yelling his name.

"I'm here! I'm here," he replied, taking several deep breaths.

"I've got him," another voice said. Magnus was still too groggy to place the speaker, but it was familiar. "Just hang tight, Magnus."

Another few seconds passed before soft light appeared, turning the watery space over Magnus blue. Then a body crashed through the ceiling in a mighty throng of bubbles. The figure turned left and right before spotting Magnus, then lunged. Magnus took the offered arm, groaning against the pain in his head. There was a sudden jerk, and then Magnus was on the surface, kicking to keep his head above the deep swells.

"Can you reach the skimmer?" Titus asked—if Magnus's head doubted the speaker, his HUD finally registered the personnel roster.

Magnus looked up and saw the recovery bar affixed to the skimmer's belly awash in the repulsor lights and salt spray. "Yeah, I think so." He kicked both legs hard and reached for the bar. His first attempt failed when his gauntlet slipped from the rung. But his second attempt succeeded, and Magnus pulled himself up with some assistance from Titus below. He climbed atop the skimmer and swung himself into the pilot's seat. Then he reached down to aid Titus as the gladia straddled the body in front of the vertical stabilizer.

"Good to go," Titus said. He wrapped an arm around Magnus's chest and tapped him twice on top of the helmet. Magnus took a second to prepare his gut for the acceleration and then punched the throttle.

"ANYONE HAVE EYES ON ROHOAR?" Magnus asked when he had finally caught his breath and his head cleared.

"Rohoar has eyes on Rohoar," the Jujari replied. "And he is riding with Abimbola, who is certainly upset with having so much Jujari up his ass."

Magnus laughed. "I'm sure he is."

"He did not mean it like that," Abimbola replied.

"Of course he did," Titus added. "And"—the gladia paused for a second while he sounded preoccupied with a task—"now I have a picture of it."

"I am going to feed you to my pet rathmonolith when we get back to the Dregs, Titus," the Miblimbian replied.

"That's fine. But this pic will live forever on the galaxy's servers."

Abimbola growled in reply as the rest of the squad sounded like they were stifling laughter.

The sea skimmers converged in formation again, and Magnus breathed a sigh of relief. The Repub hadn't sent any more Kestrels out, and according to sensors, it would be clear sailing back to Capriana.

"Hey, LT," Titus said over a private channel. "Can I ask you something?"

"Shoot," Magnus replied.

"Back there, when you were in your mech, how did you let those Marines get the jump on you like that? Those Recon troopers too, right?"

Magnus secretly hoped no one had seen the fight. Not only

had Titus witnessed the whole thing, but he'd also taken note of the enemy's specialty. *Respect, Titus,* Magnus thought. *Respect.*

"I mean, you saw them coming," Titus continued. "At least that's the way I read it from where I stood. And you were in a BATRIG, for crying out loud."

"Yeah, yeah. You read it right." Magnus looked down as the waves as the sea skimmer cut through the whitecaps. "Sometimes, love for your team makes you do stupid splick."

There was a moment's silence as Titus seemed to consider the reply. "I hear that," the gladia said, and then nothing more.

Magnus was relieved that there weren't any follow-up questions. Honestly, he didn't know how else to reply, though he did feel endeared to Titus for accepting the answer to his question.

Magnus opened the squad channel back to the *Spire.* It was better to keep everyone apprised of the conversation as it went. "You there, Colonel?"

"Go ahead, Adonis," Caldwell said.

"What's the play?"

"First, glad you're okay down there."

Magnus smiled for the helmet cam. "And here I thought you didn't care."

"I was talking to Rohoar."

The Jujari's face appeared as he spoke, grinning a toothy smile. "Rohoar appreciates this concern."

"Sure, you do," Magnus said. "The play, Colonel?"

"If I didn't have such an affinity for the capital, son? I'd tell you to get the hell out of there. You've already risked enough, and you've overstayed your welcome—way past time on target."

"But you do care about the capital," Magnus replied. "And you're going to tell me there's still time to save the planet."

"Something like that. As you heard Brass Balls mention earlier, the only remaining way to activate the PDS is from inside CENTCOM—do yourselves what you were hoping the general would do."

"Did he just say *inside* CENTCOM?" Titus asked.

"Yes," replied Rohoar. "Are you unable to hear well anymore?"

"No. No, I just—forget it."

"You're sure it's the only way, Colonel?" Magnus asked.

"It is, son. I'm sorry."

"There is some good news, at least," TO-96 interjected. "Given the fact that the capital has incurred assaults at three different sites—your initial intrusion of CENTCOM, Petty Officer Zoll's raid on the lab, and your latest attack on Elusian Base—their defenses are scrambling to respond."

"I'm not sure I see how that is good news, 'Six."

"Forgive me, sir. Sometimes I forget that my intuitive processes do not adequately articulate—"

"'Six!"

"The situation is good news because the Republic's forces are spread thin. As a result, the last place they will expect an assault—"

"Is at the first place we hit."

"That is correct, sir."

Magnus clucked his tongue. "Damn, you're a smart bot."

"I agree," Azelon said, appearing over TO-96's shoulder.

"Thank you, sir," said TO-96, his eye sockets glowing a warm shade of amber.

"So, you are proposing that we head *back* to the capital and take the elevator down again?" Abimbola asked.

"Something like that, yeah," Magnus replied.

"Rohoar still does not understand why we did not do this the first time," Rohoar said. "Your human logic is confusing."

Magnus didn't blame the Jujari for asking. "Because we were trying to keep casualties down—ours specifically. Infiltrating the Elusian Base appeared to be the easier path."

"Easier than breaking into an underground basement?"

Magnus nodded. "Yes. But, hopefully, they're paying less attention this time."

"Or more." The Jujari licked his lips. "Rohoar is ready to mat his fur with the blood of his enemies."

"Is that a thing?" Titus asked. "You actually do that?"

"Jujari expression," Rohoar replied.

"Gotcha," Titus said with a hint of relief.

"But also a thing. It is both an expression and a thing."

"Then it's just a thing," Titus said.

"And expression."

Titus rolled his eyes. "Whatever."

"One more thing, Adonis," Caldwell said, his voice low. "Ezo just let us know that they're on the way—and so is Moldark."

Splick. "How long we got?"

"With subspace transmission delay? The Wonder Twins tell me about an hour."

"Colonel, even if we activated the shield right now—"

"It's not a lot of margin, son. I know. Just do what you can and get the hell out of there."

Magnus nodded. "Roger that. Magnus, out."

"*Spire*, out."

Magnus took a deep breath and tried to focus. "Okay, gladias. We've got a job to do, and sunup isn't going to wait for us."

As the sea skimmers continued east toward the sky glow of Capriana's lights, Magnus tried to formulate some sort of infiltration plan. Attempting a failed op for the second time in a row wasn't exactly textbook. In fact, he was reasonably sure it would end poorly. But they had to try—there were too many lives at stake not to. It was in moments like this that he appreciated the Jujari's cut-throat tenacity, even if their logic was just as confusing.

But this wasn't a repeat operation, technically speaking. The first round's objective had been to convince CENTCOM's leadership to activate the PDS. Now, it was a deep infil op, and the demand for enabling the PDS was on Granther Company.

"Magnus, do you read?" said a voice over VNET. Magnus glanced at the ident tag.

"Zoll," Magnus replied. "You good?"

"Ha. We're alive, but we smell like splick."

"Come again?"

"Sewers. We have the assets, and half of us are heading westbound through the city sewers."

"You have my parents?" Awen asked, her voice filled with excitement. "Are they all right?"

"They're fine, Awen," Zoll replied. "And they're eager to see you."

"You said half," Magnus interjected. "Where's the rest of your team?"

"We split up. Delta and Echo Teams stayed topside to defend our descent into the lab's lower levels. But they're on their way out now. We're regrouping at a treatment facility Cyril found."

"Roger, copy," Cyril said. "It's just over a clickity-clack west, over."

Magnus smiled despite his growing concern. "So I take it the lab's transports were a no-go."

"Roger," Zoll said. "The facility's AI made sure of that. So we're improvising."

"Seems we're all doing a little of that," Magnus replied. "Find a way to the Simlia atoll, and we'll meet you there. Oh, and a free piece of advice: see if you can locate a Jules Sea Skimmer Rentals franchise."

13

"JULES SEA SKIMMER RENTALS?" Reimer said to Zoll. "That sounds fun."

"All part of your paid vacation, care of the Gladio Umbra," Zoll said.

Reimer laughed. "And how do these sewers figure into that?"

"It was in the excursions brochure."

"Must'a missed that."

"Nah. It was clearly marked with the line that read *This Option Is Full of Splick, You Dimwitted Derk Duffer.*"

"Guilty," said Reimer with a self-deprecating tone, and then he laughed along with everyone else.

Charlie Team continued west through the sewers while Delta and Echo Teams fought their way out of the lab's upper stories. So far, neither element had suffered casualties since entering the lab, and Zoll hoped it would stay that way. It was just a little further until Charlie Team got out of this hellhole and topside again. They just had to keep Awen's parents alive and find a new means of transport to the Simlia atoll.

"I still don't get it," Zoll said to Balin and Giyel over external speakers. "You're Elonians. So, how the hell did you two get roped into working for the Repub?"

"We were abducted from our home," Balin replied.

"Lured away under pretenses, and *then* abducted," Giyel said with a tone that suggested she was used to expounding on her husband's definitions.

"What kind of pretenses?" Zoll asked, stepping over a short collection dam that acted as a divider between the current tunnel and the next intersection.

"The Republic Ambassador paid us a visit," Galin said, and then spit into the sewage.

"Ambassador?"

Giyel nodded. "Gerald Bosworth."

"The *third*," Balin added with no attempt to hide his obvious disdain.

Zoll looked over his shoulder at the couple. "Didn't realize he made house calls."

Balin tilted his head. "You know of him?"

Zoll chuckled. "A whole lotta people know about him. I helped detain him for my boss once, back on Oorajee. Then the Repub reacquired him. Most recently, he sent us evidence of your capture, which is what led us here. I just didn't think he was the one who did the wet work." Zoll held up a finger. "Correction: didn't think he had the stamina to do the wet work."

"Wet work?" Giyel asked.

"Murders, assassinations, and sometimes kidnappings," Zoll explained.

"Well, it didn't feel like a kidnapping at first," Giyel replied. "He was persuasive."

"How so?" Zoll held up a hand as he studied a barred gate ahead. "Rix, can you take care of this?"

"On it, chief." Rix skirted Zoll and the dau Lothliniums to start cutting through the barricade with a torch. The Elionion couple shielded their eyes from the bright sparks.

"At first, he told us that Awen was in trouble and that the Order of the Luma and the Republic needed our help to secure her," Giyel said. "That it was a matter of grave consequence."

"Naturally, we would do anything for our daughter," Balin said.

"So, you went with him," Zoll said.

The couple nodded.

Rix finished cutting the bars and kicked out the hole he'd made in the gate. "After you," he said.

Zoll stepped through and helped Balin and Giyel, using his headlamp to illuminate their way.

"At first, everything seemed legitimate," Balin said. "Our daughter was taken hostage by the Jujari, and the Republic wanted to employ us to help negotiate for her life."

"Forgive my ignorance, but why would they think you could help?" Zoll asked. "He's the ambassador."

"True, but we are also Elonians."

Zoll shrugged. *Right,* he thought. "The one species trusted with peace, diplomacy, and stability even more than the Luma."

"Something like that," Balin said.

"Plus, it was our daughter," Giyel said. "And we had something they could use."

"And that was?"

"Research," Balin said. He helped his wife over a mid-tunnel dam. "Specifically, medical research on the Jujari."

"And the Ambassador was going to use that as leverage?" Zoll didn't feel the logic was adding up. "But wouldn't you have just given it to them anyway? You're Elonians, after all."

"Of course we would have," Giyel said. "But our work wasn't ready yet."

"And, in our naiveté, that's what made us so willing to help the ambassador," Gailen said.

"It wouldn't be a stretch for you to give something to free your daughter when you were already going to give it anyway," Zoll said.

"Right." Balin nodded. "Only, the whole thing was a ruse."

"As soon as we got on the ambassador's ship, we were arrested and diverted here to Capriana." Giyel rubbed her wrists as if remembering the restraints.

"And that's when Bosworth turned the tables on you," Zoll said.

"Precisely," Balin replied. "As it turned out, *he* had Awen hostage and threatened to kill her unless we did his bidding."

"Which was to create a biotoxin?" Zoll asked. "Isn't that a little extreme?"

"Of course," said Giyel. "And that's why we refused."

Balin nodded. "At least at first. Up to that point, he hadn't provided evidence that Awen was in his custody."

"But, he did eventually?"

Giyel touched her forehead and steadied herself against her husband. "Yes. Images of…"

"Of Awen being tortured," Balin said. "Chained up and unconscious."

Zoll wondered how such a thing was possible and was about to ask when he remembered how the Marauders had first taken Awen captive. But if the footage was from her temporary imprisonment in the Dregs, how had the ambassador obtained it?

"So, what was it he asked you to make for him?" Zoll asked.

"A derivative of the Simikon blight," Balin answered.

"From the old Limbian invasion?"

Balin nodded. "Like all Elonian scientists, my parents kept detailed records of their work."

"But I thought you Elonians cured that plague?" Zoll asked.

"We did," Giyel said. "But it's so fast-acting that if anyone got their hands on the generic composition and released it far enough away from the antitoxin, you're looking at—"

"Planet-level extinction," Zoll said, restating their description from back in the lab. "But you have that antitoxin, right?"

"Of course," Giyel said. "Which is why we were willing to recreate the virus if it meant buying our daughter more time."

"That's when Bosworth started asking for other things," Balin said.

"There's more?"

"But we don't have to worry about that now," Giyel said hurriedly. "Thanks to you. How soon before we can see Awen?"

"It's more like, how soon before those explosives go off," Rix stated. "And we don't got much time, chief."

"How long?" Zoll asked.

"One minute."

Zoll looked at Cyril. "We close?"

"Uh-huh," said the code slicer. "Just up ahead, copy vector bravo."

Rix shook his head. "I'll never understand you, kid."

Zoll pushed forward until he saw a ladder that led to an access hatch. "This it, kid?"

"Roger niner niner, sir," Cyril replied. "Let's scoot the coop."

"Wish," Zoll said. "We clear up top?"

The mystic paused and tilted her head slightly. "All clear, chief."

Zoll pointed at the Jujari. "Redmarrow, you first. Clear us a way out of the building as fast as you can."

"Right away, human leader." Redmarrow stepped around the dau Lothliniums then bounded up the ladder, spun open the hatch, and disappeared. Then Rix went up to guard the dau Lothliniums as they climbed, while Zoll, Wish, and Reimer brought up the rear.

Reimer resealed the hatch. "Not my worst sewer excursion, but not my best either."

"Time," Cyril yelled. A deep *boom* shook the small utility room and everyone reached for something to hold onto. Chunks began falling from the ceiling. "Let's get a pronto on our giddy up!"

"Never mind," Reimer said, looking at Zoll. "I'm taking this up with the ship's captain over dinner."

DUST SHOT out the front door as Charlie Team ran out of the treatment sub-station and onto the street. Without the benefit of helmets, Balin and Giyel coughed and doubled over on their knees.

"You okay?" Zoll asked Giyel with a hand on her back. She nodded and then waved him off.

"Zoll," Bliss yelled over comms.

Zoll looked up to see Delta and Echo Teams jogging toward him. "You in one piece?"

"Affirmative. But that's more than we can say for the enemy."

"Dominate," Zoll said.

"Liberate, baby."

"And you guys?" Robillard asked. "I see you found the assets."

"We're fine," Zoll replied.

"Just make sure you read the fine print on the excursion brochure," Reimer said.

Zoll smiled, then turned to face everyone. "It won't be long before the Repub connects the lab and this sewer plant, so we've gotta get the assets off the street and then find a way to the exfil point."

"Any recommendations now that the lab's shuttles aren't an option?" Robillard asked.

"We're headed west, to…" Zoll studied the mission map in his HUD. "Liquid Gold Marina and Sea Park."

"Sounds enchanting," Bliss said.

"We're looking for sea skimmers." Zoll could practically hear people's excitement level rise. "And, no, you don't get to keep them. It's just a day trip."

ZOLL LED his squad west toward the city limits. Boardwalk lights glimmered at the end of the block, signaling that the teams had reached the shore—and all without discovery. At least so far. The gladias kept the dau Lothlinium's concealed as best they could, but Zoll knew the efforts weren't perfect. Had this been broad daylight and the streets full of pedestrians, they would have been discovered long ago. But the early morning hours were working to their advantage. Just one more leg south, across the ocean, and they were home free.

"Is that what you were talking about, chief?" Rix asked, pointing toward a thatched hut beside the marina's entrance. The sign read Jules Sea Skimmer Rentals.

"That's the one," Zoll replied. "Cyril, see what you can do."

"Copy copy," the code slicer said, running ahead.

"Rix, go with him."

"On it, chief," Rix said.

"Where are we going?" Balin asked, running hand in hand with his wife.

Zoll switched to external speakers. "We need to get you to another atoll where a shuttle will be waiting for us."

"And we're headed to a marina because?"

"Because our A Plan is a no-go."

"So you're improvising," Giyel said.

"Yup."

Zoll and the rest of the squad charged across the sand, heading straight for the sea skimmer rental stand when blaster fire erupted from inside the hut.

"Get down," Rix yelled, presumably to Cyril. Zoll noticed both of their shields take hits. More blaster fire turned the inside of the hut bright red as the rounds danced across the sand and ricocheted off the sea skimmers. Zoll looked for Repub troopers, but there weren't any.

"What the hell's going on in there?" Zoll asked.

"Some lunatic woman has us pinned down!"

Zoll told Awen's parents to stay put behind a cluster of palms and ordered Longchomps to keep watch. "Everyone else with me!"

When Zoll reached the rental hut, the woman Rix had mentioned seemed to be reloading her weapon from behind the counter. Rix was about to stand from behind the hut's half-wall when the woman started shooting again.

"Take that, you thieving bastards," she shouted above the blaster rounds, spraying the ground with bolts. "Try and take my property, will you? Think again!"

"She's crazy," Rix yelled. "I'm gonna shoot her."

"Don't shoot her," Zoll said. "She's a damn civilian."

"She's gonna kill us!"

Zoll needed to think fast. Not only was his team in jeopardy from this vengeful entrepreneur, but the blaster fire was sure to draw attention and risked tipping off Repub security.

"Grahban," Zoll said. "Go through the back of the hut and snag her. *But don't kill her.* Wish, give our boys some protection."

The mystic put up a Unity shield to keep the blaster fire from doing any more harm to Rix and Cyril while the Jujari dashed around the back of the hut. A moment later, Grahban punched a hole in the wall—with his whole body—and grabbed the woman from behind. "Got her," Grahban said.

Zoll stepped into the hut and saw the Jujari restraining a snarling woman that seemed intent on kicking, clawing, or even biting her way out of whatever unseen force had her pinned.

"Put me down," she ordered. "I'm gonna kill you, little bitches!"

"Told you she's gonna kill us," Rix said, standing hesitantly.

"I will not permit her," Grahban said. "Though she is stronger than her size suggests."

Zoll turned on his headlamp but didn't de-cloak. "Jules, I take it?"

The blonde-haired woman froze, squinting against the bright light. She was probably attractive when she wasn't seething—perhaps thirty years old. "Who the hell's asking?"

"We're not here to hurt you."

"That's what they all say." She spit into the light. "Just give us your skimmers, and no one gets hurt. Am I right? Well, not today, you son of a bitch."

"Can I subdue her?" Grahban asked. "Please, with sweet fruit on top?"

"Negative, not yet," Zoll said, though he appreciated the attempt at the human idiom. "We might need her."

"We *definitely* need her," Cyril said. "She's locked us out." Zoll looked over at the code slicer who was already working on a sales console behind the counter. "Seems Magnus's previous hijacking tipped her off, so she instituted a core systems firewall."

Unaware of Cyril's VNET conversation, Jules nodded toward the console. "I can see some cloaked asshole on your team has discovered my lockdown. Payback's a bitch, isn't it?"

"Let me dispatch her," Grahban said. "One of those skiffs in the marina is probably easier to be thieving."

"And slower," Bliss said. "If speed is our priority, these sea skimmers are by far our best bet."

"Splick," Zoll said, biting the inside of his cheek. He decided to try the impossible and removed his helmet.

Jules winced as the light left her eyes and revealed a floating head. "What the hell?"

"Jules, my name is Petty Officer Kar Zoll. I need you to remain calm."

"Calm? What in mystics' name is going on around here? You some GR freak show or something?"

"Not even close," Zoll said. "We are the Gladio Umbra, here to rescue some hostages and help protect the planet from an impending attack by a madman who controls the Repub fleets. I know that sounds crazy, but you've just gotta trust me."

"If you're here to protect the planet, then why are the GR shooting at you?"

Zoll shrugged. "Since when does the Repub do what makes sense?"

"Fair point."

"And we're gonna need your skimmers. But we'll reimburse you for each one."

"Get lost," she said. "You know how long it took me to build this business? I ain't letting them go just because some floating-ass head asked to buy them at four in the morning."

"We'll pay you double."

Jules grimaced, then seemed to think of something else. "Nah. But, triple, and you have yourself a deal."

A Republic warning alert went off in the city.

Jules looked back at Zoll. "*And* you tell me about this Glad Umbrella, cause it sure as hell ain't the GR."

A new barrage of blaster fire hit the hut, but this time it came from the city. Longchomps roared over comms. "We have two more packs of bucketheads charging from the east!"

"Get out here," Zoll said. "Delta Team, covering fire!"

"So, we got a deal or not?" Jules said.

"Deal. Grahban, release her."

The Jujari let go, and Jules yanked her arms free then stretched them in protest. "Bitch," she said under breath.

"But I am a male," Grahban said to Zoll.

Jules raced to the console where Cyril was and then worked

through several screens. "There," she said, turning to Zoll. "The skimmers are yours."

"Thanks for your help," Zoll replied. "It was a pleasure doing business with you."

"Not so fast," Jules said, ducking as a blaster round whizzed through the hut a meter from Zoll's head. "I'm coming with you."

"That wasn't part of the deal." He put his helmet back on.

"Deal's change, especially when the GR is shooting at you. Plus, I just ensured that those skimmers will shut down once they get out of range from my comms watch." She raised her wrist and swished her arm back and forth.

Zoll cursed. "Fine. But no more questions until we make landfall."

"I can live with that."

"That's good, 'cause you're dying otherwise." Zoll flipped back to the squad channel. "Return fire and mount up. It's time to blow this sea skimmer stand!"

14

"The sewers," Magnus said to himself as his small squadron of sea skimmers approached Capriana's shore. Hearing Zoll mention the city's waste management system gave him an idea.

"What was that, buckethead?" Abimbola asked.

Magnus cleared his throat and spoke up. "Zoll said he was using the sewers to escape the lab."

"And you think we should use them to infiltrate CENTCOM."

"I do. It's the only other way I can think to gain access without going down the elevator again. 'Six, Azie, can you give me a position on the Forum Republica's waste management facility?"

"Certainly, sir," TO-96 said. "Please stand by."

A moment later, a new topo map appeared in Magnus's HUD, displaying a portion of the city just north of the capital complex. A small building glowed blue, and an ident tag featured its coordinates, distance, and time to target at current speed.

"What can you tell me about it, 'Six?" Magnus asked.

TO-96 began narrating as the building expanded and morphed into a three-dimensional schematic. "This particular public waste facility was first commissioned in 4121 by the Sentient Species Alliance in order to serve their newly founded headquarters. Upon its completion, Chancellor Ronruth declared it to be——"

"'Six, kill the history lesson," Magnus said.

"But, sir, I feel that——"

"'Six!"

"Fast forwarding to today, this facility is the main distribution hub for all waste leaving the Forum Republica's northern half." The schematic oriented to follow root tunnels as they branched out and spread to numerous locations within the capital's northern section. The view raced along one pipe in particular. "CENTCOM is serviced by this line, which bifurcates into east and west stems."

"Which one is closer to the command room?" Magnus asked.

"The west line, sir. It terminates here"—TO-96 illuminated a small chamber—"in a collection stall directly below a utility room."

"How secure?" Abimbola asked.

"Grates are locked and have standard pressure sensors."

"So no motion detection?" Magnus asked.

TO-96 shook his head. "No, sir. Nor are there thermal sensors. Given the nature of sewage, both are rather futile."

"Right." Magnus zoomed out and dropped a marker on the shore closest to the sewage plant. "Heads up, Granthers. I've updated the mission map with a new waypoint. Get clear of your skimmer as soon as we make landfall. Chameleon mode all the way to the sewage facility."

The team confirmed his orders and shifted left toward the new waypoint.

"Thanks for your help," Magnus said.

"Happy to be of assistance, sir."

Magnus thought he detected a hint of sadness in the bot's voice. "Listen, 'Six. When I get back to the ship, you can tell me all about the city's municipal engineering history."

"Only if you wish, sir."

"Pal, if we make it through this, you can tell me all the stories you want."

TO-96 seemed to perk up. "I will gladly indulge you, sir."

"I'm sure you will. Magnus out."

MAGNUS'S SQUAD ditched the sea skimmers on the beach and moved into the urban sprawl without being noticed. For all the hell the Granthers raised at the three Repub locations, the city was relatively quiet. Though, Magnus guessed, the TACNET channels had to be a mess with comms traffic. *The more chaotic, the better*, he thought.

His fire teams raced down the empty sidewalks and then dashed across the street once they'd arrived at the waste plant.

Unlike the other buildings on the block—those made of composite materials and designed with sleek lines—this facility's red brick exterior and tall windows made it look old and worn out. *Fitting for a place that refines splick.*

"'Six," Magnus asked. "What do we have for security?"

"Just cameras, though I doubt they're being monitored with any level of discipline."

"Copy that."

"I estimate two night guards and three technicians on-site," the bot added.

"Thanks." Magnus looked to Rohoar. "Can you get us in the ally-side door *without* making a scene?"

"Rohoar will do his best," replied the Jujari.

Just before Magnus gave the command to move out, he noticed Abimbola flip a poker chip, catch it, and slap it on the back of his gauntlet. "What does it say, Bimby?"

The Miblimbian hesitated, his visor fixed on the chip.

"Bimby?"

"It says this path is bad luck," Abimbola replied.

"'Course it's bad luck," Haze said. "We're about to get up to our necks in splick."

But Abimbola didn't seem to register Haze's comment. He was still fixed on the chip.

Magnus touched the giant's arm. "It's just a poker chip, Bimby. It's not fate."

"It is not just a poker chip, buckethead. It is the way of the gods."

Magnus sighed. Religion always seemed to mess with good people's rational thinking. "But the gods don't have a NOV1, do they. And they're not the ones down here making their own destiny."

"The gods don't need NOV1s to determine history."

"That may be so, but we need them to make it."

Abimbola finally looked up. "I trust the gods."

"Fair enough. And I trust my blaster."

"And if it fails you?"

Magnus smiled, though his friend couldn't see it. "I don't know if there are gods out there or not, but I've got you, Bimby, and you're practically as big as one." He slapped him on the arm. "Come on, we've got a job to do."

Alpha and Bravo Teams followed Rohoar around the side of the building and up a short staircase to a rusted out double-slider. The Jujari pierced the center seam with his claws and then pushed the panels apart. The door squeaked in mild protest, but that was all.

"Everyone through," Magnus ordered, and then double-checked their six before entering himself.

Once inside, Abimbola and Titus led the teams down a series of hallways using TO-96's schematic as an overlay guide. The team moved cautiously as they approached the security office, but it turned out there was little to worry about. One security guard was lost in a holo film while the other was sound asleep in his chair.

"As you cross into the next building, you'll find the treatment center's fourth stage," TO-96 said. "Were you not wearing your armor, I would be inclined to warn you about the smell and the need for a breathing apparatus."

"You're a great tour guide, 'Six," Magnus said.

"I do my best, sir. A bot never knows what line of work they may be forced to undertake once their current owner has reached their expiration date."

"Gotta make a living," Magnus said as his unit crossed an elevated walkway and filed through a decontamination lock. Once out the other side, the Granther's emerged into a massive room, the floor of which was a veritable sea of—

"Splick," Abimbola said.

"You can say that again," Titus replied.

"Why?" Rohoar looked between the two gladia. "Rohoar sees no reason to restate the obvious."

"Let's just keep moving," Magnus said. "Stay focused."

The teams crossed over the churning floor of waste, took the stairwell up a putrid waterfall, and then entered another lock. They followed the facility's four-story progression of rooms, waterfalls, and locks, before arriving at the last set of doors marked Inlet Matrix. Magnus motioned everyone in and they found themselves in an enormous pump room with several giant pieces of machinery occupying the majority of the floor space far below.

"There is an elevator toward the rear of the walkway," TO-96 said, adding a vector to the squad's HUDs. "Please proceed to the sixth subfloor."

The teams crossed the catwalk, and Titus called up the lift. It took two trips to get everyone down to sub-level six. From there, they found the main sewer shafts that left the plant.

"Who's first?" Titus asked.

"I am," said Abimbola. "Done plenty of this in the Dregs."

"I don't even want to know why," Awen replied as the giant leaped into sewage that went up to his waist. When she jumped in, the liquid went up to her chest. "I blame you, Magnus."

"As does Rohoar," the Jujari said. "So much blaming."

The gladias followed the Miblimbian one at a time, careful to keep their weapons aloft. Fluids didn't affect NOV1s, but there was just something about keeping a firearm clean that seemed to compel everyone to hold them overhead. *Old habits*, Magnus guessed.

They trudged up one tunnel after another, turning left, then right, then left, until Magnus was thoroughly disoriented. Without TO-96's HUD guidance, the squad would have been lost. The sewage system was a vertical labyrinth of corridors, tunnels, and passageways. They encountered several barred gates, which Haze and Doc made quick work of with low-yield directional charges and thermal cutters.

When their current shaft began to narrow, TO-96 informed them that the end was another 100 meters out. But the bot's voice was intermittent, no doubt due to CENTCOM's scrambling tech. "Then ... overhead ... find an access hatch," he said.

"We're losing you, 'Six," Magnus said, tapping the side of his helmet.

"Ladder ... to the utility ... CENTCOM, as outlined."

"'Six?"

"Careful … -ssure sensors," the bot added.

"Right." Magnus at least remembered the bit about the hatch sensors from earlier, and then looked to Awen and Nídira. "Any thoughts on the pressure sensors?"

"I have a little experience with them, yes," Nídira said.

"Do I want to know why?" Awen asked.

"Probably not." Nídira stepped under the hatch and lowered her head. Magnus was about to ask what she was doing and how long it would take when the mystic turned around. "All set."

"A *little* experience?" Magnus huffed out a chuckle. "I'd love to see what a *lot* of experience looks like."

"You're welcome," Nídira said, stepping aside for Magnus to grab the ladder's first rung.

"I'm going up first and will call down if and when it's safe to proceed," Magnus said. He felt a few gladias move to stop him, but he insisted. "I've made you endure enough with this mission, so if anyone's going to put their life on the line here and now, it's going to be me. No arguments." His shoulders relaxed. "Good. Stay here and await my signal."

Magnus called up Azelon's hand from the hard light emitter on his gauntlet and let her go to work on the keypad. The connection was intermittent, which slowed her progress down. Magnus was about ready to ask Awen to remove it but worried there might be redundant security measures. Suddenly, the deadbolts disengaged, and Magnus unwound the locking wheel. Trusting that Nídira had done her job, he pushed and flipped up the hatch. When no alarm sounded, he climbed the remaining five meters to the next hatch and opened it.

Magnus pulled himself into a large utility room filled with storage racks and maintenance equipment. He also spotted a mop sink and shower stall. Despite its advanced technology, Novian armor still couldn't overcome the olfactory sense of a human nose, so Magnus thought it best to wash as much of the excrement off his suit as he could before proceeding into the headquarters. No sense giving up the element of surprise simply because the enemy smelled him long before they saw him.

When he was done with the shower, he moved to the doorway and scanned the outer hallway with IR. Several bodies headed his way, but they seemed to be holding holo pads, not weapons. When they passed, Magnus peeked out the door and down the hallway. After switching back to optical sensors, he noticed a placard that read Command Center.

"All right," Magnus said. "Everyone up."

The gladias emerged from the sewer access hatch one at a time and then rinsed in the shower. A few minutes later, everyone assembled by the doorway.

"What is the plan?" Abimbola asked.

"Awen, I want you and Nídira to keep any blast doors from closing off the command room. I have a feeling that if those things shut, we're in trouble."

"Certainly," Awen said.

"Rohoar, Czyz, you're leading the way in. We can't afford for stray blaster fire to harm the consoles, so do as much damage as you can before they draw their weapons."

"We shall slaughter without blasters," Rohoar said, flexing his paws.

"Good." Magnus pointed to the snipers. "Silk, Dutch, you're in charge of knocking out any ceiling turrets. If there are any, and I'd bet several hundred of Bimby's poker chips on it that there are, then it's up to you to hit them before they hit us."

"Copy," Silk said.

"Doc and Haze, you're covering our rear. Bimby, Titus, you're with me. Everyone clear?"

Heads nodded.

"Good. Let's stack up and prepare to move."

The gladias lined up single file behind Rohoar and Czyz, ending with Doc and Haze. Magnus waited for the next round of personnel to pass before giving Rohoar the order to move out. Czyz opened the door for the other Jujari and then tapped him on the shoulder.

Everyone moved into the hallway and headed toward the direction placard. Rohoar turned left and headed down a long corridor that ended in a reinforced windowplex wall that looked into the command center. Three CENTCOM staffers were walking toward Rohoar while two troopers stood beside the entryway. A fourth staffer had just scanned his ID card over the lock to open the glass doors.

"Do it," Magnus said to Rohoar.

The two Jujari burst forward and smashed through the unsuspecting staffers. The people screamed as their bodies were flung into either wall by an invisible force, alerting the troopers further down. Repub MC90 blasters came to the ready, but the troopers seemed to have no idea what to aim at. A beat later and the Marines were knocked unconscious—if not dead—as the Jujari shoved the fourth staffer forward and wedged his body in the closing door.

CENTCOM's Command Center was a multi-tiered room that overlooked a twelve-meter-high holo wall. Each level was filled with glowing consoles and vibrant holo displays, boasting all manner of data routed in from across the galaxy. Only the first tier of operators seemed to notice the commotion. When their downed colleague's head flattened against the ground, several of those watching shrieked in horror.

Rohoar and Czyz were inside and thrashing within seconds. They tore into the seated operators without discretion. Necks split, chests opened, and heads cracked as the beasts leaped down the levels, dispensing their unique brand of Jujari violence.

Silk and Dutch came next, scanning the ceiling as per Magnus's orders. But, so far, no one had raised the alarm.

Several naval and intelligence officers unholstered sidearms and aimed at the carnage unfolding in the room, but like those Marines at the door, they seemed at a loss for targets. It wasn't until one CO raised a comm's device to his mouth that things got heated.

Silk cut off the reporting officer with a blaster bolt to the mouth just as the man finished yelling "Emergency" for the second time. He flipped backward, missing the majority of his face. A moment later, auto turrets dropped from the ceiling and chattered as they sought to acquire targets. At the same time, a klaxon sounded, and red lights spun up.

"And here come the doors," Awen said.

Magnus stepped into the room just as giant blast doors moved in from either side. He glanced at Awen and saw her head dip. The doors began to shutter, sending a low rumble through the floor.

"We've got company," Doc said, raising his NOV1 and firing down the hallway. Several Marines in Mark VII armor and MAR30s took a knee or set up beside hallway bulkheads, returning fire.

"Splick," Magnus said. "Recon."

"Your old unit," Dutch said.

Magnus sneered. This wasn't good. First the two at Elusian Base, and now these guys. Why had they been assigned security details on Capriana? Magnus didn't want to see them, didn't want to fight them, and definitely didn't want them on this planet if it all went to hell. As much as he tried to ignore it, he felt the pull of the brotherhood—to find out who they were, where they hailed from, and catch up on the latest news.

"You good?" Titus asked as blaster bolts smacked the blaster proof windowplex.

"I'm fine." Magnus shook himself out of his disbelief and swallowed the lump in his throat. "Keep those Marines back."

"Roger that," Doc shouted.

Dutch and Silk continued blowing the auto turrets from the ceiling as Abimbola and Titus assisted the Jujari in slaughtering the remaining operators. Rohoar was about ready to dispatch an intelligence officer in the center of the room when Magnus noticed the man's console. "Wait," he hollered to Rohoar. The Jujari withheld the death blow as the officer cowered in his chair. "Just wait."

"Why spare him?" Rohoar asked.

Magnus ran down to the man's console. "Look."

Rohoar studied the holo but seemed unable to piece together Magnus's intention.

"It's the PDS terminal," Magnus replied. He turned off chameleon mode, which clearly shocked the officer.

"Who the hell are you?" the man asked.

Magnus pressed the barrel of his NOV1 to the man's temple. "If you value your life, you'll do as I say."

The officer's lips quivered. "Or you'll kill me as you've killed everyone else?"

Magnus dismissed the question. "Activate the PDS."

"What?"

"The planetary defense system. Fire it up."

The officer squinted at Magnus, seemingly unable to fathom what was being asked of him. He sputtered several incomprehensible starts before finding his tongue. "But I must have senior approval for that."

"Consider this all the approval you need." Magnus pushed with his weapon. When the officer failed to move, Rohoar punched him in the head and kicked him off his chair.

"Rohoar!"

"He delays us. Now you can do it."

"But we could have used him."

"No." Rohoar sniffed the air in his helmet. "He was worthless."

Magnus maglocked his weapon to his back and then sat down to study the holo display.

"Room clear," Dutch said over the sound of blaster fire in the hallway.

"Then we could use you back here," Haze said, his voice strained.

Magnus knew the Recon Marines would give the gladias a run for their credits. Which meant he needed to figure out how to raise the shield and then get the hell out of there. He scanned the display and saw menus and readouts and status bars, none of which seemed to have the On button he assumed should be front and center. But he was a ground pounder by trade, not a Cyril.

"Azelon, you there?" Magnus asked over VNET. When no reply came, he tried again.

Then Azelon's voice came through. "—nus... sorry that... shielding..."

"Splick," Magnus said. "Looks like I'm running solo on this one." His eyes scanned the menu categories until he found a tab that read Core Status. "That sounds right." Magnus selected it, and up popped more data than he'd seen in a year. "You've gotta be kidding me."

"This is a negative expression," Rohoar said.

"Sure is." Magnus searched for something that looked like an activation sequence or start-up checklist, but nothing stood out. He swore again as the sound of blaster fire grew behind him. "How you doing back there?"

"These bucketheads are just as aggravating as you are," Abimbola said.

"Yeah, they're the real deal." Magnus tried another tab on the menu and scanned a live power grid schematic, hoping to find some sort of switch. But the deeper he looked, the more complicated the screens became. "Eh. I'm getting nowhere here. Anyone else want to try?"

"How can it be so hard to activate a shield?" Rohoar asked. "Shields are supposed to be easiest. Rohoar says, raise shields, and shields are raised. Rohoar says, lower shields, and shields are lowered. Rohoar says—"

"Yeah, yeah, we all know what Rohoar says." Magnus waved him off with a hand. "But this isn't Rohoar's ship." Just then, Magnus realized what he needed to look for, and then a knot tightened in his stomach. He found a tab marked Security, and then a sub-index marked Initialization Confirmation. The menu opened to a biometric input page, which included fields for a retinal scan, handprint, and voice activation. Magnus ground his teeth.

"Do we have a problem, scrumruk graulap?" Rohoar asked.

"A big one, Scruffy," Magnus replied. "You see General McCormick lately?"

"Not since the elevator. Why?"

"Because that's who we need to get this thing going."

"Good news, Magnus," Titus said, motioning from the entryway. "I think we found McCormick."

"What?" Magnus stood up. "Where?"

Titus squeezed off a few more rounds. "He's shooting at us."

15

BLACKMAN BLINKED against the light and brought a hand to his temple. His head hurt. It felt like someone had hit him hard enough to—*to knock you out, Robert?*

He blinked again and looked at the lines dangling from his arms. "Where the hell am I?" he asked no one in particular, surprised at the grogginess of his voice.

From his semi-reclined position, Blackman saw two medical professionals enter the hospital suite and move toward him. "Senator Blackman," said a tall woman in a long white lab coat. "Nice to see you awake. I'm Doctor Bannon. How are you feeling?"

"Like I've been run over by a skiff loader," Blackman replied.

"You took a serious blow to your head, Senator."

My head? Blackman blinked, trying to piece together his disjointed thoughts. There were secrets he was protecting. And an attack on Capriana. "Where—where am I?"

"You're in the Forum Republica's medical unit, sir. You've been out for almost two hours. Security found you—"

"In an elevator." The memories were booming more vivid. "Proconsul Tower."

"That's right. Do you remember what happened?"

"No." Blackman shook his head a little. "No—I mean, I do, but I didn't see—" Blackman stopped. "Where is the general?"

"General McCormick?" said the other person, this one in nurse's attire. "He's right here." The man pointed to a bed on the other side of a translucent partition that streamed with medical data.

"McCormick," Blackman said. When the man did not stir, the senator shouted his name twice more.

"Sir, please," the doctor said. "You've suffered a severe concussion, and you need your rest."

"Rest?" Blackman tried to sit up and instantly felt a wave of vertigo hit him. He pushed against the dizziness and willed himself onto one elbow. "There's no time. Wake him up."

"But, Senator, we can't just—"

"Wake him up," Blackman yelled. "Or I'll have you arrested."

Bannon drew in her lips, perhaps stifling whatever rebuttal she had, and then nodded at the nurse. "Do as he says."

The nurse produced a device from his belt and walked to the general. Blackman couldn't see what happened next, but McCormick awoke, cursing and shouting as if he was back inside the elevator. The nurse stumbled backward as the general sat upright.

"Relax, Issac," Blackman said. "You're in the medical unit."

"What?" McCormick looked over at him, eyes blinking. Then a look of recognition washed over his face. The general glared at the tubes and wires on both arms and then yanked them out, much to the chagrin of Doctor Bannon and the nurse. But neither professional seemed interested in fighting him.

"Leave us," Blackman said, pulling the lines from his own arms. Monitors scolded him, and lights flashed. Bannon looked like she wanted to attend to the monitors, but Blackman waved her off. "And arrange an escort back to CENTCOM."

"But, sir, you really—"

"Order the damn escort!"

Bannon nodded and then left with the nurse.

Blackman looked at McCormick as the man threw off the white blanket and swung his legs over the bed's edge. "You think he's coming?" the general asked, steadying himself. "You think Kane's on his way?"

"Of course he is. We're the ones who ordered the fleets to return."

"That's not what I mean, Robert."

Keep it together, Blackman encouraged himself, sensing the conversation was about to get complicated. But his decades in the Republic Senate had conditioned him on how to dress up the truth in ways that kept people from noticing it. "Do I think Magnus is right? Is Moldark coming to wipe us out?"

The general looked away. "I really hate that name. I wish you'd just call him Kane."

"But it's not Kane that So-Elku had us try to assassinate."

McCormick threw his hands up. "Another name I've come to hate."

"Be that as it may, the Luma did us a favor, did he not?"

The general nodded. "Resulting in a failed assassination attempt. And if Kane figured out it was us, that may very well be what's pushed him to do what Magnus claims he's coming to do. Plus, I believe that Kane leveling Capriana would suit So-Elku just fine, given how desperately he seems to want to extend his brand of peace throughout the quadrant. A thousand credits say he *wanted* the assassination attempt to fail."

The general had been rattled, and rattled leaders did unpredictable things. This wasn't the time for unpredictability, so Blackman needed to regain control of the situation. Moreover, McCormick was getting far too close to the truth.

"Get ahold of yourself, Issac," Blackman shouted, startling the general. It had probably been a very long time since anyone had yelled at him. "You sound like one of those damn conspiracy theorists right now! For the last time, the fleets are coming home because we ordered them to, not to even a score or satisfy some Luma leader's secret agenda. And Moldark—or Kane, or whatever he wants to be called—won't know that we ordered the assassination. You've gotta relax, Issac."

The general hesitated for a moment, and then looked at his Marine Corp uniform folded neatly on a shelf. "You're right. I'm sorry." He moved to the pile of clothes and studied them. It still seemed like there was something the general couldn't shake. "So, Magnus is lying?"

"Lying, delusional—how should I know?" Blackman slid off

his bed and then touched his forehead, fighting off a new wave of dizziness. "The man is either trying to earn his way back into the Corps or get some sort of strange revenge."

McCormick pulled on his slacks and undershirt. "I still don't like that we pinned Stone's death on him."

"It was expedient," the senator said. "Not personal."

"I know what it was just as much as you do." McCormick reached for his black jacket and slid his arms into it. "And I don't like that we tarnished the Magnus name."

"This is bigger than reputations and personal pedigrees, Issac. You know that."

"It's about setting things right for future generations—I know the talking points." The general smoothed his uniform and worked his jaw once. "Do you think they'll forgive us?"

Damn his sentimentalism, Blackman thought to himself. *How had the Corps produced such a pathetic worrywart?* "They don't have to forgive us. They have to survive."

A long silence passed between the two men as the general turned toward a mirror and examined himself. "And what if Magnus is right?"

Blackman hesitated to put on his senate coat. The general wasn't letting this go. "But he's not right."

"But if he is, then there might not be anything left for us to redeem."

"Then none of us will be alive to care, will we."

"Really?" McCormick turned from the mirror and took two steps toward Blackman. "That's your rebuttal? You're ready to throw billions of lives away on some deranged form of nihilism?"

"Of course not. I'm just trying to be a realist, and so should you. For the last time, Magnus *doesn't* know what he's talking about. Your biggest concern should be which military tribunal to try Moldark in when he gets here, and where to spend all your credits once we shake out the dirt."

"You make it sound so simple," the general said, taking a deep sigh. Blackman wondered how many other people saw this side of the outwardly staunch military commander. He was a far cry from the brave intergalactic leader who commanded the most formidable ground force in the galaxy.

"That's because it is simple." Blackman checked himself in the same mirror that McCormick had. "The fleets are returning from a successful attack on the Jujari. You and Franks will take full credit for it and be lauded as heroes. Then we will use the momentum in our favor to restructure the Senate accordingly, ushering in a new age of sovereign rule and galactic peace."

"You're too good at reciting our rhetoric," McCormick replied, but the man still didn't seem settled.

"What is it, Issac?"

"I don't see the harm in taking precautionary measures."

"By raising the planetary shield?" Blackman lifted his eyebrows as if shocked by the idea and then turned on the general. "If the defense system goes up, the Senate will want to know why. And when they call for an investigation, they'll not only look to the members of CENTCOM, they'll make the heads of the Navy and Marine Corps give accounts for the fleet-return orders—the same fleets that the PDS is defending the planet from. And that, General, puts the Senate far too close to the Nine for my liking. And we both know where they'll place the blame."

McCormick twitched his nose and then loosened his collar with two fingers. "You're right, of course."

There was a chime at the door. "Military escort for General McCormick and Senator Blackman," said a trooper's voice over the comms.

"Come," said the general. A four-person fire team entered the room single-file.

"General, you're receiving an urgent communique from CENTCOM," the lead trooper said, handing McCormick a holo pad.

"From CENTCOM?" The general looked to Blackman and then took the pad. He swiped the message open, and Admiral Frank's face appeared.

"Issac, it's good to see you," said Franks.

"You too, Penn."

"You had us worried there."

McCormick gave a curt smile. "What's this about?"

"In the time you've been unconscious, we've had two additional attacks on Republic facilities."

The general looked at Blackman and then back at Franks. "What kind of attacks? Where?"

"The first was at the biomedical research facility in sector seven."

"The hazardous materials unit?"

Frank nodded. "Seems they went after some high-level asset on level four."

"Mystics. Did we stop them?"

"Negative. They killed three platoons of Marines and then escaped."

"But—how's that possible? I thought the facility was secure?"

"Intelligence thinks they used the sewers."

McCormick sneered. "And do we know what they took?"

"Negative. But we're looking into it."

The general shared another look with Blackman. The senator stepped into the frame and acknowledged Franks. "Would this have anything to do with the assault on us in the elevator?"

"We're unsure, Senator," Franks replied. "But we do know we're dealing with a covert and highly skilled military force here."

"How can you be so sure?" McCormick asked.

"Because this is what they did to Elusian Base." A series of video clips replaced Franks's face, showing several massive explosions in and around the fort.

"Great mystics," Blackman said.

"And their target?" the general asked.

But Blackman answered the question before Franks could. "The planetary defense system."

Franks's face reappeared, head nodding. "We armed the facility housing the PDS's manual override with an auto-destruct sequence after we reviewed the footage from the elevator. We guessed they might make an attempt on it once we got word of an assault on the island."

"Who else saw that elevator feed?" Blackman asked, more forcefully than he intended.

"Don't worry," Franks said. "It's confidential."

Blackman nodded. "And the facility?"

"Eliminated before the PDS could be raised."

Blackman gave an inward sigh of relief. For So-Elku's plan to work, the PDS needed to stay down for the first part of Moldark's assault on Capriana. Blackman would eventually raise it from inside CENTCOM after the initial salvos and Republic attempts to negotiate. He could mourn the civilian casualties later, but it was a small price to pay for how much the galaxy would gain.

So-Elku and the Nine had more in common than they both knew—they both firmly believed that the Republic needed to die if true peace was to reign once again. But unlike the Nine, So-Elku wasn't belabored with protocol, bureaucracy, and majority votes—all vestiges of a tired system. Instead, the Luma leader had power—real power—to make things happen. And Blackman had been guaranteed a place at the table.

"What about the enemy?" McCormick asked. "Surely, we must have—"

"They're in the wind, I'm afraid," said Franks.

"But how is that possible?"

"As I said," Franks replied as he raised an eyebrow. "Covert and highly skilled."

McCormick turned to Blackman and said, "You still think he's delusional, Robert?"

"As a matter of fact, I do," Blackman said. "Even more so now."

"What's this about?" Franks asked.

"It can wait," the senator said. "Gather the Nine in Proconsul Tower. We'll meet you there in ten minutes."

Franks nodded and reached to close the feed when the sound of screaming people filled the background. The admiral turned from his desk—located in an executive office adjacent to CENT-COM's Command Center—and opened the door. Blackman and McCormick watched as the holo pad fell to the floor, and blood splashed across the camera.

16

First squad concentrated their fire down the hallway, taking out Recon Marines as fast as possible, but the black-suited troopers kept pulling their dead away only to send in fresh blood.

"The windowplex is giving way, Magnus," Titus said from his post on the defensive line at the top of the command room.

Magnus left the PDS terminal and headed up toward the translucent dividing wall, now glowing red hot from the enemy's relentless barrage of blaster fire. The MAR30 could dispense its share of damage, as the reinforced blast-grade windowplex was finding out. It wouldn't be long before the gladias cover fragmented into shards of molten sludge.

"What is the play, buckethead?" Abimbola asked.

Magnus had his weapon raised but stayed clear of the gap filled with blaster rounds. The bolts had already crossed the

Command Center and all but destroyed the large holo display along the far wall. "We need that guy, right there."

Abimbola followed Magnus's nod toward General McCormick at the end of the hall.

"Cover's failing," Dutch yelled. The windowplex had reached its limit.

"Awen, Wish," Magnus said. "Let the blast doors close!"

"You got it," Awen replied.

A beat later, the large partitions groaned and shuddered, engaged by their drive system. They raced toward one another from opposite sides of their recessed corners and slammed shut in the center. Only a few muted bursts of blaster fire thumped on the opposite side until someone ordered a cease-fire.

"Well, that's better," Titus said, breathing a sigh of relief.

"For the moment," Abimbola replied. "We have only traded one bad scenario for another."

"And we still need the man out there for the computer in here," Rohoar said. "Plus, Rohoar feels that we are pinned in here like desert Slanthers caught in a canyon. If we are forced to stay too long, we may start eating one another for supremacy."

"No one's eating anybody," Magnus said. "Just calm down." He needed a second to think—there had to be another way to activate the PDS. He walked down the aisle and sat behind the terminal.

"What are you thinking, Magnus?" Awen asked as she walked up behind him.

"I'm thinking General McCormick might not be the only one with the authority to start up the defense network. There needs to be a backup, in case he was MIA during an invasion." Sure enough, Magnus spotted just what he was looking for. A dropdown menu near the display's top was pre-populated with McCormick's name, most likely because he was the most senior member, Magnus guessed. But he wasn't the only name on the list. There were five more, each ranking members of the military.

Awen must have registered the same thought as Magnus, because she tapped him on the shoulder, and asked, "You think someone on that list is in here?"

Magnus nodded. "Gotta be." He stood up and made sure the squad channel was open. "Listen up. We're looking for admiral or general insignias on the injured. Search every console station and all the side offices. If you don't know what those insignias look like, ask someone. Move."

Alpha and Bravo teams broke out and started scouring the room, including the side offices and clear-paneled meeting rooms. Magnus helped as well, flipping people over who he thought might still be alive, only to find them shot or mauled on the front side. He wished they hadn't been so violent upon entering, and wondered if they'd killed the very person they needed to save the planet.

Don't think like that, Adonis, he told himself. *You're gonna find a way.*

"I think I've got someone," Dutch said. Magnus moved toward her position on the upper level, just beside a corner office. "Admiral Penn Franks."

"He's on the list," Magnus said, bending down to examine

the man. But he was unconscious and bleeding from three Jujari claws marks in his chest. "Dammit."

"He's still alive," Awen said. "But barely."

"Take him to the console," Magnus said. He grabbed Awen by the arm and put her in a private channel. "Can you do anything to wake him?"

Awen seemed to hesitate. "I'm not sure."

"Try?"

She nodded. "Of course. But, if I try too hard, I might—"

"He's dead anyway, Awen."

She looked away. "I'll see what I can do."

Together, they walked back down to the PDS terminal where Silk and Doc had placed Franks in the chair. Magnus worked with them to secure the admiral's handprint and even managed to pull his eyelids apart to obtain a successful retinal scan. All that remained was the voice indent match.

"Awen?" Magnus said.

She stepped forward, placed a hand on Franks, and went still. A few moments passed before the admiral started coughing and his eyes flew open in a spasm. He shouted and thrashed, and it took Silk and Doc to keep the main restrained. Franks coughed more, and blood flew through the holo display.

"Admiral Franks," Magnus said over external speakers. "We need you to raise the planetary defense shield immediately."

Franks blinked, seemingly unable to focus on anything.

"Admiral Franks," Magnus repeated after raising the volume on his helmet.

"Yes?" The admiral winced at the sound. "Where am I?"

"You're at the PDS console inside CENTCOM's command room. The planet is under attack, and we need you to raise the shield."

"Under attack?" Franks looked around again but saw no one due to the gladia's chameleon mode. Instead, the admiral's eyes latched onto several bodies on the ground beside him. "Holy mystics. What's—what's happening?"

"We need you to speak your passphrase to activate the PDS," Magnus said.

"Under whose—" Franks slammed his eyes shut in pain. He groaned and seemed like he might pass out.

"Franks," Magnus yelled. When the man didn't respond, Magnus looked to Awen. "Do something."

"He's dying, Magnus."

"Do something!"

Awen put her hand on the man again, and the admiral shook. Then his eyes flew open as he gasped.

"Admiral Franks," Magnus said. "Please speak your pass into the system."

"Under whose authority?" Franks managed to say through gritted teeth. "I need proper—" Franks grunted as if someone had just punched him in the gut. "Proper clearance."

"Belay that order, Admiral Franks," said a voice from the ceiling speakers.

Franks pushed himself away from the console upon hearing his name from someone he clearly knew. The moment his shoulder slipped from Awen's hand, he went unconscious and fell to the floor.

"This is Senator Robert Malcom Blackman of the Galactic Republic Senate and Chairman of Central Command," the voice said. "To former Marine Lieutenant Adonis Olin Magnus and whatever team you're leading, I order you to stand down and drop your weapons immediately."

Magnus felt his team look at him even without seeing their helmets move. He motioned for them to hold position.

"I can't see you, of course," Blackman continued. Dutch and Silk had taken care of the cameras along with the auto-turrets. "But I know you're there, listening. So I'll make myself clear."

Magnus knew this man's voice—it was strangely familiar.

"Within the next few minutes, the security team outside the Command Center will gain access to the room you're standing in. When they do, the firefight will continue until you've either laid waste to an entire battalion of troopers now converging on your location, which I highly doubt you have the man- or firepower to accomplish, or you surrender. Killing you would be another option, but the Republic never wishes for anyone's death, so I'm on record as saying that I prefer you to surrender and spare everyone even more needless bloodshed."

"Send someone in to raise the planetary defense shield, and we'll stand down," Magnus said.

"No, scrumruk graulap," Rohoar said. "We must not—"

"Quiet, Rohoar," Magnus said on internals. To his credit, Rohoar didn't protest further.

"It's really that important to you?" Blackman said. Magnus recognized the senator's voice from the elevator. This was the other man with McCormick. "You'd risk your life and the lives of your team just to activate a defense shield?"

"It's even crazier that a senator and a general would resist a credible warning and jeopardize billions of lives," Magnus replied.

The senator laughed. "Credible? Son, nothing's credible when it's done at blaster point. Stand down, and—"

"Send someone in, and we'll surrender." Ever since meeting McCormick and Blackman in the elevator, it bugged Magnus that neither man wanted to raise the PDS. Whatever happened to *better safe than sorry?*—especially when it came to defense. Where was the harm in protecting the capital, if nothing more than to give someone the benefit of the doubt?

Something didn't feel right to Magnus, but he couldn't figure out what. He was too preoccupied with what would happen if the senator refused Magnus's condition of surrender. Still, in the back of his brain, Magnus felt that the only reason to keep the PDS down was that there was something the CENTCOM leaders had to lose that was worse than Capriana's annihilation. *But nothing's worth that*, Magnus thought.

"Mysticsdammit," Magnus yelled. "What are you waiting for? Send someone in, raise the shield, and all of this ends. What the hell do you have to lose?"

"Magnus," Awen said with a pleading tone. "They'll execute us on the spot. Surely, you must—"

"Is there anything more important?" Magnus said to her over the squad channel. "We already forfeited our lives, Awen. The moment we decided to do what we believed was right. At least this way, we know we're giving our lives to protect billions of lives. I can live with that."

"And you'll die for it too," Awen said.

"And you?"

"Yeah." Awen shook her head in resignation. "Yeah, I can die for that."

"As can I," Abimbola said.

"Rohoar too," said the Jujari.

The blast doors activated and crawled apart. A shaft of light split between them as a figure appeared, hands raised. Magnus cycled through his visual sensors before he could clarify the silhouette. "It's General McCormick," Magnus said.

NOV1s followed the general as he walked into the command room. Then the senator's voice sounded from the speakers again.

"You've already met General Issac S. McCormick once before," Blackman said. "Allow him passage to the PDS terminal and see to it that he activates the system as you've requested."

"Move it, General," Magnus said to McCormick. The general looked around, clearly trying to place the speaker, but the only people in the room were dead or dying on the floor. "We haven't got all day."

McCormick kept his hands raised and made his way down the steps toward the PDS terminal on the bottom level. He stepped around several bodies that lay sprawled across the stairs. "You're all dead," the general said softly. "You know that, don't you?"

"The console, sir," Magnus said.

"For what it's worth, however, I don't mind putting the shield up."

"Happy to hear that."

"It's a small price to pay to stop such a cowardly attack."

Magnus swallowed the taste of bile in the back of his throat. "Cowardly is not taking the chance to save people you swore to protect just because you didn't like the messenger, general. Now, the terminal."

McCormick reached the lower level and stopped when he saw Franks's body on the floor. Then he stepped over the admiral and took a seat.

"Do you really think he's coming?" McCormick asked, his voice barely audible.

Magnus looked to Awen, wondering if she heard it too. "Come again, General?"

McCormick worked his jaw and looked annoyed. He inclined his head toward the display and rolled his eyes as if scolding Magnus for being insensitive. Magnus stepped closer. "Do you think Moldark is coming to destroy the planet?"

Magnus lowered the volume of his speakers. "Do you think we'd be doing all this if we weren't convinced?"

The general sighed and then reached a hand toward the holo display. "I was afraid you'd say that."

"Then why the delay, sir?" Magnus said, driven to ask by a deep sense of curiosity. He watched as the monitor scanned the general's upraised hand, and then presented a confirmation icon.

"That's a complicated answer, son. One far above your pay grade."

"More complicated than saving people's lives?"

The general huffed and then leaned forward to let the terminal scan his retina. "There was a time that was the only thing that mattered." He held still. "And I'd give anything to get back there."

A confirmation icon chimed on the holo display. All that remained was the voiceprint match.

"We've lost our way, Magnus," the general said, swiping a prompt to reveal the secret passphrase. The sentence illuminated with a countdown timer. But the general lowered his head.

"General?" Magnus said, trying to get the man back on task. "The voice print?"

But the general seemed like he was in a different world. "It started with such noble ideals, you know. But somewhere that all changed. And it made us do things…"

"General, the passphrase."

"I'm so sorry for what we did to you, Adonis." The general met Magnus's eyes—though the man could hardly know where to look besides where the sound came from. Still, Magnus felt as though McCormick looked straight into his soul. "Your grandfather would never forgive me, nor do I expect you to. But I *am* sorry."

Magnus froze. *What did they do to me?* The sound of his pulse thumped in his ears, and time seemed to slow down.

"Magnus," Awen shouted. "Snap out of it!"

Magnus shook his head and blinked. "General, the passphrase. Please."

McCormick looked back at the holo and seemed to notice

that the countdown timer only had five seconds remaining. Magnus assumed that if the general didn't act quickly, the whole process would begin again, and probably with some sort of time penalty or additional security measure. McCormick held his finger over the record icon and started speaking.

"Purple sparrows rarely dwell amidst the chambers of—"

Something metallic bounced down the stairs and landed beside the terminal. Magnus blinked. It was a Recon issued VOD. "Fragger!"

17

THE VOD BLAST blew Magnus backward down the aisle of consoles. McCormick's body had shielded him and Awen from the worst of it, but still, Magnus's shield was gone, and his armor had been damaged. Blaster fire flooded his audio sensors as Magnus pushed the general's body off his chest.

"Awen, can you hear me?" Magnus asked, shaking her arm.

Her head rolled toward him. "Are we alive?"

"For now. Can you get up?"

"Yes, I think so. My shield's at—"

"Zero. Mine too." Magnus raised a hand in caution. "Stay behind the consoles."

"Right."

Magnus helped Awen to her knees and then peered over the next row of terminals. Recon Marines infiltrated the Command Center and laid down a heavy base of fire. The best thing the gladias had going for them was that the enemy still couldn't see them. That would all change the moment some trooper with IR optics got wise and started calling out targets over TACNET and populating their HUD. Magnus could practically see the layout of the Repub software.

"Return fire," Magnus shouted, and then ordered the Jujari to flank the Marines while Awen and Wish activated some Unity shielding.

Rohoar and Czyz bounded up the side stairs and bored into the enemy's right and left flanks. A Marine left his place by the blast doors and flew through the amphitheater toward the main holo display. His body cracked against the already broken display wall, filling the air with sparks, before crashing to the ground. On Czyz's side, a Marine's scream filled the air as his helmet was ripped from his head, along with part of his face, thanks to Czyz's claws raking across it. The Jujari ended the man's suffering by knocking his head back with a wicked *snap* sound.

The Recon's fire shifted to defend their flanks, as the dead Marines provided the most visible evidence of the gladias' location. But still, Magnus and the others took heavy fire from the MAR30s.

"There's only one way we're putting these boys down," Magnus said to Awen. "When I'm done, I need you to close the blast doors. Can you do that?"

"Yes, I think so," Awen said.

"Seal them too."

"But what about—"

"We'll blast our way out if we have to."

Awen nodded.

Magnus activated his NOV1's AI-assisted multi-target fire effect mode and felt the barrel gimbal unlock. He raised his weapon above the terminals and watched his HUD pick out sixteen different targets—all Recon Marines, all about to die before they even knew what hit them. *And this still isn't any easier,* Magnus thought, remembering his conversation with Titus. Then he squeezed the trigger.

The NOV1 released a bright spray of blaster fire in sixteen different directions as the gimbaled barrel shuddered to accommodate the multi-target field of fire. The blaster bolts pierced chest plates and punctured helmets, sending each Marine to the ground in a rhythmic secession of clattering armor.

"Close 'em," Magnus ordered Awen. The doors began sliding shut, crushing Marine bodies as they did. Magnus caught sight of a man through the narrowing crack. His silver hair and dark gray senator's uniform glinted in the flicking ceiling lights. It was Blackman. And the last thing Magnus saw before Awen and Wish finished closing the doors was the senator's hate-filled scowl.

"Would somebody mind telling me what the hell just happened?" Silk asked. The rest of the gladias stood and looked around at the body count.

"More like, what are we gonna do next," Silk said. "Look." Magnus tracked her head nod toward the PDS console, or what was left of it. Sparks shot from the terminal, and a small fire coming from General McCormick's body—among others—sent black smoke toward the ceiling. Apparently, the fumes were enough to activate the fire-retardant system. Water sprinklers popped from the ceiling and showered the room.

"Any bright ideas, buckethead?" Abimbola asked.

"For the PDS?" Magnus asked rhetorically. "Not until we can see if TO-96 has any more bright ideas."

"No," said Abimbola. "For us getting out of here with our lives."

"We're not going until we activate—"

"Adonis." Awen laid a hand on his arm. "It's over."

"But there's got to be another way to raise it."

"This *was* the other way," she said. Awen held his gaze even through their helmets. "The best thing we can do now is find a way out and try to evacuate the city."

She was right, but admitting it felt like a defeat. And Magnus hated failure. "I need ideas."

"Scans show no other doors or tunnels," Haze said.

"I can confirm that," Wish said. "Our only options seem to be the vertical shafts for ventilation and cabling conduits, but everything looks too small for us."

"How about down?" Magnus asked, wondering if they could take advantage of the sewer trick again.

"Negative, LT," Doc said. "I'm showing solid cement and bedrock beyond that."

Magnus swore under his breath and turned to Awen. He wondered if she could read his thoughts, if she saw him calculating the odds of fighting their way back through CENTCOM, up the elevators, through the lobby, and out the Forum Republica's front doors. Could she sense the despair growing in his chest?

The feeling of helplessness? Of regret at knowing he'd put his team in an untenable situation, all for the sake of—

"Of trying to save the lives of the innocent," Awen said. "We knew what we were getting into, Magnus. It's all right."

"I'm not giving up this easily," Magnus said. "There's got to be another way."

Awen looked away, took a deep breath, and then stared at Magnus's visor again. "If you want to go out those blast doors fighting, then we'll go with you. Until at least one of us can sound some kind of alarm to evacuate the city."

"Rohoar agrees," the Jujari said. "And he is with you."

"As am I," Abimbola said, racking a fresh mag in his weapon. Everyone in the teams added in their approval of the last-ditch effort.

"It's suicide," Magnus said, looking around.

"This whole mission was suicide," Titus said. "We all knew it. And so did you."

Magnus lowered his head and sighed. Asking everyone to risk their lives for this op had been much easier from the safety of the *Spire*, back when success seemed within reach. Now, with no other way to raise the shield and little chance that any gladia would reach the surface in time to spare the civilian population, Magnus could hardly find the words to order his squad forward—much less to thank them for their self-sacrifice.

He was about to order the blast doors reopened when he spotted something in the general's dead hand. It was a keycard for an elevator. But unlike the security cards used daily, with their edges rounded and optical patterns scratched from constant use, this one looked pristine.

Magnus knelt and opened the general's fingers. A word printed at the top of the card made Magnus's heart skip.

Executive Office.

Magnus grabbed the card and stood. Then he looked around the Command Center's perimeter.

"What is it?" Awen asked, obviously noticing Magnus's sudden change in demeanor.

Magnus spun toward Dutch. "Where did you find the admiral's body?"

"Up there," she said, pointing to the top level in the corner. Magnus saw what he was looking for.

"That's an office," he said, skirting by Awen and heading up the stairs at the end of the row of consoles. He took them three at a time and stopped outside a door that designated the room beyond as a suite. He waved his hand in front of the motion scanner, but the door produced a dim error trill. Magnus tried sticking the keycard in a slot on the activate panel, but the door made the same inert sound. Irritated, Magnus pointed his NOV1 at the door and blew a gaping hole in it.

"What are you doing?" Titus asked.

"I'll let you know in a second," Magnus replied, stepping through the smoking hole. "Stay put."

He scanned the executive office, noting a large conference room table and chairs, several couches, a wet bar, and a large desk. "Come on, come on," he said to himself as he searched the walls. They were covered in art and boasted a few large mirrors, but not what he was looking for.

"What's going on, Adonis?" Awen asked, poking her head through the blowout door.

"It has to be here," Magnus replied, more to himself than to her.

"What has to?"

Then his eyes stopped on one of the floor-to-ceiling mirrors —about the width of a person. "There." Magnus dashed across the room and started prying against the mirror's edges. When it didn't budge, he got even more hopeful. This wasn't a simple piece of decoration. It was a door—it had to be.

"Magnus, what's gotten into you?" Awen said, her voice filled with concern.

Magnus turned and flapped the general's keycard at her. "It's for a private elevator," he said. "The general was going to raise the PDS and then get out."

"Or help *us* get out," Awen said, drawing near and taking the card from Magnus. He turned and kept searching the mirror for a slot.

"How about this," Awen said. Magnus turned to see Awen insert the card into a slot on the desk. Several LEDs blinked around the opening and a chime issued from the mirror. Then the glass slid away to reveal a small three-person room.

"You're a genius." Magnus grabbed her by the arms and would have kissed her were they not wearing helmets.

"You're welcome," she said. "And you can save that kiss for later."

Magnus smiled, and then roared over VNET, "Everyone in the office, now!"

THE ELEVATOR OPENED into a similarly styled office suite—only this one had a view of the entire capital complex. The sky was just beginning to warm the horizon, and Magnus double-checked his mission clock. It was just past five o'clock in the morning.

"Sir, is that really you?" TO-96 said, appearing in a new comms window.

"Boy, am I glad to see you, 'Six," Magnus replied.

"Magnus," Colonel Caldwell exclaimed. "Sweet mother of mummified mystics, man—where the hell have you been?"

"Long story, Colonel." Magnus motioned Awen and Titus out of the lift and then sent the pod on its nonstop trip back to CENTCOM.

"Where are you now?" Caldwell asked.

"Looks like we're somewhere in Proconsul Tower. Pretty high up too."

Titus opened the office door and then looked back at Magnus. "You're not gonna believe this, LT," he said to Magnus and Awen.

Magnus walked over and looked out the door. On one side of the open floor, there looked to be a large meeting hall, and on the other was an elevator bank, with several elevators that seemed to be designated to the tower's upper-level spaceport. He strained to look at the ceiling, which was a lavish windowplex dome. Above it loomed a massive tower with half a dozen docked shuttles. "We're on the top floor, Colonel. And the rest of the squad is on the way."

"And the PDS?"

Magnus shook his head. "I'm sorry, Colonel, but that's a no-go. We need to order a city-wide evacuation."

"You're sure?" Caldwell said, his voice lowered as if in mourning.

"The terminal is destroyed, so unless the Wonder Twins have some new bright idea, yeah, I'm sure."

Caldwell looked at TO-96 and Azelon.

"If by Wonder Twins, Magnus is referring to Azelon and me, the answer is no," TO-96 said.

"Copy that," the colonel replied. Then he looked past Magnus into the near distance. "Mung born isotropic bastards."

"What does that even mean?" Magnus shook his head. "Any ideas on how to go about doing this?"

The Colonel looked at Azelon. "How 'bout it, Smarty Pants?"

"I am less familiar with the prime motivating factors for humans and other evolutionarily adjacent species," Azelon said. "Though, I suppose catastrophic threats that provoke favorable evasion responses within the amygdala are ideal."

"What the hell kinda talk did you just spew out?" Caldwell said. "We're not trying to incite mass hysteria, lady."

"That is how you interpreted my assertion?" Azelon tilted her head. "Interesting."

"I have an idea," TO-96 said with a raised hand.

"It better not be some sort of brainiac splick like hers," the colonel said, nodding at Azelon.

"No, sir. It relies on you and planet-wide video transmission."

"You mean a PSA?" Caldwell asked.

"A what, sir?"

"A public service announcement," Magnus answered. "It's an old-fashioned way of getting news out to a wide audience via more traditional broadcast methods."

"Careful who you're calling old fashioned, son," Caldwell said.

"Then, yes," TO-96 said. "A PSA. Though I am not entirely certain Azelon and I will be able to gain access to the planet's broadcast channels."

"I'd say do what you can until we come up with a better plan," Magnus said. "Better to be prepared—"

"Than dead," Caldwell said.

"I suggest you make haste," Azelon interjected. "I've just detected several ships jumping out of sub-space." She paused and raised a finger. "Make that several dozen, and counting."

"Moldark," Awen whispered. "He's here."

18

PIPER STOOD in the middle of a street as the buildings fell around her. Her body shuddered from the fear, and she could hardly breathe from the worry gripping her chest. These were the same sensations Piper had so many times before. But she knew this was only a dream. Still, the anxiety *felt* real.

"Piper," someone yelled above her. But she didn't want to look into the sky. If she did, she'd wake up. And it wasn't time to wake up yet. She had to see if *he* would come for her. "Piper, wake up!"

"No, no," she replied, wrestling against the call of her consciousness. She punched and kicked, refusing to leave the ruins in the streets. But then her eyes caught sight of something moving in the distance, something emerging over the rubble's horizon. She squinted and blinked, resisting the voice above, and instead narrowed her eyes on the person beyond.

It was a Marine trooper. Yes, it was Magnus—he'd come to save her. Like always.

"Mr. Lieutenant Magnus," she cried out, her heart filling with an overwhelming sense of relief. Piper waved her hands. "I'm over here!"

Piper wanted to run to him, but her feet wouldn't move. They were stuck in the rubble, lodged beneath broken concrete and metal rods. It didn't matter, though. Magnus would come to free her just as he always did.

There had been a time, only a few days ago, where she'd second-guessed him. No—*worse*. She'd *believed* against him. Believed that he'd done horrible things to others—to his brother. To her mother. But those things, it turned out, were lies. Lies that she'd been wrong to accept and not question, not talk to him first. That mistake had hurt her, and him, and others. So Piper vowed never to make that mistake again. There would be no more hiding, and no more believing what people whispered in the darkness. She would always run toward the light—toward what was right.

"Mr. Lieutenant Magnus, I'm over here," she said again, waving her arms, still unable to wiggle her feet from the wreckage. *He should be here by now*, she thought, wondering what was taking so long. His silhouette was still there, head and shoulders still bobbing back and forth. But no matter how long she waited, Magnus seemed the same distance away, as if he were walking on a treadmill.

Maybe her eyes were playing tricks on her. Perhaps he was much further away than she first realized, and he was only *now* getting closer. Piper tried to content herself, willing her heart to calm down while she waited for her hero to arrive. For he *would* come. *Soon.* Any moment now.

Shadows moved out from the broken buildings, darting toward Magnus. Piper could not make out who or even what they were. But she felt they meant Magnus harm. Something about them felt malnev—manlevno—malevolent. Felt evil. Like they wanted to kill him.

"No," Piper said. "This isn't how it goes. This isn't the way!"

The shadows started attacking Magnus. They swirled around him, lashed out, and struck him on the shoulders and head.

"Stop it," Piper screamed. Magnus looked like he was struggling to stand. "You're hurting him!"

Piper tried to free her feet, overcome with panic, but each time she did, the debris cut into her skin and pushed against her bones. She screamed, and then grabbed her left knee, yanking it in a wild attempt to wrest herself from the rubble's clutches. But nothing happened. She screamed his name so loudly she thought her voice would break.

"Wake up," someone said, shaking her shoulders.

Piper's eyes flew open and saw her grandmother's face. Feeling disoriented, Piper reached for something to hold— anything. Willowood grabbed Piper's wrists and bound them to her chest. Still, Piper thrashed—she had to get to Magnus.

"Peace, child," Willowood said.

All at once, the dread left, dissolving like salt in a cup of water. Piper felt a wave of relief wash over her, calming her nerves. The warmth of the blanket returned, as did the comfort of the pillows cradling her head.

"Peace," her grandmother said again, her hand stroking Piper's hair. "All is well, my child. All is well."

Piper took several deep breaths and used the blanket to wipe the tears away. "I have to go."

Willowood scrunched her eyes up. "Go?"

"He needs me."

Willowood hushed her. "You've been dreaming, darling granddaughter. But you're safe now."

"No, no." The fear started to return. "He needs me."

"Who needs you?"

"Mr. Lieutenant Magnus." Piper tried to sit up. "He needs me."

"Piper, please." Willowood pleaded with her hands. "You need to lie still."

"No. He needs me right now."

"Peace," Willowood said, and again, a new wave of peace washed over Piper—this one stronger than the last. The anxiety vanished, and Piper felt it was safe to lie back down. "There, is that better?"

Piper nodded, taking a deep breath that made her lower lip quiver. "I saw him, grandma. I saw him."

"Magnus?"

"Yes. It's a dream I've had many times. But this time, it's different."

Willowood continued to stroke her hair, and it felt good. So reassuring. "How so?"

"He always comes to rescue me—in Capriana, I mean. I stand in the middle of the buildings, and they're all broken. And then he walks up the street and rescues me. But, only this time, like what just happened, he doesn't. Something happened to him." Piper could feel her heart beating faster and her words get quicker. "Something attacked him. They came out of the ruins and swirled around him. Hitting him. He tried to get rid of them. He tried. But there were too many, and he couldn't. And then I tried to go help him, but I was stuck. I couldn't move. And they kept hurting and hurting him! I yelled for them to stop, but they wouldn't. They just wouldn't!"

"Easy, easy," Willowood said, her face taking on a look of grave concern.

"And the worst part?" Piper choked on her tears, and coughed, perhaps realizing the meaning of the dream for the first time. "They killed him."

Willowood acted like she was about to say something, but her hand hesitated in smoothing the hair on Piper's head. So Piper said the words again, but more softly.

"They killed him, grandma. And I couldn't do anything to stop it."

A long silence passed between them as Willowood folded her hands in her lap and looked off somewhere. "How long have you had this dream? The first one, I mean, where he rescued you?"

"A couple of months," Piper said, giving her best guess. She still couldn't tell time over months like the adults did. "Ever since right before I met Mr. Lieutenant Magnus."

Willowood examined Piper's face with interest. "How soon before you met him?"

"I was on daddy's ship, from when we left Capriana. I had the first dream, and then Mr. Lieutenant Magnus showed up that night to rescue us when we were adriftering."

"Adrift."

"Uh huh."

"And you're saying you've had this recurring dream consistently ever since then?"

Piper thought about it. "How much is consistently?"

"Enough that it happens every few weeks or days?"

Piper nodded.

"But now it's changed?"

Again, Piper nodded.

"And this is the only time it's ever been different?"

"Yup." Piper took another deep sigh, and her arms and legs got the chills. "But I don't think it was a dream."

Her grandmother sat up a little straighter. "No?"

"It felt real. I mean, really real. Like I was actually seeing things like I'm seeing you right now. And I know the difference between real things and dream things—I'm not a baby anymore. I know the difference."

"I'm sure you do," Willowood said, looking away again.

"I think he's in trouble, grandma." But her grandmother didn't say anything. So Piper touched Willowood's arm. "Grandma?"

"Yes, child?"

"I said, I think he's in trouble. I think they all are."

PIPER WASHED her face and put on a new white and blue-trim suit that Azelon had made for her. Then she ate a snack, took a few sips of water, and followed the glowing lines on the floor until she found her grandmother inside a dimly lit lounge. It had comfy chairs and a wide window that looked out over a planet.

"Is that Capriana Prime?" Piper asked, stepping into the room.

Willowood nodded. "It is."

"Is—is Magnus down there?"

Again, her grandmother inclined her head. "He is."

Piper put a hand on her chest. "And do you think—?"

"They're in trouble, yes, Piper."

Piper felt herself about to burst into tears when Willowood raised a hand. It felt like a heating pad, and a soothing sensation moved down her body.

"Try and calm down, child. You said you're not a baby anymore, right?"

Piper nodded, though less confidently than she would have before hearing that Magnus was in trouble.

"Good. Then I need you to stay focused and not let your emotions get in the way of what we need to do."

"We're going to do something?" The words filled Piper with a sense of hope.

"Of course we are. Did you think we we're just going to sit around and cry after you had a premonition like that?"

"A premnom—"

"Premonition. A feeling that something is going to happen. A look into the future."

"Are you saying Magnus is going to die?"

Willowood pointed to the open chair. It was dark leather and had two white pillows in it. "Have a seat, Piper."

Piper nodded dutifully and sat down.

"Not everything you dream is real," Willowood said.

"But some of it is?"

Willowood smiled. "When you're a true blood, yes."

"Awen told me I'm a true blood."

"I'm sure she did." Piper's grandmother looked out the window at Capriana. The wrinkles on her forehead told Piper that something was definitely wrong.

"So is what I dreamed about Magnus real?" Piper sat up straight as her suit squeaked in the chair. "Is he going to die?"

"Your dreams are special, Piper. Special because they show you not only what has been, but what could be."

"So, I saw the future?"

"You saw *a* future. A possible future. But not the certain future."

"You mean, it might happen?"

"Correct."

Piper's nose wrinkled. "What makes it certain or not?"

Her grandmother smiled at the question. "People. Our actions dictate our future, and not even the Unity knows exactly how things will turn out."

"Wait. Are you saying I was dreaming in the Unity?"

"In a manner of speaking, yes. Your powers? They're very special." Willowood reached forward and took Piper's hand. "You have something that no one else has ever had before you—at least not that I'm aware of. And so, even in your sleep, it seems you are able to move within the Unity of all things. What you saw was a possible future that had to do with very real things, but not exact things."

"Like when I first met Magnus." Piper squeezed her grand-mother's hand. "I dreamed about him in Capriana, but we met on the starship. Kinda like that?"

"Yes, kind of like that. Premonitions aren't exact. They're more like shadows of what's to come. Only after events have transpired do we see what has happened."

Piper looked at Capriana. "He's down there, isn't he."

Willowood nodded.

"And he's in trouble."

"Yes. He just communicated with the colonel, and it seems things are getting serious."

"Moldark."

Willowood looked at Piper with surprise. "Why would you say that?"

"I don't know. I guess I can just feel it. He's here, isn't he."

"Yes." Piper's grandmother had a serious look on her face. "Yes, he's here."

"Then Mr. Lieutenant Magnus needs my help." Piper stood up. "I need to get down there."

"Piper, please sit down."

"But, grandmother, I—"

"Sit down." Willowood's tone sounded so much like her mother's that it sent a chill through Piper's body.

Piper sat and placed her hands in her lap. "I'm sorry, grandmother."

"There's nothing to be sorry for. I just need you to listen."

"I'm listening."

"Good. Going down there, to Capriana? It's far too dangerous. And you made a promise to Magnus."

"That I wouldn't do anything stupid again."

Willowood bobbed her head back and forth as if she wouldn't have said it the way Piper did, but couldn't dismiss the accuracy of it. "Right. But there are more ways to help him, ones that don't put your life in jeopardy."

"Like what?"

"A few hours ago, when you were awake and sharing about what happened on Moldark's ship, you said you helped him convince people."

"To destroy the Republic."

Willowood nodded. "What if there was a way to undo that?"

"You mean, like change their minds? Tell them not to destroy the Republic anymore?"

"Exactly. Though, you can never fully remove a thought from someone's mind. We always believe part of what we hear, even when we learn that it wasn't true."

Willowood's words pricked Piper's heart. Did that mean there would always be a small part of her that was suspicious of Magnus? She hoped not. But, then again, she could still feel the old Piper that was angry at him—even fearful of him. Was that what her grandmother meant?

"I'd like to propose that you and I try to undo what Moldark made you do," Willowood said.

"You're going to help me?"

Her grandmother nodded. "I think it will need both of us, yes. Would you like to try?"

Piper considered the prospect of being able to undo that evil that she'd done for Moldark. "Will it hurt him?"

"Hurt who?"

"Grandfather."

Willowood recoiled a little. "That man is not your grandfather, Piper. At least not anymore."

"But he said—"

"What he said cannot be trusted. And I'm so sorry you had to meet him the way you did. It's not…"

Piper waited for her grandmother to finish her sentence, but she seemed too lost in thought. "Grandmother?"

"I would have liked you to know him when we were young."

"When you first met?"

Willowood nodded. "Those were some happy days. But the creature you met—that is not your grandfather, nor is it even Admiral Kane. It is something altogether different. Someone we must stop."

"Then let's do it. I'm ready."

19

Commodore David Seaman sat in his quarters adjacent to the *Solera Fortuna's* bridge, staring through the windowplex at the blue surface of Capriana Prime. Coming around the horizon was the massive atoll that marked the Republic's seat of power—a crescent-shaped island chain that might well have been a series of countries, given their size. It was the place of his birth and represented everything noble and right about the Galactic Republic— at least when it had esteemed such attributes, before its fall into the quagmire of bureaucracy.

But how noble and right have you been? Seaman asked himself, tapping the glass-topped desk in his quarters.

The events surrounding the Battle of Oorajee's final hours had put Seaman in an uncommonly sour mood—most especially Fleet Admiral Brighton's orders to annihilate the Jujari fleet despite what would have been their sure surrender. The command disgusted him. He couldn't say as much, of course—it was unprofessional. But was he indeed in a profession where any disgust with killing was treated as contempt?

In the end, Seaman hadn't needed to follow through with the order. The Jujari pressed the Paragon in a final surge. *A last act of desperation*, Seaman thought. But in his heart, he knew that wasn't it—not entirely, anyway.

There had been an assault on the *Black Labyrinth*. Rumors had spread of a small spec ops team making an attempt on Moldark's life. It hadn't been the first time someone tried to take out the new leader, Seaman knew. But unlike the previous efforts, which had been conducted by a faction of Republic loyalists, this one, it was said, was carried out by a unit unconnected with the Republic. In fact, Seaman's sources in the *Labyrinth* said the unit didn't look or move like any in the quadrant. They were, to use the childhood trope, aliens.

And then there was the sudden appearance of illegally outfitted civilian vessels that made good the mysterious attackers' escape. Officially, it was ruled as an insurgent uprising—a last-ditch effort by the Jujari by which they called in old favors to ensure their retreat.

But none of that made sense to Seaman.

For one thing, why call in favors when you've already lost the war?

But for the other, the Jujari and the civilian armada weren't fighting like they were trying to retreat. They were fighting to defend something of tremendous value. Something that smelled of hope.

A trill sounded at his door.

"Come," Seaman said. The doors slid apart to reveal Lani DiAntora, the *Fortuna's* Flag Captain.

"DiAntora," Seaman said, then he gestured to one of the two leather chairs before his desk. "Please."

She purred in the Sekmit version of appreciation and slid into a chair with feline-like grace.

Seaman studied her for a long moment to the point that it was probably awkward for her. *No, not for her*, Seaman corrected himself. *She's a Sekmit. They act like they own the universe.* And he meant that in a mostly positive way—one that emphasized the species' unwavering confidence. *Though, sometimes, it is a pain in the ass.* "Why'd you join the Navy, DiAntora?"

If she was caught off guard by the question, she didn't show it. "I wanted to serve the Republic."

"Sure, but why?"

"To help maintain order in the galaxy, and to keep evil people from harming the innocent."

Seaman steepled his fingers and touched them to his lips. "Noble."

"Logical." DiAntora tilted her head and flicked her ears. "And you, Commodore?"

He rocked back in his chair. "I wanted to get off Capriana Prime. See the galaxy."

"So you had issues with your family?"

He smiled. *Damn, she was intuitive.* "My father."

"And did you see the galaxy?"

Seaman nodded. "More than I bargained for. And some-where along the line, I got lonely."

"Lonely, sir?" An inquisitive expression crossed her feline features. "But weren't you posted to—"

"A ship full of sailors?" He nodded and then stared off in the near distance. "Isn't it odd how you can still feel alone even when you're surrounded by people on every side?" He looked back at DiAntora, but her eyes darted away. "Anyway, somewhere along the line, that loneliness turned into a mission."

"And what was that, sir?" she asked.

"Help maintain order in the galaxy, and keep evil people from harming the innocent," he replied.

DiAntora smiled.

"Not only did I grow up somewhere along the way, and reconcile things with my father, but I realized I wasn't alone, so long as I flew close to others who had the same ambitions." He stared at her.

DiAntora held his gaze for several seconds. Seaman wasn't sure where his feelings for her might lead, or if she even recipro-cated them. But he liked her. And when this was all over, maybe he'd do something about it.

"What are your orders, Commodore?"

Seaman didn't answer right away. Instead, he swiveled his chair to face the window. "Have you ever been to Capriana, Captain?"

DiAntora flicked an ear. "No, sir. I attended the Academy at Tellstall, and my training never included any time on Capriana Prime."

Seaman nodded. "It's beautiful. Towering spires that shine in the morning light. The gentle trade winds that keep the heat at bay. And hundreds of kilometers of beaches to spend your sunsets on." He sighed. "I love the beach." Then he looked at DiAntora as if to see if she shared any of his appreciation.

Her head twitched. "I hate the beach. Sir."

Seaman chuckled. "You would, wouldn't you."

"Sir?"

"Cats hate the water, and you're—"

DiAntora glared at him with her feline-like eyes.

"You know what? Never mind. My point is, it's a lovely place. And I would never want to do anything to hurt it."

A moment of silence filled Seaman's quarters. He knew the Sekmit would not repeat her question about their orders, so Seaman steepled his fingers and placed them to his lips. "Admiral Brighton has asked us to prepare for orbital bombardment against the surface. Article 99. No survivors."

If DiAntora was surprised, she didn't show it. Her eyes studied him with so much intense curiosity that Seaman second-guessed whether or not he should tell her what he was thinking. But he'd played his hand. So he relaxed his arms and looked back at Capriana.

When several more seconds had passed, DiAntora finally spoke. "You seem averse to these orders."

"And how do they make you feel?"

"Feelings are irrelevant, sir."

"Are they?" Seaman studied her face for a moment. Was she really so cold and calculating? "You're back above Aluross in this same scenario. The order comes to you to fire on the capital—to fire on everything that moves. Are you telling me you don't feel anything?"

"I did not say I didn't feel anything," she replied, straight-faced. "I said feelings are irrelevant. There is a difference."

"So you would follow orders to annihilate the planet, city by city? Even take out emergency ships departing the surface?"

DiAntora was calculating every word—every micro-expression—Seaman could feel it. She didn't even blink. For a moment, he thought the woman was going to side against him. *She'd blow up her whole damn planet if it were an order*, he realized.

"No."

Seaman held his breath.

"You wouldn't?"

"Must I repeat myself to you?"

Seaman squinted at her, trying to think where to go next. "I just never figured you for treason."

"The charges would include failure to follow a direct order in a time of war, misconduct, and gross dereliction of duty. Treason would only apply should I attempt to thwart the government's attempts actively."

"And would you ever attempt to thwart your government's military activities?"

"I have never been placed in a situation where such a provocation—"

"Dammit, Lani," Seaman said as he brought his fist down on his table. DiAntora's eyes widened in what was, perhaps, the first emotional reaction above "barely breathing" that Seaman had ever seen her make. He shot a finger toward Capriana and stood from his chair. "Would you fire on that planet and wipe it out?"

"It's an order?"

"Yes, it's a mysticsdamned order," he shouted back. "And you're going to relay it if it comes down the COC."

DiAntora lowered her eyes and seemed to search the carpeted floor. Perhaps the Sekmit had a soul after all.

Seaman could feel heat flushing his face. "I need to know what my subordinate is going to do, Flag Captain DiAntora. What is your answer."

DiAntora snapped her chin up, and Seaman could have sworn he saw a tear staining the fur below her eye. "No, Commodore," she said through clenched teeth. "I will not fire on that planet."

Seaman exhaled and turned his head away. Then he returned to his chair and leaned back. "No, you wouldn't, would you. Because above all things, Lani DiAntora, you are an honorable person. That is why you're a fine commander." He looked up at her. "The uniform did not make you great. You were great before you went to the academy."

She bowed her head ever so slightly. "Thank you, Commodore." Then she took a deep breath and swallowed. "I will relieve myself of command and confine myself to my quarters."

"Like hell, you will," Seaman said.

As if in defiance, DiAntora stood in the blink of an eye. Seaman was about to order that she sit down when he saw the woman look at something in the near distance. He glanced over his shoulder, wondering if there was something in his office to catch her attention, but there wasn't.

"Captain," Seaman said with some concern. "Are you all right?"

DiAntora tilted her head and twitched her ears as if listening to something. Again, Seaman looked around the room but heard and saw nothing. But he did feel something. A wave of warmth washed over him that he couldn't explain—like the sun emerging from behind a cloud and warming his skin.

DiAntora raised her paw-like hand and held it flat in front of her. Her eyes looked at it like she was pressing against an invisible wall.

What the hell is happening? Seaman asked himself.

But then he felt such a strange sensation of peace that he could not be mad at DiAntora. And—to his surprise—neither could he be afraid. Whatever apprehension he had about resisting Brighton's orders was gone. And not gone as if it created a vacuum in his heart, but gone as if something else had replaced it entirely. It was an emotion he had felt many times before, but nowhere near as strong as now.

Courage.

"WE MUST GET WORD TO CENTCOM," Seaman said now that DiAnotra was seated again. Whatever strange thing had happened in his quarters, it was gone now, and Seaman had a job to do. "We can prevent the attack by raising the planetary defense shield."

"But won't they conference with Fleet Admiral Brighton first?" DiAntora asked.

Seaman nodded. "That is procedure. But I'm hoping that my rank will avail me a certain benefit of the doubt."

"You could also say you're acting at his behest. By the time Brighton realizes the shield has been activated, it will be too late to deactivate the startup sequence. Furthermore, any attempt to implore CENTCOM to lower it would exacerbate the situation, raising CENTCOM's suspicions of foul play."

"And reassure them of their defensive measures," Seaman added.

"Until such time as an investigation can determine the culprits." DiAntora tilted her head at him. "You'll be arrested, of course. As will I."

"Lani, I don't think either of us will be around long enough for that."

She smiled. "Neither do I, Commodore."

"David, please."

DiAnotra eyed him as if being cautious. "Sir, naval protocol dictates that we—"

"We're about to try and undermine Lord Moldark. I want the person complicit with me to at least call me by my first name if we're going to die."

She nodded and repeated her previous statement. "Neither do I, David."

He liked the sound of that—more than he would ever admit, at least until all this was over.

"Bridge to Captain DiAntora," a voice said over ceiling speakers.

"Go ahead," she replied.

"Sensors are showing that Lord Moldark's personal shuttle has departed for the surface, along with ten heavy transports. We thought you would like to know."

"I am aware. Thank you, Nyquist."

The channel closed, and DiAntora looked at Seaman as he brought up a holo. He zoomed in on a group of ships departing from Third Fleet and descending toward the atmosphere.

"It's the *Peregrine*," Seaman said. "And he's got enough Marines to hit the Forum Republica if he wants."

"Perhaps command has changed their mind about Article 99," DiAntora said, but Seaman could tell by the tone in her voice that she wasn't convinced.

"What are you up to?" Seaman said, watching the ships fade away. He thought for a few more seconds, then looked at DiAntora. "I don't like it. I'm hailing CENTCOM."

She nodded and then started typing on his desk. A control surface appeared under her fingers, and within seconds a holo window appeared in front of Seaman. He thanked her with a nod of his head, straightened his uniform, and sat up straight.

The holo frame read Connecting… but nothing happened for several seconds. A new message read Diverting… and then Senator Blackman's face appeared. He was not inside CENTCOM but seemed to be walking somewhere in a hurry.

"Senator Blackman, this is Commodore David Seaman with the Paragon's First Fleet. I was hoping you could—"

The screen went fuzzy, and the sound was muffled as if Blackman had stuffed the data pad under his arm. The mic picked up the sound of rustling clothing and shouting in the distance. And the sound of blaster fire.

"Senator? What's going on there?" Seaman exchanged a worried look with DiAntora. "Senator, can you hear me?"

"Yes, yes, Commodore," Blackman said at last, holding the screen up to his face and brushing grey hair off his forehead. "I'm sorry for the delay. How can I help you?"

Again, Seaman glanced at DiAntora. Something was wrong. "Is everything all right there, Senator?"

"Quite so," Blackman said, still out of breath. "I'm attending a training exercise as part of a public relations campaign to bolster support for the Marine Corps among some of the Secessionists. Not the best place for a call. But I can talk now."

Seaman raised an eyebrow. Either Blackman really was where he said he was, or this was the fastest thinking senator on Capriana. "Pardon the inquiry, sir, but why didn't anyone inside CENTCOM's Command Center answer?"

Blackman smiled. "You don't call CENTCOM much, do you, son."

This much was evident as Seaman had never had reason or seniority to—until now. "No, Senator."

"As acting Chairman, I receive all calls from our military forces abroad, whether or not I'm in the Command Center. Now, I expect what you have for me is urgent?"

"Yes, Senator. It appears that Lord Moldark has left for Capriana." Seaman couldn't be sure, but he thought he detected a faint tic in Blackman's upper lip.

"Ah, yes. Of course he is."

"You're expecting him then?"

Blackman lowered his voice and leaned into the data pad. "The Nine are gathering to discuss our next plans, Commodore."

Seaman hesitated. "Who are the Nine?"

"I see." Blackman narrowed his eyes at Seaman. "Son, does your CO know you're calling me right now?"

Seaman lifted his chin. "No, sir. That's why we're calling you."

"We?" His eyebrows went up. "Who else is with you?"

"I meant that rhetorically, Senator. It seems someone has issued Article 99 against Capriana Prime. Was that the Nine?"

"It's a security measure, son. Nothing more. You needn't fear a thing."

"A security measure?"

"The Valdaiga Accords as well the Naval Rules of Engagement call for certain preemptive procedures in the event of other factors that are"—he waved a hand—"far too complex for this conversation. Now, if you'll excuse me, I need to get back to the presentation, and you—I think—need to stop initiating conspicuous interchanges behind your CO's back. Am I right?"

Seaman felt at a loss for what to say—which was a rare thing given his capacity as a leader.

"I said, am I right, Commodore?"

"Certainly, sir."

"Blackman out."

"Seaman—" The call ended. "Out."

DiAntora closed the window and then sat back in her chair. She raised a furry eyebrow at Seaman. "He's lying, you know."

"I think so too."

"No, I don't mean to say I *think* he's lying. I'm saying he's lying as a fact."

"Ah," Seaman replied, rubbing his forehead with one hand. "So, where does this put us?"

"I sense fear in the senator."

"Like he wasn't expecting Moldark."

She nodded. "And he *was* inside CENTCOM, just not the Command Center."

"And how do you know that?"

"I've seen that hallway before, on other calls."

He sat forward. "You've been on calls with CENTCOM before?"

"As an observer, not an initiator."

Seaman sighed. "And the Nine—what was that about?"

"Perhaps the organization in control of the Paragon," DiAntora offered. "Though, from what I gathered during that call, they've lost control."

"So you think Moldark's really going to order it? Article 99, I mean?"

"And they're not raising the PDS." She stroked her chin. "I'm not sure what his trip down there is for, but when Moldark gets back…"

"When he gets back, it could mean the end of billions of lives."

DiAntora nodded. "I believe so, yes."

"GENERAL LOVELL," Seaman said as he stood from his desk. "Please, come in."

"Always an honor to be a guest of Fleet Command," Lovell said, stepping into Seaman's quarters. He also acknowledged DiAntora. "Captain."

"It's good to see you, General."

"Please," Seaman said. "Have a seat."

Lovell sat and smoothed his uniform. He could have hailed from Limbia Centrella, given his commanding presence and dark complexion, but he was born and raised on Capriana Prime, like most other generals of standing. The Republic could claim impartiality all it wanted, but the majority of its commanding officers had roots on Prime in one way or another—the Brigadier General was no exception.

"How can I help you both?" Lovell said. Seaman shared a glance with DiAntora and then looked back at the general. The general seemed to catch the look. "What seems to be the matter?"

"General, are you aware of the Fleet Admiral's recent order?" Seaman asked.

Lovell looked between DiAntora and Seaman. "If you don't mean the order to return to Capriana Prime following the successful campaign against the Jujari, then I'm afraid you have me at a loss."

The way Lovell said "successful campaign against the Jujari" made Seaman second guess his decision to pull the general into the fold. If he had sided with Moldark, then this was going to be a very short meeting—one Seaman doubted he'd survive. While his Navy pride was strong, he would be no match for the seasoned Marine war hero seated across from him. He knew Lovell could kill him before Seaman knew what happened. But if Seaman wanted to save Prime, then he had to take risks, and there was no time to spare. One way or another, he would probably lose his life in the conflict—it might as well be for something he believed in.

"Moldark has issued Article 99 against Capriana Prime," Seaman said. "We're awaiting the order to execute at any moment."

At first, Lovell didn't move. He looked passively at Seaman as if he were still waiting for the punchline of a tired joke. But when Seaman failed to say anything further, the general worked his jaw, and simply said, "I see," followed with a sniff.

"I take it you weren't aware then?"

"No, I was not, Commodore. This is the first I've heard."

Seaman nodded and then looked out the window toward the planet. "And if I were to ask if you would be complicit in following through on this order?"

"You're asking if I would sanction it?" He looked between the two of them.

Seaman nodded.

"Hell no, not in a million lifetimes."

Seaman let out a breath, as did DiAntora. "We hoped you'd say that, General."

"Well, apparently, I'm among like-minded people?"

"Yes, General," DiAntora said. "You most certainly are."

"Do you have some sort of plan besides abstaining?"

"We're working on that," DiAntora said. "And that's why you're here. We need your help."

Seaman outlined the call with Blackman and Moldark's departure to the planet's surface. "We're not sure what he's up to, but we would like you to send an element of Marines to monitor him and keep an eye out for anything unusual."

"Unusual?" Lovell looked to each of them again. "How do you mean?"

"We think there might be a third party involved, working to undermine the Paragon."

"As in the assault on the *Black Labyrinth*?"

Seaman nodded. "The same. We have reason to believe they may be trying to help prevent this genocide."

"How do you know?"

"Call it a hunch, General. For now, we need boots on the ground."

Lovell pursed his lips in thought. "I can activate an element right away. Tasks?"

"Track Moldark's shuttle, report on his activity, and reinforce any efforts to stop him should fighting break out."

"Can do."

"Thank you, sir," Seaman said without any attempt to hide his relief. "We're grateful."

"And I'm grateful you trusted me. I've been suspicious of that bastard for a while now. He's responsible for me losing some good Marines. And if this is what you say it is, then it's about time someone sacked up and did something about it. But I do have a question."

"Go ahead," Seaman said with an open hand.

"If this doesn't work—if we can't figure out how to stop him down there—what then?"

Seaman looked to DiAntora. She raised a single eyebrow as if to say, "Might as well tell him."

Seaman sighed. "Then we'll take on any ship that tries to follow his orders."

20

THE REST of first squad gathered in the office suite less than five minutes after Magnus had first arrived on Proconsul Tower's top floor. The plan was to proceed to the docking platforms and commandeer a transport that would get them to the Simlia atoll where Azelon's ship would be waiting. Magnus suggested to Caldwell that they simply take a shuttle, pick up Zoll, and head to the *Spire* themselves, but TO-96 warned against it. Even with CENTCOM in chaos, the odds were still high that the city's orbit defense cannons would knock out any unauthorized flights above 350 meters.

"Sounds best to stay low, get out of the city's fire window, and meet at the extraction point," Caldwell said.

"Copy that," Magnus replied.

"I do have news on a lighter note," Caldwell said. "Bosworth intercepted our care package."

"Our dummy Piper? And how'd that go for him?" In the short time Magnus had known Azelon, he'd learned she didn't do anything half-assed, so he genuinely pitied whoever was sent to do the ambassador's dirty work.

"Took out two retrieval vessels," Caldwell said with a grin. "Bosworth was nowhere to be seen, of course. Probably fled the system by now. But at least he knows we don't play nice."

"Hard copy on that," Magnus replied with a grin. Then he turned to the squad. "Time to see what kind of ride we can arrange for ourselves. Let's move."

Magnus took three steps into the lobby, heading for the elevator bank, when four pods opened—including the two that the gladias had jumped out of less than two hours before. He held up a fist. "Everyone freeze."

Marines poured out of the elevators, made a defensive perimeter, and covered several civilians as they crossed to the space port elevators on the other side of the bank. One man stood out to Magnus in particular.

"It is the senator that Rohoar dislikes," the Jujari said.

"High marks for recognition, Scruffy," Magnus replied. "Looks like he's trying to make a run for it."

"The coward," Abimbola said.

"Yes." Rohoar growled. "Rohoar likes him even less than Rohoar did before."

"Let us dispatch them," Abimbola said, racking a charge.

"No," Magnus said, lifting a hand. "They're trying to escape just like everyone else. We've killed enough today."

"You cannot be serious, buckethead."

Magnus looked back at the Miblimbian. "I am, Bimby. That man was only trying to do what he believed was right, and I can't fault him for that. Mercy dictates I let them go."

"He's right," Awen said, inserting herself between the two gladias and peering out the door. "Blackman—assuming that's who it is—may be a coward, but unless those troopers are shooting at us, they're not a threat."

"But they are leaving the city even before an evacuation has been ordered. It makes no sense to me." Abimbola's voice grew distant. "Though, I suppose, it is just like their Republic ancestors."

"It's how the higher echelons of the Republic work," Magnus replied.

"Among the Jujari, the mwadim stays until their last pup has been made safe," Rohoar said.

"Then I'd say the Repub has a lot to learn from you," Magnus replied—and if he didn't know better, he'd say Awen was smiling at him.

"Stay where you are," a trooper yelled over external speakers.

"Splick," Magnus said. "Somebody got wise and switched to thermals."

"Lay down your weapons and get on the ground," said another trooper, his blaster pointed in Magnus's direction.

"Rohoar asks permission to shoot them."

Magnus sighed. His shields were drained, his armor damaged, and he'd most likely die if the Marines opened fire. "Awen, I need a shield."

"Done," she replied.

"We're just trying to get out of the city like you," Magnus said over externals, hoping to reason with the troopers.

"I said, lay your weapons down!"

"Rohoar has a sense that they are going to shoot you, scrumruk graulap."

"Magnus has that same sense, Scruffy."

"Last warning," a trooper said.

Blackman poked his head out of the elevator. "What's the holdup, people?"

"We have unidentified cloaked personnel on the west end of the lobby, Senator," replied a Marine.

"That's the enemy, dammit. Open fire!"

A unit commander pointed forward, and blaster fire erupted from the elevator bank. Had it not been for Awen's Unity shield, Magnus would have died. Instead, he rolled to the shield's edge and fired around it. The rest of first squad peeled out of the office and returned fire, taking down several troopers before the majority escaped into the elevator pods and ascended toward the spaceport docks.

"Everyone all right?" Magnus asked. No one registered any damage, so he ordered them across the lobby and to the elevators. One Marine still moved on the ground. Rohoar saw it and dropped a knee on the trooper's helmet, killing him instantly.

"What?" the Jujari asked with raised shoulders. "Rohoar put him out of his misery. This is also mercy, no?"

Magnus waved off the comment and ordered everyone into the remaining elevators. "It's gonna be hot when we get up there, so be ready." Everyone acknowledged and pointed their weapons out, ready for the doors to open.

The pods moved skyward, racing through the docking platform's latticework tower. The warming horizon flashed between the metal cross pieces as Magnus sensed his pod slow. He rolled his head and made ready to open fire. As soon as the doors opened, blaster rounds streaked across the main deck. "What the hell?"

"Paragon," Titus yelled, firing past the Marines and into a cluster of black-clad troopers emerging from a Stiletto-class Corvette.

"Target the Paragon. Protect the senator!" Magnus squeezed his trigger and took out two troopers firing on Blackman's position. The grey-haired man covered his head, hid behind two Marines, then ran back toward the elevators.

"Rohoar can kill him now," Rohoar said.

"Negative. We need him alive." Magnus laid down heavy fire as Blackman raced toward him. Several more aids followed the senator, but at least two were gunned down as they retreated.

Magnus's NOV1 shrieked as it dropped three Paragon troopers in a row, cutting a line of blaster holes across their chest plates. The bodies thrashed as they went down, joining others who met their fates with Novian blaster rounds in their bodies. But despite how many troopers Granther Company took down in the opening seconds, more enemy combatants emerged, pressing the shaky defense. Finally, the Marines fell back toward the elevator pods.

"Give them some protection," Magnus ordered. The words

weren't out of his mouth before Nídira erected a defensive wall. It bought the Marines precious time as they scrambled for the elevators.

A man dressed in black emerged from the Stiletto-class ship. He walked down the vessel's under-nose cargo ramp and raised a hand. At first, Magnus thought he might be directing the troopers or trying to get someone's attention. Instead, Nídira began screaming. Magnus looked to his right and saw the mystic writhing in pain—feet half a meter off the ground.

"Awen," Magnus yelled. "Do something!"

But without Nídira's shield, the Paragon's attack rained down on the gladias. Magnus took a bolt to the shoulder. His torso twisted even before he felt the round's sting sear his flesh. He fired his NOV1 one-handed, boring into a trooper trying to flank the Granther's position. The man dropped as blaster fire stitched up his chest and into his helmet.

Nídira was still dangling in midair. Awen put a small shield around her, but it seemed to do nothing against the unseen attack.

"It's Moldark," Magnus said, turning his NOV1 toward the man on the cargo ramp. "Take him out!"

But only some of the gladias could target the enemy leader—if they all did, first squad and the retreating Marines would be overrun by troopers. But whatever Moldark was doing with his dark arts had to be stopped. He lifted three other Marine's off their feet as their weapons clattered to the deck. Even with their helmets on, Magnus could hear their wails.

Nídira gave out one final bawl before her body vaporized in a cloud of ash. Her power suit fell to the ground like a flag falling from a mast. Awen's shield gave out as she knelt to the ground in horror.

"Awen," Magnus yelled. "Shield!"

More blaster rounds pinged off the elevator bank's housing and blew across personal shields. Magnus ducked, trying to avoid a fatal shot. Even with superior weapons, the gladia were outnumbered and unavoidably tasked with protecting the senator and his entourage.

Magnus's last energy magazine went dry. He ejected both mags and reached for a fallen Marine's weapon when a round knocked the blaster away. So Magnus pulled his V from its holster and started firing into the sea of Paragon troopers. The weapon seemed to do little more than aggravate the enemy. He let out a string of automatic fire, swiping the pistol left and right—it was terrible fire control, but done on purpose and out of desperation, it was enough to make the enemy think twice about advancing on him.

Past caring what risk he posed to the nearby shuttles and star-ships, Magnus grabbed both VODs from his belt and hurled them toward the enemy. "Fragger out!" he yelled as the small devices flew, one after the other. The resulting explosions sent half a dozen Paragon troopers flying both times as their bodies were doused in flames and sparks. The shockwaves knocked several other troopers off their feet, but they managed to keep firing on the retreating Republic forces even from their knees. Whatever drove these combatants, it was otherworldly.

Just when the enemy press seemed to be too great, Awen put

up a new shield.

"Get below," Magnus ordered, stepping back inside an elevator and checking to make sure Blackman was behind him. Then Magnus punched the panel to send the pod back down. The image of blaster bolts dispersing against a Unity shield vanished as the doors closed. Then the pod dropped away, and a gentle whir replaced the sound of blaster fire. Magnus turned to check on Rohoar, Doc, and Titus. "You good?"

They all nodded.

Then he looked at Blackman and his senate aid. Magnus turned off chameleon mode, though he noticed it was already malfunctioning on his left shoulder plate anyway due to the blaster round he'd taken. His suit had dispersed nano-bots into the tissue that would disinfect the wound and stem any bleeding not cauterized by the blaster round. But deeper nerve and muscle damage would need cellular reconstruction therapy in a tank later on—if there was a later on.

The senator looked stunned but seemed to be trying to compose himself. "Was that—? I mean, was that—?"

"Admiral Kane?" Magnus said, opening his helmet's visor.

Blackman nodded.

"Now do you believe me, Senator?"

The man hesitated, then seemed to regain at least some of his composure. Blackman smoothed his uniform and pursed his lips. "Far from an orbital strike, wouldn't you say?"

"That man just killed half your staff and at least two dozen Marines, Senator."

"And yet, the city itself is spared."

"For now," Magnus said. The senator did have a point, though. From the way Piper made it sound, an orbital bombardment seemed to suit Moldark's level of animosity toward the Republic. So why the in-person appearance?

"You okay, Magnus?" Caldwell said over VNET.

Magnus slapped his visor down and turned away from Blackman. "Nídira's gone, Colonel. And we suffered some minor injuries."

"I saw. I'm sorry, son. We didn't detect Moldark's ships until just now."

"He must have snuck under the city's sensors like we— Hold on. Did you say *ships*?"

The colonel nodded. "We count ten heavy armored transports and a corvette."

"Troop carriers?" He glanced at Blackman.

"That's a full battalion," Dutch said from an adjacent pod.

"But why the invasion force?" Magnus asked, still glaring at Blackman. "Surely he sees the PDS isn't operational yet. Why not take the shot?"

"He must want something planetside," Caldwell replied.

Magnus raised his visor again as the elevators came to a stop. "What's he after, Blackman?"

"I'm afraid I don't—"

Magnus punched the windowplex just beside the senator. "What's he after?"

"He's a lunatic, Magnus. How should I know?"

"Because, *Senator*, he's your pet project, isn't he?"

"I'm sorry, but I still don't—"

Magnus punched again and cracked the window. "Isn't he?"

"Okay, yes. Yes. But can we please get going first?" Blackman pointed toward the now-open elevator doors.

"Stay where you are," someone shouted. A platoon of Marines pointed weapons into the senator's elevator, aiming at Magnus.

"I'm getting really tired of surprises behind every elevator door." Magnus was about to raise his hands when Blackman stepped around him.

"It's all right. He's with me," Blackman said. "They all are."

Magnus raised his eyebrows and looked at the other gladias in the pod, still cloaked.

"Lower your weapons, for mystics' sake." The senator pushed his way out of the pod and walked through the platoon. He went straight for the tower's main elevators and motioned for Magnus to follow him.

"Go ahead and let 'em see you," Magnus said over the squad channel. "Don't need these boys any more wound up than they already are."

At once, the gladias dropped chameleon mode. To the naked eye, they seemed to appear out of thin air—one second, there was open space, the next, ten alien-armored elite warriors filled the space port's elevator pods.

Blackman looked over his shoulder only once, as if completely expecting the sight, and then pressed an elevator control panel. "We haven't got much time, Magnus."

"Copy that," Magnus said, stepping forward. Slowly, the gladias followed his lead and emerged from the elevators, eyeing the Marines. The moment of tension passed, however, when Paragon troopers crashed through the domed ceiling and fired into the lobby.

"Let's get to those elevators," Magnus yelled. He re-cloaked, and then reached for a downed Marine's weapon. He stripped its energy mag, and then pulled two more off the dead man's hip. Then he reloaded, racked the first charge, and fired at the enemy troopers fast-roping through the ceiling.

The first Paragon bucket he hit let go of the rope and fell the remaining eight meters to the floor. The second trooper also let go, but the line snagged his thigh so that his body flipped over. A third attacker died when Magnus's NOV1 severed the rope. The line pooled on the ground as the trooper's body hurtled toward the floor, crashing into the deck with a loud *thud*. But even with his team's quick response, at least one Paragon platoon dropped through the ceiling, and another appeared in the remaining spaceport elevator pods.

"Defend and descend," Magnus said with his back toward the tower's set of elevators.

As he stood firing shoulder to shoulder with other Marines, a wave of emotion hit him harder than a blaster bolt. It was the first time since the ambush at the mwadim's palace that he'd fought side by side with Marines still loyal to the Republic's cause. He imagined something like this—well, not like *this*—but some miracle that would allow him back into the fold. Only, this wasn't true acceptance, only a matter of circumstance. And as soon as the immediate threat was put down, he'd be a hostile combatant again, wanted for treason.

The senator dashed into an elevator and hid inside the doorway. "Get the hell in here, boy!"

Guessing he was the only *boy* the senator might be referring to, Magnus retreated inside and made way for several other gladias and at least two Marines. Once the pod was full, Blackman shut the doors, and the elevator dropped.

Again, Magnus de-cloaked and raised his visor, but this time he pointed his NOV1 at Blackman's head. The act was met with both Marine's raising their MC90s, which made Dutch and Haze de-cloak and raise their NOV1s at the Marines. It wasn't until Rohoar de-cloaked that both Marines lowered their weapons—their bodies leaning back in silent appreciation of the Jujari in alien armor.

"Why's he here?" Magnus asked, back in control of the pod. "And why didn't your orbital defense cannons take those ships out?"

"I don't know," Blackman said. "They must've come in under sensors, or the cannons are down."

"Bad answer," Magnus said, pressing the barrel against Blackman's cheek.

"Get that out of my face, you little splick."

Blackman tried pushing the weapon away, but Magnus elbowed him in the head. "Don't touch my blaster, Senator. You didn't earmark any tax credits for this one."

Looking less fearful and more annoyed, Blackman rubbed the side of his head where a small trickle of blood appeared over his ear. "What do you want?"

"I want to know why this whole thing isn't adding up,"

Magnus said. "The general seemed to change his tone just before someone rolled a VOD beside him. And now you're trying to escape before an evacuation has even been ordered."

"That's because—"

"Shut up." Magnus elbowed him again. "If I don't like the answers you give me, then we can add three more bodies to the count, right here, right now."

"You wouldn't."

"I'm already wanted for treason, Senator. You think you threaten me? All that matters to me now is getting my team back safely and making sure the city's population has a fighting chance at an evacuation—one you're going to initiate as soon as you explain to me what the *hell* is going on."

"All right, all right, just—please—get that thing out of my face," Blackman said.

Magnus lowered his weapon and then gestured for the senator to get talking.

"I can't prove this, but I believe that Kane is here to settle a score."

"What kind of score?"

Blackman hesitated.

"What kind of score, Senator?"

"There's a secret organization rumored to be operating within the senate."

"The Circle of Nine."

Blackman's eyes went wide. "So you've heard of them?"

"Maybe. Why are they significant?"

"We believe they're responsible for creating the Paragon."

"Why?"

Blackman's eyes shifted back and forth, so Magnus raised his elbow again. "Okay, okay. For years, we thought there was a conspiracy to unseat the Republic and usher in a new militaristic government. General McCormick, as you mentioned, was thought to be a part of them."

"You're talking a military coup, Senator."

He nodded. "Yes, son. That's exactly what I'm talking about. One that has apparently gotten way out of hand."

"Out of hand?"

"My sources tell me that Kane was only supposed to threaten the Republic, not any of this." He gestured around the pod.

"So you admit Kane changed?"

"Of course. It was public knowledge that something had happened to the admiral—something out there over Oorajee. No one knows what exactly. But he went mad and stopped following orders."

"And now you think he wants some sort of revenge against the Nine? For what?"

Blackman shook his head. "Your guess is as good as mine, son. Though, if I had to say, I suppose it has something to do with whatever drove him to the point of insanity."

"Then why not just level the city if he's so mad? Why risk the invasion force?"

Blackman swallowed hard and dabbed his ear with a handkerchief. "*Moldark* isn't a man, Magnus. He's a beast. A menace. At least from what I'm told."

"How do you know that name?" Magnus raised his NOV1

and sensed the Marines tense. But Dutch, Haze, and Rohoar had them dead to rights.

Blackman shied away from the barrel, hands up. "During his final transmission with CENTCOM, he refused to be addressed as Kane anymore. He insisted that *weakling*—his word, not mine —was dead." He pointed to the ceiling. "That *thing* up there doesn't think like we do. He's not logical. And right now, I think he wants to personally see to it that the Nine die at his hand before wiping out the planet."

Magnus lowered his weapon. "It's a weak guess, at best. And, tactically, it's suicide." He didn't trust senators—and this one was no exception. They all seemed to be as slippery as Fathroni sand snakes. Magnus considered killing Blackman where he stood and being done with the whole thing. But Blackman was probably the closest he was going to come to speaking with someone in a high echelon any time soon. Magnus hoped Blackman could order the evacuation and—just maybe—tell him more about how he'd been burned. "For someone who knows so much about conspiracies, Senator, I find it strange you wouldn't take my word for it when we were in this same scenario two hours ago. So I'm not sure why I should believe a damn word coming out of your mouth."

"I don't blame you in the least, Magnus. Especially after what they did to you."

"What's that supposed to mean?" Magnus felt his pulse quicken. "Who's *they*?"

"I'm CENTCOM's Chairman, Magnus. I'm paid to know about everything that happens inside the military."

"Including military coups?"

Blackman flushed. "We've been over that."

"Who's *they*, Senator?"

Blackman dabbed around his ear again. "From what we know, you were in the wrong place at the wrong time."

Magnus's thoughts raced. "Rescuing Senator Stone?"

Blackman gave him a sad look—somewhere between empathy and pity. "We believe he had information on the Nine. Apparently, he was willing to divulge what he knew *after* getting his family to safety."

"So they sabotaged his ship and then sent a team to abduct him." Magnus clenched his teeth, remembering the Bullwraith. "And they needed a fall guy."

"We can't prove any of this yet. But we will. It's only a matter of time. Unless, of course—"

"Moldark kills the Nine first," Magnus said.

The senator nodded. "So, you see, I wanted to believe you, but as far as I knew, you were working for Moldark. After all, you *were* with the 79th Recon, were you not?"

Magnus's gut tightened.

"And attached to one of the fleets?"

Magnus gave a shallow nod.

The senator looked at the bloody handkerchief and then dropped it on the floor. "So, we had to be sure."

"Are you sure now?"

Blackman raised his chin. "I am."

"Then order the evacuation, Senator, and you may live to see the sunrise."

"That's rather difficult to do, son."

"No, it's not." Magnus unsnapped the leather pouch on the senator's hip, yanked the data pad out, and handed it to Blackman. "Start broadcasting."

The senator chuckled as if laughing at a small child's attempt to dress themself. "It's not that simple, Lieutenant. Surely, you understand that."

"Then do what ya gotta do, and make it fast."

"I must get to the communications building," Blackman said. "From there, I can send out a secure transmission to the entire planet."

"Have fun with that."

"Not so fast, Lieutenant."

"Please, let Rohoar pinch his head," Rohoar said.

Magnus held up a fist to silence the Jujari. "What do you need, Senator?"

"You're giving me a personal escort," Blackman said, smiling like a seasoned Antaran backdraw player with a pike up his sleeve.

Magnus squinted as if into a bright light. "I'm not giving you splick."

"Then you're not getting your broadcast."

The insanity of the conversation was making Magnus's blood boil. He put the barrel of his NOV1 under Blackman's chin and leaned in close. "If I didn't know better, *Senator*, I'd say you *want* this planet to go up in flames."

"I'm simply addressing the fact that I need more than the remaining Marines at my disposal to get me across the plaza to the comms building. That is all, son. Call it whatever you want, but those are the facts. No escort and I don't survive long enough to address the planet."

"Ground floor," said a female voice from the elevator's holo panel. The chime dinged, and the doors opened. But even before they did, he heard the blaster fire coming.

21

TRYING to change someone's mind felt a little like trying to get a stain off your favorite stuffed animal. Piper's old corgachirp, Talisman, had stains like that. No matter how many times her mother had washed him, the blemishes never went away—not entirely. And neither did the memories of how the marks got there. It was almost as if Piper could track the journey of her childhood through Talisman's scars.

The brown stain on his foot was from when Piper used Talisman as a paintbrush. The crusted patch of discolored fur was from when she got too close to the campfire during the family camping trip. And the reddish blotch on his cheek was from when Piper had a nosebleed in the middle of the night. These were permanent marks, and no amount of wishing was going to take them away.

Likewise, trying to undo the hate that Piper had helped foster in the Paragon fleet was an impossible task. Despite her best efforts to speak to their minds within the Unity, Piper felt unconvinced that the men and women on the ships were free of her influence. What was done was done, and now she'd have to live with the consequences.

"Maybe we're going about this wrong," her grandmother said as they floated above the three Republic fleets. It was exhilarating to float in hard vacuum without the need for a spacesuit. But Piper couldn't let the newness of the adventure with her grandmother distract her, not if Willowood had a new idea on something they could try.

"What do you mean?" Piper asked.

"Maybe it's too much to try and change everyone's mind. What if we only look for those who are unsure already?"

"Like doubters?"

"Like doubters, yes." Willowood's glowing Unity form smiled at Piper. Her grandmother was already beautiful enough as it was. But when inside the Unity?—she was absolutely and utterly *radiant.* "Perhaps if we can plant the seeds of light in some, they will touch others. Let them do the work for us."

"There," Piper said, pointing to one of the bigger ships—a *Super Dreadful Naughty,* she thought, but then scrunched her nose, knowing that class name wasn't right. "I sense something in that ship."

Willowood paused as if looking at a list. "That's the *Solera Fortuna,* the flagship of First Fleet. Yes, I sense doubt on that ship too, Piper. Well done."

"Thanks, grandmother."

"Come," Willowood said, and then surged toward the ship. Piper followed, and within another second, they were inside someone's quarters adjacent to the bridge. It wasn't exactly like being there in person, of course—things were not as clear, and conversations were not as distinct. It was a lot like opening your eyes underwater. But there was enough detail about the space to make out faces and some words. And Piper wasn't so concerned with details anyway—Willowood had told her to pay attention to feelings. *To people's hearts.*

"We can't change people's hearts," Willowood said earlier. "But we can speak to ideas, and fan the flames of belief, even if the embers are very small."

Now, it was time to blow on the embers.

Piper gravitated toward one man in particular. He seemed like he was in charge. *A master of the seas,* she thought, imagining him on one of the big ocean-bound sailing skiffs from her stories. His heart seemed to have many questions in it, ones that wondered why so many Jujari had been killed, and others that wished he could stop more lives from being taken. He was a good man.

Sitting across from him, Piper noticed a beautiful blonde-haired Sekmit. She'd only ever met one of the feline-like species, but they fascinated her, much like the Jujari did. And, like the man, the Sekmit seemed against all the horrible things that had been done to the Jujari fleets.

Piper stretched out her feelings toward the two figures and took a deep breath. She searched for the stains of her earlier work, but—much to her surprise—she couldn't find any. The finding so shocked her that she immediately called out to Willowood.

"Grandmother?"

"Yes, child. What is it?"

"My work for Moldark—it's not in these two."

"Nor in several of the crew I've found," Willowood replied with a sense of hope in her voice. "In fact, there's very little of it in the ship at all, if I'm not mistaken."

"Why?"

Willowood took a second to reply. "I'm not sure, but perhaps your work for Moldark was not as wide-spread as you first thought."

"That would be a good thing."

"Yes, Piper. That would be a very good thing."

So Piper set to work, not undoing what had been done, but encouraging what already existed. She coaxed her life force toward the couple, urging them to embrace their doubts as legitimate concerns and not treat them as imposters. They were right to question the activities of the fleets. And, likewise, they were right to want to protect others even if it meant putting their own lives at risk. This was the way of the hero.

"I believe in you," Piper whispered. "I believe you can do great things."

Suddenly, the female Sekmit stood up and looked straight at Piper. The act so startled Piper that she leaped backward, breaking connection with both people. But Piper had done what she needed to. The Sekmit woman tilted her head and twitched her ears.

"Can she see me?" Piper asked her grandmother.

Willowood appeared beside Piper, and then looked at the woman. "They are a very sensitive species, the Sekmit. So it does not surprise me that she seems to sense you now. Go ahead— wish her well once more."

Piper drew close again. "May you succeed in all that your heart sets out to do for the good of others. May you resist evil, and may love conquer all." Then she raised her hand for no other reason than to show she meant the Sekmit no harm.

The feline-like woman raised her arm in reply and placed a paw-like hand so close to Piper's it felt like they were touching. The moment lasted only a second before the man called the woman away.

"That was beautiful," Willowood said. "Where did you learn that?"

"Learn what?"

"What you said to her."

Piper shrugged. "Momma used to say it to me. And it just felt right."

Willowood smiled. "She would be proud of you—you know that?"

"Nuh-uh. But, okay."

Willowood laughed. "Come. We should search for other ships like this one."

BY THE TIME Piper and her grandmother withdrew from the

Unity, Piper was exhausted. Speaking to people's hearts was hard work. But it was worth it—at least she hoped so.

Much to her grandmother's surprise, many ships seemed mostly unaffected by Piper's original message. Specifically, most of First Fleet and some of Second. This, Willowood said, was good news. It meant that Moldark's influence over the Republic Navy was less than Colonel Caldwell and the other leaders had feared. Hearing her grandmother's assessment also helped ease Piper's heart. She didn't want people to get hurt because of anything she did. Still, knowing that she'd helped Moldark in any way made Piper feel sick.

"Given how successful that was, I will gather the rest of Paladia Company and employ the mystics to continue what we've begun," Willowood said from her chair in the observation lounge. "We may be able to talk sense into many more, perhaps a large portion of Second Fleet, but it's hard to know for certain how compliant they will be." Then her grandmother's eyebrows closed together. "Are you sure you're all right, Piper?"

"Yes." Piper bit her lip. "I just hope it's enough to help."

"Even a little help can go a long way in salvaging the fleets. What we did may save tens of thousands of sailors."

"Not the sailors." Piper thought better of the statement. "I mean, yes, sailors. But, it's more about—I mean—"

"Magnus," Willowood said, and then seemed to remember something. "*Mr. Lieutenant* Magnus."

"Uh-huh."

Willowood smiled. "Anything we do up here helps what they're doing down there. Remember that."

"I know." Piper looked down at the blue glow of Capriana Prime. "But what if it's not enough."

"That's hard to know, isn't it."

Piper nodded. "I just feel like—"

A dark feeling seized Piper's chest, causing her to lurch forward.

"Piper," Willowood said, rising from her chair and grabbing the girl's shoulder. "What's wrong?"

The sense of dread that gripped Piper was stronger than any she'd felt before. Her vision was so blurry that she could hardly see her grandmother's eyes. "It's Mr. Lieutenant Magnus," she said. "Something's wrong."

Willowood didn't answer right away. Maybe she didn't believe Piper. Or perhaps she was searching the Unity for herself. But Piper was sure of what she felt—certain that Willowood would sense it too. Because it was horrible.

"Yes," Willowood said. "I sense it too."

"I've got to—" *Got to what?* The same panic in her dream threatened to keep Piper from breathing. "I've got to save him."

"Piper, we went over this."

"No." Piper leaned away from her grandmother's touch. "I betrayed him once. I won't do that again. Not when I know I have the power to help him."

"But you just did."

"No, I didn't." Piper stood, forcing her grandmother to sit back. "Not like I know I can. I'm going down there."

"Piper, listen to me—"

"No, grandmother. Mr. Lieutenant Magnus needs my help. Not from up here. Down there."

"My darling child," her grandmother said, lifting her hand to touch Piper's face, but Piper leaned away. A moment of silence passed between them as Willowood's eyes seemed to grow sad. "It is much too dangerous for you. What Mr. Lieutenant Magnus has chosen, he has chosen for himself, not you. And there's nothing you can do to stop that without unnecessarily putting yourself in harm's way."

"I would rather die than stand here and do nothing."

"Piper, please—"

"No, grandmother. No *pleases*. I have the power to help, and I'm going to with or without you. If you try and stop me…"

"You'll what?" There seemed to be a lot of pain in her grandmother's face.

Piper bunched her fists and felt the Unity's energy flow into them. She would never hurt her grandmother—she didn't want to hurt anyone unless they were harming others. But Piper knew she had enough power to keep people from stopping her in doing what was right. "I won't let you."

22

Magnus stepped out of the elevator and dashed for cover behind some white stone planters in the Forum Republica's Grand Plaza. The rest of the gladias followed him, as did several Marines. Paragon troopers pressed in from the east—Magnus's right— while Marines held them off from the west. While Moldark's ship had docked above Proconsul Tower, the rest of the HATs must've landed in the eastern courtyards.

"What's the plan, Lieutenant?" Blackman yelled from behind Magnus.

"To not get shot," Magnus replied over externals. "Where's the communications building?"

"Over there." Blackman pointed to the north. "Through the gardens, across the plaza."

A five-story white building with undulating exterior walls and black windows sat on the plaza's far side. First squad needed to cross a large garden in the plaza's middle, but it would provide some decent cover, which was a plus. Magnus marked the foot-path as a waypoint on the squad's HUD, noting the trees and columns, and then set the comms building as the rally point. He also told the gladias to keep chameleon mode off or risk being hit by the Marine platoons firing from the west.

"What's your plan, Magnus?" Caldwell asked, appearing in his HUD.

"Looks like you can stop production on your acting debut," Magnus replied. "As you heard, the good senator has volunteered to do it instead."

"As he should, mysticsdammit."

"Still, if we don't make it, you should keep your lipstick on."

"And it's my favorite shade too." The colonel winked at Magnus and then closed out his window.

"Keep your heads down," Magnus said to the rest of the squad. "And protect the senator."

"Rohoar does not like protecting the senator," Rohoar said.

"Then just work on protecting me," Magnus replied. "I'll do your dirty work."

"Why would Rohoar wish for Magnus to fill in his splick holes? Plus, Magnus lacks the hind legs for this work."

"Just cover him," Abimbola said to the Jujari with an irritated tone. "We are ready, Magnus."

"And Awen?" Magnus said. "I could use some extra cover."

"I've got you, Adonis. Ready when you are."

"Stand by." Magnus looked over his shoulder at Blackman. "Think your Marine detail could give us a hand?"

"They're sworn to protect me," the senator yelled, plugging his ears from the sound of the blaster fire. "Where I go, they go."

"Maybe just remind them not to shoot us in the back."

"You want them to shoot you in the back?"

Magnus shook his head emphatically. "Negative. *Not* shoot us in the back."

"Right." Blackman looked at the nearest Marine and relayed the plan to move to the comms building. "And don't shoot these guys in the back," he added at the end. The Marine acknowledged the orders with a nod, and then turned to the rest of his unit, presumably passing the orders on. "They understand," Blackman said to Magnus. "We can go."

Magnus nodded and looked back at his team. "Let's move."

ALPHA AND BRAVO TEAMS moved in a line across the plaza's southern edge, firing to the east. Blackman stayed tucked behind Magnus and Abimbola while Awen kept a Unity shield running down the line, beginning with Magnus. At first, the Paragon seemed not to pay the traversing gladias and Marines any notice. But by the time Magnus had reached a cluster of palms, the enemy had started to focus their fire.

"Two Marines down," Haze said from the end of the line.

"Make that three," said Doc.

"Shoot and move," Magnus said. "Here we go." He and Abimbola moved out from cover and headed the rest of the way to the garden's footpath. Blaster fire tore through leaves and splintered tree branches as they advanced past the perimeter. Once they were well inside the foliage, Magnus gave the order to run.

With one eye on Blackman and the other on the path ahead, Magnus followed the winding route around a pond filled with nowei fish, and then over a footbridge that crossed a stream. Ahead lay an intersection of paths that diverted to other areas of the gardens, bordered on all sides by marble columns and a circular archway system that connected the pillars' tops. Magnus was just about to step forward into the circle when several blaster rounds exploded against the column closest to his head.

"Cover right," Titus yelled, marking a spot to the east on the HUD. The gladia took cover behind trees and planters, firing into the Paragon forces making their way toward the intersection.

From Magnus's position behind the pillar, he spotted a small knoll to the southeast. It's elevated summit and ferns would provide an excellent flanking position.

"Bravo Team, break off and head up that hill," Magnus said. "Let me know when you're in position. When they are, Alpha Team, we're crossing the intersection."

Everyone acknowledged, and Magnus fired into the enemy ranks taking cover along the arcade's eastern perimeter. One unlucky trooper peeked out from behind a column. When he did, Magnus put a blaster bolt through his helmet, splitting it in two. Another trooper made a run between trees but tripped over a root in the ground. He sprawled on his chest, and Magnus fired into his midsection—penetrating the ribcage. The NOV1's power punched through the man's other side and dug a furrow in the ground, filling the air with grass and dirt.

"In position," Titus said over VNET.

"Do it," Magnus said.

The moment the flanking fire rained down from the hill, Magnus pulled Blackman into the intersection and fired on the Paragon.

"Fragger out," Titus said. Magnus saw the tiny munition move on his HUD, and then detonate behind a group of palms, flushing out three troopers. Their bodies flipped through the air —one landing in the nearby pond with a splash. The pressure from Bravo Team was just enough for Magnus to make it to the other side with Blackman still crouching behind him and Abimbola.

Once on the intersection's north side, Magnus gave the order to shift fire to the southeast and cover Bravo Team. Titus came back down the hill and told the senator's Marines to follow him. But as they crossed the middle ground, the Paragon got wise and covered against Magnus's flanking fire. Then they opened up on Bravo Team and the Marines. Without a mystic to lend them additional protection, several gladias took damage to their shields, including Titus. Magnus watched him take a hit to the hip and start limping.

"Titus," Magnus shouted, moving out to meet them.

But Titus waved him off. "We've got this, LT."

In one swift motion, Haze brought up his SMS and fired a VOD straight at a pocket of Paragon troopers. The resulting blast carved a hole in the enemy's ranks that afforded Titus just enough time to cross the intersection. Likewise, Magnus ordered Rohoar, Silk, and Doc back toward the middle to cover the gladias and Marines making a run for it.

Awen made to move as well, but Magnus stopped her. "I need you here with Bimby and me to guard the senator."

"But Titus and—"

"Blackman is our priority," Magnus said.

She sniffed. "Fine." But Magnus could tell she wasn't happy about it.

Once everyone was past the open ground, Magnus continued north through the gardens until the comms buildings filled the plaza's far side. It was a straight shot across, and, so far, no Paragon forces had gotten wise to their final destination.

"Let's move," Magnus said. "Watch our right flank and six o'clock."

The squad crossed the plaza without incident and then filed into the comms building's front doors. Magnus looked at Blackman. "Lead the way, Senator."

"Third floor," he said, pointing toward the elevators.

"No. We'll take the stairs." Magnus led the unit up a switchback set of glass stairs lit with baby-blue lighting along the edges. Servos whined as the gladias ascended. That was when Magnus noticed Blackman breathing heavily. Judging by his barrel chest and ample midsection, Magnus guessed that any dedication to sportsmanship in the senator's youth had vanished, replaced with a commitment to long hours of desk- and table-sitting.

"Now where?" Magnus said, waiting for Blackman to arrive on the third floor.

"Left," he said, taking deep breaths.

"How far?"

"You'll see—" Blackman wiped his forehead with the back of his sleeve. "You'll see a sign for Studio A. There."

Magnus followed the man's pointed finger to a wall sign that indicated an entranceway around a bend in the hall. He raced along it until he saw a set of high-density doors and stepped through when they opened. Magnus stepped into a big room with black walls. In the middle stood a collection of holo-emitters, the points of which formed the imaginary shape of a cube. Above it, LED lights of all shapes and sizes dangled from the ceiling, while inside it, three small cameras floated at head-level.

"Room clear," Magnus said over comms. A few moments later, Blackman entered, practically dragged by Abimbola. "Okay, Senator, tell us how this works."

"There's an activation console over there," Blackman said, sounding as if Magnus should have already seen it.

"That means nothing to me. Why don't you check it out."

Blackman threw his hands in the air. "No wonder you've been blackballed."

"Hey, we're saving your life here, pal," Titus said after raising his visor and pointing his weapon at Blackman. "Show some respect."

"Easy," Blackman said with his hands raised. "Not sure you want to shoot the guy who needs to order the evacuation."

"Which wouldn't be a problem if the guy had chosen to do it earlier," Titus replied.

"Stand down, Titus," Magnus said with a reassuring tone. "I'm grateful for the support, but we need him right now."

Blackman lowered his hands and pulled down on the edges of his uniform. "See?"

Titus thrust his chin out toward the senator and spit.

"Get it up and running, Blackman," Magnus said. "We don't have much time."

"Affirmative, sir," TO-96 said, appearing in Magnus's HUD. "I've tapped into the Forum Republica's security cameras and see heavy Paragon troop movement inbound on your location, entering from the south."

Magnus turned to Titus and Bimby. "We've got company in the lobby."

"We're on it," they replied, calling away everyone in Alpha and Bravo Teams but Awen.

When Magnus looked back at Blackman, the man was lazily walking toward the console. "Get a move on, pal."

Blackman waved off the remark and stood before the console. "Let's see what we have here," he said, wiggling his fingers and pulling up a holo display. It took him a few seconds to log in and then call up a broadcast menu. Magnus saw all three cameras twitch as they woke from sleep mode. Then Blackman took a moment to play with some of the menus. First, an image of a beach appeared in the cube. The senator muttered something to himself, and the image switched to a sports arena. Finally, an image from inside CENTCOM appeared.

"Looks convincing," Magnus said. "Now, let's get you in there." But Blackman was still messing with the settings. When

Magnus looked over the man's shoulder to see what was taking so long, the senator seemed to be ordering the cameras in a series of pre-programmed shot changes from multiple angles. "What the hell are you doing?" Magnus pushed him aside. "This ain't a glamour shoot."

"I'm simply making sure that—"

"Go stand in the scene," Magnus said, taking control.

"But you'll need to hit that button there."

"I know how to hit broadcast." He pointed Blackman toward the CENTCOM holo display. "Go."

Blackman squared his shoulders and walked into the scene. But he didn't face the cameras right away. Instead, he paced back and forth, talking to himself.

"Blackman," Magnus yelled. But the senator was unmoved. So Magnus racked a charge in his NOV1 and pointed the weapon at him. "If I didn't know better, I'd say you *want* this strike to hit."

"Magnus, please," Awen said, placing a hand over his weapon's barrel and forcing it down.

"You should listen to her, son. Sharing information of this scope requires more tact than you might appreciate as a buckethead."

"How's this for tact?" Magnus turned to the console and slammed his fist into the broadcast button. The camera's blinking blue ready lights changed to red. "You're on."

Blackman froze. For a split second, Magnus thought he was going to have to step in. "For the love of all mystics, would you just—"

"Citizens of Capriana and all surrounding atolls," Blackman began, speaking as smoothly as if he had days to prep for his appearance. "I am Senator Robert Malcom Blackman of the Galactic Republic Senate and Chairman of Central Command. I come to you today on behalf of the entire Republic with grave news. The city and, in fact, the planet, are under orbital threat by enemy forces. While we are working to reach a swift and peaceful resolution, the Senate and the members of Central Command have unanimously voted to order an immediate planet-wide evacuation. And, rest assured, I have successfully negotiated for the safe passage of all civilians. There is nothing to fear.

"Please be aware that we are in the process of activating the planetary defense shield. To ensure your safety, we encourage you to calmly and carefully make your way to the closest evacuation center. Take only what belongings you can carry, knowing that you will be able to return to your homes as soon as the threat level has been reduced.

"As always, we will provide continual updates on the progress of our positive negotiations with these outside forces, and we look forward to your safe return. Thank you for your patience and understanding." Blackman stepped out of the frame and walked toward the console.

Magnus was so stunned by the slippery-tongued senator that all he could do was watch in disbelief as the man stepped around Magnus and depressed the broadcast button. The live transmission ended, and the Galactic Republic logo appeared.

"I'm not sure why I shouldn't kill you right now," Magnus said.

"Why? For lying?" Blackman busied himself on the console menus. Within a few more seconds, the logo was replaced by an emergency evacuation list of procedures read by an automated voice. "Please, if the general public knew the whole truth, there'd be utter pandemonium and *no one* would get out of here alive." Blackman turned to face Magnus. "Is that what you want?"

"You're sick. You know that?"

The senator scoffed. "Save your speech, son. All of us do what we need to save lives. You do it with a blaster; I do it with words. What they don't know won't hurt them, and if they knew the truth, they'd die before the first shots were fired. So don't lecture me on morality, trooper. Just do your job and—"

Magnus slammed the butt of his weapon into the senator's forehead. The man dropped to the ground like a sack of Jorin kessel radishes. Magnus looked at Awen. "He was wearing on my soul."

"Mine too," she said.

"How we looking, Bimby?"

"We are taking heavy fire in the lobby," Abimbola replied. "This exit is compromised."

"What about the senator?" Titus asked. "He get the word out?"

"He did," Magnus said. "And now he's—taking a little break. Tell those Marines they can come get him when they're ready."

"Hard copy," Titus replied.

"Hey, 'Six. You got any alternate escape routes that don't put us in the path of Paragon or Repub troopers?"

"As a matter of fact, I do, sir," TO-96 replied. "The Forum

Republic boasts a surprising amount of architectural ingenuity which lends itself to—"

"Remember how I said you could give me a history lesson later?"

"Of course, sir. Save this for that time?"

"If you don't mind."

"Not at all, sir."

"Great." Magnus smiled. "What's the escape route?"

"Forwarding to your HUD now, sir."

"Thanks, 'Six." As soon as the waypoints populated, Magnus ordered the gladias to fall back, and then he moved toward the hallway.

"Sir," TO-96 said. "The colonel and I must insist you get moving. The Paragon is surrounding the building."

"About that," Titus said, appearing on the channel."

"Scary looking guy's making his way across the plaza toward our location."

Magnus slowed. "Moldark? Toward the comms building?"

"He must know we're here," Awen said. "He wants revenge. Or maybe he thinks we have Piper."

"Either way, we're not sticking around long enough to find out."

23

"Block all the exits," Moldark said to Captain Yaeger. "No one leaves."

"Right away, my lord," Yaeger replied.

The trooper turned and began giving orders as Moldark stared down into the Senate Chamber's bowl-like amphitheater. Rings of glossy black consoles punctuated with red leather chairs descended a dozen tiers down to a central dais. In the background, Yaeger dispatched the few remaining security sentries with blaster fire that made the hall's congregation cower. The room was half-full, most likely an emergency session. But the odds favored that Moldark would find the senatorial contingent of traitors here. And he *would* find them—every last one of them. He would hunt them down and stare into their impudent eyes as they begged him for their lives.

"My fair senators of the Galactic Republic," Moldark said

from atop an aisle. He took the first few steps and studied the retreating officials as he descended. "Now that I have your attention—"

"What's the meaning of this?" someone asked from the dais.

Moldark gazed at the woman who spoke—middle-aged, pale, and hints of gray in her hair. "An excellent question, madame senator. I'd like to offer you a deal, or rather, an ultimatum."

"You are in no place to offer anything."

"Oh, but I think I am." Moldark stretched out his ethereal hand and latched onto her soul. The woman screamed as he hoisted her half a meter off the dais. The audience reacted with shouts, backing away from Moldark and distancing themselves from the woman. "I'm looking for certain traitors among you."

"Stop this madness," another senator shouted. He stepped in between Moldark and the woman.

"Noble, but stupid," Moldark said. He added the man to his feeding. His body spasmed as Moldark sucked his life out in a matter of seconds, leaving his ashen corpse to crash upon the floor in a dust heap. This brought about even more demonstrative reactions in the room as senators and their staffers clamored toward the exits.

Moldark continued his steady advance toward the woman, holding her hostage in suspended agony. But he needed her, so he released his hold. The woman fell to her knees, gasping for breath.

"As I was saying, I am only looking for six traitors." When the woman didn't answer, still preoccupied with the simple task of breathing, Moldark continued. As he approached the bottom floor, he lifted his arms and turned about. "Senators Miller, Ko-Li, Long, Jinterro, Yan Andar, and Blackman. Are you here?"

The amphitheater grew quiet save for whispers and sniffles. Moldark turned back to the woman and strode up the dais to meet her. He knelt and stroked the back of her head with his gloved hand. "Madame Senator, I will release everyone in this room so long as you point me toward the traitors I mentioned."

She coughed and then steadied herself on the carpeted floor. But she was still gasping too much to speak.

"You're wasting my time." Moldark hoisted her aloft on an invisible arm—her body shaking for all to see. "I will kill her." He spoke loud enough for the whole room to hear. "Or you may produce the individuals I specified. Do so, and the rest of you may depart. It is that simple."

"I am Senator Jinterro," replied a woman in her early sixties, stepping out from a group near a side exit. She was thinner than Moldark remembered.

"You see now?" Moldark looked around the amphitheater. "That wasn't so hard. And the others?" But no one else spoke. So Moldark yanked a measure of life from the woman. She shrieked.

"Stop it," yelled a younger man from his seat in the third tier. "I am Ko-Li. Release her."

"Not until I have the others, Senator."

Ko-Li raised his chin, took a deep breath, and pointed to various spots around the room. "Miller, Long, and Yan Andar."

"Coward," one of the other senators yelled.

But Moldark grinned. "You see? That wasn't so difficult, was it? However, I am still waiting on Senator Blackman. Which means none of you are going to walk out of here."

"He's in the communications building," said one of the Nine. *Miller*, if Moldark remembered correctly.

"Oh? And how can you be so sure?" Moldark asked.

Miller swiped a finger across a console, and a holo feed appeared. It was Senator Blackman. "He's addressing the planet from inside the communications building."

"And this is happening right now?" Moldark asked, studying the broadcast.

"Yes. It's live."

Just hearing Blackman say the word evacuation made Moldark furious. *They mustn't be allowed to escape*, he thought. *None of them must be allowed to retreat and live another day—not one.*

"Captain Yaeger," Moldark said. "Release them."

Yaeger nodded and ordered the doors open. Anxious senators and staff hurried up the aisles and out the doors. Moldark even made good on his word to the chairwoman on the dais. Finally, all that remained were Miller, Ko-Li, Long, Jinterro, and Yan Andar.

"Senators." Moldark squeezed his gloves, and their squeaky sound echoed around the amphitheater. "So good of you to join me."

"You'll never get away with this, Kane," Yan Andar said, pointing his blue-skinned finger at Moldark.

"Kane?" Moldark chuckled. "Kane's been dead for a while now, Senator."

Yan Andar hesitated, then withdrew his finger. But he wasn't finished. "Do you honestly think you can charge into the Forum Republica's Senate Chamber, hold us hostage, and not expect for there to be repercussions?"

Moldark *tsk'd* the man three times. "Senator, I'm very disappointed with you. And yet, you biologics are all the same. Always basing your power on that which you derive from the anxieties of the masses. How easy it is to undo you."

"We demand that you—"

Moldark seized Yan Andar's soul with an outstretched hand. "You demand nothing." The other senators stepped away. Moldark could smell their fear.

"What do you want?" Jinterro asked.

"What an appropriate question, Senator Jinterro." He examined each of the senators until their eyes darted away. Then, with low-toned exact words, he said, "I want to remember the looks on your faces as you witness the end of your insignificant lives."

"THE BUILDING IS RIGHT UP THERE, my lord," Captain Yaeger said, pointing toward a structure along the plaza's north end. "We have them surrounded."

"Them?" Moldark asked.

"Yes, my lord. The senator is being protected by a contingent of Marines and some cloaked combatants. We believe they're the same ones we encountered upon our arrival atop Proconsul Tower."

Moldark sneered. "The rebels."

"We believe so, yes, my lord."

Moldark quickened his pace, eager to terminate Blackman. From there, he would dive into CENTCOM and find the remaining three Circle of Nine members: Admiral Inquin and Generals Veer Quince and McCormick. And, with any luck, he'd take some of the rebels hostage then bleed them for stealing his granddaughter. *No*, Moldark snapped at Kane's thoughts. *She is not my granddaughter. She is merely a girl.*

One of Yaeger's companies assaulted the building's front entrance with a barrage of blaster fire. But most of it seemed to be dispersed by some sort of energy shield—no doubt the work of a mystic. The defenders retaliated from within, cutting into Yaeger's forces with heavy weapons fire. But there were more than just Republic blasters—there were Novian weapons. Moldark was sure of it. Ever since hearing the distinct whine on the *Labyrinth*, nightmares from his past gnawed at the edges of his thought—the sounds of his wailing ancestors mixed with mining blasts as his people were ripped from their homes.

"Give the order to charge," Moldark said. "All sides."

"But, my lord, there's—"

"Charge, Captain. Or you forfeit your life."

Yaeger squared his shoulders, gave Moldark a quick nod, and then began motioning his men forward. However, several of Yaeger's subordinates seemed to hesitate. "What is it, Captain Yaeger?"

"Nothing, my lord."

"Untrue." Moldark laid the mere wisp of a tendril on the

man's soul, causing him to freeze in place. "I will only ask again once, Captain. Is there a problem?"

"Some of the men—" Yaeger choked against the pressure closing around his chest and neck. "Some don't want to advance."

"Of course they don't. They're cowards. Who?"

But Yaeger was unable to reply, gagging.

"Never mind." Moldark released Yaeger and sought out three of the Captain's subordinates. He hoisted all three Paragon Marines off their feet, ripped their life force from their miserable bodies, and dashed their ashes against the ground. He assumed the clattering armor might have the desired effect. "Order them again."

"Yes, my lord." Yaeger reissued the command and his Paragon Marines charged the enemy—obviously more afraid of the dark lord than of the rebel scum who cowered in the comms building. *The miserable wretches.*

More reinforcements joined the advance, and Moldark felt a growing confidence that, this time, he had the enemy. He would repay them for their assault on his ship and for taking the child. They would suffer, and he would enjoy devouring each of their meaningless lives to satiate his appetite.

At the same time, however, Moldark sensed something cold— as if a dark cloud passed over the sun. Kane's body shivered, which annoyed Moldark. But this was more than a physical sensation. The dark cloud had a presence—perhaps even a personality. He had felt it once before too, on Worru.

Moldark spun to his right, then his left.

"Is everything all right, my lord?" Yaeger asked.

"Yes," Moldark said, snapping his head back to the battle.

"We're taking heavy fire," Titus said.

Magnus and Awen arrived at the third floor's balcony and looked down into the lobby as dozens of windowpanes exploded. Alpha and Bravo Teams worked with the Marines to defend the structure's main entrance, while outside at least two platoons of Paragon troopers advanced on the comms building. A dark figure in a black Repub Navy officer's cape stood further out, hands on his hips.

"I need options, buddy," Magnus said to TO-96.

"I'm afraid there aren't many, sir. The building is surrounded. I estimate that it is only a matter of time before they close in to exterminate you."

"You're in a kill box, son," Caldwell said. "Best to make like a Lorquidian pink bellied newt and scoot."

"Hey, Azie," Magnus said. "Any chance you have more of those BATRIGs on hand?"

"While there are several in production, I do have one more ready for immediate deployment," Azelon replied.

"What are the chances you can put it down inside the plaza—say, between Moldark and us."

"I have calculated landing accuracy to plus or minus ten meters, sir."

"Extra points if you drop it on Moldark's head," Abimbola added.

Magnus smiled. "Send it, Azie."

"BATRIG deployed," Azelon replied. "ETA in nine minutes, eighteen seconds."

Magnus marked the time with a second counter in his HUD. "Doc, Haze, I need you to protect our rear. LIMKIT4 mines in ground floor doorways, improvise with your remaining VODs. Go." Doc and Haze acknowledged and peeled out of the lobby.

"Everyone else, thin those ranks. And just before that crate lands, I want you behind cover. It's gonna make one hell of an entry." Magnus turned to Awen "You're up."

Awen slid past Magnus and grabbed the railing. A moment later, a semi-translucent Unity shield appeared where the lobby windows had been. The wall absorbed most of the enemy blaster fire, but the Paragon's assault was so intense that some rounds still made it through. Without Nídira's help, it seemed there was only so much Awen could do.

"Zoll, do you copy?" Magnus asked over VNET.

"Here, LT," Zoll replied.

"What's your position?"

"Looks like we're still sixty-four klicks out from Simlia atoll."

Magnus frowned. "I want you back here."

"Change of plan?"

"Affirmative. Can you manage it?"

"Of course. Why? You got some heat?"

Magnus watched the Paragon concentrate fire on a single spot in Awen's shield, apparently trying to bore a hole through it.

"We're not gonna have time to make two extractions, and we need evac sooner than you."

"Copy that. Just give us a waypoint."

"Stand by." Magnus brought up his topo map and pinged Azelon again. "Azie, how close can you get that shuttle to us?"

"Assuming the defense cannons have been deactivated, given the hundreds of civilian ships attempting to leave the surface, I'd say the closest safe LZ is located to your east, on Moore's Beach. You risk little interference with emergency flight paths and minimal detection from the Republic's security forces. Though, given the city's current threat level, I doubt resistance will be much concern for you."

"It's not the Repub I'm worried about." Magnus examined the beach and the bay it enclosed. "Sounds good. Mark it." A new map marker appeared four klicks to the east. Magnus brought Zoll up again. "You seeing that?"

"Hard copy. We're on our way."

"See you soon."

MAGNUS HAD LEFT Awen to her Unity-wielding several minutes earlier and joined the squad firing into the Paragon ranks. Alpha and Bravo Teams held the Paragon outside the comms building for longer than he expected. But another platoon had been added to the enemy's ranks as they pressed toward the comms building, with Moldark still lingering in the background. At one point, some of the Paragon Marines seemed to refuse orders, and the dark lord began using his otherworldly powers to thwart the advance. Magnus saw three enemy troopers rise into the air, shake, and then drop back down in puffs of gray ash.

"Anyone else see that?" Titus said.

"No way he's doing that crazy splick to us," Doc replied.

"Hard copy," Magnus said. "Whatever we do, we cannot let Moldark get a bead on us. Everyone understand?" The unit acknowledged and continued to fire on the enemy.

Magnus worked to keep Moldark's troops from boring a hole in Awen's shield. He thinned out anyone who lent their firepower to the task, knowing that a breach in the mystic's defense could spell disaster for the gladias. A few of the senator's Marines picked up what Magnus was doing and helped reduce the enemy's focused efforts even further. Magnus drained a whole clip by taking out nine troopers with an MTFE shot. But then he scrambled to retrieve two half-spent energy mags from downed Marines to replenish his weapon, and maglocked two more to his hip.

Two explosions rocked the back half of the building—one after the other. "That you, boys?" Magnus asked Doc and Haze.

"Did we wake you up?" Doc asked. "Sorry about that."

Magnus smiled. "I love the smell of limp mines in the morning."

"You'll also be pleased to hear that those LIMKITs not only took out a dozen Paragon troopers but made these entryways all but impassable."

So, maybe not *everything* was going bad. "Nice work, gladias. Get back here as soon as you can. We could use your firepower."

Doc acknowledged the order and signed off. Then Magnus checked his timer on the BATRIG. "Just gotta hold 'em for another fifty seconds, Granther Company."

The hope of seeing another of Azelon's mechs in action seemed to bolster the unit's fire effectiveness—or at least their fire rate. Paragon troopers fell to the NOV1s left and right. But no matter how hard Magnus's gladias fought, the enemy seemed to have more reinforcements to take their place.

Magnus brought up the squad channel. "At the ten-second mark, I want VODs going out the front. Then take cover as far inside the building as you can. Pull those Marines with you too. As soon as you feel the shockwave pass, we're back here. I need your cover fire until I get inside the crate. Copy?" Green icons went down the chat window.

"Delivery inbound in twenty seconds," Azelon said as if Magnus was getting a bouquet delivered to his house.

"You're a peach, Azie," Magnus replied.

"A peach, sir?"

Then to the squad, he said, "Here we go. Ten-second mark in five, four, three, two, one."

The words "fragger out" went out over the channel as detonators sailed through Awen's shield and then bounced along the plaza's stone. The gladias retreated into the structure, pulling as many Marines with them as they could. Magnus strong-armed two men, yelling at them over his external speakers. "Take cover!" The men didn't waste any time following Magnus through a secondary set of doors and ducking behind a load-bearing stone wall.

First came the VOD detonations, all of which activated the audio dampening feature in Magnus's helmet. He felt the ground tremor under his boots. But it was nothing compared to what happened next.

If the crate made a sound when it crashed through the windowplex ceiling of the Forum Republica's central plaza, Magnus didn't hear it—not because the action wasn't loud, but because the crate traveled so fast that its ground impact overpowered any other sound. The explosion blew in the building's front wall and fired high-speed projectile debris through the secondary rooms. Magnus watched a Marine get cut in half when a part of a metal window frame speared him through the back. Two other Marines flipped head over heels as the shockwave's force hurled them into a cluster of desks. The power even made Magnus stumble and catch himself against the ground with an outstretched hand. But once the blast was over, Magnus was on his feet and running into the lobby.

"Covering fire," he said, crossing the entryway and heading for the front doors. A few beats later, the rest of the gladias started sending blaster bolts to each side of Magnus as he charged for the giant crate. The container sat half a meter in the stone, still smoking from its orbital entry. He opened the access panel as before, shot inside like an albino dwarf chimp chased by a Venetian mawslip, and climbed into the cockpit. He was barely situated when enemy rounds started plinking against the exterior.

"How we looking out there?" Magnus asked his team leaders.

"The crate knocked them back," Abimbola said. "Very nice work."

"Most survived," Titus said. "And I think you really pissed off Moldark."

"Remind me to send him flowers," Magnus replied as he brought the mech to life.

"Yes." Abimbola laughed. "For his funeral."

Magnus flexed his arms, and the crate's walls flew out. The Paragon troopers closest to him dove for cover and stopped firing. "You want some of this?" Magnus roared over externals. The enemy stepped back again. "That's what I thought."

Magnus swung up both arm-mounted weapons—his GU90M on his right and the RTD10 on his left. Then he watched as his biotech interface acquired two dozen targets and suggested fire priority. "See ya," he said, and then commanded the BATRIG to fire.

The GU90M rattled his suit as it tore into enemy armor, riddling them with thousands of blaster holes. The Paragon Marines attempted to return fire, but their aim was wild—especially as the buddies on their left and right fell to Magnus's withering fire.

To his left, the torrent disruptor detonated three troopers at once, showering other combatants in the immediate proximity with pureed flesh. Troopers slipped on the gore as they tried to duck the BATRIG's next round, but they were unable to escape Magnus's lethal gaze. He swept the foreground with GU90M fire, raking the ranks relentlessly.

Magnus wasn't without his damage, however, as several blaster rounds did manage to strike his mech. But the beast's armor plating absorbed the energy, and no critical systems took even the slightest damage.

The troopers seemed to realize their fire was ineffective against the BATRIG, so they retreated—and made way for Recon Marines carrying three RAB25s. The 25mm rotary action blaster was a holdover from the last century but had yet to be replaced. Handheld and extremely versatile for combatting both short- and long-range targets, the rotating multi-barrel, hip-fired weapon could chew through armor like it was wood.

Magnus aimed down the widening gap between Paragon phalanxes and targeted the three RAB-wielding troopers. He fired on the first man with his GU90M and shredded him. But the second two troopers sprayed Magnus before he could react. Hundreds of blaster bolts drilled his chest plate in less than a second.

System alerts chimed in Magnus's head before a bright light appeared a meter in front of him. It was a Unity shield, absorbing the blistering blaster attack. It wouldn't last long, Magnus knew. But it didn't need to. With the precious few seconds Awen's defense bought him, Magnus aimed and fired his RTD10, blowing the two Marines to smithereens. Then he turned both arm-mounted weapons on the two remaining Paragon groups and fired, pushing them back.

"Someone must've ordered a retreat," Titus said.

"No doubt." Magnus could hear the high-pitched whine of Silk's sniper fire through her helmet's mic. "Look at those bastards run!"

"Everyone up and out of there," Magnus ordered, taking

steps toward the fleeing enemy. He searched the group for Moldark, but the dark lord was gone. Magnus thought maybe the crate's concussion did him in—after all, the man wasn't wearing any armor. *But today hasn't been my lucky day*, Magnus thought to himself. *And no reason for it to change now.* More likely, Moldark suspected something bad was in the crate and took cover, knowing not even his otherworldly manipulations could thwart it. At least, that's what Magnus imagined the freak thinking.

24

Two explosions blew out the comms building's side and rear, filling the air above the plaza with dust clouds. Increased blaster fire poured from the structure, as if the rebels were reinvigorated by thwarting the Paragon's backdoor attempt. "More," Moldark roared at Yaeger. "Fire more!"

A second wave of explosions punched holes in the Paragon's front lines as the rebels tossed VODs from the building's lobby. But Moldark smiled at the volley, seeing it as sign that the enemy was growing more desperate. He had them.

"Don't just stand there, Captain," Moldark seethed. "Get in there!"

Yaeger stepped toward the battle line, only to be blasted off his feet. Moldark, too, flew backward, struck by a shockwave. Then his back slammed into the marble floor, and he slid until he hit a raised planter. Moldark blinked, caught his breath, and regained his feet. When he looked back toward the comms building, he saw a large cargo crate standing on its end. A human trooper in Novian-style armor raced toward it then disappeared within a hatch.

"Open fire," Moldark roared. At first, nothing happened. So Moldark repeated the order until blaster shots pinged off the crate. But the armored container was impervious to blaster fire. Moldark was too far away to latch onto whoever was inside, so he ran forward. Suddenly, the crate's walls fell away to reveal a mechanized battle system reminiscent of Novian ones Moldark had seen before. Which meant he knew what the weapon was capable of, and he was not prepared to face it personally.

Moldark stopped running and watched as his troopers made way for three RAB gunners. The men's weapons wound up and then spat bright torrents of bolts at the mech. They drilled the chest for only a moment before an energy shield appeared, sparing the pilot from certain death. The mech retaliated with both weapons, quickly liquifying the three heavy gunners before turning his firepower on the rest of Captain Yaeger's company.

The dark lord cursed as he stepped out of the line of fire. Moldark's forces were not equipped to take on a mech. And at this rate, he wouldn't be able to kill Blackman or the generals either. He watched in frustration as the rebels emerged from the comms building and cloaked their armor. *This is all their fault,* Moldark said to himself, seething inside. *And the true blood child.*

Of course, there were other ways to terminate the enemy, even if they weren't as satisfying. But he was running out of options—a fact that he loathed.

"Admiral Brighton," Moldark said over comms as he turned away from the battle.

"Yes, my lord," Brighton replied.

"Inform Captain Ellis that I am returning to my shuttle."

"Right away."

Blaster fire assailed Moldark's front lines as the enemy and their mech moved toward an exit. Likewise, the dark lord headed across the plaza toward Proconsul Tower's elevators. With each step he grew more furious. "One more thing, Brighton."

"Of course, my lord."

Two stray blaster rounds tore through Moldark's cape while a third struck him in the shoulder blade. But the dark lord's pace didn't slow. "Execute Article 99."

"THIS WAY," Abimbola said, leading the unit around the plaza to the southeast along TO-96's waypoints. The path led Alpha and Bravo Teams behind the advancing Paragon troops and out the complex's east side.

"Not you," Titus said. He was speaking to the senator's Marine element over externals, pointing back toward the bulk of the Repub's defensive line along the plaza's west end. "Go on, get." He flicked his hand at them like he was scolding a dog. But then Titus took on a melancholy tone, like he was playing a part in a low budget holo film. "Go back to your home. You don't belong to me. Just go."

Magnus chuckled. "You done yet?"

"They grow up so fast."

"You humans have many problems," Rohoar said.

"Ain't that the truth." Magnus gave the order to activate chameleon mode since they weren't working with friendlies. Then he pivoted right, keeping his weapons covering their six as his squad advanced around the plaza's perimeter. "Let's pick up the pace, Granthers. We haven't got all day."

"You heard the man," Abimbola replied, running faster.

The gladias followed the long-legged Miblimbian while Magnus fended off the Paragon troopers. But the bulk of Moldark's forces seemed more preoccupied with hammering the Repub's line than pursuing the gladias. Magnus wondered, yet again, why the Paragon leader had opted for this ground invasion when he could have destroyed the entire city from above.

As the gladias reached the plaza's east entrance, Magnus noticed the heavy transports waiting outside. Just as he'd suspected earlier—based on trooper movement—this was the Paragon's LZ.

"Light resistance expected ahead," Magnus said. "Keep your eyes up." Then he had another idea. "Anyone got any VODs left?"

Several gladias responded affirmatively. Doc even said he had one last LIMKIT4.

"Good. Take out any loadmasters still defending the HATs, and then toss your ordnance in the transports. If we're not gonna stick around to help those Marines, we might as well make leaving a pain in the ass for Moldark."

"Isn't his ship atop Proconsul Tower, though?" Awen asked.

Magnus cursed. "How'd I forget about that?"

"You've got a few things on your mind right now." She patted his shoulder. "Let's do this."

Magnus led the way, tearing a hole through the entryway with two VWMs from his back. Then he strode into the flames and emerged from the capital complex with ten HATs idling in an exterior plaza. "Light 'em up."

He fired on the first two while simultaneously launching one of three remaining VWMs into a third. The loadmasters for each transport dove for cover—two outside of their respective shuttles, and one inside. But it didn't matter. All their efforts were wasted as Magnus's assault ruptured fuel cells and drive cores, blowing the ships sky-high. Deep black plumes of smoke billowed into the morning air as fragments of the wreckage pelted the ground.

Abimbola led Alpha Team to the left while Titus motioned Bravo Team to the right. Together, both units popped fraggers, and Doc threw his LIMKIT4 like an old satchel charge. The explosives created a multi-beat roar as each weapon exploded, one after the other. Cargo bays burst. Wings flew off. Cockpits shattered. Even down to the pilots who tried to crawl away, Magnus's squad left no survivors.

Magnus continued through the maelstrom's center, marking himself as the next waypoint for the teams. On the far side of the open ground with the exploding ships, a street ran north and south—one filled, not just with early morning traffic, but with thousands upon thousands of pedestrians fighting to get off the planet.

"So much for not creating pandemonium," Magnus said.

But Titus thumbed over his shoulder. "Yeah, I don't think we helped much." As if on cue, another fuel cell detonated, casting the street in an orange glow. Several people screamed, hugging loved ones close and veering away from the plaza.

"I think deactivating chameleon mode will let us move through the city better," Dutch said. "People might be more prone to stepping aside if they see us coming."

"It's not a problem for Rohoar," the Jujari said. "Rohoar has stepped on people before without feelings."

"These are the ones we are trying to save, Scruffy," Magnus said. "Remember?"

"They all look the same to Rohoar."

"Fair enough." Magnus chuckled. "Let's go full visual, as per Dutch's suggestion. Stay low. Move fast. Should be clear sailing from here."

FIRST SQUAD CROSSED the four klicks of urban chaos in much less time than Magnus expected. Despite the mad civilian rush to find transportation, people were still people and made way for things bigger and louder than themselves. It took only a few warning shots aimed skyward to clear some of the thickest intersections, but otherwise, the gladia's route was unobstructed. Additionally, there were no substantial threats from city police, who probably couldn't tell a Novian gladia from a Repub bucket given the stress they were under.

When Magnus finally crossed the main island's eastern

boardwalk and ventured into the sand, Zoll stood beside a sea skimmer, along with Charlie, Delta, and Echo Teams. There was even one new face that Magnus didn't recognize—until he remembered the framed pictures inside the sea skimmer rental hut. But she would wait. It was Awen who caught his eye next.

She took off running toward the shore as two people ran from Zoll's ranks to meet her. Then Awen pulled off her helmet, dropped it in the sand, and threw her arms around the two people that Magnus guessed were her parents. There wasn't the best light to see by, but the two dau Lothliniums certainly looked Elonian—like he imagined Awen's parents might appear. They embraced several times, holding each other's faces, as Awen consoled them and checked them over.

"Mr. and Mrs. dau Lothlinium?" Magnus said as he drew near, clomping through the sand in his BATRIG.

"Mom? Dad?" Awen said. She pulled away from them and looked up at Magnus. "I'd like you to meet Adonis."

Without thinking, he waved the GU90M at them. Balin and Giyel both seemed horrified. They winced and pulled Awen toward them.

Magnus tried to think of some way to recover the moment, but it was gone. *Nice first impression, Adonis,* he told himself. "Pleased to meet you both."

Awen's father raised a tentative hand in reply, and Giyel offered a weak smile.

"Mr. and Mrs. dau Lothlinium, I'm so sorry to break this up," Magnus said. "But we can continue the reunion on the *Spire*. For now, we've got—"

"Is your fearless leader the one in the big toy?" the woman next to Zoll said. Even from some thirty meters out, Magnus could hear her voice clear as day.

Zoll nodded. "He has a thing for fun splick."

"No kidding," she replied as she walked around the Elonians and toward Magnus. "Bastard stole almost a dozen skimmers from the west side." She pulled a blaster pistol from her waistband and pointed it at Magnus. "You have some nerve, whoever you are."

"She does know you're in a BATRIG, right?" Titus asked.

Magnus raised his eyebrows. "Apparently that doesn't seem to—"

A blaster round bounced off his shoulder plate.

"What the hell, lady?" Magnus said over externals.

"What the hell, me? No, what the hell, you! *You're* the damn fool who ripped me off."

Magnus raised his arms as if to plead his case, but the woman shot both of them in quick succession. *So, she's good with a blaster*, Magnus noted. The rounds did little more than spray some sparks in his face. But the woman's assertiveness was formidable. "Listen, I don't know who you are or—"

"My name's on the damned hut, bucketheaded mech brain. *And* on the side of every skimmer I own. What do you mean, you don't know who I am?"

"Jules," Magnus said.

She threw her hands up in the air and turned around as if addressing a stadium full of people. "By mystics, the little boy's got smarts!"

"Listen, Jules," Magnus said, trying his best to soften his tone. "We already planned on reimbursing you for—"

"Your man Zoll over there has agreed to pay me three times their value."

"Three?" Magnus looked to Zoll.

"Sorry, LT. But she drove a hard bargain, and we had some Repub heat."

"I guess three times it is," Magnus said, though he wasn't sure where they were going to get all the credits. Maybe Abimbola could pay her in poker chips.

"*And* a free pass to wherever you're going," Jules said.

"Now hold on a second, lady."

"Jules," she said, correcting him.

"She did the same thing with me," Zoll added over comms. "Pain in the ass."

"We're not taking you anywhere," Magnus said.

"Like hell, you're not. You think I wanna hang around here after all the crazy splick going on? Plus, you really think I trust you people to pay me once you're off-planet? Uh uh, no way."

"I hate to break up this enchanting conversation, sir," TO-96 said.

"Oh, by all means, please do," Magnus replied, turning from Jules.

"Azelon's shuttle will be landing at your location in ninety seconds."

"You're a god, 'Six," Magnus said. "I might just kiss both you bots when we get back to the *Spire*."

"That won't be necessary, sir."

"I wouldn't mind," Azelon said. Magnus could have sworn he heard every head in Granther Company turn. Azelon seemed to discern a look from TO-96 and then looked off-camera at him. "I'm detecting hostility from you, TO-96. Is there something we need to discuss?"

"Can you two baskets of digital hormones keep it in your metal knickers for one damn minute?" Caldwell said. He looked at Magnus, and the colonel's face grew grim. "Adonis, sensors are picking up a significant power increase in Third Fleet's weapons systems."

Magnus noticed a ship streak across the sky much faster than any civilian transport was permitted to travel. Granted, this was an emergency. Still, the ship was the quickest object in the sky. "Moldark," he whispered.

Caldwell spat toward his boots. "If I didn't know better, those ships are either fixing to play a planetary game of spank your momma, or they're prepping to—"

"Fire on the city," Magnus said.

Caldwell nodded.

How had it come to this?

For some reason, Magnus felt sure his team would be able to raise the PDS and save the planet. Even when all three attempts failed, he thought something would come through for them in the end. After all, this wasn't about saving the Gladio Umbra, or even a valued member of their team like Piper. This was about keeping billions of people from harm. Surely the cosmos favored their side.

"Magnus?" Caldwell's voice snapped Magnus from his thoughts. "Get aboard as soon as that ship touches down."

"There's got to be another way," Magnus said.

"Son, you tried. We all tried." Caldwell pulled his cigar from his mouth. "Some days, you gotta know when to initiate a tactical retreat. And this is one of those days."

"No, Colonel." Magnus chewed on his lower lip. "We're not quitting."

"Dammit, Magnus!"

But Magnus closed the channel and turned back to face the city. As soon as he did, six Rhino-class armored personnel carriers emerged from the avenue Magnus had taken from the capital complex.

"APCs," Dutch shouted, raising her weapon. Everyone else turned and raised their NOV1s too. But the vehicles weren't firing on them.

Not yet, anyway, Magnus thought. "Hold your fire," he shouted. "Activate chameleon mode." The enemy could track the gladias because of their movement in the sand and through IR sensors. Still, Magnus figured his team needed every advantage they could muster in such an indefensible position. "Keep the civilians covered up."

"What about you, LT?" Zoll asked, no doubt referring to why Magnus hadn't cloaked his mech yet.

"I'm staying visible in case these bastards wanna chat."

"And if they don't?"

Magnus looked at Zoll. "That's what I have you for."

"La-raah," Zoll replied.

As APCs got closer, Magnus couldn't tell if the units were the answer to his prayers or the executioner come to put him out of his misery. Either way, these Rhinos were about to change the game.

The vehicles slowed, and still, they kept from firing. Magnus felt sure that if they were Paragon troop carriers, Granther Company would be under attack. Which meant they were Republic. Perhaps this was a member of CENTCOM coming to tell them the PDS was going up. Or maybe that the fleets were back under Republic control. Magnus was up for any good news.

Or it's Blackman, Magnus thought, imagining the senator double-crossing them.

Just then, all six APCs opened their port, starboard, and aft ramps, and released two Marine fire teams each. They formed a semi-circle around Magnus's unit, confining them to the water's edge, weapons raised. With the sound of the waves crashing behind him, Magnus waited for someone in authority to emerge from one of the Rhinos.

The large hatch above the driver's cockpit popped open on the centermost APC. Then hydraulics flipped the lid back until a fat face emerged, illuminated by the interior lights.

25

"COMMODORE," General Lovell said, hailing Seaman on the bridge from his unit's headquarters within the *Solera Fortuna*. "My team is headed toward the rebel forces east of the capital district. They're reporting heavy weapons fire, and IFF shows one Gerald Bosworth, a Galactic Republic Ambassador, in the mix. Are you aware of his involvement?"

"Negative," Seaman replied. "That said, please advise your units to get away from the city. An LO9D strike from the *Labyrinth* is imminent, and several other ships in his fleet are diverting power to weapons."

Lovell's face froze.

For a split second, Seaman thought there was a transmission glitch. "General?"

"I understand," Lovell replied, snapping out of his trance.

"You don't think that Moldark will actually fire on the planet, do you?"

Seaman frowned. "I do."

"Mystics, help us," Lovell whispered.

Seaman nodded at the sentiment. "Bring those Marines back and prepare your divisions for ship assault, as previously discussed."

"We'll be ready. Lovell out."

Seaman turned to DiAntora. She inclined her head as if in acknowledgment of what was to come. "The captains are with us," she said in an assuring tone. "Every one of them."

"What about Second Fleet?"

DiAntora's eyes narrowed. "Admiral Lin Phaq is still ignoring our hails, as are all his captains." She took a deep breath. "We tried."

Seaman could do what needed to be done without Second Fleet, but Lin Phaq's help would go a long way in stopping Moldark from annihilating the planet. "Then it's time we get this done. Open the fleet-wide channel."

DiAntora looked at the comms officer.

"Right away, Captain," replied the officer.

As soon as Seaman saw his face in the main holo, he began. "Attention all personnel of the Republic Navy's First Fleet. This is Commodore David Seaman aboard the *Solera Fortuna*. All hands, battle stations. I repeat, all hands, battle stations. This is not a drill.

"Third Fleet, under the command of Admiral Kane, also known as Moldark, has ordered all ships in all fleets to stand ready to implement Article 99 against Capriana Prime. That is not an order we will carry out. Moreover, it is an order we will resist with force.

"I am ordering a full-scale assault on any ship that engages in hostile activity against Capriana Prime. Target weapons systems and engines before life support and communications. I want these ships disabled with minimal casualties. But we will destroy them if necessary. Marine divisions are awaiting orders to board and retake ships as able. Talon squadrons are standing by. Command attack authorization level alpha. I repeat, this is an alpha-level command attack authorization. Mystics helps us all. Commodore out."

Seaman stared at a man twice his years in the holo display before the transmission ended and the screen went blank. There was no precedent for what he was about to do—for what any of them were about to do. But then again, no commander had ever issued an Article 99 against Capriana Prime or any other planet in the quadrant. It was a measure saved for unanimous senatorial approval during extreme and highly specific wartime scenarios. Some argued it wasn't needed at all and fought vigilantly to have the article banned. But, as with most governments, once a measure was on the books, it was tough—if not impossible—to have it removed. Bureaucratic ink had a way of sinking into the desk that laws were signed on.

"Captain," the sensors officer said. She was a young female Nuromin named Teloni. "The *Labyrinth's* forward LO9D cannon is fully charged and ready to fire."

Seaman clasped his hands behind his back as an image of

Moldark's Super Dreadnaught filled the holo display. He knew this decision was coming: Issue a preemptive strike or wait for Capriana to take the first hit? One meant instigating a multi-fleet conflict, while the other meant hundreds of thousands of civilian lives lost. In the end, however, Seaman knew which he would choose. He was paid to give his life—civilians weren't.

Blaster fire would be the quickest option for disabling the *Labyrinth's* forward LO9D cannon. But Seaman knew Moldark's shields would be up, which would stop the *Fortuna's* blaster rounds —but not guided ordnance. "Take out that cannon, Captain. Fire torpedoes."

"Aye-aye, Commodore," DiAntora replied. "Weapons, target that LO9D with torpedoes, three birds."

"Target acquired, Captain," the weapons officer said.

"Fire."

Three small icons appeared on the fleet map as the torpedoes streaked away from the *Fortuna*. They skirted several ships before leaving First Fleet's ranks and charging into Third's. For a moment, Seaman felt hopeful that the ordnance would find their mark. Third Fleet wouldn't be expecting this, and he hadn't given them a reason to believe First Fleet would refuse the Article 99 order.

Anti-missile blaster fire streaked across the holo display. Several Frigates attempted to shoot down the torpedoes.

"Captain, we're being hailed by the *Limitless Reach*, *Jericho's Triumph*, and the *Trifecta*."

"Ignore them," DiAntora said.

"All ships are raising shields," Sensors Officer Teloni said.

"The torpedoes will get through," DiAntora replied. The words were barely out of her mouth when one of the torpedoes exploded on its way toward the *Labyrinth*. Seaman double checked the fleet map. The icon blipped out.

"Two torpedoes remaining," the weapons officer announced.

"Come on," Seaman said in a whisper.

"Sir," DiAntora said. "Now that our strike has been detected, the chance those torpedoes will be rendered ineffective is over 86%."

"We only need one to make it," Seaman said.

A second torpedo blinked off the map. It appeared as a small fireball against the *Labyrinth's* backdrop as defensive fire ripped through its housing.

DiAntora took a quick breath. "Sir, I recommend we—"

"Wait." Seaman put a hand up, then lowered his voice. "Come on." His eyes moved between the fleet map and the holo feed, willing the tiny projectile toward its mark.

On the map, the last torpedo's icon disappeared under the *Labyrinth's* hull. For a split second, Seaman thought the torpedo had been shot down. Then a bright explosion flared under the Super Dreadnaught's bow.

"Direct hit," Teloni said. "Target eliminated."

A bridge-wide sigh of relief was shared as Seaman turned to DiAntora. "Your ship." He stepped aside and called up separate holo displays so as not to distract DiAntora for her job of commanding the *Fortuna*.

As DiAntora began calling for shields and ordering new targets, Seaman started receiving tactical information on all ships in the fleet. He commenced by ordering the Dreadnaughts to form a semi-circle between Third Fleet and Capriana. If Moldark wanted to eradicate the planet, then he would have to get through Seaman first. He tapped the category of ships and then drew a line to the intended position, finishing with a tap of the Execute Command button. Acknowledgment icons went down the dialogue window as the carriers fired up their main thrusters, including DiAntora's, which came in the form of a verbal response behind him.

"On our way, sir," she said.

Next, Seaman ordered the fleet's ten Battleships and twelve Battlecruisers into two equally mixed groups—one to stand at the orbital north of Third Fleet, the other to orbital south. The result was a blockade for the enemy to fire through should they wish to carry out the Article 99 attempt. His fingers grouped the ships and then drew more lines through the holo display's shimmering light before hitting the execute prompt.

The Destroyers and Frigates he tasked with more aggressive runs, inserting them like Boresian corral dogs to apply pressure on any attempts for Third Fleet to avoid his blockade. What the smaller ships lacked in capacity and resources, they made up for with stronger shielding, allowing them to take a beating while getting their anti-ship munitions closer to their targets. It meant putting more sailors in harm's way, but there was too much on the line not to be bold. If anything, Seaman hoped the abrupt maneuvers would make the other commanders think twice about carrying out any proposed attacks against the planet.

Seaman brought up his communications menu, selected his

pre-recorded transmission to Second Fleet, and sent it again. Maybe now that First and Third were engaged, their commanders would view and reply. This was no longer a game of what-if scenarios—this was happening in real time. Sailors and civilians would die today—fewer if something were done sooner than later. It was time to pick a side and take off the gloves.

"Fleet shuttle detected coming from the planet's surface," Teloni announced.

"Designation?" DiAntora asked.

"Stiletto-class. The *Peregrine*."

"Moldark," Seaman said to DiAntora. She nodded.

He looked back at his map of icons and grabbed his chin. Even though his fleet outnumbered Third, they had the advantage of a large target—both the planet in the background and a plethora of ships in the foreground. For Seaman, it would be a battle of containment; for Moldark, it was a race.

"I'm detecting more LO9Ds above standby capacities," Teloni added. "I'm marking targets on all five carriers."

Now that Moldark was off the planet, it seemed he wasn't wasting any time in attacking the surface. With the enemy ships' shields rendering immediate blaster fire ineffective, torpedoes and Talons were the best options.

Seaman tapped three torpedo-class categories from his munitions list and selected all highlighted ships equipped with the desired weapons. Then he assigned values to each LO9D target option and hit Auto Assign, allowing the AI to allocate combinations with the highest favorable outcomes. Seaman double-checked the assignments and tapped Accept.

Once those were sent, he called up a command prompt to scramble the Talon squadrons. First, he had to manually override the system, which took priority of all Talon assignments from strategic fighter command. With SFC hosted on the *Labyrinth*—a position he'd held not so long ago—there wasn't a way to order First Fleet's fighters without bypassing command priority.

Seaman entered his passcode, held his breath, and then exhaled as the system confirmed he had wrested control from the *Labyrinth*. Whoever had replaced him at SFC, apparently they were too new to refuse the action. Seaman brought up the fighter assignment and tactical maneuvers overlay, and then doubled down on the LO9D targets, allowing the AI to auto-assign First Fleet's squadrons to them. The AI would calculate attack vectors, compensating for both distance and speculative resistance. Satisfied with the assault plan, Seaman hit Execute, and then accompanied the order with a verbal command to the carriers.

"Attention all carrier commanders, this is Commodore Seaman. Scramble all squadrons. I repeat, scramble all squadrons. Squadron configurations and target assignments dispatched."

Behind him, DiAntora echoed the order to her airwing commanders and forwarded Seaman's plan of attack. The commander acknowledged, and DiAntora replied with the required status update. Seaman appreciated her diligence even though she could have just as quickly replied to him personally. But protocol was in place for a purpose, and Sekmits were anything if not perfectionists.

Within moments of the Talons appearing on Seaman's tactical map, Third Fleet replied by launching its own squadrons.

"Sirs, enemy fighters launched," Teloni said from the sensors console.

Both DiAntora and Seaman nodded.

"I see them." Seaman tapped the Alert icon on all enemy fighter groupings as a precaution. The designation was redundant, but he knew from experience that the pilots wouldn't mind. Plus, First Fleet couldn't afford to lose this fight—*Capriana* couldn't afford for them to lose this fight—so there could be no mistakes.

"LO9D amidships on the *Labyrinth*, preparing to fire," Teloni said, her voice tight.

Seaman turned to the woman. "Where are our torpedoes on that cannon?"

"The first wave was taken out, sir. And the second—" The officer's eyes double-checked something. "Also gone."

"That can't be." Seaman scanned his own map, clearing everything but the *Labyrinth* and the torpedoes from the *Fortuna*. But both the first and second waves had been terminated during his ship assignments operations. He added the squadrons assigned to the *Labyrinth*, but they were still several seconds away from maximum effective range.

"The *Labyrinth* is firing," Teloni shouted.

Seaman watched the main holo display in horror as a bright ball of light built under the *Labyrinth*'s belly, followed by a long energy streak that burst toward the planet.

Seaman's efforts had been too late.

"No," he roared, stepping toward the display. His heart sank, his hands balled into fists. "It can't be." He watched in terror as a bright spot appeared on Capriana's largest island. Even from this height, the shockwave was visible, sweeping outward toward the ocean. "Mystics—what has he done?"

26

"LIEUTENANT MAGNUS, how nice to see you again," Bosworth said from atop the central Rhino's cockpit. He looked like an overripe pangfruit stuck in a Quinzellian miter squirrel's nesting hole, ready to burst if he tried any harder to squeeze through.

Magnus looked to his right and left. They were surrounded by nearly four companies of well-armed, highly trained Marines. Even if Granther Company could take out half of these Marines, the risk of civilian casualties was far too high between Awen's parents and Jules. Plus, the Rhino's M109s increased the chances that any resistance would end in a bloody mess.

"What do you want, Bosworth?" Magnus yelled.

Bosworth looked down his gut and into the cockpit. "I can't hear him." There was a brief pause. "No, I don't want to walk out there. Drive me closer, you fools."

The Rhino's repulsors applied some forward thrust, and the APC hovered closer to Magnus.

"Keep going, keep going," Bosworth said with a disgusted tone. The APC continued to crawl until the ambassador raised a hand. "That's enough." But the drivers clearly didn't respond fast enough for his liking. "I said, that's enough. That's enough!"

The repulsors reversed, and Bosworth's torso disappeared in a swirl of sand. When the dust finally settled, the ambassador—atop his Rhino—was even with Magnus. The two stared at one another's mechanized versions of their biological selves.

"What do you want, Bosworth?" Magnus repeated, now close enough for the ambassador to hear.

"You have something that belongs to me," Bosworth replied.

"So you got our care package?"

Bosworth scoffed. "Oh, that? Please. I knew you weren't ever going to send the child."

"And yet, from what I understand, you still sent several Marines to their deaths by investigating."

"But I had to, you understand, in the off chance you actually sent the child. I've met stupider people."

"Ouch," Magnus said with a tone that might accompany rubbing his arm—had he been able too.

"No, you can have the girl, and so can Moldark for all I care." Bosworth pointed past Magnus. "I want my lovely scientists."

Scientists? "You want the dau Lothliniums back?"

Bosworth nodded. "Call me sentimental, but I've grown very attached to them."

"Or attached to what they can do for you." Behind him,

Magnus could hear Azelon's shuttle approaching. He glanced at his HUD for confirmation.

"Trivialities," Bosworth said. "You have them, and I want them back."

"Sorry to disappoint you and the boys here"—Magnus gestured to the Marines—"but they're going with us. Seems like you got all dressed up for nothing."

"The ship is landing now," Azelon said to Magnus as Bosworth shielded his eyes from flying sand.

"Thanks, Azie."

"But that's not all," Caldwell said, his voice filled with concern. "We have hard confirmation that a LO9D cannon is preparing to fire on Capriana."

Magnus had a flashback to Oorajee, where he nearly died from a low orbit cannon round. The blast had cost him his eyes.

"You copy, Magnus?" Caldwell asked.

"I read you."

"Get out of there, son," said the colonel. "*Now.*"

"The dau Lothliniums," Bosworth said with a sneer. "Or we open fire."

"Bosworth, listen," Magnus said, taking a step forward. Maybe—just maybe there was a chance he could talk some sense into the ambassador. "Moldark is preparing to fire on Capriana. You've got to get out of here."

Bosworth laughed, and his jowls shook when he did. "You think I don't know that, Magnus? I'm the one who helped formulate this plan."

"And did it include you being down here as his LO9Ds powered up?"

Bosworth chuckled some more and then wiggled his arm in the air. "You see this?" A silver bracelet locked tight around his pudgy wrist. An LED blinked, and the device appeared to have a small touchscreen. "This is my insurance policy. Moldark and I have a deal."

"I hate to tell you, but I think he ripped you off," Magnus said.

"This little gem keeps fleet cannon fire away from me. Anyone without a bracelet, however—take, for example, oh, I don't know, say, *you*—well"—he patted his belly—"they're out of luck."

"Then I don't see any incentive to give up the scientists since you're not going to give me your little magic bracelet."

"No," Bosworth said. "But I will give you this one." He produced a second bracelet from his inside breast pocket and flicked it back and forth.

"Nah," Magnus replied. "I'm rather partial to the one on your wrist. Something tells me it works better. So, if you give me yours, then maybe we'll talk."

"No more talking. The dau Lothliniums or I open fire."

Magnus opened his mouth to reply. But he couldn't. A bright light appeared in the sky directly above him, washing the beach in broad daylight. But it wasn't the sun—Magnus had seen this blinding glare before.

It was LO9D fire.

Magnus wanted to tell everyone to take cover. He wanted to ask Azelon to move the shuttle back. But there wasn't time. In the split second the thoughts went through Magnus's mind, the orbital round pierced the core of Proconsul Tower some four klicks away. It was as if a shaft from the sun bore into the building, ignited every floor, and then shoved the contents outward.

Gigantic billowing fireballs erupted at the top and moved down, detonating level after level until the entire structure was engulfed in flames and blew apart in a giant shockwave that rippled through the city. A beat later the force of worlds colliding knocked Magnus's mech into the sand. His ears rang, and his vision filled with objects flying over his head.

An ocean wave struck his shoulders and washed over his helmet. Magnus activated the auto-stand mode in his HUD and felt the mech's AI take over. A quick scan determined that the pilot, Magnus, was in nominal condition. Then the unit rolled over, pushed itself up to its knees, and stood. Control reverted to Magnus, and he looked around to gain his bearings.

His gladias had been blown into the water, as had most of Bosworth's Marines. Magnus's NBTI was rebooting, but he could see lots of Novian armor treading water. On the beach, the ambassador's six Rhinos had moved across the strand but were still intact. And overhead, Azelon's ship had been forced out over the bay but remained aloft.

Then it hit Magnus—*the civilians*.

At first, he thought only of Awen's parents and Jules, all three of whom seemed to be thrashing about in the sea. His gladias would recover them in moments. But then he looked back toward the Forum Republic. Where proud structures stood moments before, fire reigned. Buildings were decimated—blown to shells of their former glory—and energy systems exploded, sending more flames and sparks shooting out of the inferno.

Then Magnus noticed the avenue that led back to the capital. People laid on the pavement—hundreds of people. *Thousands* of people. Magnus stumbled, trying to see if any of them had survived. He swore and then swore again, but all he heard was the sound of ringing—ringing so loud he thought he might go mad from it.

He took a few steps forward, then a few more, until he was running toward the avenue. Bodies were stacked upon bodies, mounded at the boardwalk end of the street like a massive ground mover had plowed the pavement. Magnus felt his gorge rise, and just when he thought he might vomit, he saw a person move. Then another. And then more, until hundreds of people tried to untangle themselves from each other, struggling to regain their feet. People wept, others screamed, and still others walked around aimlessly, shellshocked.

Magnus felt tremors go through his body as memories of other people in this condition flooded his mind. He'd seen this before on battlefields across the quadrant. Marines and civilians alike, staggering like stupefied versions of their once dignified selves. In the wake of horror, they meandered like the walking dead—forever traumatized by the evils of war. As with the faded streets of his memory, for every living person in this Caprianian avenue, there were many more dead. Their bodies were strewn out along the pavement and against buildings like leaves blown down the road from a cold autumn wind. And now, like the old days, Magnus felt helpless in the face of such destruction.

An agony without description crawled from somewhere deep in his soul, clawing its way out of his spirit and writhing to find a voice in his head. He roared, screaming at the scene played out so many times in his past—and the one now, assailing him in vivid detail. He shouted and shouted until he tasted blood in his mouth. Then he spat into his helmet and coughed, stumbling toward the urban sea of victims.

"—do you copy?" said a voice in his head. It was familiar, and —somehow—reassuring. Like the person could be trusted with everything Magnus was witnessing. Like the speaker had been here before. Seen this. Felt this. "Magnus!"

"I'm here," Magnus said, barely recognizing the sound of his voice. It was coming from inside his head rather than through his ears. Maybe because his ears weren't working. But his biotech interface was. "I'm here," he said again, more forcefully.

"What's your status, son?"

Son. This was Caldwell speaking. "I'm—I'm—" *You're what, Adonis?* Magnus swallowed and then fought to order his thoughts.

"Adonis! Can you hear me?"

You're what? Magnus was still trying to answer the question— still trying to separate himself from his memories. From his pain.

Then he heard his true self. *You're a Gladio Umbra, and you've got a mission to complete.*

Magnus blinked. "Yes. I can hear you, sir."

"And your team?"

Magnus turned toward the sea. A few gladias were struggling out of the waves. "I see some. They're—" He glanced at the roster. Most icons were green, a few yellow, and no red. *No red, not dead.* "They're all alive."

"Holy milk-sucking bastard children of the mystical saints," Caldwell replied. "You're one lucky son of a bitch, Magnus. And Awen's parents?"

Magnus scanned the waves. He spotted Abimbola and Zoll helping Balin and Giyel out of the surf. Likewise, Titus was trying to help Jules, but she shoved him away. "Alive," Magnus said, relieved by his pronouncement. "They're all good, sir."

Caldwell whistled and then inserted his cigar back into his mouth. "Azelon's bringing the ship back in. I want you loaded up and out of there ASAP."

"Copy that, Colonel."

"And Adonis?"

"Yeah?"

"I'm glad you're okay."

Magnus chuckled once. "Me too."

"I'm sorry to break up this sentimental moment, sirs," TO-96 said.

"But you're going to, aren't you, Brass Balls," Caldwell said.

"That's an affirmative, sir. Sensors show several ships converging on your location, Magnus."

"What kind of ships?" Magnus asked.

"They appear to have departed from the fleets in orbit."

Magnus swore under his breath. "Paragon."

"I'm terribly sorry, sir."

"So am I, 'Six." As if taking on Bosworth and his Marines wasn't enough, now Granther Company had to tangle with Paragon troopers. "Things on this op just keep getting better and better."

"Do I detect sarcasm, sir?" TO-96 asked.

"What gave it away?"

"Well, given the statistical probability of how many unforeseen events have negatively affected—"

"'Six?" Magnus said.

The bot paused. "Bad timing to answer what was most likely a rhetorical question?"

"Nailed it."

"*Spire* out," Caldwell said. His and TO-96's faces disappeared.

Magnus looked up as Azelon's shuttle neared the beach. It was a Novian designed XTS Transport Shuttle, featuring two down-swept wings and a V-tail. The hull looked like it had been raked by blaster fire, and two newly opened holes sent sparks into the waves. But unless Azelon informed Magnus that the shuttle couldn't fly, he had no reason to think it wouldn't get them back to the *Spire*.

"Magnus?" Azelon said.

"Go ahead."

"Please know that, like your Republic vessels, this shuttle's shields cannot be operational while the ship is aground and will, therefore, be vulnerable to enemy fire while we take on passengers. I recommend you make haste."

"We'll make lots of haste, Azie."

Magnus ran toward the shore to help gather his gladias when blaster fire slammed into his back. Proximity alerts flashed in his cockpit, and Magnus spun around. There, atop one of the Rhino's behind an M109 turret, was Bosworth. Magnus's bioteknia eyes zoomed in, and he could see the gun's recoil shaking the ambassador's snarling face as the blaster emission lit his bloodshot eyes like they belonged to a rabid animal. Magnus lifted his GU90M to fire on him, but Bosworth raked the weapon until Magnus's arm went limp.

More blaster fire slapped against Magnus's flanks. He glanced to his left to find several Marines had regained their feet and their blasters. "As soon as that ramp comes down, I want everyone loaded," Magnus said.

"Rohoar will ensure it," Rohoar said.

Bosworth continued to fire and then was joined by a second Rhino's M109 turret. Rounds penetrated the BATRIG's left thigh. Magnus willed the mech toward Bosworth, but it limped far more slowly than he expected. The mech's RTD10 came even with the second Rhino and Magnus fired. The man behind the weapon exploded, and the M109 went silent.

Bosworth's weapon continued to chew into Magnus's armor. By the time Magnus was within striking distance, his RTD10 had given out—broken in half, and spilling sparks into the sand. But the fight wasn't over. Magnus roared as he swung his oversized right arm into the M109's barrels. The turret spun sideways— Bosworth jerked with it. He yelped. "You have nothing left to shoot with, you stubborn idiot."

"Who said anything about needing to shoot?" Magnus activated Eject on his HUD. The cockpit's emergency release doors flew aside, and a small charge launched him forward. He landed like a cat on the M109 turret and then withdrew his Novian combat blade.

"Even if you get off this beach, Moldark's ships will blow you from the sky," Bosworth said, spittle flying from his mouth.

"I'm not so sure about that." Then Magnus grabbed Bosworth's wrist with the tracking bracelet and chopped straight through the forearm. He pulled Bosworth's hand away as the man shrieked.

"What have you done?" Bosworth said, clutching the stump to his chest.

"Just taking out an insurance policy," Magnus said. "Moldark and I have a deal."

"You'll never stop us," Bosworth spat. "What Moldark and Blackman and I are doing is so much bigger than all of you! *Fools.*"

"Aw, splick," Titus said over VNET. "We've got more company."

"What?" Magnus turned around as four additional Rhinos hovered down the street from the north. That was eight more fire teams and four more M109s. "You've got to be kidding me." Magnus leapt from the APC, pulled his NOV1 from his back, and raced toward the evac shuttle.

Azelon set the ramp down on the strand just above the waterline, blasting sand in every direction. The rest of the gladia fired on the surviving Marines as Abimbola helped Giyel up the ramp. Jules and Balin would be next, but the ship was taking heavy fire as more Marines recovered from the LO9D blast.

As if things couldn't get any worse, the Paragon ships arrived. They touched down to the north and south of Magnus's location, off-loading what looked to be black-clad Marines—*in Recon armor.*

"Son of a bitch," Magnus yelled.

"Sir," Azelon said. "I regret to inform you that I am taking too much fire and must get clear of this beach immediately or risk losing the ship."

"Just hold on a mysticsdamned second!"

"I have to pull away now. I'm—sorry."

"Azie, no," Magnus roared. But the ship pitched forward and accelerated away from the onslaught of enemy fire. Magnus thought he heard Awen scream her mother's name, but it was hard to hear over the sound of the thrusters and blaster fire.

"Awen," Magnus shouted. "We need a wall!"

"But my mother's on—"

"Awen, please!"

Awen ducked as blaster fire whizzed over her head. Apparently, the Marines found the gladias far better targets than the retreating shuttle, especially now that the vessel could raise its shield again. That fact seemed to startle Awen into producing a translucent glowing wall on three sides. Wish, Telwin, and Finderminth stepped to her side and, presumably, aided her. Figuring out what or how the mystics did what they did was above Magnus's pay grade. So he stuck to what he knew: reassessing the enemy while designating fields of fire to the rest of the company. But things did not look promising.

With Bosworth's original six platoons finding their way out of the surf, combined with the additional four platoons, Magnus's unit was outnumbered almost twenty to one. This wasn't going to be a fight. It was going to be a bloodbath.

And then there were the Paragon ships.

27

AWEN'S SHIELD wouldn't hold for long, even with the other mystics' help. Not with the onslaught Bosworth's Marines were giving it. Plus, the shield gave the enemy a clear target as their blaster rounds dashed across the plane. Magnus gave the Unity wall another twenty seconds tops. The gladias' only other option was to retreat into the sea, and none of them were equipped for ocean warfare—not with this armor configuration. If they backed into the water, they'd be sitting ducks.

There was only one option: violence of force.

Blaster fire erupted from behind Bosworth's Marines. At first, Magnus couldn't tell what was going on. There seemed to be some sort of commotion among Bosworth's men toward the northern flank. A miscommunication, perhaps, resulting in a friendly fire incident. But with both units so close together, that seemed unlikely. But something felt familiar about the style of assault.

As another few moments passed, the blaster fire from the north ebbed as Bosworth's Marines faltered. Heads turned left and right and orders seemed to go out over TACNET. Even the M109s on the Rhinos went silent as Bosworth's men tried to sort out whatever mishap was distracting them from annihilating Magnus and his teams.

Without warning, a squad of Recon Marines crested a dune with blaster rounds that shredded the Marine's left flank, dropping troopers along the beach like Paglothian dominos. Bodies hit the sand as Bosworth's Marines tried to fire on the new troopers closing behind them, but they were too slow. The aggressors were, after all, Recon Marines—lethal in their efficiency and brutal in their tactics—albeit loyal to the Paragon now. *Weren't they?* Magnus wondered. Because there was one glaring fact: these new Recon Marines weren't firing on the gladias.

"What is happening, buckethead?" Abimbola asked over VNET.

"Not sure. But I'm not waiting around to find out," Magnus said. Then he raised his NOV1 and kept firing on Bosworth's forces. "Keep the pressure on Bosworth's Marines!"

As more Marines fell under both gladia and Recon trooper fire, the black armored fighters grew more plentiful—they were starting to break through Bosworth's northern lines. Magnus could hear the distinct MAR30 whine as the weapons chewed through Repub armor. It wouldn't be long before they fired on Awen's shield and made quick work of it.

Just then, something caught Magnus's eye—a detail so small, no one would have recognized it. *No one except a Marine who served in the 79th Recon Battalion,* he thought. There, stenciled on each Mark VII's shoulder plate, was the yellow icon of a crescent moon and a duradex combat knife. It was the symbol of the Midnight Hunters.

"Ho-ly splick," Magnus said, unsure if he should be terrified, relieved, or just shocked at the galaxy's sense of irony.

"What is it?" Awen asked. "What do you see?"

Magnus stopped firing and inclined his head. "See the yellow symbol?"

"That's your old mark, isn't it?"

"Uh-huh."

Just then, a senior Paragon trooper accompanied by three guards ran along the surf, apparently unnoticed by Bosworth's Marines. They weren't firing, and the commander had maglocked his MAR30 to his back in a sign. *Which means he wants to talk,* Magnus knew. They double-timed it through the waves until all four troopers were within the relative protection of the Unity shield.

"Hold your fire on those four," Magnus ordered as Reimer and Bliss took a few shots on the advancing foursome. The commander was trying to say something over external speakers. Magnus activated the Enhance feature of his audio sensors and heard a voice he had not heard in a very long time.

"Adonis Olin Magnus," the Marine yelled. "Is he here?"

"Who is asking?" Abimbola replied.

"Whoa." Wainwright raised his weapon and his empty hand. "Easy there, big fella."

"Captain?" Magnus stepped forward. "Captain Wainwright?"

"None other," Wainwright replied.

Magnus grasped the captain's hand and then pulled him close.

"Uh, what's going on here?" Bliss asked. "Why is Magnus hugging the bad guy?"

"This here's my old Captain," Magnus said over comms and externals. "Introductions later. Azie?"

"I'm sorry, sir, but there's still too much *heat*, as you say, to bring the ship in."

"Not that. Can you establish a link with Captain Wainwright's comms so we don't need to use externals?"

"Please remain still," Azie said.

"Don't move for a sec, Cap," Magnus said to Wainwright.

"There, done," said Azelon. "You have an encrypted squad channel with Captain Wainwright."

"Do you read me?" Magnus looked at the captain and pointed to the side of his helmet.

"Loud and clear, Magnus," Wainright said over comms. "Nice hacker you got hidden away somewhere."

"You don't know the half of it." Magnus looked north toward Wainwright's Marines. "Care to explain what's going on here?"

"We're not with the Paragon, for starters," Wainwright replied.

"But our sensors detected—"

"That we were deployed from the fleets? Well, it turns out that not all the fleets are of one mind."

"So you're—"

"Here to help kick Moldark's ass and anyone else who threatens our friends."

"La-raah," Bliss exclaimed.

"La-raah," a few others replied.

"It's a war cry," Magnus said to the captain.

Wainwright raised a fist toward the gladias. "La-raah, damn straight." Wainwright looked back at Magnus. "But I'm afraid we can't stay long. And neither should you."

"The LO9Ds," Magnus said.

"Hard copy. And they're just getting warmed up. But First Fleet is trying to keep that from happening. Second too, from what I hear. Our Commodore sent us to try and help you, but we just got orders to return ASAP." Wainwright nodded at the thinning Marine ranks, which almost seemed enough for Granther Company to take now. "We've done what we can, but it's time to go. And I suggest you call your shuttle back too."

"Thanks for coming, Captain," Magnus said, gripping the man's hand again. "It's good to see you."

"You too, Magnus. And just so you know, we never doubted you. Not for a second."

Had M109 fire not been pelting the Unity shield, nor the beach been awash with Marine fire from two different factions, Magnus would probably have gotten choked up. Instead, he swallowed the lump in his throat and let the captain pull him into a one-armed embrace.

"And thanks for saving my life back on Oorajee, Magnus," Wainwright added. "I owe you one."

"After this, I think we're even."

Wainwright laughed. "You're making some good points."

"Let's give them some covering fire," Magnus said to his Granthers.

"Thanks, Magnus. We'll see you topside."

"See you topside." Wainwright pulled his escort back toward the surf and then headed up the shore to rejoin his northern contingent. As Magnus turned back to continue defending the extraction point, he offered a silent prayer of thanks to the mystics. *For all of the reasons*, Magnus thought.

Wainright's forces pulled back and boarded their shuttles. They'd managed to thin Bosworth's forces to such a degree that Magnus thought Granther Company had a real shot at getting off the beach. It wouldn't be easy, but it would be doable.

"How we looking, Azie?" Magnus asked.

"I estimate additional enemy reductions of twenty percent before I can attempt another landing."

"Twenty? What about Awen's shielding?"

"It does not appear to be large enough to cover the shuttle."

Magnus called for Awen. "Can you make it bigger?"

"We're maxed, Magnus," Awen replied. "And taking a beating too. I'm not sure how much longer we can hold them off."

It looked like Wainwright had bought them time, but not enough. In the end, his old Captain had only managed to keep death at bay a little longer. But Magnus still refused to give up—this fight wasn't over yet.

"There's no way we are getting off this beach in time," Titus said, stepping beside Magnus and firing on the enemy.

"Yes, we will," Magnus replied. "Azie, I need another favor."

"Of course, sir," Azelon said.

"Remember what we did at Elusian Base with my BATRIG?"

"Affirmative."

"Same thing."

Azelon paused, then tilted her head. "I'm sorry, sir, but your mechanized battle system's remote assignment capabilities are no longer operable."

"So, no VWMs?"

"That is correct, sir."

Magnus cursed.

"We're losing it," Awen said with panic rising in her voice. "Right side."

Magnus looked to the north just as part of the Unity shield gave out along the right edge. Blaster bolts riddled Bettger's body, driving her back two steps. Then her armor went full-visual as she landed on her back.

"Bettger," Magnus yelled. But her status icon switched to red right away. She was gone.

"I'm hit," Jaffrey shouted, falling on his hip in the sand beside her. His chameleon mode went down, and his status icon changed to yellow.

"Pull him back," Robillard yelled.

As the enemy fire continued to rake the Unity shield, Magnus could feel a sense of desperation trying to tunnel his vision. "I need options," Magnus said to his team leaders.

"We keep fighting," Abimbola said. The other leads seemed to agree, but Magnus knew it wasn't an answer.

"So, that's how it's gonna be?" Titus finally said. "Splick, I've got an idea."

"Then let's hear it," Magnus replied.

"Eh. I better just do it, and you can thank me later." Titus stepped past the Unity shield and took off running toward Magnus's BATRIG.

"Titus," Magnus yelled. "What are you doing?"

"Improvising."

"Get the hell back here! That's an order."

"I ever mention how much I hate being told what to do?" Titus dashed through blaster fire, climbed up the mech, and patched himself in.

"Cover him!" Magnus called, firing his NOV1 at any Marine who dared look in Titus's direction.

Magnus heard Bosworth, still stuck inside his turret, cursing Titus up and down. Two medics tried in vain to pry the irate man from his trap as he railed against Bravo Team's leader. But without a weapon, the ambassador's words were little more than pebbles thrown at the tidal wave of Titus's determination.

When Titus leaped from the BATRIG, Magnus felt a wave of relief. "You do it?"

"You bet your ass I did. Now bring that shuttle in, Azie."

"Affirmative," Azelon replied. "Landfall in thirty seconds."

But instead of running back to the shuttle, Titus beat a line to an unoccupied M109 turret in the nearest Rhino.

"Titus!" Magnus started walking toward the Unity shield, but something stopped him. He looked down and saw that his feet were stuck in the sand.

"Magnus, no," Awen said—in his head. At first, Magnus thought it was the biotech interface interacting with his brain. "He's chosen his path."

"Please let me go, Awen," Magnus said, trying to fight against the mystic's power.

"I'm afraid I can't do that, Adonis."

"But Awen, he's gonna get himself killed! You've gotta let me go."

"I won't." Even within the Unity, her voice broke up with emotion. "I love you, so I won't."

Magnus opened his mouth but couldn't think of anything else to say.

"Go," Titus yelled. "You've got sixty seconds!" The turret pivoted, and Titus blasted Marines across the beach. The M109 tore through armor, popped off helmets, and detonated energy mags.

"Let him go, Adonis," Awen said, more softly this time. "He's doing this to save us, and you wouldn't want anyone to stop you if the roles were reversed."

As much as Magnus hated to admit it, Awen was right on both counts. He started to backpedal and found his legs unlock from the sand. He watched as Titus dropped Marines with unparalleled accuracy. Then the gladia turned toward the additional incoming APCs and fired on the Marines as they emptied the Rhinos.

Azelon backed the shuttle in for a second time, and the gladias piled onboard, assisting Jules and Balin first.

"No hero splick, Titus," Magnus said over comms.

"Wouldn't dream of it," Titus replied as his weapon glowed red in the morning light. Under his withering assault, the Marines used the APCs as cover, and then fired at Titus. His personal shield took several direct hits before the only thing left between Titus and his aggressors was his Novian armor and the weapon's metal defense plate.

The enemy fire teams also fired on the XTS shuttle, threatening to disable the repulsors and main engine thrusters. Magnus returned fire as he walked backward, but the enemy numbers were too significant. He was the last to climb up the ramp, ducking inside the cargo bay as the shuttle lifted away from the beach. When he lost visual, he tapped into Titus's feed and watched the Marines close on his position. Several blaster rounds shook Titus's body. His hands fell away from the M109's dual handles—but only for a moment. His right hand reached for the grips, followed by his left. But the movement was slow, and Magnus saw Titus's blood pressure and heart rate spike.

"Titus," Magnus yelled as the shuttle pulled away from the city.

"You know how it is, LT." Titus coughed as the M109 finally went dry. "Sometimes, love for your team—makes you—makes you do stupid splick."

Titus's helmet jerked back as his camera pointed straight up in the air. The BATRIG's two remaining VWMs blasted skyward, pulled high-G 180° turns, and then returned to the beach. Magnus felt the explosions from inside the shuttle as Titus's feed went to static. He punched the cargo bay wall with his gauntlet and lowered his head.

"Everyone, please hold on," Azelon said over the company channel.

"What's going on, Azie," Magnus asked as he made his way to the bridge.

"More ships from Third Fleet are preparing to fire."

Magnus caught his breath. "Ships? As in, many?"

"That is correct, sir."

TO-96 popped up in a comms window. "I place your chances of survival at less than—"

"I'm better off not knowing this time, 'Six," Magnus said.

"That's probably for the best, sir, because they're extremely low."

"I said, I'm better off not—"

"Perhaps the lowest you've ever had in all the time we've known each other."

"Dammit, 'Six!"

"Strikes imminent," Azelon said. "Prepare for impact."

28

A SINGLE LO9D strike could temporarily knock out electronics for a few seconds. But with the number of hits that Capriana had just endured, the resulting EMP could be catastrophic.

Correction—*was* catastrophic. Fortunately, his bioteknia eyes were shielded against such attacks, but little else was, including the shuttle's flight systems.

The vessel's nose pitched down as white light hit the vessel from behind. Magnus slammed into the bridge's floor and watched through the front window as a pale-lit ocean raced to meet him. A feeling of helplessness tightened around his chest as warning indicators went dead across the instrument panel. The shuttle lost orientation, and all flight systems went down.

"Brace for impact," Magnus yelled, but then realized his HUD was also down. He flipped up his visor and roared into the cargo bay, but he wasn't sure if anyone heard him. So he closed his visor, braced himself against the console with his legs, and then grabbed onto crash couch bases. The shuttle careened toward the ocean with only the sound of the wind beating against the hull. No thrusters. No repulsors. No control surfaces. Just open air, and then—

Impact.

Magnus's knees buckled, and his head whipped forward. He heard things crack in his head, but couldn't tell if it was the craft, his suit, or his body. Everything went black. Magnus hoped he was unconscious, but the pain shooting down his spine told him he was very much alive—buried in ocean water that surged through the ship as the shuttle plummeted into the abyss. He tried to find a point of light, tried to see which way the bubbles were traveling. But all was black, and his efforts were pointless. Inertia pinned him against the ship as it sank deeper. There would be no escaping this deathtrap until it settled on the ocean's floor.

All the way down, Magnus felt the frustration of not being able to communicate with his team. How many of his unit were awake? How many had been knocked unconscious? And how many weren't ever coming back? He fought the panic that tried to smother him—tried to overwhelm his reason centers. He might make it out alive *if* he could think clearly.

Focus, Adonis. Just stay focused.

He felt his lungs expand and contract. This meant he had air in his rebreather unit. That was good. He could survive at depth for several minutes, maybe even an hour, depending on the pressure.

His body felt dry, except for the sweat on his forehead and against his chest. This meant his suit hadn't endured a catastrophic breach.

And he could move despite having no idea which way was up. That meant he had a chance of freeing himself from the death trap once it settled.

The ship jerked to a halt. They had finally hit the ocean floor. Inky blackness swirled around him. Magnus bumped into the bridge's crash couches and then used the seatbacks to orient himself. As far as he could tell, the shuttle was resting on its belly —*which makes things easier*, Magnus thought to himself.

Next, his thoughts turned toward his team. He needed to find survivors and then help them get to the surface. Magnus spun toward the aft and pushed himself into the cargo bay. A helmet bumped into his, but he couldn't see who it was. He remembered the torch on his hip and pulled it off. When he activated the light, Doc's lifeless face appeared. Magnus jerked back. The medic's visor was cracked, and his helmet was filled with water and blood.

Fearing others might be dead, Magnus swept the light beam through the cargo bay. Everything was bathed in a lurid green-blue haze, and bodies floated everywhere. His first thought was to find Awen, but there was no time to be partial, only practical. He called out, but his HUD was still down. So he gritted his teeth and started a manual inspection of each body.

The first person he rolled over was Dutch. Her eyes were closed, so he shook her—gently at first. Within a few seconds, her eyes fluttered open. Magnus shined the light in his face for her, temporarily blinding himself. But the last thing he needed was for her to panic, so it was best to assure her that at least one other person in this rig was okay. Dutch nodded, and then righted herself. She grabbed her own light and followed Magnus's lead to search for survivors.

Movement caught Magnus's attention from above. A pair of unarmored legs kicked below an air pocket. *The civilians*—he'd completely forgotten about them. Magnus pushed off the cargo bay floor and surged upward until his head popped above the surface.

"What the hell?" a woman said, pushing away. It was Jules. Blood poured from a cut on her head, but she was alive.

Magnus flipped his visor up. "Jules, it's me, Magnus."

"Great. That means nothing to me."

"I'm Zoll's commander."

Jules swore. "The bastard in the mech?"

"Yeah. We gotta get you out of here."

"Not without them," she said and pointed to two bodies hanging from a cargo net. It was Balin and Giyel. By the looks of it, Jules had wedged their arms into the webbing to keep their heads above water. They were unconscious and bleeding from head wounds—which meant their hearts were probably still pumping.

"Alive?" Magnus asked.

"For now," she replied. "You got any big plans?"

"Big plans?" Magnus squinted. "To get out of here?"

"No, for the weekend. Of course, to get out of here! What the hell's the matter with you?"

Magnus shook his head in amazement. "Just sit tight. We're still looking for survivors."

"If I'm not here, I'll be on the Lido deck reading a magazine."

Magnus raised an eyebrow, closed his visor, and dropped below the surface again. Seeing Balin and Giyel made him think about Awen, but Magnus knew if he weren't careful, he'd panic, and panic was the fastest way to die.

Slow is smooth. Smooth is fast, Magnus reminded himself. *Save the ones you can, move on to the next.*

Two large bodies were still strapped in their crash couches while a third looked wedged against a bulkhead. He loosened someone's arm from their chest belt and shined his light into their helmet. It was Abimbola. His eyes fluttered open at the light. Magnus lit his own face again and then watched the Miblimban nod. Abimbola turned to the person on his left—one of the Jujari, based on size—while Magnus floated over to a gladia wedged against the bulkhead.

It was Awen.

Magnus's heart thumped in his ears as he shined the light in her eyes, trying to get her to wake up. She *had* to wake up.

"Come on, Awen," Magnus said. "Wake up." He shook her shoulder and tapped the torch on her visor. "Come on, baby. You gotta wake up."

Suddenly, her eyes opened in a panic. Her left arm struck Magnus in the head while her knee met his groin. Had it not been for the armor, he'd have been doubled over. Instead, Magnus tried to fend off her attacks while shining the torch in his face. The beating continued for a few seconds. Then Awen's movements slowed, and she grabbed Magnus's helmet, pressing her visor against his.

He saw her lips move, saying his name, but he couldn't hear anything. He tapped the side of his head, hoping she'd notice that her own HUD was out. Recognition dawned on her face.

"Magnus?" she asked inside his head.

"Hey there."

"Are you—what happened? Is everyone—"

"We got hit by a shockwave. Orbital strikes."

"Capriana." Awen tensed. "Oh, mystics. The city."

Magnus nodded as a wave of grief swept over him. But this was not the time to mourn. They needed to get out. "You good? Are you hurt?"

"I don't think so. Just—scared." Awen continued holding his helmet, staring into his eyes. "But I'm okay."

"Good. We need to get—"

"Have you found my parents?" Awen looked around the cargo bay, but the effort was pointless without a light in her hand.

"Yes," Magnus said, trying to pull her back. "And they're alive. For now."

"Where?"

He shined his light toward the air pocket where Jules trod water. "The sea skimmer chick saved them."

"Thank the mystics."

"Listen, is there anything you can do to, you know, help us?"

Awen paused. Her eyes darted around the ship. "I'm—I'm not sure, Magnus. I've never—I mean, what should—"

"Hey, relax. Breathe."

Awen took in two deep breaths.

"We need to get to the surface." Magnus stared into her eyes. "And there's enough air in our suits to get that part done. But we still have your parents and the skimmer chick."

Awen seemed to think about the situation for a second. "I suppose I could create some sort of bubble around them? But I've never done that before."

"Awen, in the time I've known you, it seems you're always attempting things that no one has ever done."

She smiled at him and then pressed her helmet against his again. "I'm glad you're okay."

"Me too, but about you."

The ship lurched. Magnus reached for the bulkhead and looked back at Awen. "Was that you?"

"No." Awen grabbed some webbing. "What's happening?"

"We're falling." Magnus imagined the ship sliding off a shelf or dropping into a sinkhole. The only problem was that his and Awen's bodies were pushed into the floor. "No—we're—we're rising."

The ship lurched again, this time in a definite upward direction. Awen held onto Magnus as the shuttle ascended. He glanced toward the bridge to see if some sort of flight system had engaged, but the consoles were as black as before. The only explanations he came up with were crazy ones—like images of a giant Midnoric balloon whale dropping grappling hooks from their mouths and hoisting the ship. But that was as ridiculous as it was improbable.

"Something's grabbed the ship," Magnus said, which was as simple a conclusion as he could draw. "Maybe a rescue boat?" But that seemed just as improbable. Given how much damage they'd taken, Magnus doubted anything else had survived on the surface for kilometers.

"No, it isn't a rescue boat," Awen said. "Not even close." Her voice sounded like it was filled with wonder—as if she were speaking of a new present or a miraculous revelation.

The light in the water was growing brighter. The surface was near. "What is it?" Magnus asked.

"It's Piper," Awen said, grabbing Magnus's helmet again. "It's Piper, Magnus. She's here."

"But—how?"

"I'm not sure but—"

"Are you there, Mr. Lieutenant Magnus, sir?"

Magnus froze, eyes locked on Awen's. "Did you hear that?" He looked away. "Piper? Is that you?"

"Of course it's me, Mr. Lieutenant Magnus," Piper said.

"Piper!" Magnus looked at Awen. "It's Piper!"

"I know," Awen replied.

Magnus couldn't tell whether it was because they were under-water or not, but he thought he saw tears in Awen's eyes. "Piper, what's going on?"

"You don't have to worry, Mr. Lieutenant Magnus. I'm here to rescue you. Like in my dream. Well, my new dream, where I rescue you." She giggled. "It's fun, right?"

"Piper, where is *here*? Where are you right now?"

"You'll see."

The water around outside continued to lighten the closer the ship got to the surface. Soon, Magnus could see the cargo hold without his torch. To his amazement, it seemed like everyone but Doc was alive.

"You should probably hold onto something," Piper said.

Magnus nodded at Awen and then grabbed a handful of webbing. The ship ascended until the hull breached the surface. A deep sucking sound followed by several *thunks* shook the vessel as air and light rushed in. At first, Magnus thought it was the sun. In the distance, however, he could see fire.

It was Capriana, burning like the surface of the sun, stretching from north to south as far as he could see.

Magnus caught his breath. He tried to think of some curse to mutter or some sinister prayer to hurl at the cosmos, but nothing seemed adequate. Words fell short. The city looked like the charred skeleton of an ancient beast that clawed its way from hell to seek refuge in the sky. But its ankles were bound in the depths as if the sea would swallow it whole.

The civilian transport ships that had managed to escape the city and survive the blasts were faced with a new threat—orbital bombardment from ship-to-ship cannon fire. Moldark was not content with demolishing the city, it seemed. He wanted everyone dead, including those who thought they'd made it out alive. Large-caliber blaster rounds appeared from the upper atmosphere and picked off hundreds of vessels, zapping them from the sky like mosquitos.

Then Magnus remembered Bosworth's wrist relay. He knelt in the water as a strong current pulled on his body. Water raced toward openings in the bridge, and along the aft ramp, the higher the ship rose from the sea. If he didn't act fast, Bosworth's hand might be swept out of the vessel along with Granther Company's only hope of surviving a direct cannon strike.

Magnus plunged into the water, eyes darting left and right in a wild attempt to find the bracelet. He peered under crash couches, looked in nooks and bulkheads, all while trying to think where the grotesque memento might have gone to.

The bridge, he thought to himself. Of course, that was also the part of the ship that had suffered the most damage—where water was gushing out of the craft. His heart sank as he considered the very real possibility that the item had been lost to the sea. In which case, they'd all need to dive in the ocean and abandon Piper's heroic but miscalculated rescue mission. Perhaps the Fang would be fast enough to get to orbit and escape the Super Dreadnaughts, but anything else was doomed.

As Magnus searched the bridge, he could feel the dread start to creep into his chest. How had they come so far only to die over the loss of a simple bracelet? The frustration was palpable, and he cursed the ambassador and his plump little wrist. Then again, the EMP from the LO9D blasts would have knocked it out too —*unless it was shielded*, Magnus thought, knowing that particular high-grade emergency hardware was built to withstand all manner of interference.

A single LED blinked in a crevice under the central console. Magnus caught his breath and then flowed with the outgoing water until he slammed into the panel. He fought against the current, bracing his legs and back against the captain's crash couch, and then reached under the console. The ambassador's fat fingers brushed against his gauntlet, but they were enough to hold onto. Then Magnus pulled until the pudgy bracelet-covered wrist in front of his visor. "Gotcha."

Magnus stood and fought against the current to assess the rest of the team. Across the hold, Jules struggled to keep the dau Lothlinium's bodies secure. But the sudden disturbance seemed to rouse Balin. He coughed and looked around, frantic. Jules tried her best to calm him, but he struggled in the netting and threatened to hurt himself, especially as the water level dropped. In a moment, Awen's parents would be dangling from the ceiling.

Magnus flipped up his visor. "Help get them down," he yelled for anyone who could hear him. Dutch was closest, as was Czyz, so they both assisted Jules in lowering Balin and Giyel to the shuttle's floor.

"Say, say, whaddya got there, sir, Mr. Lieutenant, sir?" Cyril asked Magnus, his teeth chattering, probably from the cold water that had flooded his helmet.

Magnus looked at the bloodied stump in his hand. "This old thing?" He grinned at Cyril. "It's our insurance policy."

"Weird. Because it totally totally looks like Mordan Products interplanetary relay beacon. Third gen, I'm guessing. And with it still on whoever's wrist you hacked the arm off of, I'd say it's exactly like the scene in *Ultra Commando III* when Sal Viceman cuts off Dictator Diplarioth's—"

"Can you catch me up on that later, pal?"

"Sure, sure, Mr. sir, sir. No problem."

The sound of rushing water turned to that of waterfalls.

Magnus glanced out the bridge window—the ship was a few meters above sea level. He still could not figure out what was going on. "Is everyone all right?"

"We lost Doc," Awen said, kneeling in the water beside the medic's body.

Magnus nodded. "Everyone else okay?"

"I think we're all good," Dutch said. "But what's happening to the ship?"

"It's Piper," Magnus replied. "Don't ask me how, but it's her."

"Piper?" Rohoar said from under his raised visor. "Rohoar does not witness any Piper here. Where is she?"

All at once, a Fang dropped into view, silhouetted by the fiery horizon. "Right here, everyone!" Piper's voice sounded out over external speakers. "Hi!"

The first rays of sunlight from the east fell on the Fang's cockpit, and Magnus caught a glimpse of Piper's smiling face behind the window. "Are you—are you flying a starfighter?"

"No, of course not, silly," she replied with a light-hearted laugh. "Ricio is."

"Hey there," Ricio said, struggling to sit up underneath Piper. Magnus could barely make out his face, but it was him.

Magnus waved. "Thanks, Ricio."

"Mr. Lieutenant Magnus says thanks, Mr. Ricio," Piper said.

"Not a problem," Rico replied over the speakers.

"So, the tiny human is doing this?" Rohoar asked, spreading his hands across the cargo hold.

"Yes," Awen replied, her voice still filled with amazement. "She most certainly is."

"And whaddya got there, LT?" Dutch asked, pointing toward Bosworth's hand.

"Consider it a good luck charm."

"Whatever you say, boss."

AZELON's second shuttle arrived less than ten minutes later, and everyone transferred into it while Piper kept the damaged shuttle aloft. Once inside, the child let the damaged ship fall into the sea, which soaked Magnus's feet with a spray of saltwater. He walked up the ramp and punched the button to seal the lock, but not before casting a sorrowful look at Capriana.

"So many lives," Awen said, holding his arm.

"Too many," Magnus replied. Every island in the atoll had taken one if not more direct LO9D hits. The loss was—*was what?* Unprecedented, certainly. Magnus had never heard of anything so devastating. There was not a chapter in Galactic Republic history that recorded an entire fleet collectively firing their cannons on a planet like this—let alone their own capital.

But the loss was more than unprecedented. It was unspeakable. Never in the Galaxy's history had so many lives been snuffed out at once. He tried to calculate the population of Capriana's atoll alone, but the figure alluded him—it was millions. Hundreds of millions.

Even as Magnus thought about the number, more streams of light appeared from the sky and plunged to the surface far in the distance. They came like bolts of lightning, searing the atmosphere and detonating the ground. An orb of light billowed from each strike, expanding into the sky like bubbles of fire unwilling to burst.

The ramp sealed shut.

"This is genocide," Magnus whispered, feeling his teeth clench.

"Moldark," Awen whispered.

It seemed unfathomable that one person, one *being*, could will so much destruction. How anyone could be entrusted with so much power was one thing, but how that person could wield it so terribly was another.

Moldark, Magnus realized, was not a person, or even a being. *It* was evil personified.

"We must stop him," Magnus said. "We have got—" He choked on his words. "We've got—"

"We will, Magnus." Awen laid her head against his arm. "We will."

As Magnus turned to hold Awen, he realized something else that he hadn't before—not that there had been much time for reflection. The Galactic Republic was gone.

29

"Direct hits on the planet, sirs," Teloni said. "Estimated casualties at—"

Seaman followed DiAntora by glancing at the sensors officer. "Teloni," DiAntora said with an edge in her tone.

Teloni looked up, but the look in her eyes communicated everything Seaman needed to know. "80%, Captain. And rising."

Seaman's mind went numb with implications. The entire population of Capriana was in the hundreds of millions. And there were still more islands to go on other parts of the planet. And then there was the senatorial alliance of worlds that was— *gone. The Forum Republic, CENTCOM—all of it, gone.*

"Your orders, Commodore?" DiAntora asked.

Just then, Seaman realized this wasn't about defending Capriana anymore—she was gone. Neither was it about disabling cannons or trying to impede Republic ships. This was about wiping out a source of unspeakable evil. He must stop the monster at the *Labyrinth's* helm and anyone who joined him.

"Destroy those ships," Seaman said. "Destroy Third Fleet!"

"We're detecting movement from Second Fleet," Teloni said. "Weapons systems powering up."

"Finally," Seaman said.

"Not so fast," DiAntora said, pointing to the main display.

Seaman snapped his head and saw the ships turning to face First Fleet. "They're—" He could hardly believe his eyes. "They're joining in this insanity?"

"It seems so, sir."

Seaman went back to his holo windows and—to his dismay—added all of Second Fleets ships to the target roster. This felt like Republic war-games gone wrong. He remembered targeting friendly vessels in training exercises, where the coders had given target ships fake monikers and bogus system alignments. But this wasn't an exercise—this was all too real.

The knot in Seaman's stomach reached such a level that he could hardly breathe, and he was about to vomit. The Republic was no more, and the Fleets were imploding. He could not imagine a worse scenario—only that he would live to tell of it. *This can't be happening*, he said to himself but dared not share his anxiety with his crew. Then a hand touched Seaman's shoulder, and a wave of warmth spread down his chest. His head jerked in shock, not from any pain, but from the sudden relief he felt.

"It's all right," DiAntora said just above the sound of her purring.

Seaman heard that Sekmit had particular calming abilities

but had never been subject to them. Until now, he'd supposed it was more myth than not. But as his anxieties ebbed and his clarity of mind returned, Seaman would never again doubt the rumors, knowing they were anything but myth.

When DiAntora removed her hand, Seaman looked her in the eyes and whispered, "Thank you, Lani."

She dipped her head. "My pleasure, Commodore."

Seaman looked back at his holo displays and swallowed. With a clear head, he reconfigured defensive positions and then added more targets to the attack priority list. With Second Fleet's addition of five carriers and forty-five support ships to Third Fleet's resources, they exceeded Seaman's seventy-six starships by six. But where First Fleet still had an advantage was in starfighters, outgunning Second and Third Fleets' ninety Talons by seventy-five. Seaman felt that if there were to be any victory, it would come by way of the starfighters.

"What are your orders, sir?" DiAntora asked.

"Take out the remaining LO9D cannons," Seaman said. "We must minimize damage to what remains of the planet. Then have the starfighters target all communications. I don't want them talking to one another. Once that's accomplished, we'll hit their sensor arrays to get them flying blind. And if we can keep any more civilian vessels from getting shot down, do it. But I don't want any ships leaving this system. It ends here."

"Understood, sir."

Seaman packaged the orders and sent them to the appropriate ships. Not having to verbally command his units according to the old conventions meant not having to parse the myriad of details associated with such tactically complex missions and sub-missions. The result was more time to strategize in anticipation of the enemy's ever-changing actions.

DiAntora didn't waste a moment. She engaged the first Battleship on her objectives list, the *Independence*, targeting its comms array as well as its forward torpedo bays—she would leave the LO9Ds for the fighters. The *Fortuna's* consolidated blaster fire beat a hole through the forward shield, allowing DiAntora's weapons officer a limited opportunity to assail the torpedo bays. The result was a chain reaction that rippled across the ship's nose, taking out several decks and hampering the *Independence's* attack capabilities.

At the same time, two Talon squadrons ran strafing runs beneath the Battleship, slicing along its belly like a knife. But their primary targets were the Battleship's two LO9Ds—one amidships, the other aft. Concentrated blaster fire from their NR330 and T-100 cannons disabled both LO9Ds in quick succession. Assigning two squadrons to the objective was overkill. Still, Seaman liked that DiAntora kept the starfighters together, allowing them to not only guard one another but move on to the next objective quickly.

DiAntora finished the Battlecruiser with two torpedoes delivered to the communications array housed just under the stern-mounted bridge tower. The resulting explosion not only disabled the ship's ability to connect with the rest of the fleets but caused secondary explosions that rippled into the command center. While its hull integrity was still high, the *Independence* was out of commission and would soon succumb to the pull of Prime's gravity.

Two Destroyers—the *Williamson* and *Calatain's Freedom*—became unintentional casualties of taking down the *Independence*. Since both vessels were tasked with escorting the Battleship, the *Williamson* suffered a hull breach when the *Independence's* forward torpedo bays were destroyed. Shrapnel and unexpended munitions buried themselves in the smaller Destroyer's port side. Warheads detonated, ripping holes in the upper decks and taking out critical life support systems.

While *Calatain's Freedom* avoided both direct and indirect fire, it did find itself in the Battlecruiser's path as the larger starship careened toward Prime's atmosphere. The Destroyer's captain realized only too late that it couldn't get out of the way. Subsequent attempts to divert power to engines resulted in the *Freedom* hooking itself around the *Independence*, binding it to the Battlecruiser's hull. Seaman nodded at DiAntora—speed, luck, pilot error, and fire superiority had just combined to make quick work of three warships.

DiAntora had already instructed her wing commander to send her two Talon squadrons toward the *Limitless Reach*—a Super Dreadnaught along Third Fleet's front edge to orbital north. Seaman watched as the Talons split up to take on the *Reach's* fighters. But DiAntora's twenty-eight fighter contingent had the numeric advantage. Not only did the *Fortuna's* Talons take out three enemy fighters in the opening seconds, but two of the *Reach's* five LO9Ds were obliterated with help from *Ardent Eclipse's* second squadron. The fighters buzzed around the *Reach* like Helmordian kite raptors on a kill.

DiAntora directed primary cannon fire to the *Limitless Reach's* underside, taking advantage of the enemy captain's overestimate of direct fire to the bow. As a result, amidship shields were under capacity and buckled quickly under the *Fortuna's* withering barrage. A second and third LO9D took direct fire, detonating in bright displays of free energy left over from the weapons' storage cells.

But even with the rapid assault on Second and Third Fleets, the enemy ships still managed more LO9D strikes against the surface. The blasts burned holes through the atmosphere and pummeled islands as if the ancient gods of past civilizations had summoned the energy of the sun in judgment of the mortals' crimes. Fireballs billowed over the islands as the strike's shockwaves raced across the open seas.

The inhabitants of Capriana Prime weren't the only casualties. First Fleet lost the Dreadnaught *Octavia II* in a coordinated Talon strike comprised of four squadrons. The starfighters focused all their fire on the aft engineering decks, drilling into the core. The detonation fractured the stern and cleaved it from the ship, killing over half the crew in seconds.

Another Dreadnaught, the *Enduring Hope*, lost its bridge tower while charging Second Fleet's Dreadnaught, the *Breedlove*. The *Hope* had tried to navigate under the *Breedlove* in an attempt to take out its LO9D cannons. Sensing the maneuver but without the proper distance to target critical systems, the *Breedlove* decided on a more drastic defense—one that damaged its foremost decks by pitching down and driving its bow into the enemy's conning tower.

The *Hope*, critically wounded, was unable to disengage its engines and rammed with two other Second Fleet ships. The enemy vessels took substantial damage, but with the *Hope* so far behind enemy lines it was quickly set upon and destroyed. Seaman winced as the starship exploded, showering nearby ships with massive chunks from its hull.

The most dramatic losses, however, came by way of the enemy LO9D cannons.

The Dreadnaught *Cortisan Dawn* maneuvered into position as Seaman prescribed, blocking direct planetary fire from Third Fleet's *Jericho's Triumph*. But the *Triumph* had no intention of tiptoeing around the *Dawn* to line up its shot against the planet. Instead, it charged its cannons and fired a single LOD9 round into the *Dawn* amidship. The vessel exploded spectacularly, first by way of two orbs of fire that emanated above and below the impact point. The hull ruptured from inside-out as the top and bottom decks flowered into hard vacuum. Finally, the titanic wave of energy rippled across the surface until it erupted out the *Dawn's* sides in all directions. Only a trace of the original round's energy made it to the surface, but it was lost amidst the sea, far from its intended planet-side target—*if it had any to begin with*, Seaman noted.

Jericho's Triumph's action wasn't without repercussions. That much energy in such close proximity was more than the enemy Dreadnaught had probably bargained for. Shrapnel berated the *Triumph's* belly like a fragmentation detonator trapped under a

Marine's gut. Seaman had seen such infantry horrors relayed via holo feed before, but never in person. He supposed this was the closest he'd ever come to seeing a ship suffer a corollary fate. Thousands of small punctures riddled the Dreadnaught's under-side—none of which were fatal by themselves. But taken collectively, the *Triumph* hemorrhaged air, energy, and sailors into hard vacuum. While the starship wasn't necessarily "dead in the water," it certainly was out of the fight, including all of its belly-mounted LO9D cannons. Like every other disabled ship this close to Prime, it would share the fate of tearing through the planet's atmosphere and colliding with the surface. It was only a matter of time.

Second Fleet's *Telmadorian* was another enemy Dreadnaught to fire its LO9Ds on one of Seaman's ships. Whether just the circumstances of the two ships' positions or that the enemy ship learned from the *Triumph's* mistake, the *Telmadorian* was farther from its victim before firing two orbit-to-surface rounds. The target was Seaman's Battleship the *Pride of Albertan*, which took one round to the bow and the other to the bridge. The blasts breached the ship in half, folding the ends down as if pulled by too much weight. Still, the resulting explosions struck local ships with debris and took out several unlucky Talons.

The *Triumph's* and *Telmadorian's* use of LO9D cannons against other starships revealed an element of desperation that Seaman was not expecting. The acts were brutal, to be sure. But the fact that commanders had diverted so far from the rules of engage-ment—both in firing on Prime and other warships—spoke of immense collective anxiety. While the two Fleets' combined resources were more than a challenge for First Fleet, Seaman couldn't help but feel that Moldark was losing control. Perhaps his men were coming unnerved too—coming to grips with what they'd done. Such brutal and indiscriminate violence wasn't human. Genocide was a fetish of monsters.

And all monsters need to be stopped, Seaman thought. But with the *Black Labyrinth* retreating further into the safety of the other fleets, Seaman felt his opportunity for cutting off the snake's head slipping away from him. Inwardly, he hoped that the opposing captains would come to their senses and wake up from whatever stupor Moldark had put them in. He hoped they would turn on the venomous leader and put an end to this insanity. After all, when Moldark was done with Prime, what was the next system he would assault?

"Nooo," Seaman said under his breath as two Dreadnaughts closed over the limping *Labyrinth*. He clenched his fists. The very thought of Moldark escaping to decimate some other world made Seaman sick to his stomach. He'd rather plow the *Fortuna* into the *Labyrinth's* conning tower and sacrifice his entire crew before letting that ship get away. But Seaman knew he'd be taken out before he ever got the chance. "No!"

"Sirs," Teloni said from her sensors console. "We're picking up significant weapons fire from a new location."

"From where?" Seaman spun on Teloni and strode toward her console.

"From behind the enemy fleets, Commodore. And they seem to be attacking…" Teloni paused as if to double-check her readings. "On the *Labyrinth*."

DiAntora looked at Seaman. "But we have no ships in that direction."

"That's correct," Seaman replied. "Teloni, can you give me a visual?"

"Yes, sir." Teloni busied herself on three different holo screens, attempting to clarify an image. "On screen, sir."

What Seaman saw on the main holo display baffled him. An alien vessel, the likes of which he'd never seen, appeared on the far side of the conflict, pouring weapons fire at Third Fleet. Specifically, on the *Black Labyrinth*. Additionally, it deployed several starfighter squadrons of unknown configuration as well as dozens of unidentified vessels.

"Someone tell me what we're looking at," Seaman said without taking his eyes from the main display. It was hard to make out the details since enemy ships continued to pass in and out of the heavily zoomed image and obscure the foreign vessels.

"I think I see a decommissioned Sypeurlion Jackal-class fighter," said the weapons officer, speaking as though unsure of the information's help.

"And an old Wilda-class starfighter," the navigation officer said.

"That yellow ship appears to be a modified Gull-class heavy freighter," Teloni added. "In fact, most of those ships seem to be retrofitted."

"So what you're telling me is that they're not flying for any one particular faction," Seaman said, looking back at the sensors officer.

Teloni nodded, but with a sense of reservation. "I mean, the only ships that appear to have any cohesion are those alien starfighters."

"And you don't have a listing for them?"

"Negative, sir. The only—wait."

"What is it?" Seaman and DiAntora moved behind Teloni's console.

"We've seen these fighters before, but at a distance."

Seaman studied Teloni's results. "Over Oorajee."

"Yes, sir."

"You think they're Jujari?" DiAntora asked him.

"I don't know what they are, but they attacked Third Fleet before, and now they've followed it from Oorajee. Which means—"

"They're tracking Moldark."

Seaman nodded. "I don't know how, and right now, I don't care. All I know is they seem to be on our side." He turned back to his holo screens and started regrouping ships and aligning new target priorities. "DiAntora, let's help clear a path to the *Labyrinth* for those ships."

The Sekmit whipped her tail once. "Aye-aye, Commodore."

30

"Granther Company has reached low orbit, Colonel," Azelon said. She stood beside Caldwell on the bridge, eyes darting between several holo screens.

"What's their ETA, Smarty Pants?" Caldwell replied.

"Eleven minutes, twenty-one seconds until safely onboard the *Spire*, sir."

Caldwell studied the main holo, monitoring the Republic Fleet's movements. First Fleet engaged Second and Third Fleets, as per Willowood's forecast. The sage mystic had employed her entire company to work alongside Piper in the hopes of winning over the Repub's largest fleet. And it seemed to work. First Fleet was repositioning themselves to act as a blockade between Moldark's ships and the planet. The strategy was desperate and risky, but the right choice if the Fleet Commander wanted to save more lives.

"Whoever's in charge of First Fleet is as brave as bare balls in a blizzard," Caldwell said.

"But sir, what if it's a female?" Azelon asked.

"Then she's still got balls."

Azelon tilted her head but did not reply.

"I want us in that fight," Caldwell said after a moment. "They're going to need support if they want to stop Moldark."

"But, sir, it will take us quite a while to navigate around the battlespace in order to—"

"I don't want to go around, sweet cheeks. We're gonna apply pressure from the rear."

"An ingenious strategy, sir. Split the enemy's attention."

"Something like that." Caldwell turned to TO-96. "I want your squadrons driving straight through that mess. Hit the *Labyrinth* with everything you've got. No other target matters. You hear me?"

"Of course, sir," TO-96 said with a reassuring tone. "You're standing one meter, twenty-one centimeters from me, and speaking at ninety-two decibels. Of course, I hear you."

"Smartass. Prepare to deploy your damn Fangs, son. And get Sootriman back out there while you're at it. We're gonna need as many guns in this fight as we can muster."

"As you command, sir. All fighters are refitting now."

"Good. Flow, Cheeks. You ready to blow some splick up?"

The former Marines grinned ear to ear behind their weapons consoles. "We thought you'd never ask, Colonel," Flow said. "Been a hot minute since we toasted anything."

"I hear that. Once Brass Balls' fighters are clear of the *Spire*, I want you covering the squadrons' advance. Nothing touches them. Copy?"

"Hard copy, Colonel. We'll give 'em hell."

"That's what I like to hear." Caldwell turned to Azelon. "Decloak once the fighters are clear. I want to split the enemy's attention and get them worried there might be more of us. I also need to know the second Magnus's shuttle is within a safe range."

"You will be the first to know, sir."

"Good. Now use that magical brain of yours to help keep our fighters safe."

"My magical brain, sir?"

"It's a term of endearment," TO-96 said with a consoling tone.

"Consider me endeared," Azelon replied with a nod of her chin.

Caldwell withdrew a plasma lighter from his pocket and rolled the tip of his cigar through the blue flame. Satisfied with the pre-light, he placed the cigar back in his mouth and toked several puffs until he could draw thick white smoke. "Time to kick ass, people."

EZO HAD BARELY enough time to hit the head while his Fang got refit. He'd been able to splash some water in his face, down a protein sup bar, and then return to the hangar bay. He ran across the flight deck, whirling a hand in the air. "We're going back out," he shouted, just as the deployment alert sounded down the hangar bay. "Helmets on!" All thirty-nine Fang pilots sat upright and then bolted for their starfighters.

Sootriman waited beneath Ezo's Fang with her hands on her hips. "And just where do you think you're headed, husband?"

"You didn't hear? Caldwell's ordered a full assault on the *Labyrinth*. 'Six says you and the Magistrates are needed too."

"Oh, I heard. It just seems like you were planning on leaving me again without some sugar."

Ezo blushed. "Sugar?"

Sootriman leaned down and kissed him. Whatever expectations Ezo had of a quick smooch were dashed when she grabbed his shoulders and held him in place. At first Ezo resisted the prolonged affection, but soon warmed to it as the kiss became more impassioned. Sootriman finally let go, but Ezo's lips were still puckered.

"What was that for?" he asked.

"To remind you to stay alive out there."

"I might need one more reminder—so I don't forget."

She smiled at him. "There's plenty more when we get back to Ki Nar Four."

Ezo stood up a little straighter. "You know, I've been so preoccupied with winning, with surviving, that I think I've forgotten about…"

"About life after war?"

Ezo nodded.

"Me too," Sootriman said. "But we can't forget. The whole reason we're fighting is because we have something to go back to."

"And there are only so many tax incentives you can give your Magistrates before they—"

"Start throwing it in my face. Trust me, they already have."

The two of them shared a laugh before the sound of Fangs starting up brought them back to the seriousness of the moment.

"I miss it," Ezo said, his eyes looking off in the near distance. "Not just life before all this. I mean, I miss life with you." He shook his head. "It's weird how all this has brought us together again. All this fighting."

"It does have its place." She reached out, grabbed Ezo's flight suit, and pulled him close. "But you and I? We're not professional soldiers. Not like the others. So when this is over, we have a life to make together."

"Ezo copies."

"No, not Ezo. *You.*"

Ezo nodded. "I copy."

Sootriman held him there a moment longer and then kissed him again. When she was done, she released him and walked away. "Let's finish this."

RICIO FLEW beneath the XTS shuttle's shadow all the way out of orbit, as per Magnus's instructions. From what he gathered, Magnus's ship had been marked "friendly" to Moldark and would not suffer the same fate as every other transport trying to make orbit. Ricio felt it was best simply to comply and ask questions later. All that mattered was that Piper's rescue mission had been a success, and everyone was making it back to the *Spire* in one piece. Had Willowood not threatened Ricio to take her, he never would have signed on for the wild idea, but he knew better than to cross the mystics, no matter their age or size.

"Sir, this is TO-96," the bot said, appearing in Ricio's HUD.

"I can see that, but thanks for the heads up, 'Six."

TO-96 nodded. "As soon as Piper is back inside the *Spire*, your orders are to refuel, rearm, and then deploy with the rest of Fang Company. The Colonel has ordered an all-asset assault on the *Black Labyrinth*."

"It's about time."

"What is?" Piper asked. Her bony elbows had been digging into his sides the whole trip.

"We're making a run on the *Labyrinth* as soon as I get you back on the *Spire*."

Piper seemed to hesitate. "You're going to kill him."

"Moldark? Hell yeah, we are."

The child seemed to retreat into herself.

"He's your grandfather," Ricio said, reminding himself. "Listen, kid, I'm sorry."

"You don't have to be sorry, Mr. Ricio. He's a bad man. And we've got to stop him."

Ricio slowed as they approached the *Spire's* starboard side, aiming for a forward hangar bay. "I'm still sorry, Piper. You've had to see more than any kid ever should."

Ricio felt her tiny shoulders shrug. "Thanks for helping me save Awen and Mr. Lieutenant Magnus."

"No problem, kid."

Piper leaned forward and pulled the printed picture of Ricio's family from the flight console. For whatever reason, it seemed she hadn't noticed the image until just now. Perhaps the anticipation of rescuing Magnus had been too all-consuming.

"Who are they?" she asked.

"That's my wife, Celine, and son, Arthur."

"She's very beautiful. And he's handsome."

"Thank you. That's kind of you to say."

"Where do they live?" she asked. "They weren't on—down there, were they?" She pointed over her shoulder toward Prime.

"They were on Capriana, yes. But they're safe now, heading to another system."

Piper got quiet for a moment. "Do you love them?"

"Of course. Very much."

"Then why did you leave them?"

"What do you mean, kid?"

"Well, you left them to fly ships and fight, right?"

"Right." Ricio sighed. "I left them because I love them."

"That doesn't make sense."

"No, I suppose it doesn't." Ricio tried to think of a different way to say what it meant for him to join the Navy. "Love is a strange thing, Piper."

"How?"

"Well, there are lots of different ways to express it. The best way is to be close to those you love. Physically and emotionally, I mean. But you can also show people you love them by doing things to protect them, even if those actions take you far away from them physically."

J.N. CHANEY & CHRISTOPHER HOPPER

"But not emotionally."

"Right." He nodded and then took the picture from her and slipped it back under a bezel on the console. "So even though I'm far away right now, fighting for—" He almost said, "The Republic," but caught himself. "Fighting for freedom, this picture reminds me that the real reason I fly, the reason I risk my life, is for them."

"I think that's what my daddy did for me," Piper replied, almost inaudible.

"I wouldn't be surprised, Piper. Not at all."

All of a sudden, the child twisted around to look at his face. "And don't die out there, you hear me?"

He laughed. "Wasn't planning on it."

"Good. 'Cause if you do, I'm gonna—"

"You're gonna kill me yourself?"

She smiled. "Yeah."

"Deal. Now, let's get you back to your grandmother. Hold on."

CALDWELL WATCHED the Fangs and Magistrate ships pour out of the *Spire's* hangar bays like Limeridon azure locusts, engines burning bright against the void's deep black. He whispered a prayer to the mystics as he watched them speed toward *Labyrinth*. He hoped their efforts would be enough—they *had* to be. They weren't going to get another chance like this again.

First Fleet's 74 warships and 165 Talons had paired up

against Second and Third Fleet's combined 82 warships and 75 Talons. It was as even a fight as Caldwell could imagine, set against the blue backdrop of Capriana Prime. Both sides were losing warships and starfighters at an even rate as First Fleet attempted to keep the enemy from destroying any more of Prime's surface.

As for the *Labyrinth*, Moldark's flagship was retreating—still suffering damage from the battle of Oorajee. And if Caldwell had to guess, Moldark was going to try and jump away as soon as the *Labyrinth* got far enough from Prime's gravity well. As chance would have it, the *Spire* was blocking its way, as were eighty fighters.

"Colonel, the support ships are targeting our fighters," Azelon said. "It seems the feline is out of the satchel."

Caldwell eyed her. "The cat is out of the bag?"

"Whatever gives buoyancy to your water-based vessel, yes."

"Covering fire, Smarty Pants," Caldwell snapped, trying to keep her on task.

"Right away, sir. Also, the *Black Labyrinth's* shields have been diverted to their stern."

"Then let's give 'em a bloody nose," Caldwell replied. "Brass Balls, tell your ships it's now or never. Azie, fire what you can without hitting our pilots."

"As you command, sir," Azelon said. "De-cloaking and preparing to fire."

Caldwell watched as a volley of blaster fire erupted from the *Spire* and slammed into the *Labyrinth's* defenses. "Mystics, help us."

"And why's that, sir?" TO-96 asked.

"I just hope it's enough to give our starfighters the time they need."

"It appears the mystics have heard your prayers, Colonel," Azelon replied. "Observe."

Caldwell squinted at the conflict's far side as anti-ship blaster fire began targeting every vessel around Fang Company's path toward the *Labyrinth*. Flashes of light encircled the starfighters as they plunged headlong into the battle's center. "Sweet mother of Ceradian whores, would you look at that."

RICO LED Red Squadron at the *Labyrinth's* nose, dodging auto-turret fire as the AI helped anticipate the enemy's attacks. Several rounds glanced off his Fang, but his shields absorbed most of the energy, minimizing the damage. He had been more worried about flanking fire from the surrounding support ships, but a sudden barrage of covering fire from First Fleet gave them the advantage they needed.

"This is Red Leader," Ricio said to his squadron over comms. "We're taking the topside run. Targets displayed on your HUD." TO-96's tasks for them included auto-turrets and a strike against the bridge. "No matter what happens, we put rounds downrange on that command center, copy?" Green icons went down his chat window.

"Red Leader," Gill Quo said. "Enemy fighters."

"I see 'em, Red One. Marking." Ricio auto assigned the ten enemy fighters to his squadron and still had four ships left over for the bridge. "Red One through Ten, break off. The rest are with me."

Ricio accelerated as he crossed the *Labyrinth's* nose, weaving toward the first point defense turrets. He fired two salvos of secondary blaster fire at the first three turrets, blowing them off the deck. Red Twelve and Thirteen took out two more, while Red Eleven absorbed a critical hit, knocking out its weapons systems.

"Red Eleven, get back to the *Spire*," Ricio said.

"Negative, sir. I'm—" The Fang took three direct hits, detonating the fuselage into a torrent of superheated projectiles.

"Splick," Ricio said, flying past an auto-turret that he'd missed. "Twelve and Thirteen, stay low and tight."

"Roger that," they replied.

The three Fangs wove across the foredeck, raking it with secondary blaster fire. They took out six more turrets before lining up on the bridge amidships. "Hold this line," Ricio ordered. "Target acquired." But before Ricio could shoot, another Talon squadron rolled up from the *Labyrinth's* port side and opened fire. Red Twelve was hit from three different Talons. The Fang rolled over and drove into the *Labyrinth's* deck, carving a deep furrow in the plating.

"On me," Ricio ordered Red Thirteen. "We're pulling out to engage those Talons."

"Aye-aye," Dye Vallon said. "I'm on your tail."

"LET's give those Fangs some support," Sootriman said, marking new targets for her Magistrates. "Looks like Second and Third Fleet's carriers diverted their Talons from the front lines."

"They really like their nasty looking leader, don't they," Chloe said from inside her blue and black Sypeurlion Jackal-class fighter.

"I hate to disappoint them, but I say we put an end to their fetish," Diddelwolf said—the oldest of Sootriman's pilots. He flew a yellow Lawrence-class heavy freighter that he'd won in a lucky hand of Antaran backdraw.

"Sounds good to me," Chloe replied.

"I want everyone staying clear of those point defense turrets," Sootriman said. "We can do plenty of damage from here."

"But, my Queen," Phineas Barlow said. "We'll manage better if we get closer."

"Not all of us are flying a black-market Mk. I Talon like you, Barlow," Diddelwolf said.

"You wanna go down there and risk your hide?" Sootriman added. "That's on you. My job is to help the Gladio Umbra where we can, but it's also to keep you alive."

Barlow sighed. "As you wish, my queen."

"Good. Then let's do this."

CALDWELL WATCHED as Sootriman's Magistrates took on the newly arrived Talon squadrons. She provided invaluable cover for the Fangs, allowing TO-96's squadrons to disengage from dogfighting and continue with their strafing runs against the

Labyrinth. But despite First Fleet's covering fire, more than one enemy Destroyer put rounds on target. Several of Sootriman's starships took direct hits, casting the scene in radiant light. The bright spots burst to life for a few seconds and then collapsed into darkness—pilots and ships erased from the roster.

"Tell me you have something to shoot at, Smarty Pants," Caldwell said.

"Yes, Colonel. Now that the fighters are congregating toward the *Labyrinth's* aft, a target window has opened which satisfies the statistical likelihood that—"

"Hit that ship, dammit!"

"Yes, sir." Azelon dipped her head, and her eyes shifted color from blue to red. Then the *Spire* shot out a barrage of large-caliber blaster rounds and several groupings of torpedoes.

Caldwell squinted as the ordnance streaked across space and closed on target. "Come on, baby." He pulled his cigar from his lips. "Come on."

Multiple light flashes emitted from the *Labyrinth's* bow as the blasters took out the minimal shielding. Any unspent bolts slammed into the nose and destroyed the ship's first few sections, blowing apart compartments and tearing through critical systems. The torpedoes arrived seconds later, boring into the holes the blaster rounds made. Without point defense turrets to thin their numbers, the torpedoes burrowed deep into the hull before exploding in a concussive force that blew the *Labyrinth's* nose apart.

Caldwell let out a shout that seemed to startle Azelon and

TO-96 alike. "That's how it's done!" He slapped the Novian bot on the back as her eyes changed back to a soft blue glow.

"This is a strange reaction," Azelon said, looking at Caldwell and then TO-96.

"It is," TO-96 replied. "But fitting for the elevated adrenaline and dopamine levels most humans experience in such high-intensity moments."

"Ah," Azelon replied. She looked back at Caldwell and then produced a loud noise, which seemed to be an exact duplication of the colonel's voice.

"What the hell?" Caldwell said.

"I am attempting to empathize, sir." Then she struck him between the shoulder blades, which made him gasp and drop his cigar.

"DISENGAGE THOSE TALONS," Rico said. "All squadrons, on me! We're hitting that bridge."

Sootriman's starships had given Fang Company the relief they needed to refocus their efforts on the *Labyrinth's* bridge. It wasn't a lot of support, but it was enough—and costly too, as far as Ricio could tell. He saw several of Sootriman's ships blink out as the Talons and gunships targeted them.

"Mystics bless you," Ricio said under his breath. Then he double-checked Fang Company's whereabouts and verified the target coordinates. "Open fire as soon as you're in range!"

From Ricio's HUD, it looked as though a swarm of mad fire

wasps converged on a paralyzed ground squirrel. Now free of the Talons, the Fangs streaked in from almost every angle, each gunning for the command tower. Ricio dropped back to the deck, skimming along its length toward the stern. Above him, the bridge's wide windowplex wall looked out across the Super Dreadnaught. *Perfect view for your end,* Ricio thought. His targeting reticles blinked in conjunction with all-weapons lock, and he fed the AI one word.

Fire.

At once, his Fang bucked from the violent release of missiles and energy weapons. His ship was like a viper spewing poison at its victim. The munitions crossed the short distance to the bridge as Ricio pulled perpendicular to the hull, flying straight up the tower's face. A cloud of fire and debris exploded from the bridge. Ricio charged through it and emerged above the *Labyrinth* as more Fang fire decimated the bridge. He veered to one side and glanced over his shoulder just in time to witness a chain reaction of explosions work their way through the command tower. He also noticed another Dreadnaught charge the *Labyrinth's* stern with a hail of torpedo fire.

THE *LABYRINTH* RETREATED from the front lines, but it was to be expected. Between the damage the ship had taken during the closing moments of the Battle of Oorajee, and the blows it had suffered today, Moldark's Super Dreadnaught could not take too much more. Seaman wanted to go after it, but they were too far away. That, and it was a suicide mission. The best thing they could do was continue to provide covering fire for the brave souls who assaulted from the far side.

"Sir," Teloni said. "The *Terra Rosa*. She's charging!"

"What?" Seaman spun toward the battle map and eyed the Dreadnaught in question. Sure enough, the warship was accelerating at full burn, headed into the center of the conflict. Seaman glanced at the Captain's name. Smalley. She was either crazy or had more courage than anyone Seaman had ever met. Perhaps a little of both.

"Visuals," Seaman said, snapping his fingers. "On screen." The main holo displayed a zoomed-in view that tracked the *Rosa* as it surged after the *Labyrinth*. "Mystics, she's going for it." How Smalley had convinced her bridge crew to go along with her spoke to her leadership capabilities—as well as the desperation that all of First Fleet presumably felt.

The *Rosa* released a salvo of torpedoes through the vacuum, crossing the short distance to the *Labyrinth's* stern. At first, the enemy ship retaliated with a staggering volley of anti-torpedo blaster fire. Seaman wondered if there would be any torpedoes left as explosions filled the space between the two vessels. But the *Rosa* wasn't done.

Most likely sensing the prize that awaited her, Captain Smalley sent every torpedo she had at the *Labyrinth*, exhausting the ship's forward bays. The *Rosa's* aft bay capacity indicators drained as the ship threw more torpedoes at the retreating Super Dreadnaught. Three Frigates and two Battlecruisers helped the *Labyrinth* target the incoming ordnance—they would not let the most notorious ship in the Paragon Navy go down without a fight. Their blaster rounds coalesced just behind the flagship's stern in a chaotic mass of near-constant explosions.

Seaman wrote the *Rosa's* assault off as noble but unsuccessful effort. Even though he could not see through the brilliant flashes of light, he knew Smalley's attempt—though valiant—was not enough.

Then a light brighter than blaster fire and exploding torpedoes erupted on the holo screen. Seaman winced as his crew gasped. When the light diminished enough for him to see shapes again, the *Labyrinth's* engines were gone—blown apart. The remnants shot away, striking other ships in the immediate vicinity. Divested of all propulsion—and also its bridge—the *Labyrinth* started a lazy roll to starboard.

"She's done it," DiAntora said, arriving at Seaman's side. "I can't believe—she's done it."

Secondary explosions started moving toward the bow. Plumes of fire blew armored plates off the top decks, shot out the landing bays along the sides, and ripped holes in the belly. Energy cells beneath cannon emplacements ruptured, popping the weapons from the hull, while air pockets filled with flammable gases burst up and down the hull.

"We've done it," Seaman said, turning to face DiAntora. He grabbed her by the shoulders and—*and what?* He was elated, and terrified, and euphoric. And Lani was as marvelous a creature as he'd ever seen. If they survived the final exchange in the wake of the *Labyrinth's* loss, he would find a patch of peace somewhere in the galaxy, and he'd ask her to marry him.

"Commodore?" she said, eyeing his hands.

"Right." Seaman let go and smoothed her sleeves. "Forgive me. Target all remaining ships. Let's end this."

"Aye-aye, sir." Then DiAntora leaned in to his ear. "Then let's pick up where you left off."

CALDWELL STEPPED toward the main holo display as the *Labyrinth's* stern exploded into a thousand fragments—give or take several hundred bits and pieces. "Well, I'll be a speckled dick's dinner," he said with his cigar stuck in the corner of his mouth.

"A touch derogatory, isn't it, Colonel?" Azelon said.

"I believe he's referring to the songbird, native to Albatron Three," TO-96 supplied.

Caldwell ignored the bots' exchange and continued to marvel at the catastrophic display unfolding before him. It wasn't just that a Goliath-class Super Dreadnaught was suffering a bitter death, nor that it took the Gladio Umbra, Ki Nar Four's Magistrates, and the Galactic Republic to bring it down, but that it was Moldark's flagship.

That sniveling bastard. He deserved this, and a thousand deaths more for the destruction he'd reigned down upon Capriana Prime. Then the Super Dreadnaught exploded, temporarily turning the holo display bright white. Caldwell raised a hand and squinted against the burst. Then, as the light faded, thousands of fragments flew off in every direction and left a gaping hole in the Paragon's fleet formation. The *Black Labyrinth* was gone.

Caldwell blew out a thick cloud of smoke and then returned to the captain's chair. "Target the next closest Dreadnaught," he said to Azelon. "And if you can work your fancy-ass magic on commandeering any of those Talons to lend us a hand, do it."

"It will mean less computational power in protecting our Fangs and Sootriman's Magistrates, sir," she replied.

"That's fine. I don't think they'll need as much cover moving forward. Watch for any enemy ships looking to jump away from the system. Make those our highest priority."

"Understood, Smoking Hot Man."

As one, Caldwell and TO-96 turned to stare at Azelon.

"You fry a circuit or something?" Caldwell asked.

"I must concur with the Colonel's line of questioning," TO-96 said. "Though in slightly less antiquated terms."

Azelon jerked back in a very human expression of genuine surprise. "He smokes, his body temperature remains above average, and he is a human male. I fail to extrapolate your negative assumptions of my new nickname for the Colonel."

"Son of a bitch," Caldwell said, removing his cigar. "I like it."

"But, sir," TO-96 said, raising his hands in protest. "The inference is that she thinks you are attractive?"

"It is?" Azelon replied.

"That settles it then," Caldwell replied. He pointed the stump of his cigar at the Novian bot. "From now on, I'm Smoking Hot Man. Or Hottie, whichever suits you at the moment."

TO-96 turned to Azelon. "What have you done?"

EZO CHASED a Repub Talon around the topside of the Battleship, attained weapons lock, and fired his primary blasters. It took two direct hits to penetrate the shields and one more to pierce the armor plating that housed the starfighter's drive core. The cylinder went nova and split the fuselage like an egg, propelling the pilot forward before vaporizing him.

A second Talon crossed Ezo's path near the Battleship's conning tower, so he rolled left and came in close. But just when Ezo was about to fire, a third Talon dropped in behind him. The first few blaster rounds from the Talons T-100s peppered Ezo's stern, but his shields held.

Then the fire stopped.

Ezo glanced at the battle map and saw the starfighter accelerating toward him—it had the shot, yet the Talon's guns remained silent.

"Ezo's got one right on top of me," he said over comms, his voice frantic. But it was a pointless request. By the time anyone got close enough to help Ezo, the enemy would toast him. The Map showed the Talon's icon overlapping with his own. "What the hell?"

Ezo looked to port and saw the Talon pull up alongside him. The pilot pounded on his dashboard and seemed to be throwing an overall fit inside the cockpit. Without warning, the enemy fighter pulled ahead and came in behind Ezo's latest target, and then fired a missile. The locked-on Talon attempted to avoid the shot, but the proximity didn't allow enough time. Ezo's ship flew through the fiery debris field before rolling over the nose, and headed back along the belly.

"What the hell was that?" Ezo said to no one in particular.

"Did my assistance startle you, Commander Ezo?" Azelon said through his neural link.

"That—that was you, Azelon?"

"Indirectly, yes. We'll see you back aboard the *Spire* soon," she said.

Ezo gave a half-smile and a quick nod of his head. "Ezo like your style, bot. No wonder 'Six likes you."

"I do have the ability to perform many useful and pleasing tasks."

"Okay, stop right there."

Just then, TO-96's voice broke over the channel. "Azelon, we need your Talons' assistance in sector three, grids twenty-three and twenty-four."

"I see them," Azelon replied.

"Ezo doesn't," Ezo said. "What's happening?"

"The Magistrates are taking heavy fire from three retreating Destroyers," TO-96 said.

Ezo did the mental gymnastics required to pull up the grid in question and then reorient his Fang. "Blue Squadron, on Ezo!"

"But, sir, we have plenty—"

"Can it, 'Six. If my lady needs backup, there's nowhere else you're going to task me."

"Understood, sir."

"Is that how you feel about me?" Azelon asked TO-96.

"Answer carefully, buddy," Ezo said to him, accelerating his Fang.

"Of course, Azelon," TO-96 replied. "Only I would come to your aid twice as fast."

"Good answer," Ezo said.

But Azelon didn't seem impressed. "That is a pity."

Ezo studied Azelon's face in his HUD and noticed that TO-96 seemed equally perplexed. "And why is that a pity?" the bot inquired.

"I wouldn't need the help."

SOOTRIMAN and about twenty of her Magistrates found themselves in the unlucky position of being hemmed in on two sides by two Destroyers, with a third behind them. Even though the ships seemed bent on retreating from the system now that Moldark and his flagship were destroyed, it didn't mean they weren't going to take out whoever they could in the process.

A heavy base of blaster fire kept Sootriman's forces dashing back and forth between the two flanking destroyers while Talons made passes from the front. Even despite her best efforts to get the *Radiant Queen's* Panther-class canons on target, the enemy seemed to be twice as fast. So for every Talon she took down, the Destroyers took out two of hers.

Frustrated with the toll her squadron was taking, Sootriman decided to change tactics. She closed on the nearest Destroyer and raced along the port side. The *Queen's* blasters blazed against point defense turrets, silencing their assault on her remaining ships—now only eight strong.

Oncoming Talons forced her to double back along the Destroyer, so she used the opportunity to scout an idea she had forming. If her squadron couldn't get past the Destroyers, maybe she could fly *through* them. As she ripped along the Destroyer's port side again, she stole a glance inside the hangar bay. Sure enough, her suspicions were confirmed.

"You still with me, Chloe?" she asked.

"Yeah. But we just lost Boris and Pell," Chloe replied, her voice tight.

"Splick," Sootriman said. How had the enemy's imminent defeat turned into such heavy losses for her people? She ground her teeth and tried to keep tunnel vision from getting the best of her. *Ironic*, she thought, considering what she was about to do.

"But you still have me," Diddelwolf said. "I'm like the rash you get from—"

"Don't need to finish that, Wolfy," Chloe said. "We all know."

"You've still got me too," Barlow replied. "Whaddya have in mind?"

"Follow my lead," Sootriman said. "We're getting out of here." She pulled the *Queen* back and shot away from the Destroyer's hull, then arced around until she was pointed back at the port side.

"I mean no disrespect, my queen," Diddelwolf said. "But what are your intentions?"

"Keep your heads down and all your dangly bits tucked in," she replied, and then punched her Panther-class starfighter forward. Her bow was pointed directly at the hangar bay, which ran through the entire ship and opened on the other side.

"You're one crazy-ass queen-bitch," Chloe said. "I'll follow you anywhere."

The *Queen* broke the atmosphere shield at full thrust but slowed from the sudden appearance of both air and gravity slowed her ship as well as pulled it toward the deck. The ship struck the hangar bay floor on her belly, sending out waves of sparks as it skidded across the deck. Flight crews dove out of the way as Sootriman's ship annihilated supply trains and cargo containers. What concerned her the most, however, was a grounded Talon on the far end of the hangar bay.

"This might get bumpy," she said.

"It's not already?" Barlow asked. "Splick."

Sootriman manually aimed her main ion cannons at the upcoming obstacle and then squeezed the triggers on her flight controls. The ion cannons sent bolts of charged particles sizzling through the hangar bay's air, sending small whips of lightning into everything they passed over. But when the rounds met the Talon, they tore through the fuselage and blew the ship out of the way.

Sootriman did her best to guide her ship across the deck before it shot from the other side of the hull and rendered the void. The flames vanished, and the sudden acceleration pushed her back in her seat.

"Hell, yeah," Chloe shouted. "I'm through."

"Penetration successful," Diddelwolf said.

"You're old and gross," Chloe replied. Then she cursed.

As the *Queen* arced out and away from the Destroyers, Sootriman eyed the hangar bay, spewing fire into hard vacuum. Starship pieces flew from the hole, including painted sections she knew all too well.

"We lost Phineas," Chloe said. "As well as—"

"The rest," Sootriman said, sparing Chloe the list of names. She made two fists and bashed them down on her console three times, yelling as she did. "No!"

How had she just lost eighteen ships in less than five minutes? Sootriman brought up her squadron roster. The other half was still on the far side of center, assisting TO-96's Fangs. Still, she counted only five ships there—five, plus her three—that was eight out of an original fifty.

It was impossible.

Completely outrageous.

And inexcusable.

"I'm here," Ezo said over comms. "Where do you need us?"

Sootriman swallowed the tears that she'd licked off her lips. "You're too late, husband."

There was a moment's hesitation before Ezo replied. "But I only count three of you."

"And that's all there is here. Five more in grid forty."

"But that can't be right."

Sootriman felt her anger burn like a volcano about to erupt in paradise. Her thoughts flooded with memories of Caledonia, of charred bodies washing up on shore, of Republic ships leaving the planet, and of her family being left to pick up the pieces. She switched over to a private channel. "Isn't that what happens when you try and fight someone else's war? You lose. You always lose."

"There must be some mistake," Ezo said, his face searching the holo screens around his cockpit. Sootriman could see his eyes growing wider as the reality of the Magistrate losses dawned on him. "This can't be right."

"No mistake, husband. We may have defeated Moldark, but it seems our people—*my* people—paid the highest price, once again."

Ezo's ship pulled up beside her as the first enemy ships began jumping into subspace. The flashes of departing light lit their faces as husband and wife looked at one another across the void.

"I wanna leave," Sootriman said at last. "I just wanna go home."

"But, love sauce, we've got—"

"Don't you love sauce me, husband." She wasn't about to let him sweet talk her into staying. "There's nothing left for me here. Nothing left for me with the Gladio Umbra."

"That's not true, and you know it. What about the people who survived down there? You're saying you don't want to be a part of rescuing them when you have the chance?"

Sootriman looked out her cockpit window and studied the burning islands hundreds of kilometers below. How anyone could survive such massive destruction was beyond her. But helping the innocent survive Moldark's dark reign was precisely what she'd set out to do—what she'd convinced her Magistrates to do too.

There was something else about the islands that stirred her heart. The scene reminded her of Caledonia, and her mind flashed back to the how her people had watched the Repub aid shuttles leave long before their work had been concluded. *The costs were too high to continue,* she was told. *They've done as much as they can.* But there were still tens of thousands of displaced Caledonians from the war.

If Sootriman left now, she wouldn't be any different than the Republic. "And I'll be damned if I have that on my conscience."

"What was that, love?" Ezo asked.

She sighed. "It means I'm staying. But only until the rescue efforts are under control. Then I'm out."

"I can live with that."

"Good, 'cause if you can't, you're sleeping on *Geronimo Nine* when you get back to Ki Nar Four."

"Not the worst quarters."

"I stripped out the ship's core."

Ezo swallowed hard. "I stand corrected."

MAGNUS AND AWEN walked onto the *Spire's* bridge, still covered in grime and dried saltwater. They were exhausted, having seen their share of death, and ready for a shower, food, and a lot of sleep. But Magnus wanted to report to the Colonel, and Awen said she wouldn't let him go alone.

"Lieutenant Magnus," TO-96 exclaimed in a chipper tone. "And Awen! So good to see you." The bot walked toward them and threw his arms around their armor in awkward hugs.

"You too, TO-96," Awen replied. Her head jerked sideways, attached to the bot's elbow. "And—that's my hair."

"My apologies."

"You've still got my—ouch! My hair."

"I'm terribly—"

"Stop pulling away, 'Six!"

"Here," Magnus said, grabbing the bot's arm to keep him from yanking Awen's head any more. "Relax your elbow. Now, slowly pull it away. There you go."

"Ah, thank you, sir. Again, I'm terribly sorry, Awen."

"It's fine," she said, rubbing her head. "Compared to everything else I've been through today, it's the least of my concerns."

"You have been busy, indeed." TO-96 looked at Magnus. "Sir, you mentioned that I could share Capriana's municipal engineering history with you upon your return. Would this be a suitable time?"

"Magnus, Awen," Caldwell said as he prompted the bot to step aside, and then offered his hand to Awen. "It's good to see you."

"And you, Colonel," Magnus replied. Then to TO-96, he whispered, "Later, 'Six. I promise."

"I see Piper saved your wet asses," Caldwell said.

Awen smiled. "That she did. And to be honest, sir, we're both a little surprised you let her go."

"Awen, if there's one thing I've learned over the years, it's don't mess with a woman when she has her mind set on something."

"Piper, sir?" Awen asked.

"She certainly counts. But I mean someone far more intimidating."

"Willowood," Magnus said.

The colonel nodded. "Said the kid was going with or without my approval. Which meant I'd better give some express consent or there was going to be a lifetime of hell to pay. Fastest option was to stick the kid with Ricio and see what happened. The rest, I think you know."

Magnus nodded, reminding himself to thank Ricio when he got back. "What's the latest with the planet?"

"Well, how dark do you like your coffee, son?"

Magnus knew the meaning of the colonel's expression. "The only real way to drink it. Straight up."

Caldwell blew smoke out his nostrils and through his mustache. "We expect few survivors on the planet. Azelon gave victims on the far side the best survival rate. Thinks maybe 20% of the inhabitants will survive."

"I've revised that to 17%, sir," she added.

"Well, splick." Caldwell raised a hand as if giving up on the numbers game. He refocused on Magnus and took a deep breath. "It's bad, son. That's what we know right now. The fallout from the blasts is worse than we expected too."

"Thus my revised numbers, sir," Azelon said.

Caldwell ignored her. "Up here, we lost six Fangs altogether."

"That ain't too shabby, Colonel," Magnus said.

But Caldwell took the cigar stump from his mouth. "Sootriman's Magistrates took the heaviest losses."

"How bad?"

"Lost forty-two ships."

"Forty-two?" Magnus touched his forehead. "How?"

"Half her squadron got pinned down by three Destroyers

leaving the sector. The other half took heavy losses while defending our clean up after the *Labyrinth* went down."

"Mystics. And how's she taking it?"

"Very hard, as I believe the expression goes, sir," TO-96 said. "But she has at least agreed to help with rescuing any survivors on the planet."

"Then she's headed back to Ki Nar Four," Caldwell said. "Can't say that I blame her."

"And Ezo?" Awen asked.

"He's still out there finishing off the Paragon Talons that couldn't jump away," Caldwell said.

"What about when he's through?" she said. "Is he going to stay with us?"

"I believe he's staying for me," TO-96 said. "But I assume he intends to take me back to Ki Nar Four as well."

Magnus looked at Awen and then to the bot. "And will you go?"

TO-96 tilted his head as if giving the question serious consideration. "Since my maker has not yet offered me a proposition, I cannot rightfully provide a meaningful answer to your hypothetical inquiry."

"Meaning, you want to check in with Azelon first," Awen said, nodding toward the other bot. The mystic had an uncanny way of reading between the lines of code.

"No." TO-96 looked over at Azelon. "She and I have already discussed all possible scenarios."

"When?" Caldwell asked.

"Just now. She will support my decision, whatever it may be."

"Well, just be sure to let us know too," Magnus said.

"I will, sir. Thank you."

The idea of splitting the team up didn't sit well with Magnus. But then again, did he really expect things to stay this way forever?

Caldwell took another drag on the stub in his mouth. "As for Moldark's fleet, only fourteen warships and six Talons survived, and they just jumped out of the system."

"Five Talons, sir," Azelon said. "The last one was just destroyed."

"Five Talons," Caldwell said.

"Those are some heavy losses."

"You're telling me, son. We owe most of that to First Fleet, but they fared only a little better. Thirty-three warships, including just five carriers, and sixty-one Talons."

"That's a quarter of the Navy's original fighting force," Magnus said, more to himself than to the colonel. Caldwell still nodded, trying to keep his cigar from burning the edges of his lips. "So, what now?"

"I suppose that's a call for all of us to make together," Caldwell said, looking at Awen and then the two bots. "We'll wait for Willowood, of course. But our options include sticking around to help whoever's left on the planet or going after Moldark's remaining ships."

"Don't forget So-Elku," Awen said. "He won't have been sitting idle during all this."

"Agreed," Caldwell replied. "So there's plenty to discuss."

"And Moldark?" Magnus asked, trying not to jinx the question everyone wanted to know the answer to.

"We have every reason to believe he was on board the *Black Labyrinth* when it went down," Caldwell said. "And I'd like to hope that's the case. It would sure spare us all a splick-load of trouble."

Magnus looked at the bots. "Any probability that he escaped?"

"Of course," Azelon said. "Nothing is certain without sufficient proof. I place Moldark's survival at less than 3%. I am reviewing all sensor data from the conflict, looking for evidence of his escape."

"3%," Awen said softly. "I don't like those odds."

"Neither do I," Magnus said. "Let's hope for the best."

"I'm sorry to interrupt, Hottie, but we are being hailed across all channels by Commodore David Seaman of First Fleet. He's onboard the *Solera Fortuna*."

Caldwell gave Magnus and Awen a raised eyebrow before turning toward the main holo display. Magnus looked at Awen and mouthed the word "Hottie?" Then the colonel dropped the cigar on the deck and crushed it with his foot. "Put him on, Smarty Pants. Let's see how the Repub feels about us now."

EPILOGUE

MOLDARK SAT in the chair on his observation deck, glaring at First Fleet as it sought to defend what remained of Capriana Prime. He bit his lower lip in rapt wonder as two enemy Dreadnaughts suffered point-blank LO9D strikes. The blasts tore both ships apart in a spectacular release of energy, cleaving the vessel in pieces, and blasting the remains toward the planet's gravity.

Commodore Seaman's attempts to stop Moldark were admirable, in so much as a hurricane admires a bird's attempt to fly through it. But in the end? *Fruitless.*

The fool, Moldark thought.

The dark lord had handed the Republic officer the opportunity of his short and insignificant lifetime—to live out his remaining days as one of the most powerful men in the galaxy. *And what did he choose to do with it?* Moldark spat blood on the floor. *Has he no ambition?*

Seaman's betrayal mattered little, ultimately. The man was merely a means to an end—as were all these ships, people, and planets. They played their parts, served his purposes, and then it was over. They were all expendable.

The important thing today was that the Nine had been decimated. *The traitors.* Moldark had tasted their fear and drank of their lives. Well, most of them, anyway. Moldark despised that fact that he had to resort to the orbital bombardment instead of face-to-face retribution. Killing wholesale was so impersonal, like the way the Novia Minoosh had ripped his people's lives away. However, even though not all deaths were equal, Moldark's personal reckoning with the Nine was complete, and the traitors had breathed their last breaths. *Blackman, most of all.* It was what it was.

That Blackman had not died at Moldark's hand roiled the dark lord to no end. It was Blackman who had betrayed him most, after all. But in so doing, the man had inadvertently revealed just how evil the human species was. Like the Novia Minoosh, they were takers—scavengers—stealing from the weak to satiate their endless appetites. So, in the end, Blackman had done the cosmos a favor. He'd revealed the need to wipe out the species.

Capriana Prime's destruction was by no means the end of the humans, just as the Oorajee's fleet collapse was not the end of the Jujari. Both losses would set their species back hundreds of years, but that meant Moldark had more time—time he would need to replenish his resources and strengthen his numbers. Only then could he finish exterminating the Jujari and the humans wherever they hid—just as he would finish doing to his greatest foe, the Novia Minoosh.

So many wars to conduct, so many ways to end them.

Despite First Fleet's heavy losses, Admiral Brighton had informed Moldark that Second and Third Fleets were faring even worse. *As if it's my fault?* The dark lord refused to believe that the losses had anything to do with his excursion to the surface. No, this was on Brighton.

"My lord," Brighton said through the holo window that floated in front of Moldark's chair. "I must insist that you proceed to your shuttle."

"I thought I told you to move the *Labyrinth* back, Admiral," Moldark replied.

Brighton cleared his throat. "We have, my lord. But we've also run out of—space."

Moldark blinked in dismay. "Admiral Brighton, the environment outside our ship is called *space* for a reason. How can there—"

"There seems to be a ship blocking our retreat."

Even before Brighton showed him images of the Novian warship, Moldark knew the surprise attack was from the same rebel vessel that opposed him over Oorajee—the same rebels who fought against him in the capital.

"Force your way past them, you fool," Moldark spat.

"Yes, my lord. However—"

A violent force threw Moldark back in his seat as the *Labyrinth* slowed. Brighton, likewise, flew off-screen, jolted by the ship's sudden change in inertia.

"Admiral," Moldark roared as tremors shook his chair. "What is going on with my ship?"

Brighton reappeared, his hands trembling as he brushed the hair off his forehead. "We have sustained severe damage to sections one and two, my lord, all decks."

"From what?"

Brighton swallowed. "The unidentified ship, sir."

"It's Novian, dammit! Stop saying it's unidentifiable! I told you the species—"

More explosions shook the *Labyrinth*, jostling Moldark in his chair. When Brighton reappeared for the second time, his face was pale.

"As I said, my lord, I must insist you evacuate. I have readied your ship—"

"I'm on my way."

"Very good, my lord."

"And you, Brighton?"

The admiral paused, as if unsure of what to do with the personal question. "Me, my lord?"

"What are your plans?"

An awkward silence followed as Brighton's lips struggled to form words. "I will stay with the ship until the end, my lord."

Moldark couldn't decide if Brighton's decision was bravery or cowardice—the former being the mark of an extraordinary though nearsighted commander, the latter, the easy escape from life under Moldark's thumb. "Very well."

"Thank you, my lord," Brighton said hurriedly.

"Whatever for?"

"The opportunity to serve you, of course." The man stood to attention and saluted Moldark with an extended arm and a clenched fist—the Paragon's position of power. Moldark shook his head. Clearly, Brighton had spent enough time in proximity to the dark lord that the underling's reason centers were co-opted.

For a fleeting moment, Moldark considered rescuing the man. The dark lord would still need commanders, and Brighton had proved faithful. Then again, his promotion *had* been a matter of convenience, and the admiral did seem to exude a particular weakness, one that kept him from making the hard decisions. Perhaps his loss was for the best.

Moldark flicked a hand at Brighton. "Yes, yes. Get on with it then. Farewell, Admiral."

"Farewell, my lord."

THE *LABYRINTH* SHUDDERED AGAIN as Moldark made his way to the *Peregrine*. The four-person fire team that escorted him moved without saying a word. They navigated the bustling corridors quickly, stopping only once when the ship's shaking grew too severe. The lights flickered, and several people screamed in the distance. But the moment the vibrations settled, Moldark bid the men keep moving.

Despite feeding not more than two hours before, Moldark could already feel his body—*Kane's body*—growing weak. He would need a new host before long. But people feared him among the Republic, what little of it remained, and reputation had its advantages. Plus, he had labored diligently to find the perfect host in this part of the cosmos—it would be a shame to lose it now.

The escort led Moldark into a busy hangar bay where the *Peregrine* awaited. The ship sat like a blackbird of prey eager to take flight. Outside, starfighters crisscrossed the void, filling space with blaster rounds and missiles.

Captain Yaeger stood beside the *Peregrine's* under-nose ramp with his helmet beneath his arm. "Lord Moldark," he said, saluting.

"Good to see you again, Captain."

"And you, my lord. My orders are to escort you wherever it is you wish to go."

"Very well. And do you intend to fly this ship as well as guard me?"

"No, my lord. Captain Ellis and his First Officer are already onboard and ready to depart."

"Shall we, then?" Moldark motioned toward the ramp, but Yaeger gestured for the dark lord to proceed ahead. No sooner was he on board than bright lights appeared in the hangar bay. Something significant was happening outside the *Labyrinth*.

"Please be seated, my lord," Captain Yaeger said as the fire team filed up and closed the ramp.

Moldark headed for the bridge where he found Captain Ellis at the helm and a co-pilot beside him. The dark lord took a seat behind the co-pilot so that he could see Ellis. "What is it, Captain?"

"Reports of heavy torpedo fire to our stern," Ellis replied. "The Dreadnaught *Terra Rosa*, my lord."

"Then, I suggest you proceed with haste."

"Yes, my lord." Ellis activated the ship's repulsors, hovered, and then backed through the atmospheric shield and into hard vacuum. The *Labyrinth's* death tremors were replaced with the steady hum of a shuttle underway, but Moldark also had a clear view of the *Rosa's* assault. The behemoth ship had closed to within three or four kilometers of the *Labyrinth*, and it appeared to be firing every torpedo in its arsenal.

Point defense fire from the *Labyrinth*, as well as from several other nearby ships, kept the majority of the projectiles from striking the Super Dreadnaught's stern. But given the volume of enemy ordnance, even a minority of the torpedo-fire was more than the *Labyrinth* could endure. Dozens, if not scores of torpedoes collided with the *Labyrinth's* stern, bathing the aft section in light. A chain reaction of explosions moved toward the bow, coming dangerously close to the *Peregrine*.

"Do you intend to watch all day, Captain?" Moldark asked.

"Apologies, my lord." Ellis steered the craft away from the impending destruction and accelerated.

"You may, of course, view the images on holos."

"Yes, my lord." Ellis nodded at his first officer, and then brought up two display screens, both with different views of the *Labyrinth*.

Moldark gazed at the ill-fated ship as explosions rippled along the hull, racing toward the bow. Fire enveloped the *Labyrinth*, deck after deck, section after section until the entire vessel blew apart and its remains flung into the remaining warships.

The advantage of the whole scenario, Moldark realized, was that the *Peregrine* had the perfect cover. No one would be watching his escape—how could they in the face of such inexorable and magnificent destruction?

Captain Ellis maneuvered away from the battlefront, past the Novian ghost ship, and away from Capriana Prime. Then he turned to address Moldark. "My lord. Where do you wish to go?"

Moldark had already been pondering the question, of course. And there were many options, to be sure. One was to head to Worru, to exact revenge against the *other* traitor, So-Elku. But doing so would require more planning and more power. The mystic was not to be trifled with, and Moldark would need time before engaging the Luma Master.

The ultimate choice, of course, was to head back to metaspace and complete his original mission of wiping out the Novia Minoosh and their singularity once and for all. It seemed such an easy task, yet one that had eluded him as of late. Still, the chance would come—he could feel it. Plus, Ithnor Ithelia couldn't be a destination any more than a fictional realm could, not until he'd obtained coordinates for a quantum tunnel. And without the child, creating a tunnel or finding coordinates back to metaspace —to his home universe—would prove impossible.

Which left the most obvious option: returning to Oorajee. If he could salvage even some of the ships from this costly encounter, he might succeed in exterminating the Jujari while he bided his time for the Novia Minoosh. A final assault on the desert world had another benefit too—luring the rebels to him. Perhaps then he would get their mystics to create a quantum tunnel for him—if not willingly, then possibly through deceit.

"Oorajee," Moldark said at last.

Ellis raised an eyebrow in surprise. "My lord?"

"We have unfinished business there, do we not?"

"If you're referring to the Jujari still left on the planet, then, yes, my lord. We have unfinished business."

"Lay in the course, Captain. Additionally, I want you to order the rest of the fleet back to Oorajee."

Ellis seemed stunned. "Me, my lord?"

"Yes, you. Is there a problem?"

"Well, no. But, isn't that a job for—"

"A senior commander? Ellis, look around. Are you not the most senior naval officer on this ship after me?"

"Well, of course, my lord, but I—"

"And wherever I go, do I not bring the heart of the Paragon with me?"

"Of course, my lord."

"Then you are my commanding officer, Ellis. At least until all our remaining ships are accounted for. Now, send the orders, and let's get free of this tomb."

"Yes, my lord. As you wish."

Moldark sat back in his seat and watched the final moments of battle play out. As soon as Ellis gave the order for retreat, the *Peregrine* slipped into subspace, and the scene above Capriana Prime vanished.

MAGNUS and AWEN will return in TERMINAL FALLOUT, available to preorder now.

For more updates on this series, be sure to join the Facebook Group, "J.N. Chaney's Renegade Readers."

CHARACTER REFERENCE

Gladio Umbra - 1st Battalion - Colonel Caldwell

Granther Company - Special Unit / Elites (25)
Lieutenant Magnus
1st Platoon

FIRST SQUAD

Alpha Team

- Abimbola (RFL)
- Rohoar (JRI)

- Awen (MYS)
- Silk (SNPR)
- "Doc" Campbell (DEMO/MED)

Bravo Team

- Titus (RFL)
- Czyz (JRI)
- Nídira (MYS)
- Dutch (SNPR)
- Haze (DEMO/MED)

Second Team

Charlie Team

- Zoll (RFL)
- Longchomps (JRI)
- Wish (MYS)
- Reimer (SNPR)
- Rix (DEMO/MED)

Delta Team

- Bliss (RFL)
- Grahban (JRI)
- Telwin (MYS)

- Bettger (SNPR)
- Dozer (DEMO/MED)

Echo Team

- Robillard (RFL)
- Redmarrow (JRI)
- Findermith (MYS)
- Jaffrey (SNPR)
- Handley (DEMO/MED)

Taursar Company - Rifle (150)
Captain Forbes

- 1st Platoon (50) - Wagoner, OIC

(Includes Ricky, Handley, Ford)

- 2nd Platoon (50)

(Includes Arjae, Dihazen)

- 3rd Platoon (50) - Jackson, OIC

Hedgebore Company - Rifle (150)
Lieutenant Nelson

- 1st Platoon (50)
- 2nd Platoon (50)
- 3rd Platoon (50)

Drambull Company - support and Intel (83)
Azelon

- 1st Platoon (21) - Intelligence - Cyril
- 2nd Platoon (36) - Logistics - Berouth
- 3rd Platoon (26) - Fighter Support - Gilder

Attached to Fang Company

Fang Company - Starfighter Attack Wing - (39)
TO-96

- Red Squadron (14) - Commander Ricio
- Gold Squadron (12) - Commander Nolan
- Blue Squadron (13) - Commander Ezo

Raptor Company - Naval Operations (19)
Azelon

- Command (6)
- Fire Support (13)

(Includes Flow and Cheeks)

Paladia Company - mystics (40)
Master Willowood

- 1st Cadre (14) - Sion
- 2nd Cadre (14) - Incipio
- 3rd Cadre (12) - Tora

List of Main Characters

A. H. Lovell: Human. Age: 51. Planet of origin: Capriana Prime. Brigadier General, 1st Republic Marine Division, I Marine Expeditionary Force, Galactic Republic Marines; includes 79th Reconnaissance Battalion. Dark complexion, commanding presence.

Abimbola: Miblimbian. Age: 41. Planet of origin: Limbia Centrella. Commander of Bravo Platoon, Granther Company. Former warlord of the Dregs, outskirts of Oosafar, Oorajee. Bright-blue eyes, black skin, tribal tattoos, scar running from neck to temple.

Adonis Olin Magnus: Human. Age: 34. Planet of origin: Capriana Prime. Gladio Umbra, Granther Company commander. Former lieutenant, Charlie Platoon, 79th Reconnaissance Battalion, "Midnight Hunters," Galactic Republic Space Marines. Baby face, beard, green eyes.

Aubrey Dutch: Human. Age: 25. Planet of origin: Deltaurus Three. Commander of Alpha Platoon, Granther Company. Former corporal, weapons specialist, Galactic Republic Space Marines. Small in stature, close-cut dark hair, intelligent brown eyes. Loves her firearms.

Awen dau Lothlinium: Elonian. Age: 26. Planet of origin: Elonia. Commander of Echo Platoon, Granther Company. Form Special Emissary to the Jujari, Order of the Luma. Pointed ears, purple eyes.

Azelon: AI and robot. Age: unknown. Planet of origin: Ithnor Ithelia. Artificial intelligence of the Novia Minoosh ship *Azelon Spire*.

Cal Wagoner: Human. Age 31. Planet of origin: Capriana

Prime. Lieutenant (Officer In Charge), first platoon, Taursar Company, Gladio Umbra. Leads defense of north tunnel in the assault on the *Black Labyrinth*.

Chloe: Human. Age: 29. Planet of origin: Tresseldor. Magistrate of Klon, aka "the Terror of Tresseldor." Short red hair flipped out under a black Repub officer's cap, Sypeurlion admiral's jacket. Pissed at everyone, a vendetta around every corner. Challenger. Flies a black and blue Sypeurlion Jackal-class fighter.

Cyril: Human. Age: 24. Planet of origin: Ki Nar Four. Assigned to Bravo Platoon, Granther Company. Former Marauder. Code slicer, bomb technician. Twitchy; sounds like a Quinzellian miter squirrel if it could talk.

Daniel Forbes: Human. Age: 32. Planet of origin: Capriana. Captain of Taursar Company, Gladio Umbra. Former Captain of Alpha Company, 83rd Marine Battalion, Galactic Republic Space Marines, on special assignment to Worru. Close-cropped black hair, but a swoop across his forehead. Brown eyes. Clean-shaven, angular face.

David Seaman: Human. Age: 31. Planet of origin: Capriana Prime. Captain in the Republic Navy, commander of the *Black Labyrinth's* two Talon squadrons, Viper and Raptor, and the head of SFC—Strategic Fighter Command. Promoted to Commodore (Flag Officer) of First Fleet aboard the *Solera Fortuna*.

Dieddelwolf: Human. Age: 54. Planet of origin: Unknown. Magistrate of To-To, under Sootriman; oldest of the Twelve. Long grey beard and a gold ring in one eyebrow. Known as a bit of a player with the ladies. Pilots a yellow modified Gull-class heavy freighter.

Dozer: Human. Age: Unknown. Planet of origin: Verv Ko. Assigned to Bravo Platoon, Granther Company. Former Marauder, infantry. A veritable human earth-mover.

Gerald Bosworth III: Human. Age: 54. Planet of origin: Capriana Prime. Republic Ambassador, special envoy to the Jujari. Fat jowls, bushy monobrow. Massively obese and obscenely repugnant.

Hal Brighton: Human. Age: 41. Planet of origin: Capriana Prime. Fleet Admiral, First Fleet, the Paragon; former executive officer, Republic Navy.

Idris Ezo: Nimprith. Age: 30. Planet of origin: Caledonia. Assigned to Alpha Platoon, Granther Company. Former bounty hunter, trader, suspected fence and smuggler; captain of *Geronimo Nine*.

Issac S. McCormick: Human. Age: 58. Planet of origin: Capriana Prime. General, Galactic Republic Marine Corps Commandant, CENTCOM. Flat-topped redhead, pale complexion. Large gut, double-chin.

Jules: Human. Age: 31. Planet of origin: Capriana Prime. Sea skimmer racing champion, and proprietor of Jules Sea Skimmer Rentals franchise. Blonde and fit with a fiery attitude.

Kar Zoll: Human. AgeL 35. Planet of origin: Oorajee. Petty Officer, team leader for Charlie Team, Second Squad (Officer in Charge), 1st Platoon, Granther Company, Gladio Umbra. Tall, dark hair. Competent leader and tactician.

Lani DiAntora: Sekmit. Age: 29. Planet of origin: Aluross. Flag Captain of the *Soloar Fortuna*, under Commodore Seaman. Feline-like humanoid species, blonde hair. Inquisitive, analytical, and unafraid of senior officers.

Lin Phaq: Nimprinth. Age: 48. Planet of origin: Caledonia. Fleet Admiral of Second Fleet, Galactic Republic Navy.

Michael "Flow" Deeks: Human. Age: 31. Planet of origin: Vega. Assigned to the *Azelon Spire*. Former sergeant, sniper, Charlie Platoon, 79th Reconnaissance Battalion, "Midnight Hunters," Galactic Republic Space Marines. One of the "Fearsome Four."

Miguel "Cheeks" Chico: Human. Age 30. Planet of origin: Trida Minor. Assigned to the *Azelon Spire*. Former corporal, breacher, Charlie Platoon, 79th Reconnaissance Battalion, "Midnight Hunters," Galactic Republic Space Marines. One of the "Fearsome Four."

Moldark (formerly Wendell Kane): Human. Age: 52. Planet of origin: Capriana Prime. Dark Lord of the Paragon, a rogue black-operations special Marine unit. Former fleet admiral of the Galactic Republic's Third Fleet; captain of the *Black Labyrinth*. Bald, with heavily scared skin; black eyes.

Mauricio "Ricio" Longo: Human. Age: 29. Planet of origin: Capriana Prime. Republic Navy, squadron commander of Viper Squadron, assigned to the *Black Labyrinth*.

Nel Teloni: Nuromin. Age: 25. Planet of origin: Plydithera. Sensors Officer aboard the Solera Fortuna.

Nubs: Human. Age: Unknown. Planet of origin: Verv Ko. Assigned to Bravo Platoon, Granther Company. Former Marauder, infantry. Has several missing fingers.

Penn Franks: Human. Age: 60. Planet of origin: Minroc Santari. Admiral, Chief of Naval Operations, Galactic Republic Navy, CENTCOM.

Phineas Barlow: Human. Age: 36. Planet of origin: Ki Nar Four. Magistrate of Kildower, under Sootriman; most respected of the Twelve. Burgundy cloak over one shoulder, a black Repub-style chest plate, beige pair of cargo pants with tall black boots, black beret. Has a thing for Chloe. Flies a blue retrofitted Light Armored Transport.

Piper Stone: Human. Age: 9. Planet of origin: Capriana Prime. Assigned to Echo Platoon, Granther Company. Daughter of Senator Darin and Valerie Stone. Wispy blond hair, freckle-faced.

"Rix" Galliogernomarix: Human. Age: Unknown. Planet of origin: Undoria. Assigned to Bravo Company, Granther Company. Wanted in three systems, sleeve tattoos, a monster on the battlefield.

Robert Malcom Blackman: Human. Age: 54. Planet of origin: Capriana Prime. Senator in the Galactic Republic, leader of the clandestine Circle of Nine. A stocky man with thick shoulders and well-groomed gray hair.

Rohoar: Tawnhack, Jujari. Age: Unknown. Planet of origin: Oorajee. Commander of Delta Platoon, Granther Company. Former Jujari Mwadim.

Saasarr: Reptalon. Age: unknown. Planet of origin: Gangil. Assigned to Echo Platoon, Granther Company. Former general of Sootriman's Reptalon guard. Lizard humanoid.

Shane Nolan: Human. Age: 25. Planet of origin: Sol Sella. Assigned to Alpha Platoon, Granther Company. Pilot, former chief warrant officer, Republic Navy. Auburn hair, pale skin.

Sig Jackson: Human. Age 32. Planet of origin: Capriana

Prime. Lieutenant (Officer In Charge), third platoon, Taursar Company, Gladio Umbra. Leads defense of south tunnel in the assault on the *Black Labyrinth*.

Silk: Human. Age: 30. Planet of origin: Salmenka. Assigned to Bravo Platoon, Granther Company. Former Marauder, infantry. Slender, bald, tats covering her face and head.

So-Elku: Human. Age: 51. Planet of origin: Worru. Luma Master, Order of the Luma. Baldpate, thin beard, dark penetrating eyes. Wears green-and-black robes.

Sootriman: Caledonian. Age: 33. Planet of origin: Caledonia. Assigned to Alpha Platoon, Granther Company. Warlord of Ki Nar Four, "Tamer of the Four Tempests," wife of Idris Ezo. Tall, with dark almond eyes, tanned olive skin, dark-brown hair.

Titus: Human. Age: 34. Planet of origin: unknown. Commander of Charlie Platoon, Granther Company. Former Marauder, rescued by Magnus. Known for being cool under pressure and a good leader.

TO-96: Robot; navigation class, heavily modified. Manufacturer: Advanced Galactic Solutions (AGS), Capriana Prime. Suspected modifier: Idris Ezo. Assigned to Echo Platoon, Granther Company. Round head and oversized eyes, transparent blaster visor, matte dark-gray armor plating, and exposed metallic articulated joints. Forearm micro-rocket pod, forearm XM31 Type-R blaster, dual shoulder-mounted gauss cannons.

Torrence Ellis: Human. Age: 31. Planet of origin: Capriana Prime. Serves as the *Peregrine's* captain under Moldark.

Ty Yaeger: Human. Age: 30. Planet of origin: Minrock Santari. Captain, the Paragon. Moldark's personal bodyguard and lead enforcer for the assault on Capriana.

Valerie Stone (*deceased*): Human. Age: 31. Planet of origin: Worru. Assigned to Alpha Platoon, Granther Company. Widow of Senator Darin Stone, mother of Piper. Blond hair, light-blue eyes.

Volf Nos Kil (*deceased*): Human. Age: 32. Planet of origin: Haradia. Captain, the Paragon. Personal guard and chief enforcer for Moldark.

Waldorph Gilder: Human. Age: 23. Planet of origin: Haradia. Assigned to Alpha Platoon, Granther Company. Former private first class, flight engineer, Galactic Republic Space Marines. Barrel-chested. Can fix anything.

William Samuel Caldwell: Human. Age 60. Planet of origin: Capriana Prime. Colonel, 83rd Marine Battalion, Galactic Republic Space Marines; special assignment to Repub garrisons on Worru. Cigar eternally wedged in the corner of his mouth. Gray hair cut high and tight.

Willowood: Human. Age: 61. Planet of origin: Kindarah. Luma Elder, Order of the Luma. Wears dozens of bangles and necklaces. Aging but radiant blue eyes and a mass of wiry gray hair. Mother of Valerie, grandmother of Piper, mentor to Awen.

ACKNOWLEDGMENTS

Special thanks to the Ruins Alpha Readers:

Matthew Titus, Mauricio Longo, Kevin Zoll, David Seaman, Shane Marolf, John Walker, Jon Bliss, Walt Robillard, Elijah Cole, Joseph Wessner, Aaron Seaman, Matthew Dippel, and Ollie Longchamps. You make every chapter better.

Additional thanks to our AR Team:

Darin J.
Roxanna T.
Doug B.
John V.
Joe B.
Bill H.

James T.

Javier L.

Jeremy D.

Nora L.

Kitty M.

Nick R.

Drew D.

Natalie L.

Mike H.

Brandon O.

Alan S.

Lonn P.

Susan S.

Diane D.

Ken W.

Michael A.

Bruce R.

Tracey B.

Lynn B.

Tony R.

Geoffrey M.

GET A FREE BOOK

J.N. Chaney posts updates, official art, previews, and other awesome stuff on his website. You can also follow him on **Instagram**, **Facebook**, and **Twitter**.

He also created a special **Facebook group** called "JN Chaney's Renegade Readers" specifically for readers to come together and share their lives and interests, discuss the series, and speak directly to me. Please check it out and join whenever you get the chance!

For updates about new releases, as well as exclusive promotions, visit his website, jnchaney.com and sign up for the VIP mailing list. Head there now to receive a free copy of *The Other Side of Nowhere*.

https://www.jnchaney.com/ruins-of-the-galaxy-subscribe

Enjoying the series? Help others discover the Ruins of the Galaxy series by leaving a review on **Amazon.**

ABOUT THE AUTHORS

J. N. Chaney is a USA Today Bestselling author and has a Master's of Fine Arts in Creative Writing. He fancies himself quite the Super Mario Bros. fan. When he isn't writing or gaming, you can find him online at **www.jnchaney.com**.

He migrates often, but was last seen in Las Vegas, NV. Any sightings should be reported, as they are rare.

Christopher Hopper's novels include the Resonant Son series, The Sky Riders, The Berinfell Prophecies, and the White Lion Chronicles. He blogs at **christopherhopper.com** and loves flying RC planes. He resides in the 1000 Islands of northern New York with his musical wife and four ridiculously good-looking clones.

Made in the USA
San Bernardino, CA
12 June 2020

73077708R00287